T0196518

# To Be Damned

A Journey into Horror and Temptation

Kenneth Miller

iUniverse, Inc.
New York   Bloomington

Cover Artwork:
Edvard Munch: Vampire 1895
oil on canvas
91 x 109 cm
Munch Museum, Oslo

Copyright work of art:
Munch Museum / Munch Ellingsen Group / ARS, NY 2010

Copyright photo:
Munch Museum

iUniverse books may be ordered through booksellers or by contacting:

iUniverse
1663 Liberty Drive
Bloomington, IN 47403
www.iuniverse.com
1-800-Authors (1-800-288-4677)

ISBN: 978-1-4502-4273-8 (sc)
ISBN: 978-1-4502-4274-5 (hc)
ISBN: 978-1-4502-4275-2 (ebook)

Printed in the United States of America

iUniverse rev. date: 09/24/2010

Dedicated to my mother,
whose love and compassion
could be the basis for a
novel far greater in size
and scope than this one.
I love you, Mom.

"Those who have done right
shall rise to live;
the evildoers shall rise
**to be damned.**"

JOHN 5:29

# Prologue

ENGLAND – 1665

The plumes of black smoke rose high, dissipating in the gray-shrouded evening sky over London. Large vessels of boiling tar burned on street corners and in back alleys, in open defiance to the recently passed "no fires" law by the city magistrate. The fume of the simmering tar was believed to be the only effective response against the Great Plague, which continued to ravage the city mercilessly.

The Plague had come as a thief in the night, through some back door left carelessly ajar. Like a ravenous beast, it had taken thousands to their deaths each week. Its hunger unabated, the death toll continued to rise.

With the advent of the fall months, it being September, the city settled into a general state of avoidance in the daytime and ignorance in the night. The unafflicted dared not render aid to the afflicted for fear of contamination, and many fell back upon the old ways and superstitions of their pagan forefathers in a desperate effort to preserve their health.

The evening belonged to the sick and demented, for no sane person ventured onto the streets after nightfall. The exceptions were the watchmen who sat outside marked houses to make certain the infected within did not leave, and the operators of the dead carts. The latter collected all dead bodies and disposed of them in mass graves. Beyond these gruesome occupations, only those on urgent business could be propelled into the dark.

As the sun hung low in the sky, many hurried to the false security of their homes. Now was the time of the dreaded silence, when none uttered a word and prayers were whispered with thick tongues. The only sound reverberating through the deceased streets was the ominous creaking of the dead carts, filled with corpses after another day's collection.

Occasionally, the bellman who accompanied the dead carts would ring his large handbell, signaling their presence in the neighborhood. This would cause doors to open and grieving relatives to offer up their dead, thus adding to the carts' grisly cargo.

"Bring out your dead," the bellman droned incessantly. He was filthy, the back of his neck covered with the smashed remains of dead flies. His body odor rivaled the stench of his grotesque contraband.

Several large men, stooped over as they pulled the carts along behind them, grimaced at each addition to their load. They, too, were as the bellman: smelly, dirty, and weary-looking. They treated the bodies without any form of civility or reverence for the dead.

Whenever a house surrendered a corpse, the little children that followed the carts would gaily run up and paint sloppy red crosses on its door. This warned others in the area that the house had been contaminated.

Moving on, this macabre procession eventually came to the end of town, where the dead carts filed out of the city and into the surrounding fields. High upon one of the grassy slopes, three men watched their approach.

The first man was an artist. He stood behind a makeshift easel gingerly applying paint to his canvas with delicate dabs of his brush. He wore a painting smock which was coated with layer upon layer of oil paints. A faded blue neckerchief topped his head and his sleeves were rolled up to the elbow. He worked fervently on his painting, otherwise oblivious to the world around him.

The second man reclined on a slight hillock. He was a poet, and accordingly wrote with equal passion in the small booklet resting upon his lap. His feather pen scurried across each page, pausing only long enough to be dipped in the inkwell that sat between his legs. He, too, was shabbily dressed and cared little for what surrounded him, the center of his universe being the booklet in his lap.

The third member of the bizarre trio was a small boy, misshapen in body as well as in mind. Though he bore no load, his carriage was not unlike that of the men who drew the dead carts, bent over as if by some weight upon his shoulders. He was a hunchback, and the deformity which wracked his body also rendered him an idiot. He waited with the patience of a dog obedient of his master at the feet of the artist.

"Ah, the beauty of it all! Never could I envision such scenes of pure brilliance, of such divine pathos!" cried the artist at the sight of the subject of his painting, the parade of dead carts.

The poet paid him no attention, instead reciting his current poem. "Always you are in our bones, oh great decimator, awaiting that hour of our weakness. Death ... even your name rings cold."

"More! More!" implored the artist, looking up from his canvas. "I could stand here and do nothing but paint dead carts and listen to you all my life. This is Heaven! Quick! Hunchboy, fetch me my knife!"

The hunchback nodded stupidly several times and then whisked down the slope of the hill. Reaching the hill's foot he descended upon a small, beaten-up canvas bag, his nimbleness searching through its contents hampered only by his mental deficiency.

The artist engaged the poet in further conversation while he awaited his servant's return. "Just a year ago I was absent of creativity. My mind was as useful to me as my indolent hands. But now! Now all I have to do is look! The charnel houses, the mass graves," he pointed to the grim cavalcade, "the dead carts! What more could artists such as we ask for?"

"Another civil war, perhaps?" the poet replied with a sly grin.

"We may have one if the situation doesn't improve."

"Indeed. What with the king and his court moved to Salisbury, leaving us commoners here to rot."

"But we shall not rot, my friend. We shall create!"

The men ended their talk with the sudden reappearance of the hunchback, panting loudly from his run up the hill. He held his hands behind his back as if playing some childish game and looked at the two men, a large smile adorning his face.

"Well? Do you have it?" the impatient artist snapped.

The hunchback nodded vigorously with pride.

"Then give it to me!"

Sluggishly withdrawing his hands from their hiding place in the small of his back, the deformed boy slowly raised them for all to see. His smile shrank when he saw the faces of those he tried to please.

In his hands he held a small spade – not a knife.

The poet looked at him with disgust. "The incompetent," he muttered, resuming his writing.

A worried look crept across the face of the crookback; his hands, and the prize they held, slowly descended from their loftiness.

The artist stared at his bowed helper in silence. Then he exploded, hitting the boy across the face with the back of his hand. The poor freak flew backwards, landing hard on his hump, a soft moan escaping from his blistered lips. Dazed, he glanced up at his master, a hurt expression upon his face.

The artist was livid as he bent over the abused boy, who, still clutching the spade, raised his hands in self-defense. Angrily, he yanked the tool from his cowering assistant's grasp. "Not this, you idiot!" he uttered with contempt as he held up the spade, "My knife! My knife! The one that I cut you with!" He proceeded to viciously kick the little humpback several times, screaming almost incoherently, "Let me kick that hump off you! Roll over and let me beat you sane!"

Accustomed to this sort of abuse, the bent boy lay still making no attempts at protecting himself. He waited for the artist to finish venting his anger.

After several good blows to the ribs, the artist turned to the poet, his foot aching. "How 'bout a go at it?" he said as he motioned to the wheezing hunchback twisting in pain at his feet.

The poet looked over with deep disdain, and shook his head. "I should think you've done all that need be done to the poor whelp. Leave him be and return to your masterpiece."

"I believe you are correct," remarked the fatigued artist, turning his attention once more to the cowering lump at his feet. "You get the hell out of here before I change my mind. Perhaps you may become the subject of my next work, eh?" He gave the quivering boy one final kick before turning away.

Sore, the hunchback pulled himself up as best he could and groped his way down the hillside. His hand was bloody and torn from the spade being ripped from his grasp and his ribs blushed a dark purple.

"You shouldn't let shit like that disturb you," said the poet, trying to calm his friend. "At least he brought back a spade. What would you have done had he brought a brush?"

"The same."

Both men burst into laughter.

After having composed themselves, the poet offered up yet another of his poems: "Her heart slowed … Death … Death … oh, come to me my love, and take away this great burden called life."

"Magnificent," declared the artist, returning to the canvas before him.

The time he was distracted from the incomplete painting allowed him a new perspective. Something was not right with his artwork. His eyes scanned the minute lines his brushstrokes had created on the barren piece of flax. What was it? he thought to himself, thoroughly examining every detail.

*There! That was it!* His eyes strained in the poor light to confirm his error in tint. The blood of those in the carts was too light. He went to work adding darker colorations of oil to his mistake, but to no avail. "Damn it! I can't get the bloody thing right! The blood is too light. Christ! It looks orange in tone!"

The poet raised his eyes from his writings only to lower them, silently deciding that engaging the artist in additional conversation might further enrage him.

In his hand the artist still held the small spade mistakenly brought to him by the hunchback. The spade's sharp edge rested firmly in his palm, its handle pointing freely up at him. In his anger and frustration he forgot what he held and forcefully squeezed down upon the keen blade.

The abrupt pain that raged through his hand diverted his attention from his painting to his wounded extremity. He opened his hand, allowing the tool to fall from his grasp and onto the ground, and examined the deep, straight slice in his palm.

The thin gash ran across the width of his hand. As he looked at his injury, gently opening wide his palm with the forefingers of his free hand, blood welled up and overflowed the incision's embankments.

He watched the cascading crimson run from his palm to his forearm. At his elbow, the precious red droplets showered the dusty ground.

The pain he felt was overshadowed by the timely boost his creativity had received. In wonderment, his gaze shifted from the bloody mess in his hand to the canvas, an unusually large grin breaking his veneer. He whispered softly to himself with a hushed, religious-like zeal, "What better for blood, than blood?" With the release of those words he shot forth his hand against the canvas board, allowing liberal quantities of blood to splash on select areas of his painting.

Once again the poet allowed his eyes to venture in the direction of his friend. He saw the ragged man, a gleeful expression on his face as he attempted to empty his veins into his work. "What incarnation of the bloody pits of Hell have you allowed your 'silent poetry' to become?"

"What better for blood than blood, eh?" the ecstatically deranged painter professed. "I am becoming one with my work. I actually stain the fabric of this canvas with myself!"

The poet scrutinized him in silence. He then looked to the quill in his hand. Its tip was coated with black ink and peppered with small, wind-blown particles of debris. Looking once more to the artist for inspiration, he then dutifully wiped clean as best he could the ink pen on his trousers. When he was through he carefully pricked the tip of his left index finger with the pen point. His blood sputtered out in a scant quantity. It required repeated stabbings to achieve a sufficient amount with which he could write, after which he held up his gory finger proudly for inspection. "Look here, friend artist. I, too, shall follow your creative lead."

The artist paid him no attention. Something was wrong again. His blood had ceased to flow as it had previously, being in the natural process of coagulation. Desperate, he attacked his wound, trying to recreate the red river that had only a moment ago been the source of an innovative waterfall. "Need more blood," he mumbled to himself.

It was at that instant, upon the utterance of those words, that once again his ingenuity prevailed. As if struck by a bolt sent from Hades, his brain formulated an idea so diabolical in conception that he dared not breathe a word of it to his companion. It was a concept that would allow him to shower his paintings with as much blood as he deemed necessary, and he would not have to be injurious to his own person.

He calmly set aside his brush and bent down, picking up the discarded spade from the dirt. His eyes searched the horizon for the subject of his wrath and the ultimate donation to his artwork.

He saw the small hump of insignificance crawling carefully down the slope of the hill, its bruised and battered form gently swaying to and fro in a mockingly heroic attempt at avoiding sharp rocks and camouflaged sinkholes.

The artist clutched the spade close to him, cunningly burying it beneath his smock. His eyes never leaving the distant blot on the landscape, he moved toward it, calling out, "Boy, come here! Come here at once!"

The shrillness with which the artist applied himself ruffled the poet, who had exhausted his finger well and was in the process of obtaining more blood from his left thumb. On his lap rested his booklet, its pages no longer in black ink, but in red.

He noted the artist, stalking slowly down the slope of the hill. Inhaling with pride the smell of burning tar mingled with the stench of decay, he gazed at his new poem with obvious affection.

As the orange sun slipped beneath a horizon of death and despair, shadows joined in the shell that was London. And with the onset of night, exhausting the last rays of sunlight, the poet read aloud the first line of his newly completed ode.

"All hail the Great Plague ..."

# Chapter One

It was her again. The strange but wonderful woman who had infested his dreams since childhood. Always it was the same, always she called to him; beckoning him unto her open arms, pleading for his love. She whispered his name, her voice a night breeze, slow and murmured with the cool tinge of death.

"Christian ... Christian ..."

He could not resist her, he could never resist her. Slowly he moved towards her, his every step an agony between horror and desire, repulsion and attraction. He was close to her now, he could smell the fragrance of her body: doses of incense with underlying smatterings of rotted flesh.

Her exquisite body, bathed in moonlight and twisted shadows, was unadulterated by the obscenity of clothing. He was within her arms now, feeling her cool breath wash over him as he buried his face deep in her abundant breasts. He felt her enclose around him, her arms hugging him tightly. He could not escape, he could never escape.

He raised his head from her chest, her hands toying with his long brown hair, and looked into her eyes. Her eyes! Those eyes! Bereft of life, and yet so alluring they had him powerless to withstand her. His gaze then fell upon her scarlet lips: red, velvety folds which opened to reveal two ivory daggers sharpened on the neck bones of many a lover.

The tension mounted; she had him utterly and absolutely. He could neither resist nor assist, but only lie limp in her arms, staring into her.

Her mouth opened wide in accommodation and expectation, and in her jaws he saw his fate. One tooth held his death, the other his damnation. He closed his eyes as her mouth clamped down upon his neck and the cold of her saliva mixed with the warmth of his blood.

In her sucking he felt his life leaving, his essence coming to rest in her belly. Between her ingestions of him she sighed and he could smell his blood on her breath. She cooed through crimson-stained lips, "You are mine ... you are mine ..."

Christian Coleswitten woke from his restless slumber drenched in his own perspiration, his every pore drowning in a sea of sweat. His hands danced over his face as he attempted to wipe the sweat from his countenance. This being futile, he resorted to using his damp sheet.

The room was hot. It was early September and quite cool outside but he dared not open the window for fear of allowing a contagion of the Great Plague into his room – or worse, into his lungs.

Even now, as he sat on his crude wooden bed in the stillness of the room, he could hear the cries of the doomed in the streets outside. The closed window did little to stifle their piercing screams, their wailing pleas for salvation. His own security comforted him little, for he felt not safe but that he was hiding, cowering behind wet blankets.

Once more, his mind turned as it had innumerable nights before, to contemplating his dream-woman. *Who was she? Why does she torment me through loss of sleep and cause me such distress?*

He rose naked from his bed and walked to the window, his large, slightly lanky frame glowing in the moonlight raging through its glass. The wooden floor creaked under his weight and splints of rough floorboard bit into his feet. Peering out into the London night, the vats of burning tar illuminated well the expected horrors on the streets external.

He looked past his own image caught in the window glass, his twenty years wearing poorly on him as his sunken brown eyes took in sights of which even the great Dante could never have imagined in all his nine circles of Hell. Scattered people groped in the cobblestone streets, their bodies wracked with pain and despair. Some spouted incoherent pieces of psalms, others simply cried out for help from up above. The shrieks of women troubled Christian, but they did not rattle him as deeply as the wails of babes afflicted with the sickness.

He listened for the children and silently counted the numbers in his head. *What was that? Three? No, four. Four little ones on one city street alone. How many were there in the entire city? The entire country? Precious newborns barely dry and already they die, never to have known the wonders of life, to have experienced love, or to have known God.*

*God? What kind of God allows this to happen to his people, let alone innocent children?* Father Stemmons had pronounced his belief that the Plague was a display of God's anger at the people of England as a result of their refutation of the Roman Church. God saw fit to deal with the Anglican heretics in Old Testament fashion. "Nothing's better than a good plague to bring the strays back to the flock," Stemmons famously proclaimed.

"Now they're in Limbo," Christian muttered aloud to himself as his thoughts returned to the children and their plight. Many went unwashed of their original sin to the grave, in death being barred from partaking in the pleasures of Heaven. "They are in Limbo, while we are in Hell."

A sudden rapping stirred him from his troubled thoughts. He looked blankly at the door, waiting to see if he had, in actuality, a visitor or if the accursed woman of his dreams was now afflicting him in reality. The unknown caller once more attacked the door and Christian let out a sigh of relief. It wasn't her, for he was quite certain the knocking was real and not the product of his rampant and libidinous imagination. He then proceeded to his clothing, piled neatly on a chair opposite his bed, and selected his well-worn, white shirt. Hurriedly tossing it over his head he pulled down at its bottom, ensuring that the long shirt would cover his nude body completely. Moving to the door, he challenged the unexpected solicitor: "Who art thou who trespasses at so late an hour?"

From the outside came the dampened reply, "'Tis Bremen, the ship's steward. I have an urgent message sent to you by Father Stemmons."

Bremen, Christian thought, the pudgy, little weasel who fancied he could escape the Plague by hiring on with a warship. His ship must have docked and he, being the cowering lump of shit that he is, had gone immediately to Father Stemmons for some form of religious protection. God doesn't play favorites, Bremen, you alone should know that.

"Come now. Open up! 'Tis with urgency and great import that I am sent unto you," whined the steward through the heavy wooden door.

Christian turned the locks and released the bolt, waiting momentarily as he listened for Bremen, who moved nervously about outside. Gauging the distance between his unwelcome visitor and the door, which swung outwards, he vigorously thrust it open, catching the seaman square on the jaw.

Bremen reeled backwards and toppled over a particularly large pile of rubbish sitting in the street. Christian stood in his doorway, his shirt ruffling with the nippy nighttime breeze, observing the man's fall with a smirk.

"You intended to do that!" an incredulous Bremen stammered as he rose covered in dung. "You shan't witness the glory of Paradise if you continue in your roguish ways!"

"Don't you preach to me, you sniveling, rotund coward!" Christian roared. "If I were to commit a thousand sins daily, blaspheming through mere existence, I would rather be preached my condemnations by a common whore than you, sir, you who deserts his family in such times as these. 'Twas I who held your good wife's hand when she succumbed to the sickness, who cradled your children into the arms of Saint Peter while you were off examining Dutch frigates."

Bremen stepped back speechless, his eyes filling with tear and his head lowering in shame. The feces smeared all over his shirt seemed somehow fitting.

"You've delivered your message," Christian mockingly intoned, "now return to the safety of your vessel."

Bremen turned and slowly walked away. Christian did not see the storm that broke over the steward's cheeks, nor did he care.

"I hope you drown," Christian whispered under his breath as he watched him disappear down an alley. Returning to the heat of his room, he secured the door behind him. *What could it be that Stemmons wanted? And at this time of night?* He continued to allow his mind to ruminate as he dressed himself in the darkened interior.

The clothes he put on were work clothes, the grimy coverings he wore when visiting those afflicted. He glanced over at the plain wooden chest that occupied the far corner of his room, its bronze padlock glinting at him in the poor light. That was where he kept his fine apparel, the expensive attire which was willed to him by a grateful, but unrepentant, Catholic seafarer. He reserved the unlocking of that chest for extremely important occasions.

After fumbling in the dark for his stockings, he sat himself on his damp, little bed and placed upon his feet his father's old boots. As he stared at the well-worn boots that encased his feet, he thought of his father. It had been about two years since he had passed, his heart abandoning its chore. God, how he missed the stern old man.

Invariably, thinking of his father prompted Christian to revive images of his mother. Images pieced together through long conversations with his father and his own ideas of what a mother should look like. His mother had died in childbirth. She was the cause of his life as he was the cause of her death.

His hand gently steadied the broad crucifix dangling from his neck. It had belonged to his mother and, aside from a few pots and pans, was all he owned of her. He tucked the ornate cross into his shirt and rising from the bed put on his coarse wool coat. After sweating inside, he feared catching his death with the chill of the night.

Leaving this humble sanctuary for the wilds of the dark played havoc with his mind. Will I die tonight? he wondered. Will I take into my lungs an inhalant of the Plague? What kind of a world is it in which we live when one cannot leave his dwelling without fearing the mark of Death?

He then prepared himself, praying for the sick's salvation as well as for his own. As his hand grasped the cold door handle he felt a strange chill tingle down his spine. It wasn't from the frigid cast-iron handle, nor from any other external device or phenomenon, but from some inexplicable source within. He felt his throat dry and his body quake as his mind came to rest on the only logical explanation.

It was *her.*

He quickly fled his abode hoping to leave his lurid thoughts inside. Upon the locking of his door he yielded a more troubling notion. What was it that could cast him so into this dreaded dark, forcing him to readily quit his sanctum? What was it that he feared more so than the Plague, more so than death itself? As he rushed down deserted streets, he once again could not avoid the truth. It was her.

The winding corridors, shadowed here and there with the deranged and dying denizens of the night, flew past Christian as he hurried on his way. Foul limbs reached out from their places in the darkness, silently beseeching him to either save or destroy them, to assist, somehow, in the obliteration of their pain.

Peering into the obscure blackness which surrounded him, he caught a whiff of that which was all too familiar: the aroma of putrefaction.

Following the scent, he was led to a vat-lit side alley, where the fire beneath the boiling tar warmed the air and cast dancing silhouettes on the rough brick walls. Amidst the fire's festivities Christian eyed the far wall, taking notice of several crates stacked one upon the other.

Approaching the boxes, the rotten stench mixed with the smell of tar, growing so strong as to bring tears to his eyes. Blinking erratically, he pulled the collar of his heavy coat high and buried his face within its stifling wool folds, raising himself on the balls of his feet to gaze into one of the open crates.

In the flickering firelight, he perceived the wooden boxes to be filled with spoiled cabbage. He breathed a sigh of relief, pleased that he had uncovered rotting greens and not rotting flesh.

Out of the corner of his eye, he detected movement in the ruined vegetation. The moldy, brown leaves of the cabbage had become a nest, and the security of the crates a fortress, to a family of rats. Their beady stares angered him. The damn vermin were everywhere, he thought. They shall become the inheritors of the city before long. This brief conception transfixed him, producing the compulsion to act, and grasping the crate's corners he tipped it over.

The crate hit the ground with a loud clatter, eliciting a noisy response from the rats. The screams that poured forth from the rank mouths of the rodents sounded eerily human-like, a fantastic chorale composed of malicious spite and intense revulsion.

They scurried, fleeing their overturned keep for refuge elsewhere. There must have been twenty to thirty of them, an ensemble effusion of filth and disease.

The remaining rats from the toppled box cried out in alarm, prompting the other cabbage crates to spew over in a sea of grimy fur. The mass exodus from the upended hovels seemed endless, sending hundreds of the small beasts into the dark recesses of the night, leaving Christian to stare in disbelief.

Even with all he had seen during the Plague's residency in England, he was still amazed at two things: the capacity people had in them for cruelty, and the disproportionately large number of rats infesting the city.

The desertion complete, Christian slowly returned to the now vacant rat commune. He walked stealthily, foot over foot, in his convergence on the crates. He did not fear the rats; rather he feared his own good sense, honed on his experience and past dealings with the dead. He did not smell moldering vegetation, as he would prefer to believe, but rather the sickeningly sweet smell of deteriorating flesh.

He surveyed the disheveled boxes but could see nothing. He then maneuvered around so as to enable him a view from behind. Carefully, he scanned the shaded area that had been previously barred from his vision.

What he beheld shocked and repulsed him to no end. There amongst the crates and cabbage lay the decaying shell of a little girl. Her face, though drastically reduced through rot and devouring, maintained its expression of terror.

As his eyes imbibed the ghoulish sight, he took notice of the heaving of her chest, which seemed so irregularly spontaneous that he entertained for a brief moment the horrific possibility that she was still alive.

He knelt at her side and, moving the crates that cast her in shadowed darkness, examined her paltry body in the open firelight. He at once felt foolish for even thinking her alive for her left foot was missing, as were her digits, nibbled to the bone.

*The wicked fiends had made a meal of this poor, defenseless child! They probably came across her, weak with the Plague and seeking refuge behind these crates, and descended upon her, gorging their hunger on her living flesh.*

Upon further examination of the nude corpse, Christian made a discovery that additionally added to his horror. Finding no swellings about the groin or neck area, no bulbous mark of the bubo anywhere on her person, he fearfully surmised that she was not to be counted amongst those stricken with the Plague. Probably caught in her sleep, she had been set upon by hundreds of ravenous rats and eaten to death.

My God! he thought, the little bastards were no longer scavengers, but hunters as well. Who could be safe when in darkness and shadow there lurked so well numbered an enemy? An enemy that did not discriminate against women and children, but attacked them with equal ferocity. An enemy that fought not for king and country, but for its belly.

The heaving of the dead girl's chest gnawed on Christian's brain as the rats had her body. What was it that caused the illusion of life, the charade of circulation? He studied her for a moment longer before deciding to act.

Gently wrapping his fingers around her pasty calves, he slowly rose and carefully dragged her remains from the array of surrounding crates to the openness of the fiery alley. He had dealt with the dead before and knew well of skin slippage and other damages to the body incurred through improper handling. He treated her with all the gentleness and care one would expect to be shown the living, not the dead.

Having removed her corpse to the center of the small area, as near as he could to the firelight, he set her legs down, careful not to allow the stump of her left foot to brush against him. The absence of rigor had made her transportation less of a task. With the increased abundance of lighting he could accurately scrutinize the atrocities which had been committed on the child.

The myriad bite-marks were more pronounced, as were the dark blotches and discolorations of her decaying skin. Her hair was matted with rat excrement, filth, and clumps of her own coagulated blood. Grime stained her, a thick layering of smoked tar having settled on her stationary cadaver. The missing digits and amputated foot further added to the grotesqueness of her form.

Christian felt the burning of tears once more assault his eyes, but this time it wasn't from the putrid smell or his close proximity to the heated tar. *What had they done to this pathetic child? What horrific pains did she undertake at the clutches of the lowliest of villains?*

Not content, he charily turned her onto her stomach.

Her back was relatively untouched by the ravenous rats, although that was not to say it was in fair condition. Dark blemishes of lividity tarnished her, weaving a cobblestone patchwork into her upper posterior. Her buttocks were no longer rounded and smooth, but compressed; flattened and wrinkled though extended proneness and dead weight.

As he looked mournfully at the shredded beauty before him, he turned his thoughts to the oft-repeated movements of her chest. He had heard of demons and evil spirits inhabiting the dead, using their corporeal forms to scour the countryside for innocence to malign. Stories of the dead rising from their graves filled his head. These were ridiculous superstitions, he reasoned with himself, created by imaginative old women. Besides, in all the tales he had heard, only those wicked in life rose to be wicked in death.

Just as he was about to envision the dire predicament London would be in if all those dead of the Plague came forth from their mass graves, he caught sight of a strange movement near the girl's leveled rump. The aberration was fostered in the harsh but varying glow of the fire. Christian strained his eyes and bent at the knees in an attempt to ascertain what it was that drew his concentration to her buttocks. It was as if the pulsing of her breast had moved to the depths of her bowels.

Consternation, laced with dread, wafted on the smoke whirling about his head. The hair on the back of his neck rose in unison to the chilling thought his mind formulated to conspire against him. Was it possible? Could it be? No, he assured his rebellious brain, let that not be so! In denial, he rolled the girl back onto her posterior.

But his darkest fear was fully and most graphically realized when the head of a rat protruded from the girl's open mouth; its gore-caked snout sniffing the air and its eyes flashing nervously about. It tried with great difficulty to turn itself around, but the smallness of the child's oral cavity impeded its progress. Its beady, little orbs fell on Christian, who stared frozen with shock and anger.

The two of them, man and rat, eyed each other in silence. All that could be heard was the crackling of the fire, taunting the two foes to prolong their piercing stares. The rat seemed to smile at Christian, as if he was proud of his handiwork and reveled in his warm maw. Christian ended the sullen sport with a methodic step forward.

Instantly the rat let out a high pitched squeal and the girl's body came convulsing to life. She writhed and wiggled on the hard cobblestone, the muffled screams of a horde of rodents emanating from within.

"Good God!" Christian blurted in hollow invocation. *They have made a home of her innards! They recline in the warmth of her decay and nestle in the rot of her swellings! By God, I'll not have it!*

He then quickly, and with none of the delicacy shown prior, grabbed the monstrous dwelling firmly by the ankles and dragged her closer to the flame. He would not tolerate the further desecration of this child's body.

As he approached the flaming tar vat the rats, sensing their rapid movement towards the extreme heat, attempted to flee the girl through any exit possible. Christian saw to it that no attempts were successful; kicking back in those absconding through the vagina, and shifting the body so as to not allow them exit through the anus.

He caught one final glimpse of his foe as he hefted the corpse high into the thick air, its form like that of a rag doll. The leering rat, the one with the audacity to stare him down from the mouth of a deceased child, glared at him as it frantically tried to free its stuck self from the binds of the girl's jaws. Their eyes meeting, the vermin let out a lamenting wail before being submersed in the boiling tar.

Christian hastily pushed the entire body headfirst into the hot vat. He forced the only visibly remaining part of the girl, her sole foot, into the liquefying black. He didn't want the rats to have any opportunity at salvation, he wanted them to burn – burn for their sins in the cremating tar as he feared he would in the searing pits of Hell.

With the profane deed accomplished he staggered wearily into the street, resuming his hazard fraught journey to the residence of Father Stemmons. He was cold, tired, and wet from his nervous sweat. Regarding strangers with treachery, he eyed all. The feelings of discomfort and stress colluded with the vulgarities he witnessed to upset his stomach. When would it all end, he sorrowed silently.

People dissipated into darkened crannies at his approach. Filled with fear, they slunk away with his every footfall. The poor had no place to go, and were joined in death on the streets of London with the turned out and wandering afflicted. Pity was undue most of them, they having turned their backs on Christ for quacks, mountebanks, conjurers, palmists, fortunetellers, and magicians. Witchcraft and the unholy abidance of Satanism were rampant. How quickly those in fear forsook even He who died for them, Christian noted grimly.

Turning onto a larger block, he could not help but observe the overabundance of red crosses on dwelling doors. The sight of them tore into his senses. It seemed as though when one house in a neighborhood became marked the other houses were soon to receive paint as well. So it was that the bloody crosses spread throughout the city like a wildfire. If ever he despised anything religious, it would surely be those damnable crosses.

Several homes had written in paints of differing colors the motto, "Lord have mercy upon us". He was thankful these households were still in obedience to the Lord, for many a house had pagan relics or symbols of black magic embellishing their doorjambs. Even now, as he strode up the slick street, he could make out the word "Abracadabra" above various doorways. Just as the Plague was infiltrating every household, so was Satan the souls of its occupants.

As he crossed the worn cobblestone, his boots' thunderous clicking announcing his coming, he was overtaken by a train of dead carts. He bobbed in between the sluggish carts, dodging the glares cast his way by the annoyed men who pulled them.

Although he had tried to avoid doing so, his eyes wandered to the bed of one of the carts and to the gruesome cargo contained therein. He beheld the piteous dead: clothed in rags, their mouths gaping open in screams forever silent. In the erratic lighting of the rocking cart's lamplight he glimpsed the eyes of the demised glaring into his soul, condemning him in their quietus. He saw the young, the old, the weak, the strong, the male, and the female. Death was not fastidious in his trade. Like the crippled indigent, he took what he could get.

Christian had been so transfixed by the deploring departed that he did not realize he was standing in the middle of the street, impeding the flow of the dead carts. A large, burly man reeking of vinegar and body odor grabbed him forcefully from behind.

"Would ye care to join 'em?" the odious man whispered close to Christian's ear. His breath was heavily laced with leek and garlic and his closeness to Christian further enhanced its potency.

Christian felt queasy at the smell of him. As he turned to face him he was entreated to the overwhelming stench of the man's body mingling with that of his breath. Coupled with the surrounding decay filling the dead carts it was too much to bear. Once more dots of perspiration formed on Christian's clammy skin and his knees buckled under him as his feet were displaced on the slippery-smooth cobblestone.

He did not fall, for the large man held him up and spun him around. Christian weakly stared into the man's face. His eyes were a steely gray, filled with tremendous spite, and his dry, cracked lips bled. Caked, white spittle concealed the corners of his mouth and his teeth were hued in browns and yellows, not a one being a natural white. His rank tongue flopped in and out of his mouth triumphantly butchering what remained of an already degenerated English language.

"Ye want to join 'em?" the man leeringly solicited.

Christian was speechless. It was not due to fear, although there was a substantial uneasiness felt by him in the presence of the ruffian. It was that he did not wish to open his mouth and additionally inhale the stink. Looking over the man's shoulder, Christian saw that he was in fact an operator of a dead cart, his devil's wheelbarrow lying motionless behind him.

"Answer me, ye sod!" the man demanded of him, "Do ye want a closer look?"

Christian vigorously shook his head. He felt as though he was suffering from the fever, his heart beating in anxiety to his helpless condition. He summoned all the resistance left in him, from the rising of his bile to the strength-sapped arms dangling limply at his sides. With a vengeance he tore at the hands that held him by his arms.

The foul man only laughed at his attempt, picking him up and whirling him about. He marched with Christian to the rear of his abandoned cart and paused, easing him down upon the street.

"Ye find the dead so interesting, eh?" the man growled, "Then why don't ye join 'em?" He lifted Christian into the air despite Christian's lively protestations, setting him down atop the bodies in the cart's bed. There Christian rested with those eternally resting.

Christian breathed heavy, gasping breaths and held his eyes tightly closed. He could not believe this was happening to him. He felt the corpses beneath him bend and break, accommodating his body weight. Summoning up his courage, he opened his closed eyes and turned them downwards.

He saw in the pale light the faces of those he so dishonored by sitting on. They were the faces of children, of young women as of yet unreleased from the stony clutches of rigor mortis; all of them robbed of their lives, their youth, and now undergoing in death an even greater ignominy. Christian squirmed to acquire his freedom, but to no avail. The man had grown strong in his daily drawings of the dead.

"Might it be that ye were a-lookin' for a fair dame amongst these worm biscuits?"

Christian painfully shook his head.

"Well, here's a fine lass. A day old, but not too moldy for ye." The man released him with his right hand, but tightened the hold of his left around Christian's neck. With his free hand he fished around the ghastly pile, producing an auburn-haired young woman.

Christian looked into the poor woman's face. She was not much younger than he, perhaps eighteen or nineteen, and even in death retained her beauty. Her red locks were clumped together, entangled with the hair of another of the cart's passengers. The vile man took the woman by her skull and forced her on him.

"I think she wants ye," the man said with a smirk, "I think ye want her."

He pulled on Christian's neck, compelling him to come face-to-face with the dead woman. Christian tried to back away, his feet kicking and lashing out at the corpses in the cart that offered him no sure footing. Closer and closer the man drew him towards the woman. She was almost upon him, their lips nearly touching. He saw in her mouth the white writhing of maggots and a line of ants descending from her hairline into her eyes. Was this her? he thought. Was this his dream made real? He finally forced out a sharp scream that echoed in the surrounding alleys.

The man simply guffawed and chided him, "Don't be rude, give her a kiss!"

Christian could feel his fever raging through his head. God help me, he thought, spare me this gross indignity! His mind swarmed with various biblical passages but he could not mentally recite one. *I am being forced to rape the dead! I am about to touch lips with a woman who — what was that?* He thought he heard a noise. It was a noise — that of small children laughing with glee.

He glanced over the side of the cart and there saw three children, red paint in hands, giggling at his predicament. They watched him with open mouths and frantic, joyous movements, their eyes watering not from pity, but from pleasure. *What hell is this where little ones delight in other's terror?*

The man witnessed the children's behavior and grew fierce, scolding them accordingly. The children ran off, their paint cans splashing red paint all down the street. Still incensed, the man muttered, "Children should not see such things."

He released his hold on Christian and let the woman's corpse drop amidst her kindred. He then walked back to the front of his cart and reached down and picked up the cart's hafts. Turning to Christian, who lay dumbstruck with the dead, he advised, "Ye had better leave, lest ye want to be buried with ye friends."

At this, Christian bounded out of the cart and ran away, stopping to rest only after overexerting himself. Leaning against a brick wall for support, he cried long and hard. He cried because of everything — because of the dead and dying, the Plague, the rats, the cruelty. He was on the verge of an emotional and mental collapse: a nervous breakdown. All reason had momentarily left him. He was saved from kissing a corpse through the truculent humor of three inhumane children.

Once he had gathered his wits, he felt slightly ashamed, his manhood tarnished through his essentially nonexistent defiance to the stinking man. He walked with soft, shallow steps, catching his breath and attempting to regain his pride. How could he defend himself against so large a brute? his rationale soothed. How could anyone have done any different? It still bothered him, scratching at his skullcap as if it were a festering wound. Arthur would have done different, he mused, recalling his *History of the Kings of Britain.* A whole lot of people would have done different. His esteem dashed, he turned his concerns back to the real world, returning to the nightmare of everyday existence, ascending once more into his shell of self-loathing and vile pity.

Sobs, screams, and wails filled his ears as he trudged on through the dense dark. Unseen choirs bartered with God or whoever would listen to spare their souls or the souls of loved ones sickened with the tokens of the Plague.

Christian was constrained to recall a tale he had heard, supposedly true, of a young girl recently rendered unto motherhood. Her babe was still in the suckling age when she became contaminated with the sickness. Sending her husband one night to fetch the doctor, for she was one of those who did not show the sickness right away, she complained of a bothersome fever. When he returned with the physician, to their horror they discovered the woman lifeless, dead of the Plague, her babe vainly suckling on a cold, dry teat. He did not know the fate of the child, but surely the drinking of milk from the breast of one infected must be perilous. Here, he reflected, death comes even in that most sacred of fleshly forms: the nurturing nipple of motherhood.

He hearkened to a riotous calamity of great lamentations just north of him. The Old Street Fields pest house, he figured. That and the one in Westminster were the only two pest houses he knew of in all England. It was believed that by rounding up the poor and homeless sick and placing them in one area, the Plague would be contained. All it had accomplished was to breed two abodes of hellish filth. As an attendant to Catholics of the Plague, Christian had occasion to visit the houses and deliver messages from lamenting relatives. He never dared enter, but stood outside, a good distance away, and shouted the messages to the intended within. The place smelled of death, of many people rotting away in unison. Unclean, unwanted, and unloved, they cried synchronously aloud in pain and self-mourning, their grief equaling that of Judas' on the day of his betrayal of Christ.

From pest house to charnel house, he thought as his eyes focused in the direction of the screams. He was so engrossed in his recollections that he nearly stumbled over a body lying in the middle of the street. He quickly stepped to the left and, arms flailing, caught his balance. He then surveyed the immediate area and, finding no one present, determined an examination of the remains was in order.

It was a young boy, probably not more than ten years old and not long deceased. Christian softly wiped the curly mop of black hair from the boy's face as he rolled him over from his stomach onto his back. He looked intently into the boy's glazed eyes, as if hoping to somehow resurrect him, or simply catch a glimpse of Death himself. Expectedly, no response was forthcoming, and much to his distaste he closed forever the boy's imploring eyes. He had seen a thousand similar pairs of eyes, all of them demanding of him reasons for his continuance and their close. He did not know why he himself hadn't died; perhaps he was meant for something more, something grand.

As he had done countless times before, he prepared the boy for Last Rites. It was a ritual to which he had grown despicably accustomed. Words poured forth from his mouth as water released from a floodgate, being so used to their formation that he pulled them from his mind without complicity of thought. He blessed the nameless boy, absolving him of whatever paltry sins he had committed in his abbreviated life. As he was about to finish his discourse in Latin he was interrupted by rapidly approaching footsteps.

Christian turned, his tongue still tumbling words past his lips, and searched the darkness behind him for the unknown visitor drawing near. His eyes spied a small man emerging from the pitch shadows and stumbling into the dimly lit street. The man had what appeared to be old potato sacks draped about his person, and the closer he came the older he grew. He minded the aged man, whose occupation it was to beg, but did not rise, choosing to stay at the side of the boy.

"Why bother with Last Rites? 'Twill do him no good," said the dirty beggar, repugnance masking his face.

"Let me be. 'Tis my duty as 'tis his privilege," Christian impassively intoned, not bothering to even glance up.

"He's been there for over three hours."

"Time is of no consequence in these matters."

Christian's behavior infuriated the beggar. "You churchers, you're all the same, every one of you. All pompous, all so very sure of your … your salvation!" He gestured to the boy. "You are not worth an ounce of life in this poor boy's body!"

Christian halted his ritual and sharply faced his denouncer. The man was ill, he thought as he looked into his wild eyes, probably ranting to anyone who'll listen. Better be careful. "I mean no harm. Why must you badger me so?"

"Open your eyes, man! The time is near, so very near. We are past prayers, there is no God in Heaven to save us, let alone you. Heed my advice, while you still have your health. Live life to the fullest before you watch and smell yourself rot."

Christian knew it was against his better judgment, but he had to engage this deranged heathen in argument. He rose, abandoning the boy, and set upon the pauper. "And what would you have me do, old man? Rape? Murder? Plunder? Sin against our Lord and Benefactor?"

"Yes! Yes!" hissed the beggar, moving closer. "Sin against your Lord, our Lord. That great and holy Personage responsible for all the good in the world." He motioned to the chaos that was London: the cries of the dying, the shut up houses, and the dead at their feet. He then clasped his hands in mock prayer and extolled, "Thank You, oh Jesus, for delivering unto us, Your undeserving servants, the Great Plague. Please, oh Lord, might we also have another flood, or a fire perhaps?"

"Blasphemer!" Christian protested. "The Lord holds no love for thee."

"Nor I for He! How can your God, a loving God, allow this to happen?" He threw himself on Christian, grabbing him by the collar and pleading most longingly, "Kill me! Succumb to your temptations, you shan't go to Hell."

Christian peeled the beggar's worn-down fingers from his neck, pushing him away. "You're mad!"

"And who isn't?"

"Off with you! Leave me to commend this poor lad's soul into the hands of God." With that being all he intended to say on the matter, he sank to the boy's side.

"You shan't utter one word to that boy," threatened the beggar, the insanity growing in his eyes.

"Who are you? By what rights have you to sanction this boy's eternal soul?" Christian parried, unaffected by the beggar's malevolent gaze.

"I am his father!" the alms-taker proudly proclaimed, his voice hoarse and choked with emotion.

Christian's anger melted into remorse. He felt as though he had committed some travesty by bickering with the old beggar, the old father. Through supplication he tried to ease the pain he felt he had caused the old man. "I am sorry. If 'tis your wish—"

"Away, damn you! Be gone!"

Christian lowered his head in shame and rose in silence. He could not bring himself to face the old father, let alone the dead son. As he left the unhappy family, he quickened his step in an effort to leave them behind, to do the impossible and forget them.

The old father would not let Christian forget. He cried in anguish after him, "Go back to your church, your sanctuary. Go back to your God! How can He help you and not us?" He then turned his attentions towards his son, and kneeling, raised the boy's head onto his lap, "Why has my son died? Why will He not take me?" He stared through teary eyes at Christian's shrinking form and murmured to himself, "Why not me?" The grieving man caressed the face of his son, and as his eyes passed down the vestige of his boy he spied large rats chewing at his child's feet. Pulling his son near, he wildly batted at the unclean ghouls. "Away!" he sobbed. "Away, damn you! Away from my wee one …"

Meandering through the weaving streets, Christian shamefully knew well where he was headed. The name of the pub was The Bloodied Lamb, in reference to the fact that it was located on what was once the sight of a pagan sacrificial altar. It was, much to Christian's disgust, where the Father Samuel Stemmons resided. The thought of a priest, an esteemed member of the Lord's flock, being reduced to living in such a place of ill repute angered him. Being Catholic in England had always been difficult. He had to hide his beliefs from others for fear of persecution at the hands of the ruling Protestant government. The talk he had heard recently of the Catholicism of the king's wife, and that of his brother, the Duke of Wales, had caused a stir in the Protestant elite. Fear of the king's conversion back to the religion of Rome prompted Parliamentary leaders and city magistrates to crack down on Catholics in an effort to squelch the king's reform policies, which ended many discriminatory laws against Catholics. Despite the king's good intentions, times had only gotten worse for Christian and others like him. Fear of being accused of plotting to overthrow the government hounded Papists everywhere. It was why Christian disgracefully hid his religious convictions and why Father Stemmons lived in a pub.

Emerging from the shady byways that incised the city into a network of intersecting and connecting alleys, Christian strode across a small common as his eyes sought out the familiar pub. There it was, nestled between a cobbler's shop and an importer's emporium. He grew upset at the mere sight of it, its outer walls befouled with the stains of vomit and urine, hallmarks graciously left behind by departing patrons. He turned his nose up at the detestable place and accelerated his pace. He averted his gaze from the small building itself, instead focusing on the unkempt courtyard surrounding the dirtied face of the pub with a rusted, wrought iron fence. Stopping at the fence, he mused that it was as if it were a cage fashioned to keep cretins within and those of a moral persuasion out. He looked hard at the rotting wooden placard which hung above the entrance. It was a clumsily carved rendition of the pub's namesake, that of a slaughtered lamb. Although the paint was cracked, chipped, and in many spots nonexistent, the form of a lamb, its head separated from its body but joined through a bridge of faded scarlet about the neck area, was still quite clear – an unwitting affront to God, a profane *Agnus Dei*. It was as if the paint administered to coat the heathen emblem was so embarrassed at being used in such fashion that it had retreated into the cracks and cuts etched into the wood grain, effecting a lined caricature rather than a whole form.

Christian pushed onward, opening the creaky front gate carefully so as to not cut himself on the sharp, rusty edges. The gate rattled in its worn hinges, moaning a long and mournful lamentation to its being opened. Entering the courtyard, he was struck with an almost imperceptible chill at the base of his spine. He released the gate from his hands foolishly, preoccupied with his sudden coolness. As the gate hastily slammed behind him, the hinges' moaning was raised to a sinister, shrieking laughter.

He held his right forefinger up for inspection. The cursory examination revealed that the gate had bitten him, extracting a slight amount of blood, which trickled from his fingertip. He glanced from his finger to the silent gate, which seemed somehow to return his wounded gaze with a malevolent stare.

*Death is everywhere, all around me! I am being besieged on all sides by forces that do not make themselves known, forces which hamper my every little progression, forces which I do not know. 'Tis through these forces that I live in fear of something worse than death, something which my mind perceives as the visage of a most beautiful, if not mysterious, woman. A brief jaunt becomes a treacherous journey into the night, assailants assaulting me at every turn, strangers crying out for my blood. The opening of a hoary gate transcends into a monumental undertaking, rivaling Samson's destruction of the Philistines. And I can seek no solace in sleep, that simple pleasure granted all men save for me, my rest being robbed of me by that cruel lady somnambulist.*

Christian shook the chill from his bones and cleared his cluttered head before walking to the pub's door. Standing for a moment outside the entrance, he made ready his appearance. He then reached out and turned the door handle, all the while looking into the pub's window, which was closed and curtained. He could only make out hideous shadows cast upon the gray curtains by the lamplight within. Through the thick door he heard the rumblings of laughter, the laughter of besotted slobs.

As he gradually eased the door open, ever so slightly so as to not draw attention to himself, he fancied he heard someone whisper his name. He whirled his head around and faced the empty courtyard and the common he had just crossed. Who was it? he thought to himself. Who called my name? His eyes squinted as he strained to see into the dark. A soft but cool breeze rippled through the little courtyard. Perhaps that was what it was, he rationalized, a misconstrued wind. This did little to settle his mind, for he was quite sure some person sighed for his attention. As he returned his eyes to the door before him, the chill he had so recently dislocated developed anew within him. His logic fought with his ears and painfully suffered defeat as Christian yielded to the fidelity he had heard: it was a woman's tone that beckoned to him.

As it had before, the slightest meditation pertaining to the dream woman catapulted his senses into action. He frantically pushed open the pub door and slammed it closed behind him, unintentionally becoming the focus of every eye in the place. Once inside, he saw his lack of composure in the blank stares he received from the curious patrons. His eyes darted from face to pugnacious face as he distanced himself from the pariah door.

The long silence was abated and harsh glares averted by the shrill cry of a goosed barmaid. The dishonored woman dutifully laid her hand across the miserable drunkard, slapping him to the pub floor. Laughter erupted from the slovenly patrons. Christian stared into their open mouths, untold realms of filth within every gaping orifice: diseased saliva, decaying teeth, and rotting gums all awash with foully brewed ale. Their maws were a breeding haven for every form of virulent pestilence. Their lips released the contents of their jowls as they uproariously spewed forth speckles of spittle and torrents of corrupted ale. Christian closed his eyes in disgust and walked past the rank sots.

As he headed for the back rooms of the pub, which were reserved for the private uses of the staff, he caught the suspicious gaze of the owner, who stood behind the counter tending bar. Christian met the wary man with a slight, well-intended nod, and ducked behind the portiere that separated the back rooms from the public. He did not care for the owner. Although the man was a fellow Catholic and did provide refuge for Father Stemmons, Christian found him base. He liked not the look of the man, how he carried himself, nor how he made his living.

As Christian quietly walked toward the father's room, he passed the other rooms without even a glance. His eyes were glued to Stemmons' door. It was as if that was all that mattered to him, that by knocking upon that door he would set in motion events which would lead him from his dreary existence, events which would fulfill his literary-induced fantasies. By the facile opening of a door his life's course would be set and his destiny realized.

Upon reaching the serendipitous door, he paused for a moment to collect himself. It had been a particularly strenuous night and he did not wish it to reflect on his appearance. Father Stemmons had something important for him, for the last time he had sent for him was to witness the public execution of Major General Harrison.

He recollected Harrison, sentenced to die for participating in the wars against the King. He was traditionally hanged, drawn, and quartered to the delight of the crowd. Christian remembered watching with horror the gleeful faces of the spectators. Their joyful shouts upon being shown Harrison's head and heart bothered him many months afterwards. A man had been butchered before men, women, and children, and they all responded as if it were a Shakespearean comedy. He then thought of the disinterment of Cromwell, Ireton, and Bradshaw from their repose in Westminster Abbey, and of their gibbeted desecration.

He was about to ruminate upon Cromwell's toleration of differing religions when he heard an erratic noise from within Stemmons' room. He pressed close to the door, placing his ear against the wood grain, and labored to listen. Soft murmurings from within gave way to a lusty cackle. He heard Stemmons' deep voice, vibrating the air with his bass bellow. There was another sharing the room with him, he thought. His interest piqued, Christian strove harder to ascertain who it was that occupied the room with the Father. As he leaned forward he rattled the door in its frame, the noise causing the room to fall silent. Disheartened, and angry with his own clumsiness, he had no other recourse but to knock and announce his presence.

"Who's there?" came the muffled bass from inside.

"'Tis Christian, Father Stemmons."

At this the room once more sprang to life with giggles and the accompanying sounds of a hurried reorganization. Christian could make out audible distinctions. He knew that someone was rearranging the bed and that another was fixing the chairs about the table – chair legs scraping across the floor and the billowy snap of cotton sheets attested to this.

He then heard Stemmons scolding and the hurried approach of someone from within drawing near. He backed away from the door and hoped his chagrin at almost being caught spying did not show.

The door abruptly opened with the cessation of the footsteps, and Christian met the owner's wife; her chestnut hair a mess, blouse undone, and her clothes rumpled. On different occasions she was quite a handsome woman, but now, under the shame of adultery and the wanton appearance she presented, she was considerably less appealing. She smiled at Christian and let out an embarrassed chuckle. She then pushed her hair from her face and nervously fumbled with it, endeavoring to set it right. When she did this her left breast protruded through her open blouse.

Christian's eyes eagerly fell on the well-endowed breast and he had to catch himself from gawking. Lifting his gaze uneasily from her bosom, he saw that she was watching his fascination with a mild curiosity of her own. They peered into each other. Then she broke away, allowing her interest to settle on Christian's crotch, her brow rising in pleasant intrigue.

It had been so long since Christian had physically loved a woman. The last time had been over a year ago, with Rebecca. How he missed her: her eyes, her breasts, her caress.

The unfaithful wife then departed, leaving Christian with a wink and the warm beginnings of an erection. He watched her leave, hips swaying licentiously. I would never lay one finger upon your naked skin, he haughtily declared to himself. After saying this in his mind he experienced none of the moral superiority he usually felt, feeling instead the annoyance of an unfulfilled penis bloated with lust.

"Come in, my boy, come in!"

It was Stemmons, soliciting his attention from inside the room. Christian entered the small quarters and pivoted, closing the door behind him. He inspected the room; the bed thrown together and loose bedding crumpled in a corner. The smell of lovemaking pervaded the air, further sickening his already disturbed stomach. He looked at Stemmons, sitting nonchalantly at his table, a few books propped open before him and some papers scattered about.

"You come quick," the priest breathed disappointedly without raising his eyes from the tomes in front of him.

"Time is one commodity none of us have."

"How true you are." Stemmons closed the books and pushed them to the side of the table. He then gestured for Christian to be seated. "I was just in the process of furthering that fine lass' religious education when you made yourself known. I tutor her as part of my service to her husband for allowing me this fine hospice."

"You tutor her often?"

"At least twice a day."

Christian looked into Stemmons' leering face. *A fine tutor you'll be, plying your craft in the Inferno, you foolish old lecher. A man gives you shelter and you return the favor by taking his wife under the same roof he resides and generously shares. In your observance of the Lord you so dishonor Him, in your deceit you so mock Him. 'Tis good to know that one whom I so secretly detest has committed a crime deeply etched in stone and every bit worthy of an eternity aflame.*

Christian removed his wool overcoat and set it on a nearby chair. He sat at the opposite end of the table, as far from Stemmons as possible. In the cleric's wrinkled features he saw years of abuse and debauchery carved deeply into sagging, grayed flesh. He peered into the countenance of a holy man and saw only a sinner. The man must be approaching sixty, he thought, he'll die soon. Good.

"When I heard you had need of me for work in the service of the Lord, I came at once," said Christian, shifting uncomfortably in his wooden chair.

Stemmons did not immediately reply, but instead lifted a quill pen and placed his signature on a letter totally composed in Latin. When finished, he briefly looked it over for any mistakes and then sealed it with red wax, imprinting the still pliable wax with his signet ring. He then returned to Christian, much to the youth's displeasure. "Ah, my Christian, never was there one more aptly named. The Lord loves His flock and you art His most beloved of lambs."

"Thank you, Father."

Stemmons scrutinized his guest reclining in the chair opposite him, his long legs stretching out beneath the table and slight but manly build pronouncing itself through his garments. He was a most handsome boy,

Stemmons fancied. How he should like for Christian to be his pupil in every way, as was the pub owner's wife. What he would not do just to glimpse that boy's manhood. His perverted thoughts raced from his head to his groin, and he stirred uneasily in his seat.

Christian returned Stemmons' stare, looking into his craving eyes. He's probably thinking about buggering me, he revoltingly mused.

"Rest yourself, my lovely, lovely child. Your work shall take you far into this night."

This alarmed Christian, and he quickly sat up in his chair. "Father?"

Stemmons had not counted on such a distressful reaction to his words. He attempted to quell Christian's sudden anxiety by motioning to some nearby food. "Would you like of some bread? Wine, perhaps?"

Christian shook his head.

"Very well, then. Let's get to the mutton, shall we? You do know of the Church's efforts to find a cure for the Plague?"

"Yes, they are quite vast. 'Tis difficult to ascribe a cure when the wandering poor spread the sickness to the remotest parts of the kingdom. The Plague destroys the economy as it does the people."

"How very right you are," said Stemmons with a fading grin, "however, there are some of us who no longer trust the Church, who have lost faith, given up hope. They are resigned that this is the end, that we shall languish on until the next year, the year of three sixes. Then the world will catch fire and pestilence will reign. Father O'Rourke is awaiting the rapture. He spends his evenings in the cemetery awaiting the rise of the dead. I am not one of them, Chris. My faith is not trivial. I have been spending my time not preparing for the end, but for a miracle, *the* miracle, and I believe I have found it."

He looked at Christian, impatiently waiting for a reaction. Come now, you fair dolt, Stemmons brooded, isn't this where your ambitions have always aspired to be — at the helm of sainthood?

Christian blankly stared at Stemmons. What was this most pious of adulterers up to now? He wanted to lash out at Stemmons, to call him a rake and berate him for his conduct, but he could not risk ruining the position for which he had worked so hard. With Stemmons' signature he could attend a seminary in France or Spain and devote his time to the acquisition of knowledge. Through knowledge one gained wealth, and with wealth one lived a more satisfying life. Keeping this in mind, he forced an excited look over his face and, brandishing a toothy grin, hopefully exclaimed, "The return of our Lord!"

"Nothing quite so grand, I'm afraid," replied Stemmons apologetically. *Lord, he was an impetuous boy! Has he learned nothing under my supervision?*

"What is it then, Father?"

Stemmons did not answer him, but once more fumbled with his books. His fingers flew over their bindings, searching for one tome in particular.

"Whatever task have you for me?" Christian pursued the matter further. "Surely there are many more qualified than I."

At this Stemmons ceased his fumbling and solemnly looked up at him. "Even if there were, they are all dead now – nay! You are young, spared from the ravages of the Plague, strong and hearty." He reached across the table, resting his elbows on a small pile of books, and took Christian's hands in his. "In this time, this hour of dread, there are few of such distinction, certainly fewer with such reverence for the Lord."

Christian looked away, troubled by Stemmons' praise. Was he the good Christian? The aptly named Christian? Or was he a charlatan, as much a hypocrite in his doubt as was the pig holding his hands. He hated Stemmons' cold, clammy hands always groping him, touching him.

"I have written of you to His Excellency," continued Stemmons, mistaking Christian's shame for humility. "He has found it sufficient to agree with me that you are truly chosen for the great and holy task which our Lord has seen fit to set before us. If I were but ten years younger, I would have volunteered, but as 'tis, you must go in my place. For Satan has unleashed upon me the contemptible affliction called gout."

Are you sure it was Satan and not the Lord that doth damage you so? Christian mused. The Lord takes not kindly to those who abuse His laws, let alone defile His priesthood.

Stemmons released Christian from the flabby confines of his sweaty palms and Christian immediately wiped his hands clean on his trousers.

As Stemmons busied himself with finding a certain book amongst his large pile, Christian eyed the scattered tomes as a waif does money or food. *All that bound knowledge wasting away in the possession of an old fool such as Stemmons.* He cringed when the priest pulled a book from the bottom of the pile and caused the other volumes to tip off the table and spill onto the floor. Stupid sot! Christian raged within as he bent to retrieve the sprawled books.

"Ah! Here 'tis," Stemmons remarked, holding up a black, leather-bound tome severely worn and water damaged. "What are you doing down there, my child?" he asked, peering down at Christian with a sly smile.

"I am just collecting your books spilled here on the floor, Father." he curtly replied, restraining himself from commenting further.

"Let them be and come hither. We have far more important things to discuss than time allows."

"But, Father—"

"Christian! Leave those books where they lie and come here this instant!"

Christian looked down at the books and painfully surrendered to Stemmons' wishes. He slowly rose and took the seat to the right of his superior. Closer to the monster, he thought.

Stemmons' face took on that all-too-familiar air of supremacy. He looked out at Christian through his beady little eyes. He dared attempt defiance with me? he thought incredulously. I will not tolerate disobedience, Christian. Perhaps when I am through with you I will have you killed.

His thick hands caressed the heavy black tome. "This is a bound manuscript, precise and exacting, containing the census of all recognized towns and villages in England. 'Twas compiled through tax records and Plague reports." He opened the book and flipped through several of its pages. "It has intervals in every chapter of five years, for a total of twenty-odd years at the book's close." Then, with some degree of difficulty, he handed the book to Christian. "Look up the town of Manasseh."

Christian took the volume from Stemmons' hands and cracked it open down the middle.

"No! Not at the middle! Start at the beginning chapter, silly boy," scolded Stemmons.

"My apologies, Father," replied Christian, complying with the old man's wish and commencing his analysis of the book at its title page.

"Well taken, my son," remitted Stemmons, transferring his immense girth from his chair to directly behind Christian. He placed his decrepit hands on the nape of Christian's neck and slowly massaged. Leaning forward, his face close to Christian's, the pious masseuse cooed in his ear, "Now, what have you found?"

The body odor that rose from Stemmons' frock infuriated Christian's nostrils. The man reeked of woman. He smelt as if he were abiding within the pleats of a vagina, coated with the nasty fragrance of an unclean female. The aroma of wine so permeated his breath that he could induce intoxication with a scant puff. A glutton for all sins, Father? he lamented.

The stench of the priest paled in comparison to his touch, icy fingers prodding Christian's neck in a sloppy attempt at sensuality. Christian hated being touched by the man. It always made him feel queasy – sick that he allowed Stemmons to feel him. It was as if he allotted parts of his body to be fondled; Stemmons could massage the neck, touch the shoulders, and hold the hand, but anywhere else was off limits. At times, Christian felt like an allocating whore, giving up parts of himself in order to pacify Stemmons. He would never give himself totally to Stemmons, nor would he perform any aberrant act, he just needed to keep the old bastard happy. He needed his signature. Once that was obtained, he would leave and never return. Never to lead a beleaguered existence, never to reside in squalor, and to never, ever submit himself to such gross indignity.

He carefully examined the long list of accounted names which comprised chapter one before slowly and in disbelief answering, "There were no reported deaths for the year of twenty years ago."

"Look at the following chapters, Chris. Look at every five years," instructed Stemmons, his voice laced with glee. "The entire population of Manasseh has not decreased by one 'til this very day!"

"Nor has it increased," replied Christian dryly, trying to steal the joy from Stemmons' heart.

Stemmons was pacing the room now. He was almost incoherent in his ranting. "Granted the town is a small one, being not more than seventy in population, but they have not lost a one! Not one man, woman, or child has fallen a prey to the sickness! To make the town an even greater significance, there has been none touched by Death within the town's confines! You see?" he optimistically queried, pointing to the large book in Christian's hands, "A town that has not had a single case of the Plague, nor a death, in all of twenty years."

Christian gazed incredulously at the pages before him, flipping through the chapters, searching for a discrepancy. This cannot be, he reasoned. No one dying in twenty years? On and on he continued turning pages, comparing Manasseh's records to other towns. Oxford, London – all the major metropolitan areas had severe losses either incurred through natural causes or through the Plague. Even the smallest of towns were affected by some taint of death. Bath, Bantingham – Bantingham? His mind reeled and was flooded with memories of Rebecca. Was she one of Bantingham's fatalities? He could not force himself to accept the validity of the documentation before him. He clenched his teeth and uttered, "Impossible."

Stemmons looked at him sharply, "But true, Christian. There has been no record of a death, be it natural or otherwise, in a twenty-year period. Your eyes do not lie to you! Look there on the cover, see the certified mark of officialdom? This is a miracle! This is *the* miracle! By the Divine Grace of God, this town has been spared the damnation and hellfire which has spewn all over London town."

"Almighty Father!" Christian blurted, Stemmons' excitement beginning to latch on to him as he arose to the truth.

"Exactly! This is the sign we have been praying for! God has seen fit to deliver us from that spawn of Lucifer and the Black Death, to bestow upon us the means of obtaining a cure. No deaths in twenty years would seem improbable at any time, but now? With the Plague?" Stemmons further accentuated his point with frantic arm movements, "Surely 'tis by an act of God, of Divine Intervention, that these souls are spared."

Closing the book on his incertitude, Christian was bothered anew by troubling thoughts. Even in the midst of the apparent miracle before him his elation was minimal, encumbered by his deeper compassion. While the convincing census abolished his recent skepticism, it unburied the old doubt he harbored within. How could God sanctify Manasseh and permit all of Britain to suffer? How could a compassionate Lord, a wise Lord, spare a town of seventy and destroy an isle? It did not make sense to him. The old anger flushed afresh. How could he worship a senseless and cruel God? The Lord worked in mysterious ways, but this was ridiculous. Old Testament rationale, he seethed. How belittling of a Supreme Being to keep us in line through fear and devastation.

He saw Stemmons, a laughably stupid expectant look upon his face, and suppressed his rage. He then cleared his throat and tailored his reply to Stemmons' obvious anticipation. "You want me to verify the census."

"Always so quick! I have never regretted giving you extra lessons, my boy, for my time was never wasted. You are to verify the report and ascertain by what means the villagers ward off the Plague."

"What do you feel 'tis, Father?"

"I've no doubt 'tis a product of good, of the Lord's doing, but how the town is safeguarded is beyond me. Perhaps 'tis some form of holy relic or talisman, through which the Lord's power is channeled."

"But what if 'tis beyond any mortal comprehension?"

"Do not ail yourself with concerns that are above you. Upon your return I shall notify the Pope of your findings, whatever they may be. He will then consign several of the Church's most wise and learned men to our care. They will arrive under the cover of darkness, so as not to arouse suspicion. We shall then accompany them to Manasseh and aid them in all ways possible."

Christian's heart leapt at this. He was going to be in the presence of some of the greatest geniuses of his time! He was sure he could latch on to one of them, returning with him to Rome as an apprentice. He wouldn't need Stemmons' recommendation and he could climb out of this abyss he was mired in. He would have to do an excellent job, though. He would have to conduct himself most professionally in order to be noticed. He constrained his thoughts to return to the present and his visions of glory were shelved in the recesses of his mind. "Must I leave tonight?" he asked, concerned now of the short time he had been given to prepare.

"The faster your return, the more lives can be saved."

"Is it wise not to inform the Anglicans?" Christian ventured. "They might suspect something is afoul in our secrecy should they discover—"

"They will not discover anything! Do you understand me? Few know of this plan. Only those trustworthy have been entrusted. Say nothing and nothing will come of it." Stemmons was livid, his jowls quivering. "I cannot believe you would suggest such a ludicrous idea as to notify the Anglicans. They would have us killed and take what was rightfully ours!"

Lowering his head to avoid the fat man's venomous glare, Christian thought it best to change the subject. He could not risk losing this assignment by angering his immediate supervisor. "How far away is this town?"

The sudden avoidance of a prolonged confrontation took Stemmons by surprise. Usually Christian was much more quarrelsome than this docile sheep before him. *What's the matter, Christian? Are your ambitions slaying your decency?*

"The town is fairly far. If you leave now you can reach the neighboring village by dawn. There you shall rest." He slowly approached Christian, curious to see his reaction to what he was about to tell him. "I've given all the necessary instructions to Cotton Smith-Patton, the old smith who owes us penance."

Christian threw his face up. "I know not this man."

Smiling, Stemmons was proud of the response he had garnered. *Christian, he chuckled to himself, you are so very predictable.* "He is an old soldier, perfect in his role as your attendant in all matters. He will act as your coachman and protector, so treat him accordingly."

"And you trust this man?"

"Never was there a sturdier man, nor blacker sheep, in all the Lord's flock. As your aide he has been instructed to follow your every wish. If he fails you, 'tis his immortal soul."

That last utterance put Christian at ease. He had only one more thing to ask of Stemmons. "And what if I find some divine relic or talisman to be the causation of the town's security?"

Without a moment's hesitation, Stemmons replied, "Steal it, of course."

"Of course." Christian's anger smoldered. *How foolish I should be not to realize I am a thief! I am sure one can thieve what was given by the Lord, isn't that right, Father? How unaffected Stemmons seems by the prospect of robbery. I understand that in the overall best interest of Britain one must make sacrifices, but must he be so nonchalant? He asks of me to steal as if it were to pray. What is wrong with you, Father? How can one so corrupt wear the cloth? How can you betray the trust placed in you and corrupt the innocent? How come you do not die when others, far your superiors, do?*

As both men headed for the doorway, Stemmons lightly placed his hand upon Christian's lower back. Christian flinched to avoid his offending touch, and in doing so offended in return.

"And Christian, use discretion. I'll not go to Tyburn!" The wayward cleric spoke in reference to the place where martyrs were executed. "If I am to hang myself on my own failings, then I pray my shoes to leaden weights and an angel come down to pull on my legs." Stemmons was somewhat frantic, sweat rolling over his triple chins. "If you are discovered, say not that you are a Catholic! Things being misconstrued, we may be put to death under a Popish plot. I want not to be eulogized *Te Deum*."

Christian looked at the quivering obesity blocking his exit. Perspiration accumulated in the folds of Stemmons' flabby flesh. His pores belched forth more of the glistening impurity, and his thick lips were wetted with a parched tongue. How terribly wretched you look, Father, he quietly observed. How you look like a spitted pig, roasting over coals of your own design.

He nodded affirmatively, much to Stemmons' pleasure, for the older man had been rendered uneasy by Christian's desire to educate the Anglicans. Cheer once again welling up inside him, Stemmons moved aside and allowed his companion egress.

As Christian opened the door, his flight from the hovel was hampered by the amorous right hand of Stemmons, which tenderly patted his departing buttocks. Christian's loathing was overflowing, and he could contain his repulsion no longer. Seizing Stemmons' right forearm he twisted it around. He felt the man pull away and caught him wincing. The knowledge that he had caused his molester pain filled him with delight. *Feel my wrath, Father. 'Tis nothing compared to His.*

Mortified at the violent rebuff and desiring the return of his right arm, Stemmons conceded to him, placing upon his face a mask of feigned innocence. "Be off with you now! Here," he appeased, valiantly reaching out and grasping a large loaf of bread from a basket of many on a shelf near the door, "take this to contain the hunger of a long journey."

What is he doing?! Stemmons shouted in silence. I have never seen him like this, so violent ... so vicious! God above! Look at his eyes! He's going to kill me! He's going to kill me and carry on without me!

Christian stared at the bloated face in front of him. The pleading in Stemmons' eyes did wonders for his sickly constitution. Beg for redemption, cur, he exalted. Beg for what I cannot give you.

Feeling satiated in his brief demonstration of power, he yielded to Stemmons' pain and released his arm from custody. Taking the offered bread from Stemmons' left hand, he mockingly articulated, "Much thanks, Father. I shan't disappoint you."

Rubbing life back into his injured limb, Stemmons forced a smile across his gap teeth. "I am sure you won't, Christian. Meet Smith-Patton at the smithy down the street at ten o'clock, and fare thee well!"

Christian needed little prodding to expel himself from Stemmons' presence. He whisked down the hall, impatient in his release and his good fortune.

Stemmons watched him leave from the safety of his doorway. Stroking his violated arm, his eyes filled with contempt for Christian. *Go to Manasseh, you beast!* he silently ranted. *Go and return only to die!* It would be easy to dispose of him, he schemed. A properly addressed speech to a group of drunken soldiers about the evils of the rogue Catholic disgracefully named Christian would be all that was required. They would murder him in deference to Parliament. It would be quick, spur-of -the-moment. Should anything go astray, there would be no way Christian could implicate him because he would be unsuspecting of his involvement. Caught off guard, he would be torn apart as a fox caught by hounds. *And I will watch your murder, Christian. With relish I will walk in your blood! I will watch, Christian, from the shadows I will watch.*

Christian emerged from behind the portiere a changed man. No longer would he curtsy to the whims and commandments of those beneath him. No longer would he allow himself to be subjected to the wishes of dolts and idiots. He would return with whatever was necessary to his attainment of knowledge. He would so impress the theologians with the exactness of his work that they would not leave England without him. All he had to do was visit the obscure town of Manasseh. How difficult could that be? he pondered pleasantly with a slight smile upon his lips.

The pub patrons were inconsequential to him now. Their jaded stares affected him little, he having no time in his thoughts of glory to weigh them in consideration. He was a man with a mission and an opportunity to fulfill what had up until now existed as a fantasy, a dream. No longer would he have to pollute his mind with visions of death, chaos, and inhumanity. No longer would he have to associate with drunkards and lechers, or visit pubs in the middle of the night. No longer would he live in constant fear of Death.

He reached the front door and opened it wide, allowing it to strike the side wall loudly. All in the pub turned to face the source of such a disturbance to their peace. He saw the owner, his adulteress, the barmaid, and all the vile patrons. He could not resist their indignant looks without a verbal retort. "Cast not your eyes upon me in such fashion! I will not be berated by those who find God at the bottom of a bottle! Drink your ale, and you, sir," he pointed to the owner, "continue your sale of such beverages. You shall join your good customers in the inhalation of Gehenna's smoke and profit not by the licks of flame which singe every inch of your flesh!" Finished venting, he whirled about and slammed the door behind him, causing more thunder at his departure than his arrival.

A dismayed quiet suffused the room and saturated every brow. They did not, as Christian might have expected, mock or parody him in any way, shape, or form. Those of the pub simply sat or stood, staring at the doorway, long after the object of their attentions had vanished. Christian had spoken with such conviction, such veneration for his every utterance, that he managed to chill the hearts of even the rowdiest of villains and most inebriated of alcoholics. He had forced them into silence by compelling them to look at themselves and at the truth of their miserable existences. Eventually, they would resume their humble debaucheries and drunken rants, but for now they were suspended, alone in a room of many.

As he walked briskly across the small courtyard and carefully through the vicious gate, Christian couldn't help feeling proud of himself. He was already changing with the restored hope bequeathed to him. His constant striving and vaulting ambitions had led him here – the crossroads of his life. This expedition to Manasseh was his last chance, and he knew it. He would be too old before long, unserviceable in his set ways to be of use to even the most indiscriminate of patrons. The openness of his mind would be forced shut by the malice of time, loss of hope, and unfulfillment of aspirations. He felt as though his soul would leave him if he did not attain his fruition. He did not mind dying; he merely did not want to perish unlearned.

An abrupt noise appealed to his consideration and he accordingly faced its origin. There, amidst a rubbish pile, almost camouflaged in her poverty, sat a little girl. She sorted through the garbage very hastily, picking and parting through the mess as if looking for buried treasure. When she would come across a moldy rind of bread or a sparse chicken bone she would crowd them into her tattered apron, for her pockets had holes in them. For every scrap she scavenged, her head would dart about in fear of being caught.

Look at her, Christian thought, even in her abominable indignity she fears reprisal. The good pub owner must not be beneficent to her, for her eyes are constantly filled with alarm at the pub entrance. It would be just like him; to deny a child scraps from his trash but allow a priest refuge. In a time when the populace should be banded together, fools such as he committed further atrocities in the face of the Plague.

He watched her continue in her pitiable quest for dinner, and the loaf in his hands grew heavy. She did not notice him, for she was too consumed with nervous fright and he did not make himself known. His heart grieved when he saw her express joy over the discovery of a half-eaten pie, and he was compelled to act. "Here, little one," he spoke softly, holding out the bread loaf, "look what I have for you."

Upon hearing his voice, she rose quickly to her feet. Standing, she confronted him, coated in refuse, with a wary look affixed to her face.

"Fear not, little one," Christian soothed, seeing that she was cautious, "I do the Lord's bidding." He pulled out his large crucifix from under his shirt and shook it for effect.

The girl remained still, the jingle-jangle of the crucifix having little or no influence upon her trepidation. She eyed the loaf of bread ravenously, but would not come forth.

She has obviously met Stemmons, Christian revoltingly thought. She scrounges through refuse for her meals and when presented with a freshly baked loaf does not come hither? The child so fears the sign of the cross that she would rather stand in hunger than sit in repast. What has Stemmons done to this child that the mark of our Lord so repels instead of attracts?

Placing his crucifix back within the confines of his shirt, he bent at the knee and, continuing to eye the child, gently laid the light loaf on a clean-looking cobblestone. He then rose and slowly backed away.

For every step he took in decline, the girl took two in advance. When he was about six feet away, the girl was upon the bread. She seated herself on the harsh cobblestone and shallowly examined it, turning it to and fro in the poor light. When sufficiently satisfied, she assailed the poor loaf with such vigor that not a crumb was safe. Her loud chewing filled the air and brought pleasure to Christian's ears.

While the child sat engrossed in her light but hearty meal, he could not resist but to approach her. He took long and cautious strides, laboring in his silence. My Lord, he marveled, how she treats the simple loaf as if it were a banquet, catching every crumb and savoring every dry swallow.

His close proximity suddenly dawned on the child and she rushed to raise herself from the street. Christian quickly reached out and caught her by the left arm as she was turning. He swung her around and peered into her face. In keeping with the rest of her appearance it was filthy. Large brown eyes looked up at him from under the dirt, and her nose was hardly distinguishable. Her mouth formed a small circle lined with bread crumbs and she breathed in fearful gasps.

Christian gazed into those frightened eyes and decided to remedy her fear. He softly and affectionately patted her head, his fingers gingerly smoothing and combing her greasy hair. Her tresses were probably blonde, he reasoned, but were so in need of a washing and powdering that she appeared brunette.

Under his tender grooming, the child's alarm was banished, and she was overcome with emotion at her gentle handling. It had been so long since someone had held her, calmed her. She had not received similar compassion since the deaths of her mother and five brothers well over two months ago. The warmth she was receiving from Christian's touch was too much of a strain on her eyes, and tears welled forth, cascading in cleansing rivulets down her cheeks.

The sight of the poor wretch crying laid ruin to Christian's insides. His breath became strained, and in short, quick inhalations he realized his own doubts and fears and waged war against the tide that was rising in his eyes.

It was at this time that Christian, his hands adjusting the girl's long and wild locks, made a tragic discovery. Pulling the length of the child's hair in back to the front, over her right shoulder, he was granted a look at the girl's naked neck. There, on the exposed left side, his eyes ascertained the fear which had temporarily vacated him. Several large, bulbous swellings, tokens of the Plague, embellished her virgin neck. The tears which Christian had until now so successfully fought stormed out of his eyelids. He cried in long, lamenting wails, as if in imitation of those in the pest houses. He choked on his sobs, gasped for his breath, and clouded his vision.

The little girl was startled by Christian's accompaniment in sorrow, but then returned to her sad state, crying all the louder in her woeful duet. She did not know this man, he was a stranger to her, but they were cousins in their grief. She wept for her family departed, and he wept for her.

Unable to contain his heartache, and defiant of the Plague, Christian drew the child into his arms and embraced her. He hugged her tightly and close to him, as if attempting to transplant the disease from her to him. The child, unaware of her mortal condition, clasped him snugly about the waist and buried her head in his chest.

It was here, in the arms of a sickly child, that Christian recognized what he would miss most should he leave England. He would miss the aid he serviced to the poor, the old, and the sick. He would miss helping relieve the fear and stress experienced by the dying shortly before death, and the consolation of the bereaved, some afflicted themselves. He would miss assisting others, the sacrifices he made for people made him feel worthy. Although he had no friends he would miss, they being already mourned by him, he would dearly miss the British people. He would miss England, once the fairest country in all the world. He would miss this hell ... his hell.

As his grievous outpouring gradually began to level itself, he squeezed the little child tighter. He did not want to let go of her. She personified all that he held dear. She was but a child, afflicted and on the streets, and yet she invoked in him such sentiment that if he could he would gladly forfeit his life for hers.

He held her and she held him. In her arms he felt like the child, foolish for his vain thoughts of selfish glory. In her arms his true course was set, his mind cleared, and his heart lifted. He would go to Manasseh justly, not allowing his ambitions to conquer his passions. And whenever he was in doubt, whenever his mind wandered over territory vainglorious, he would envision this child's beautiful face, and that of her tarred sister's, and quell the demons that raged inside him. She would be an icon on his path to righteousness, he would find the cure and return with it for her and all of Britain. This child shall be my redeemer, he proclaimed, as I shall be hers. Through her anguish I shall be England's salvation. My name shall be mouthed on the lips of many.

As the night once more pleased him, he cuddled the child, rocking her in his arms. He lulled her to sleep and endeavored to keep her body from the cold ground. Looking at her peaceful countenance as she lay slumbering in his arms, he was drawn once more to the pustules protruding from her neck. It would not be long, he thought, before she is initiated into the world of the dead. If they had been caught earlier, perhaps they could have been lanced and cauterized, then maybe she would be spared. As it was now, not even he could save her. His only consolation was that if he hastened in his discovery of a cure a similar death could be averted. But how he longed to save her! He did not know her ten minutes prior, but she had captured his heart. Even now, unassuming in her sleep, she demanded his affection. He stroked her hair and tenderly placed a kiss upon her forehead.

"I shall not forget you, little one," he whispered more to himself than to her. "I will never forget."

A cold breeze blew down and stirred the child. Christian wrapped her in the warmth of his coat and hushed her back to slumber. Looking from her to the icy night sky, he perceived the stars as the all-seeing eyes of God. Shifting his gaze to the full moon, still somewhat low in the black heavens, he felt a familiar shiver. Damn it, woman! he silently raged, can you not allow me one night of reprieve? For in the whistle of the wind he heard her sigh, and in the luminosity of the moon he saw her teeth.

Returning to his home with the girl in his arms, Christian carefully opened his door and quietly stepped inside. He did not wish to wake the child, who continued to sleep soundly. Lightly placing her on his bed, he covered her with his warm blankets. In all his attentions to her he had forgotten how hot the room was. Seeing the girl turn in discomfort, he cracked his window. It didn't matter that he allowed foul air into his room, all that did matter now was the comfort of this girl who would soon be in such agony.

He did not fear his bed's contamination, nor his own in the handling of the girl. In the past hour, with all that had befallen him, he had realized that despite his nagging doubts as to the existence of God, what really mattered was the way in which one conducted himself. Acting charitable on behalf of gaining entrance into Heaven was very ignoble. Whether or not a caring God existed in the soulless black of night was irrelevant. The way in which a person carried himself, the way one felt about himself, that was important. Being at ease with one's self would be nirvana, the closest a mortal could be to that Blessed Abode.

He smiled at the sleeping child, stooping to her side. It had been so long since he had done such an irresponsible and selfless act of benevolence. It felt good. He patted the child's head once more before rising from his position and throwing off his coat. Lighting a candle on his nightstand, he removed its harsh glare from its proximity to the girl and placed it on the dresser adjacent to his bed.

He was going to Manasseh in his best apparel. He would appear the epitome of a servant of the Lord, wearing his competence on his sleeve and bearing his convictions on his breast. He would daunt the townsfolk with his illustrious facade, bending them into submission through his fine raiment and silver-laced tongue.

He crouched at the padlocked chest and examined its rough exterior. This chest is older than I am, he mused, but our abuses have been equal. He removed a small key from underneath a carving his father had made of the Virgin Mary and slipped it through the lock's keyhole. Turning the key counterclockwise, the shackle was released and the padlock unlocked.

Easing the chest's lid open, the old, rust-cankered hinges laboring to shriek the child awake, Christian smiled with pride at the finery revealed to him. Reaching into the chest he withdrew his royal blue jacket, its brass buttons sparkling in the candlelight as he slung it over his left forearm. Silk stockings delighted his fingertips as he cautiously unrolled them to their full length. Sparing them his rough hands, he searched for runs with his eyes rather than his fingers. His underwear he judged would be too uncomfortable to wear, days being hot and nights not overly cool. He left them in the chest.

His dress shirt was among the finest he had ever seen, its full shirtsleeves terminating in a prolific lace weave. From the wide unbuttoned V-neck to the thin frill of the collar, the blouse was beyond reproach. With a slightly boyish grin, he laid it across the jacket and stockings.

His breeches were full, with dangling ribbon trim. Matching his jacket in material and hue, it presented him with a complete suit. He took the pants and added them to his mass of finery, then withdrew the last remaining implements of his grand appearance.

These were his shoes, finely crafted in Portugal and as yet unbroken. They would be hell on his feet, but how they looked! Shiny black leather with wooden heels and good, stiff bows; their high tongues stood straight, as if in defiance to onlookers.

Palming his pocket watch, he opened its bronze lid and squinted in an attempt at reading its hands. He was running late, much to his disapproval. Replacing the lid over the watch face, he took in a deep breath and looked down at the little sleeper dwarfed by his bed.

The pearly moonlight shone down on her, lightening her dirty hair and illuminating her filthy skin. It was as if he were witness to a remarkable transformation, a gutter girl changed into an angel. He saw how her chest quivered slightly after each breath, her diseased body beginning to labor even in sleep. It would not be long at all, he bitterly thought, before she was an angel, not simply the facsimile of one. Bowing his head, he turned from her holy form and guided himself to his chair.

Leaning forward on the chair's armrests, he stared into the tormenting shadows of his room. God, he mentally beseeched, let Stemmons be correct in his findings — let there be some tangible cure so that the little ones may be safe. Recall how you fled to the security of a manger when others your age were being slaughtered. Let Manasseh be these children's manger. Let me find the refuge they seek. Let me find the cure, God. Do you hear me? Let me save the children.

Spurned on by his elevated thoughts, he threw his work clothes off and tackled the bundle which he had just recently treated with such care. Naked, he seated himself on the cool, wood floor and thrust his big feet through his hose. Rising, he stepped into the seafarer's breeches, tying them tight about his abdomen. It would be quite the embarrassment to drop one's pants in public, certainly so when one wore no undergarments.

Slipping the white blouse over his head, he breathed in its aroma — a clean, fresh scent, despite its long abeyance in the chest. How could anything appear so fresh after so long a dormancy in a rank, wooden box? he marveled.

Stuffing the long shirt into his pants was a difficult chore under the harried conditions. He mustn't be late, he admonished himself, not when dealing with something of such importance as this. His fingers darted up and down his breast, buttoning his shirt to the collar. When finished, using the backrest of the chair as a guide in the dark, he stepped around to its front and plopped himself down.

Reaching for the Portuguese shoes, he lifted them by their stiff tongues, putting them on the floor before him and slipping into their confines. The shoes were not made for his feet, but for those of the long dead seafarer, and as such he was severely cramped in the beautiful, black footwear. Because of the discomfort they caused him, he found himself cursing the man he had so recently praised for his benevolent bequest.

Placing one arm at a time into his jacket sleeves, Christian felt as though he were placing on his person the *piece-de-resistance* of his appearance. As he slid the jacket into place on his tall build, he happily noted that it hugged him well, and was not ill-fitting as were the shoes. Resplendent in his finery, he carried himself with newfound vanity.

Pocketing his watch, he paused for a moment, looked around his little abode, then gave thought to the trip to Manasseh. He would not return to this house. Ever. He would have to take any and all valuables he so desired now or leave them to whoever found them. With this in mind, he emptied his dresser drawers into leather baggage he had come by over the years. Through the sacrifice of a few old shirts and torn britches, he managed to fit all of his mother's pots and pans as well.

His father's beautiful woodcarvings of Christ and His saints caused several more garments to make their exit. As he was fitting the last of the small statuettes, the sleeping girl sighed mournfully in her slumber. He looked at her and knew he could not leave her in such a way. He did not wish to wake her, for God knew how long it had been since she'd slept, but he did not want to depart leaving her only this house, its crude furnishings, and a small bundle of discarded clothes.

He wanted to give her something that would remind her of him and help maintain her faith, even until the end; something that would bring her comfort in her lonely, suffering death. Reaching into one of his bags, he removed his father's sweet rendition of the Blessed Mother. With a thin smile positioned on his lips, he walked to her bedside and tenderly placed the Virgin under her arm.

The moonlight continued in fostering her heavenly appearance, and it was with teary eyes that Christian kissed her soft forehead farewell. Belongings in hand, he turned from his act of mercy to soundlessly open his door and loiter in its portal. Casting his eyes about his place one final time, he bid it and its little occupant good-bye. The last his eyes saw as he closed and locked the door was that dear little girl resting on his bed with Mary in her arms and Death on her lips.

# Chapter Two

Walking briskly from his tiny house, Christian felt fully every hurried footstep. Hopefully the shoes he wore would become accustomed to his feet, or his feet would have to condition themselves to continual grief. The thought of having to appear in these shoes for several days haunted him. How well could he work with sorely blistered feet? Regardless, what else had he to wear? He could not appear in his filthy, oversized boots, and all his money (the little that Stemmons gave him) was spent on the purchase of necessities such as food. If Stemmons had given him prior notice of this sudden and exigent expedition, he might have been able to scrounge up a more comfortable and suitable pair of shoes. As it was, he could do little but flinch at every step.

In agony, he stepped up his stilted pace. With knowledge of a short cut, he turned down a street lined with houses. Once more the red crosses leaped out at him, forcing his eyes down. As he hurried on his way, he took notice of a watchman seated lax in his chair.

The man was dozing off, only raising his heavy lids to see who it was that approached. His big belly thrust out of his open pants, and in his limp left arm he sported a bottle of ale. Derelict in his job of guarding the house from the escape of those shut up inside, he performed his ineffectual task with gross negligence. For the people he was to keep within had been without several days, fleeing while he was in a drunken stupor. And while he further bloated himself on ale and idleness, his wards brought the sickness to those they met in the streets of London.

As he passed, Christian looked with contempt on the loafer. How could anyone be so indolent in times such as these? There was plenty to do for those willing to help. Indeed, the worst sin that could presently be committed in England was that of slothfulness. He had heard rumors, stories suppressed by the extraneous government, of the conduct of certain watchmen and nurses; how they would often murder their quarantined patrons – sometimes for profit, occasionally for spite.

Continuing on his way, he observed how those few people he met walked away from the houses, preferring the middle of the street. Fear of contamination was so great that they would rather be run down by a coach than chance infection. It was almost comical, he thought, that they would take such measures and arrive home to a neighbor stricken with the distemper.

He was nearly there now. He could feel excitement churning in his stomach and anticipation creeping up his spine. He was just a block away from destiny, just yards from his dreams. Whatever happened on this journey would be his to command, what he could make of it he would. It seemed appropriate that after years of magnanimous giving he should receive his wishes through a further good act. Through curing Britain he would cure himself. Pursuant to his own ethics, he would attain his life's desire. Without willful malice, but with continual decency, he would rise above his present conditions, his ambitions being channeled through good deeds rather than deceptive words. To save himself, all he had to do was save all of England.

Standing at intersecting streets, he squinted through the cloudy dark. A fog had begun rolling in, and just as it spread itself over every cobblestone, so would the Plague spread over every Briton. Looking past the fog, Christian saw the smithy and the large, black coach parked in front. He saw a man taller than himself on top, loading what appeared to be supplies onto the coach's roof.

Cotton Smith-Patton was a true Scot. He spoke with a lilting brogue and owned a fierce temper. He was in his late fifties; shoulder-length gray hair hanging unkempt, a close-cropped pointed beard and mustache, and a face lined with experience and a lifetime of hardships. In his youth he had been a mercenary in the employ of foreign service.

He had volunteered to fight under Christian IV in 1626 during Germany's Thirty Years War. After Christian's defeat at Lutter by the Imperial General Wallenstein he returned home, only to re-enter the war in a Scotch regiment under the Marquess of Hamilton. When he had tired of Germany, he sought his adventures elsewhere, fighting for whoever shared his beliefs or filled his purse.

He had first visited England in 1644, arriving with twenty thousand other Scots aiding Parliament in their civil war against the king. Three years later he fought for the king against Parliament, changing his loyalties because of Parliament's hollow promises. After the wars, he returned to Scotland and defended his homeland from an English invasion.

Residing in Scotland under Puritanical reforms, he found himself embracing Catholicism and alienating his Lutheran family. It had been years since then, years since he had seen his wife and boys. He missed them dearly, as he did his beloved homeland. He hated the English and yet was forced to reside in their city, a price on his head barring him from that which he loved. His differing religious views causing his family grief and forcing him to flee for his life, he vowed he would return someday, praying every night for God to keep and protect his clan.

While struggling to secure a package in the rack on top of the coach, Cotton accidentally sent a similar carton plummeting to the cobblestone below.

"Damned to the bloody hell of feebleness, I am," he cursed. He laboriously got to his feet and began his descent to retrieve the item. No sooner had he taken one step down when the carton was held before him. He looked hard at the young man standing below him. A sturdy-looking whelp, he thought. This must be the apprentice Coleswitten.

Christian smiled at the old man who greeted him with silence, "Master Smith-Patton, I presume?"

"I am." Cotton cautiously took the carton from Christian's hand, careful not to allow their fingers to touch. "Ye are not me penance, by chance?"

"That I am," said Christian with a pearly grin. He then moved closer and extended his already raised hand in gestured salutation. "Christian Coleswitten, more a pauper than a penance."

Cotton was taken aback. "Ye would give your arm to a stranger? In these times?"

"Why ... yes," sputtered a rebuffed Christian. "How can one do the work of the Lord when one distances himself from the tools of His labor?"

"Have ye no fear?"

"If I am to die, then so it shall come to pass. One cannot go against the will of God."

"Or the scythe of the Reaper." Cotton grinned in acceptance. He liked a man who wasn't afraid of death and was carefree in the handling of his life. "We shall travel well this night."

Christian sighed in relief. He had no time for quarrels and games, he wanted to go and return as quickly as humanly possible. The tarnished appearance of the coach bothered him. He had heard of coaches being used to cart the dead to the Mount Mill burial ground. He held his tongue in asking if this was so, for his stated approach to life and death so pleased his companion that he did not wish to betray that pleasure.

Cotton motioned to the baggage at Christian's feet as he fitted the toppled carton into the rack, "Have ye all your needs?"

Glancing down, Christian nodded, "Yes, I am prepared."

Cotton gestured for Christian to bring his baggage forth. "What think ye of this Plague, how is it fed at our expense?"

"The Plague feeds off our souls," the scholarly youth assured him, handing his heavy bags up.

"That is impossible," Cotton said, mocking seriousness. "Taxation is the soul of England, and if the Plague fed off that, the better we'd all be."

"How long shall we journey, Cotton?"

"Tonight? Not more than three hours." He took the last of Christian's bags and bound it with leather straps to the rack. Descending from his lofty height, he faced his ward on even ground and still peered down. Alluding to his glorious past, he sighed, "I've served under a Christian before."

"In that case, I certainly hope I do the name justice."

"I am sure ye will." With that, Cotton affectionately tended to the two horses attached to the coach. They whinnied in approval of his touch and buried their faces in their feed bags. Their coal-black coats reminded Christian of a moonless night.

"We will encamp on the side of the road, I take it?" persisted Christian in his questioning.

"Nay," mumbled Cotton, not even bothering to divert his gaze from his horses, "we will be stopping for what remains of the night in Bantingham. The horses will need the rest before proceeding onwards."

"Bantingham?" Christian blurted in shock. That was where Rebecca lived, where she settled after their forced separation. He had always put off visiting her for fear she would ensnare him with her love, thus enslaving him to her charms and forcing him to bid farewell any chance at entering a seminary. He would visit her tonight, though. He had to face her, to tell her what he never could. With this new revelation a further incentive, he longed to be already on the road. "Let's be off," he masterfully intoned. "I tire as we speak."

Cotton looked up from his horses. See how he gives orders already, he thought, even though he knows me not. Good, that is the mark of one sure of himself, one worthy to serve.

Christian opened the coach door by himself and took his seat near a window. He held in his hands his Bible, having removed the Good Book from his baggage before giving them up to Cotton. He did not plan on reading, for it was very dark sitting in the coach's interior. He held the Book as a comforter, something to ease his fears and nerves.

Surprisingly, in contrast to its grim exterior, the inside of the coach was comfortable. The seats were padded with a plush, though worn, black velvet. Although cramped if more than two were within, the coach was very accommodating to one.

Christian surmised that the coach's previous detail had been in the service of a funeral procession. The black exterior, the black velvet, the black drapes tied up, and the black carpeting all pointed to this being a mourner's hack. It made him slightly uneasy to know that he was to arrive at his rendezvous with destiny in that which paid homage to the dead. He prayed it only a coincidence and not an ill omen of things to come.

Cotton removed the horses' feed bags, much to their displeasure and grunting objections. He gave them each a rough pat on the head, exhorting them, "You're a-gettin' too fat, me ladies." He held the bags up in front of them. "If ye want more o' these oats, then ye'll have to work for 'em!"

Cotton gave the horses a final inspection, making sure they were attached to the coach securely and that the bits he placed in their mouths were not overly snug. He then went over to his smithy and locked it up tight, returning to the coach and looking in on Christian through the window. "If there's anything ye be a-craving, let me know by calling out or rapping on the roof," he said, demonstrating by pounding on the outside door with his fist.

Christian nodded accordingly and closed his eyes, thus dismissing his driver without speaking a word.

Cotton wasted no time in raising himself to his seat at the forefront of the coach. Placing a thick, gray coat over his person in expectation of cold forest roads, he then put upon his head a rumpled, tall-crowned hat absent of ribbons or feathers. With leather work gloves protecting each hand, he took the reins, prodding his horses onward.

Christian belied a composed, restful countenance. While appearing placid outwardly, his mind was churning with thoughts of what he would do and what he would say, not in Manasseh, but in Bantingham. It had been so long since he had seen Rebecca, since he had been ensconced in the curtain of her hair. He would not blame her, or hold malice against her, if she did not wish to see him. He should have written, but didn't. He could claim that he had never received her note detailing her whereabouts, but that would be unmanly of him. He knew it was in his best interests to avoid resuming involvement with her, but his hot loins told him otherwise. She could be taken, he supposed, married to some villager. Or worse, dead of the Plague. He prayed this was not so, for the more he pictured her bountiful breasts and alluring lips the more he wanted to be within her arms. Sinning with Rebecca wasn't hard, it was good.

Shaken from his thoughts by the coach's sudden lurch forward, he looked out his window at the slowly gaining fog. It had surrounded the coach now, submerging its wheels in a torrent of cloud. We must appear to be levitating, he fancied, afloat on the meekest of rivers.

Cotton maneuvered the carriage down the invisible street. Its wheels churned the fog, its spokes whipping up puffs of white. The clatter of the wooden wheels on the street's stone combined with the clicking of the horses' hooves produced a monotonous resonance that was soothing to Christian. Calmed by the sound, he was apt to be lulled asleep.

Eyelids resting heavy, his breathing slowed and he felt himself slip with sweet submission into Sleep's open arms. Semi-conscious, he was still cognizant of the real world surrounding him. He still heard the clattering wheels and clicking horses, still felt the gentle rocking of the coach, its light pitching to and fro further tranquilizing him.

His thoughts unraveled and his concerns abandoned him. He felt no stress or sense of urgency, only a sense of peace. His mind envisioned a supremely quiet place, a stone garden under the moon's twilight. He saw it as if he were there, walking amongst the orderly rows of gray to a large marble mosque desirous of his lips' touch. A bizarre pilgrimage to an obscene Mecca, he sensed rather than thought. His mind no longer his own, his private thoughts belonged to someone else.

As he lethargically walked toward the marble palace, being drawn trance-like rather than of his own accord, he felt as if he had been here before, as if he knew this place. In the darkening evening sky he beheld no stars. The realization as to where he was came to him in a sudden rush. The only constant in his captive mind was a sensation of death, that which linked all of his dreams, all of his nightmares. He was in a graveyard! A cemetery enriched with the rotting corpses of all who had fallen to her, the one whose marble crypt he was in the process of uncontrollably entering!

Standing before the massive mausoleum, Christian looked up at its weathered exterior. Aside from a few defaced statuettes of saints and a vandalized escutcheon, the only discernible engraving was a motto inscribed in Latin. It read: *Mulier est hominis confusio.* Woman is man's ruin.

He saw his hand thrust out and push open the rusted, iron gate. As he withdrew it, he noticed he had reopened the wound on his finger, his blood dripping slowly onto the unconsecrated ground. With the gate no longer impeding his progress, he stared into the pitch-blackness of the crypt and then entered.

Christian's mind screamed out in horror, but to no avail. He was powerless to stop or hinder his nightmare in any way. It was as if he were a detached observer, unable to interfere – yet able to feel, to sense his impending doom. Hopelessness thickened the air, making it difficult for him to breathe. Perspiration dotted his entire body, drenching him in his clothing. He shook apoplectically as he felt himself descending the stone staircase and being swallowed by the hungry dark. Was it fear he felt, or excited anticipation?

The stench of the place was incredible. As a testament to its power, he nearly gagged in his sleep. A combination of stale and dusty air tinged with the wretched smell of fleshly rot. In his dream, but against his will, Christian continued on.

He felt his feet on the hard stairs, but could not see them in the darkness. He felt his hands on either side of the crypt walls, steadying himself to keep from falling. It was so real and yet hideously unreal at the same time. He could sense that he had reached the bottom of the stairs, and glancing up could see a faint light pouring in from somewhere up above.

To his supreme terror, he could make out in the weak diffusion of moonlight several desecrated sarcophagi, their bodies strewn about all over the interior of the crypt in a most miserable fashion. Some were in more advanced states of decomposition than their kindred. Skeletal grins and hollow stares greeted him, as if in death they had learned something he had not. He heard them whisper through closed mouths and open necks, "You will join us, you will be one with us in Death's arms." The hushed chanting continued as he looked from face to shriveled face. They spoke and yet not one moved its lips in utterance. Their incantation soon resembled a demonic choral arrangement, replete with alternating pitches and differing tones. Upon reaching a crescendo that tormented Christian's mind as much as his ears, they assumed their rightful roles and fell silent.

Wake up! he tried to think. Wake up, 'tis only a dream! 'Tis not real!

His valiant attempts at resuscitating his consciousness proved fruitless, and an effort at prayer also failed. He stood alone in his nightmare, alone in a crypt decorated with the ignoble corpses of a noble family. In the disturbing quiet of the tomb, well hidden in the darkened shadows, lurked something that equally alarmed and aroused him. Something that married love with death and gave birth to a cemetery that stretched beyond one's vision and encompassed all nationalities.

Ecstatic moans and sensual sighs echoed in the crypt. From out of the darkness came such sounds of female pleasure that Christian soon felt his burning blood gathering in his crotch. Low, monosyllabic grunts reverberated around him, occasionally breaking into erotic giggles. Heavy breathing and a shrill, orgasmic cry consummated the vocal teasing. After a moment's rest, the dark contentedly sighed, "Christian . . ."

It was her! The unmistakable, sensually-sighed whisper of the woman of his dreams! She was here, in this vault, waiting for him. His spine turned to ice, but his hot blood continued to warm him. She so frightened him, but God, how he wanted her! How he longed to fall into those arms! If Death was so lovely a lady, then he wished he could die a thousand deaths!

In the dream he strained his eyes, searching the darkness for her. He stood with piqued expectation near the shaft of moonlight spearing the dark from above. His nearness to the light impeded his night vision, but just as his lust inflamed his heart so did his fear keep him from straying from the light. He quivered to think of what would happen to him should he step away and let himself be devoured by the shadows.

A light shuffling sound from in front of him, on the other side of the moonbeam, quickly drew his attention. He looked hard through the veil of light, but to no use. The brightness only blackened the already pitch darkness of the shadows behind it. She could be within ten feet of him and he would not see her. The shuffling grew closer as Christian nervously forced down a dry gulp. The stillness of the crypt furthered his anxiety. Was it her? Was it her?!

His answer came in the form of an ancient beauty stepping into the moonlight before him. She was beyond reasonable description, an incomparable lady of a classical demeanor. Her ravishing nude body was fairer than all works of art. She was Venus personified, Aphrodite in the flesh. Her ample breasts were further exaggerated under the overhead lighting of the moon. Dark shadows thrust her beauteous endowments out as if they were separate entities. Her nipples were swollen and erect, their faint pinkness abolished in the harsh, white glare. The naturally dark muff of her pubic area did well to shade her crotch, its hair glistening in the light. Her luscious hands caressed her beauteous form; fondling her breasts, massaging her hips, delving deep within her dark femininity. Her long and tangled hair was as jet black as the shadowed vault, as were her eyes; only one of which he could presently see, the other being hidden with the entire right side of her face under a shock of hair. Her facial features mirrored her body in all its glory. Full, pouting lips parted to reveal a pleasant tongue; a licked invitation to untold pleasures. Her quaint nose was the perfect centerpiece to such an exquisite face. Its nostrils flared in arousal, inhaling loudly the oppressive sexuality of the charged air. Her brow was tense and drawn in ecstatic agony over want of his touch. Her eyes ...

Her eyes. Those eyes – void of life. The black of her irises reflected the emptiness of her soul. One could stare into those orbs and see all eternity, or see nothing: no compassion, no desire, no love. Once one made contact with those dead eyes, a form of loose abandon came over him. Men would forsake duty, honor, love, and life to lie in her arms. It was not her beautiful body that so captivated her prey, although it aided her greatly – it was her eyes. Their hypnotic charm put to use a most democratic methodology; she seduced all, regardless of sex, race, creed or color. All humanity was her pleasure.

"Christian," she panted, "Christian, come ... come with me."

She held out her hands in appeal, open palms facing up, awaiting the fulfillment of his flesh. She spaced her extended arms widely so as to allow him a continuing view of her naked beauty. Everything about her suggested erotic sex. Her lips, her tongue, her breasts, her hands, her breath, and her hushed voice: all labored to express her longing. She was the epitome of all that is carnal, her body desirous of only one thing. Yet while her body made well its intentions clear, her eyes suggested a different craving.

Looking at him through shrouds of deception, her eyes did not resemble the eyes of a wanton, but rather those of a butcher examining a fatted calf. She wanted him for more than simple lovemaking; she required more of him than his stiff penis. She yearned for his soul. He saw certain death in those eyes, and it did not faze him in the least. What is life in exchange for her? he thought. Who would not give himself up for just a taste of those lips, however brief? Ah, to die in her embrace!

He felt himself move toward her, foot over sluggish foot, stumbling in the dark. He did not shift his gaze from hers, unable to break his eyes' transfixion. After what seemed like an eternity – but in reality was only several seconds – he entered the light.

She immediately fell on him, massaging him and caressing him in every way. Her hands ran across his body, seemingly touching him in many places at once. Her legs took turns rubbing his, and her enchanting hips gyrated against his groin, enraging his captive member to the point of insurgency.

Christian gladly mimicked her in the caressing of the body. His adept but nervous hands flew over her form, feeling her heavenly, milky-white (although somewhat clammy) skin. His quaking fingers alternated between the tender squeezing of her derriere and the vigorous kneading of her generous bosom. He conducted himself very shamefully with the utmost profligacy.

He then forced his lips on hers, kissing her with such emphatic passion that only the need for air unlocked their twisted mouths and tangled tongues. Taking short gasps, they continued in their ardor.

She was delicious! he mentally raved. She tasted sweet and bitter at the same time, a scrumptious mouthful with an unrelenting tongue.

In his fervor, his thrashing tongue brushed across her upper palate, producing a sharp, stinging sensation. He withdrew from her lips, tasting a wet saltiness in his mouth, and discovered he was bleeding. Staring at her in bewilderment, he saw her smile reveal those damned fangs. His blood made crimson stains on her red, red lips.

Sensuously licking the blood from her lips, she stared into his face and took his right hand in hers. "Tickle me ... touch me deeply ..." she cooed. She then thrust his hand up her moist womanhood.

Her inside felt strange to Christian's probing fingers. Even though it was a dream he was experiencing, its vividness allowed him to ascertain she was unlike any woman he had been with before. Her vagina was not feverish, as were most females in similar conditions, but rather lukewarm. He had aroused her, her juices and her hedonistic manner attested to that, but she remained tepid below.

As his fingers fiddled inside her, she forcefully resumed their kissing. Her mouth gulped down his bloodied spittle, her lips sucked his lacerated tongue. "Yes," she sighed, momentarily pulling away, "Yes. Love me, Christian … love me forever!"

Uncontrollable in his lust, he removed himself from her and with both hands ripped open his shirt, exposing his neck. "Take me!" he wept, more for sorrow than for joy. "Take me and do what you will, my fair lady! Take everything I possess, all that I am! Only love me. All I desire of you is your love. For all eternity, I beseech you most humbly to love me."

She smiled sadly, a glimmering tear trickling down her cheek, and whispered, "I have loved you since before you were born, and will love you long after you have died." With that being said, she kissed his lips softly and nestled against his warm neck. At the prick of his carotid he awoke, out of breath and out of his mind.

*Who was she? Why am I so drawn to her, by what powers does she hold sway over my unconscious brain?* He moved uncomfortably in his clothes. They were dampened by his frightened sweat, and chilled him to the point of shivering. My God, he thought, I quiver in a coldness of my own making.

How could a mere dream, a nightmare, have such an impact on his body as well as on his waking mind? She could cause him such distress that the peace of sleep became fearful to him. Awakening swathed in saturated bedclothes, his body trembling and his breath quavering, he would swear estrangement from that which enabled her to fill his head. And although black circles ringed his weary eyes as testament to his valiant attempts at staying awake, in the end he always succumbed: nodding off with a strange smile upon his lips, a countenance of serene pleasure.

The most troubling aspect of Christian's mysterious dream lover was that although vivid when asleep, he could not recollect the slightest about her when conscious. As hard as he tried, he could not remember her appearance, only that she was extremely beautiful. He could meet her in broad daylight in a market square and not recognize her in the least. It terrified him to know that there haunted his dreams a woman he could not identify, for he knew she was real; lying in repose somewhere, as in his dreams, awaiting him.

The only remembrance he had was of the woman's voice. This was so because he often heard her while roused — whispering his name on a night breeze, or giggling in a rainstorm. It did him little good, however, for although he recollected her every spoken word, the way in which they were spoken, their inflection, eluded him. He could not ascertain whether or not she was English (or any other nationality, for that matter), only that she spoke in a hushed whisper. One thing was certain, however; upon meeting this lady, should she ever disclose herself in such manner, he would know instantly who she was.

Christian turned his eyes from the black interior to the dour outside. Gazing from the windows, he was afforded a generous view of both sides of the street. The moderately slow speed of the horses permitted him a leisurely examination of his decadent London.

In the safety of the moving coach, he could stare without fear of abuse, verbal or otherwise. The thin pane of glass in each of the windows somehow made it all seem unreal, as if he were viewing strange refractions of light and nothing more. The painted crosses bothered him little now, as did the neglectful watchmen. Was it because he held no personal contact with them, cowering within the enclosed safety of a coach? Or was it that he was leaving this city of the diseased, this monument of the deceased, for his true lot in life? He would have liked to believe it was the latter, but as was his nature he tended to believe it was the former.

They were nearing the denser parts of London now, he calculated by the marked increase in activity and noise in the streets. The loss of serenity was presaged by the piercing wail of a disturbed woman. Christian drew close to the window to better view the hysteric and acquired yet another wretched memory to haunt the innards of his mind. The poor woman was mindless with grief, her crying accompanied by uncontrollable fits of melancholia. She walked, trance-like, down the street, clothed only in a nightgown, oblivious to all and beside herself with pity. Her arms hung limp, her left hand firmly clasped around the wrist of a small, departed child that she absently dragged behind her. Christian could not ascertain the sex of the child, for its mishandling on the brutal cobblestone had rendered it a faceless, sexless, bloodied mess. The sad woman hauled her sorry offspring out of view and into darkness.

Christian pressed his face up against the cold glass in an effort to catch a further glimpse of the woman, but she was gone. Suddenly thrust into his line of vision was a tall, thin old man with a long white beard. He was totally naked save for a pan of hot coals strapped to his head. Christian recalled the queer man's name, Solomon Eagle. The ancient loon always raved in such manner, declaring the end of the world, the punishment of sins, and the need for a new atonement with God. He stated the obvious.

Christian strained to sift out the naked Quaker's voice from the din surrounding the coach. He listened hard and was rewarded with the tremulous chords of deranged repetition. "We need a baptism of fire to burn away this pestilence! To cleanse our bodies and our souls! Lord, raise up a flame and raze all of London to the earth! Cease the atrocities committed within these city walls, let the flames of hellfire dissuade all from grievances against You! Burn us, burn us all!"

What an incredible fool! Christian fumed. Why should his madness manifest itself in such a sacrilegiously absurd form? Why did he not simply cry out as the others do, make private amends with God instead of public beratings and murderous supplications to Heaven above? He was the one who would burn, who would be tickled by hellfire for his false piousness and public indecency.

As the coach continued undaunted on its way, Solomon Eagle soon faded into the blurred distance, the burning coals of his head pan being the last of him to be swallowed by fog.

Christian stayed at his place near the window. The whole lunacy of it all unfolded like some bizarre circus. Through the coach's glass he could safely observe the tragic and the horrific, the full panorama of life and death on London streets. He watched with hidden expectations and concealed fear, his face as dispassionate as stone.

Turning down a larger avenue, the black coach cautiously wheeled through the befogged thoroughfares. Cotton led the horses carefully, for the fog had obscured the street beneath him. His only guidance as to remaining on the established roadway was his distance from the houses and shops lining either side of the street. He hoped to leave the fog behind with London once they hit the open forest road.

On the broad expressway, Christian's curiosity was not dissatisfied. Already he had caught sight of what appeared to be several bodies sprawled on a single side of the street. A whole family, perhaps? he pondered. The fog obfuscated most of their grave expressions and made indistinct the total number of their party. Either errant dead carts had passed them up or the entire family had only recently fallen to the sickness.

As his eyes strained in the dim light and foggy haze, Christian noticed one of the bodies moving. From the broad back and naked shoulders he knew it to be a man. What a way to perish, he contemplated, dying surrounded by the bodies of loved ones. He was nearly moved to tears for the poor man when he noticed him in no way acting in a frail manner or weakened state. "My God," Christian breathed aloud, "he's fornicating with one of the dead!"

With vigorous and quickening thrusts, the madman pumped himself into the body of an older female. Having already succumbed to a contagion of the Plague and careless of further contamination, or mindlessly indulging himself believing it to be the end of the world, the man would not stop until he had satiated himself with the corpse.

Have we descended into godlessness? Are we to become a present-day Sodom and Gomorrah? Christian asked himself. How could anyone have sex with the dead? How strong could a libido be that it would drive a man to such acts of monstrous indiscretion, such acts of gross carnality? He could never understand how men could forsake their souls for an hour of adulterous pleasure, but this? How could he empathize with one who so dishonors a deceased woman, who commits a crime far worse than Onan through his sowing of seed in a cold ground?

Continuing on and leaving the indiscriminate lover to his reprehensible pleasure, the coach moved through the byways and connecting streets of greater London. Inside the coach's compartment, Christian closed his eyes and ears to the outside world. He would not, could not, tolerate any further acts of such loathing. He wanted to be away from here, to leave all this behind him and run away, escaping into the night. He was weary of the inhumanity and death that constantly plagued him from all sides. He longed for the blessed serenity of an Italian seminary, to only concern himself with the acquisition of knowledge, not of a shared grave. How he would love to study the complete works of Homer, Virgil, Dante, Boccaccio, his own Shakespeare and Chaucer. How he wished his only considerations were trivial thoughts of mind and not life-or-death decisions such as walking down the street or eating in public. Living without fear: that to him was a paradise unto itself.

His efforts to block himself from the pathetic outside failed. A not-too-distant scream captured his attention and opened his eyes. Staring out into the cloudy streets once more, he felt trapped. What was it about death that so frightened, yet intrigued, him?

A face familiar to him appeared from out of the fog. She was an ancient creature, bent over with age and the burden of past sins. Dressed entirely in black, she mourned for a husband that had been dead for thirty-odd years. The withered and bony fingers of her right hand curled around the gnarled head of a tiny cane. Although frail, it was laughable to see her rest her entirety on that small, wooden stick. Her left hand fumbled through her pockets, searching for something. Goody Gretcham, what are you doing here at this time of night, you old hag? Christian mentally queried. Are you looking to join your beloved?

Gretcham fished from her pockets several scraps of food. To Christian's strained eyes it appeared to be strips of cooked meat with bits of biscuit. The old woman then called out for someone to come near. Two children, an older girl and a young boy, peered out at her from a sheltering doorway. As were most street urchins, they were covered head to toe in filth. Their famished, imploring eyes shone forth from their dirty faces like beacons of hope, their emaciated appearance flaunting their hunger.

As Goody Gretcham waved the food in her hands, the children slowly stepped out from their doorway. Christian felt joy rising in his heart. This old woman who had devoted her whole life to ruining other's lives through gossip was now, in the final hour, atoning for her sins! She was going to feed these impoverished children!

Goody Gretcham continued with her calls, acting as if she did not see the children standing ten feet before her. To her entreaties several large hounds rushed out from under the cover of fog. She then proceeded to feed the voracious beasts in full view of the undernourished children.

Christian sat, mouth open in dismay, looking at the old bitch petting and cuddling the unclean mutts. She continued feeding them from her pockets as they swarmed around her, licking her hands and feet. He saw the children; the girl putting her arm around her little brother, whispering words of consolation. Those animals should be dead, he raged within, all dogs and cats are to be killed, as they are carriers of the disease! If only I were a dog-killer! I'd kill the bloody beasts and use their bodies as kindling for that witch's fire!

He glared at Gretcham and the feeding frenzy she had created. Over twenty dogs now surrounded her cruel little body. In the scuffle to be fed, one of the smaller dogs was knocked against the Goody's cane, causing her to topple into the pack of hungry jackals. The smell of food stuffed in her pockets induced the already inflamed dogs to a bloody binge. Amidst her punctured screams, the dogs sated themselves on her flesh, tearing her apart and gorging themselves on her warm innards. It was ironic to see the very same animals she fed fighting over her corpse for pieces of her intestines.

Christian could not resist a smile. Despite his religious upbringing, he could feel no pity for the old woman. Justice was blind, but not without a sense of humor. Good-bye, Goody Gretcham, he mused, give the Devil's beard a yank for me!

The starving children felt none of the satisfaction that Christian experienced at Goody Gretcham's brutal demise. They felt only fear, and turning, ran from the horrid scene. Running parallel to the coach at a slightly faster speed, the children managed to stay in Christian's view for some time. Stopping in a doorway to catch their breath, he saw the two look fearfully about for the dogs. The door behind them abruptly opened and they were pleasantly greeted by a husky man.

As the coach passed by them, Christian saw the man invite the children into his home. The children, still fearful of the dogs, hurried under the man's welcoming arm and into the immediate safety the house offered. Christian began to let out a sigh of relief for the poor children, but halted his breath when he took notice of the deviously broad grin on the husky man's face. The man looked suspiciously about and then, with a relaxed composure betraying an underlying glee, he retired within.

Christian wondered why it was that the man so disturbed him. Looking up, he read the sign posted above the man's door. His heart froze and his spine tingled, he did not want to believe the awful truth he had surmised. It was a butcher's shop! The kind man was a butcher!

Christian knew well the scarcity of meat products in the city, could it be that this man was employing black means in order to stay in business? Was this man a butcher of society's dregs, of the outcasts, the homeless, the unwanted? Did he market meats never meant to be eaten? Christian couldn't bear his vile thoughts any longer. He rapped on the coach's ceiling.

"What is it?" Cotton yelled down from above. The external noises made it difficult for him to hear Christian.

"Stop the coach. I wish to get out," Christian commanded loudly from within.

"I can't do that. 'Tis to dangerous to halt even for a moment here."

"But I must get out!"

"Ye can relieve yourself once we're on the open road."

"No! You don't understand, I must get out to help the children."

"I'll not stop and endanger ye for one instance! Think not of a couple of urchins, but of all of England … of Scotland as well!"

Christian sank back in his seat. He knew Cotton was right, that he must look at the whole picture. His only concern should be for the cure. Nothing must get in his way, he must obtain it as soon as possible. The cure would banish such acts as he had witnessed as it obliterates the Plague. It is the Plague that causes such evils to be committed. To abolish the sickness would be to outlaw the necessity for that kind of malicious behavior. Returning with a cure would bring about a return to civil order. Magistrates would regain their powers, the king and court would return from Salisbury, and he would see to the butcher's prosecution.

Confident in his mind as well as in himself, he took a deep breath and stayed by the window. The Bible in his hands did nothing but feel heavy. It did not allay the aching in his heart or the grief in his soul. As the coach continued on through the city, he saw many more horrific sights, but he weathered them all. Pillagers stole from the dead, some going as far as foolishly removing clothing, leaving the dead dishonored and themselves open to contagion. Men fought with men, women fought with women, and various combinations of both prevailed. It seemed as though in the face of Death people lost all decency.

"The living cannot bury the dead," he said aloud, "but the dead shall bury the living."

Sobs, screams, and wails filled the night air. Lamentations of indescribable woe moved Christian to tears. He clutched his Bible tightly to his chest, as if to protect his heavy heart from any further weight. Why are You allowing this to happen? he asked God. What have we done to deserve this great evil?

He could not accept this as the will of Christ, his Savior. This was Old Testament wrath, as damaging as a swarm of locusts or a rain of burning sulfur. Did not Jesus die for our sins so we would not be subject to plagues such as this?

It bothered him when he scrutinized his religious doctrine, but how could he not? How could any man, sane or otherwise, not ask why this was happening? Whenever he was exposed to such sights as he had seen tonight, he inevitably was confronted with doubt. It all came down to one bothersome question: if Jesus was God, how could He allow this to occur?

The impact of a rotten leek against the window stirred Christian from his troubling thoughts. Looking past the splattered bits of vegetable, he saw a middle-aged man with an angry face.

"Too good to walk like the rest of us, are ye?" the man angrily protested. "Afraid of catching the fever now, are ye? Can't be walking with us low folk … give us your horses, we need food."

Christian could hear Cotton's deep voice threatening from above. "Leave off," he intoned. "We seek no trouble, only safe passage." Cotton sounded most God-like, Christian fancied.

"Bah!" cried the man, making an obscene gesture. "May the dead cart come and carry ye to your grave!"

"Not before stopping at your door, sir!" shouted Cotton over his shoulder.

Christian slumped uncomfortably in his seat. He did not wish to gain comfort, for doing so would lead to sleep, sleep would lend itself to dream, and he would once again be hers. He closed his eyes in avoidance of any subsequent horrors. When will it all end, Lord? he pleaded. When will the madness, the dreams, the nightmares all stop? Somehow, he reasoned, she had something to do with it. When he met the woman of his dreams it would all become clear to him.

The lonely black coach maneuvered through the cloud-white streets of London until it itself was ingested by the fog. Into the bosom of the night went the bold travelers, questing for an unknown good, the importance of their journey burdening already frayed nerves and heavy brows. Alone into the wicked, wicked night they went, the dark and sinister secret night that had long preyed upon the fears of young and old alike. In their travels they would discover the macabre truth sequestered in this unbearable darkness.

London and all its lunacy was long behind them now. It was darker in the deep forest, the tall trees creating shade from the light of the moon, dimming an already black night. The gnarled and ancient wood looming above made small the coach, their swaying limbs projecting frantic shadows on the earth below. The filtered light created movement where there was none, making ghosts out of tree trunks and hewing hobgoblins from simple stones.

The wind whistled through the foliage, leading loose leaves on an aria of nature. The gossiping leaves seemed to spread tidings of the coach's coming, muttering from clustered branch to clustered branch with every gust. The night breeze spread their discourse like a rolling wave upon the sea. And while this same wind succored the infernal forest evensong, so had it dissipated the following London fog. In nature there was no good or evil, only dispassionate fate.

Christian leaned his back against the unpadded inside wall of the coach. He resisted sleep, but it was a hard fought battle. The swaying trees, cavorting shadows, lulling wind, and magical moonlight were no allies to him. It seemed as though the entire outside intrigued against his waning consciousness. He struggled to maintain a positioning of his body that was most uncomfortable. Shifting here and there inside the coach he sought any posture incommodious. Like the monk absolving himself through flagellation, so did Christian seek pain to avoid slumber. Gradually battering himself in his efforts, his aches and pains were belittled in his victory. Physical hurt was inconsequential when compared to the mental anguish he avoided.

Cotton cowered from the forest breeze in his long, snug overcoat. The collar of the coat was drawn high, to assist his neck and face in guarding against the cold, and his wide-brimmed hat was tilted low. He did not like traversing forest roads at night. Highwaymen and worse evils lurked in the dark, waiting for an unlucky coach to draw near. His honed eyes inspected every twitching shadow, every rustling leaf. Under such circumstances as the forest was this night, his anxiety rose markedly. Putting his perturbations to the reins in his gloved hands, he drove the two mares harder. The coach sped down the rough, dirt road and through the tumultuous forest.

The increase in speed prompted Christian to rise from his uneasy slouch and look out the window. The frolicking moonlight invaded the coach, spilling onto the floor and all over his feet. He glanced down at it, enchanted by its beauty. Releasing his Bible from his numb fingers, he set it down on the seat beside him. Pressing his forehead against the window, he raised his eyes to the heavens and strove to catch sight of the wondrous moon. He could barely see its brilliance, it being nearly directly above them.

Far off in the dark, deep within the woods, a solitary, mournful cry arose. It lingered long in the crisp September night.

Wolves! Christian fretted, the hair on the back of his neck rising. Am I to meet the same fate as Goody Gretcham?

Above him, Cotton was similarly unsettled. It had been a hard summer for the wolves in these parts. He had heard talk of whole packs attacking farmers, devouring entire families. Hunting parties had been elected to rid the local counties of the carnivorous beasts, but had met with little success. All summer long they entered the forest with pointed staves and sharpened swords. Few returned alive. All summer long the wolves grew fat off the flesh of the country people. They had developed a taste for human flesh and favored it above all others. With fall already here, and the winter months drawing nigh, the rapacious beasts would need to fill their bellies and stock their hovels.

Another cry ruptured the now thick air, then another.

God! Christian lamented, they're getting closer! They're getting closer to us!

Outside, Cotton whipped the horses into flight. He beat them as hard and as fast as he could, forcing them into a dangerous gallop. We could overturn, he contemplated, then we'd really be done for. But if we don't outrun the wolf pack, the horses will surely be overtaken. Where would we be then? Once again he lashed into the backs of the swift steeds.

Inside, Christian was tossed about with such fury that his fear somewhat shifted from the distant wolves to his immediate battery. He's trying to outrun them, he rabidly assessed. The old fool's going to get us killed!

A rut in the road caused his head to smash against the top of the carriage. "Damn it all to hell!" he screamed. Steadying himself with his left hand planted firmly against the door, his right hand massaged and protected his battered head. I'm getting beaten to death by the insides of a cab! he fretted.

Racing against the night, the small vehicle carved its trail into the well-trodden forest road. The horses, fearing the howling dark, strained themselves into a lathery sweat. Their rich, salty whiteness glistened in the moonlight as they flew through the hungry woods.

Cotton knew that if he continued running the mares hard they would tire quickly. He also reckoned that the coach's frail wheels could not withstand another rut. Having not heard any further wolf calls, his mind was decided. He pulled back on the reins and slowed the horses down to a trot. His eyes wildly searched the tree lines on either sides of the road. He saw nothing and heard the same.

Christian sat slumped on the coach floor. He could feel the bruises on his body aching for attention. His left shin and his right elbow quarreled for the larger part of his consideration, both hurting equally. He felt as though he may have pulled something in his abdomen, a sharp pain appearing at his every pivot. His head felt unpleasantly numb, a foretaste of the tremendous headache he would soon be receiving. He rose carefully to his seat. Why have we slowed? he asked himself.

Reining in the horses further, Cotton sought to decrease the sound of their hooves on the hard dirt road. His ears labored in the windy forest to hear the wolves. They were coming, he was sure of that.

Peering nervously out his window, Christian stared into the shadowed forest. Where were they? he wondered. Why did they torment him with their waiting, lurking there, in the darkness just outside the light? Why did they not come rushing forth and attack them?

Taking his eyes from the dense foliage, he tried once more to glimpse the full moon. He could see it more clearly now, hanging lower in the sky: its shimmering, perfect white surface resembling a gigantic skull afloat in space. Is it a harbinger of our impending doom? he speculated, overcome with a fit of shivers.

Something coming out of the forest caught his attention through the corner of his eye. Fearfully, he dropped his gaze from the moon to the ragged line of trees just outside. Its initial movement caused him to notice it, and now, sitting quiet in the dark, it became harder to see. But see it he did — its snout protruding into the silvery light, its starving eyes meeting his.

It was a lone wolf, waiting perhaps for its company to arrive before ripping them asunder. It looked ragged and old, far too weak for a tiring assault without help. It simply sat there, half covered by the brush and shadow, looking at Christian with cold hunger.

All of a sudden the whole pack erupted from the dense wood. They had come from behind the solitary wolf and paid him no attention, as they were tangling with a captured prey. There must have been a dozen or more wolves, all tearing into the same animal. They fought with each other for pieces, reducing the poor creature, whatever it was, to something beyond all recognition.

Christian watched with both revulsion and delight. He was repulsed by the savage slaughter they inflicted on their victim, but was overcome when it appeared all their interests were vested in their immediate meal and not in any way the taking of the coach. 'Tis quite a large animal, he surmised, too fatted for a deer and too large for a boar. It must be a calf, taken from a nearby farm. Observing this all from the safety of the interior, he took in the mangy wolves' feeding frenzy. How brutal the squalid monsters were, he marveled. How they held only selfish concerns, wrestling with one another over bits of flesh and blood. How could any of God's creatures be so— Oh my God!

There, emerging from the enshrouding copse, was a little girl. All in white, the reflecting moonlight deemed her a cherubim. She stood innocent of the wolves, unaware of their savagery at her feet. She espied the coach and Christian within, and smiling bewitchingly at him, waved. The wolves encircling her paid her no notice and she did the same. They were more concerned with fighting over prey already slain.

Christian's mouth dropped open in terror. His blood became ice in his veins. His eyes took in the graphic reality of the scene and the immediacy it demanded, but he was unable to act, being frozen with fear for the child.

Her right hand reached down and scratched the head of the lone wolf and he looked up at her with a toothy grin. Her eyes still locked on Christian, she let out a playful giggle as if in a schoolyard full of peers, not a forest surrounded by wolves.

"Dear Lord ... sweet Jesus!" Christian whispered, his bated breath seeping out.

The act of her touching the wolf propelled him into action. She had crossed the line, coming into physical contact with the beasts. He did not know whether or not the poor girl was deranged, but he had to get her away from those predators. He pounded his fist into the roof, yelling, "Stop! Cotton, stop at once!"

The coach showed no signs of halting. Cotton must be ignoring me, he thought. He could pay me no attention, but how could he be heedless of the child's plight? Stooping down and craning his neck, he returned his eyes to the little girl.

He saw her face light up when she recognized him at the window. Her grin could melt Cocytus, he speculated, momentarily taken by her youthful virtue. He watched her wave at him again and he hurriedly returned her greeting. She then bent at the knees and, never shifting her gaze from his face, attempted to retrieve something from amongst the wolves.

His heart quickened as fear pumped adrenaline through his veins. She was sticking her hands betwixt the pack! his mind reeled. Her fingers were tickling their maws!

"No!" he cried out uncontrollably. "No!"

The child never let her smile droop or fade in any way as she thrust her arms in the midst of the eating animals, meeting Christian's concerned glare with a carefree wink and an accompanying giggle. She plucked a rumpled and tattered something from beneath the wolves' prey and held it proudly out for Christian to see.

He could not make out exactly what it was until she, seeing his indecision, placed it upon her head.

It was a hunter's cap, his mind saw what his eyes tried to avoid. *The wolves' prey . . . 'twas a man! They were gorging themselves on human flesh!*

Upon seeing the ghastly look of realization come over Christian's face, the little girl broke into an outburst of laughter. She held her stomach and rocked back and forth on her toes with glee. Raising one hand to her mouth in an attempt to quell the erupting hilarity, she used her free arm to signal an energetic and pleasant farewell.

The peculiarity of her nonchalance, as well as the bizarre scene before his frightened eyes, was too much for Christian to bear. He forced himself from the window and began assailing the ceiling with his naked fists. "Stop!" he cried out, his voice crackling with emotion. "Stop this coach immediately!"

He felt no slowing of the ride, no easing of the horses' pace. Cotton is ignoring me, he fumed. He kept me from saving those urchins in London, but I'll be damned if I allow him to do it again! Renewing his vigorous pounding, he let all his emotions pour forth. Hate, anger, and frustration oozed from his bloody knuckles. He was not battering the roof for Cotton's attention; he was in a melee with all that ailed him. He lashed out against all the inhumanities and injustices he had witnessed. He landed blows for the poor, the sick, the dying, the dead, and the orphaned. He would not let his logic wash clean his hands of this child. He would rescue her, and damn all of England if Cotton thought it not prudent!

"Stop this instant, you old bastard!" he screamed in desperate lunacy. "Hold those horses or I'll not wait for you to stop!"

Instantly the coach slowed. Christian could not remain inside any longer, he threw open the door and burst out into the dangerous night. He must save her, regardless of whatever barbarities the wolves inflicted upon him.

"What in the hell's wrong with ye?" Cotton bellowed from his seat, chastising Christian for his pounding. "Are ye mad? Ye scared the—" It was then that he noticed Christian's fleeing form heading towards the thicket. "Wait!" he cried out. "Wait! Hold! Wolves I've heard! Do ye hear? Wolves!"

Christian cocked his head sideways, screaming his reply in earnest, "I've seen them! They have a child! Quickly, we must hurry!"

Leaping from his seat, Cotton raced after him. Catching him twenty feet from the coach he stood before Christian and blocked his way. Grabbing him by the shoulders, he forcefully restrained the eager youth. "What say ye? A child?"

"They — the wolves," sputtered Christian, trying to manipulate himself out of Cotton's clutches, "the wolves have a little girl!"

"Where?" Cotton queried with a skeptical raise of the brow.

"Over yonder ..."

Christian pointed to where he had seen the child, the wolves, and the poor man, but there was nothing. Nothing but silence and the occasional titter of wind. Even the crickets had lost their melody.

"I see nothing and hear the same," Cotton stated, his voice congested with annoyance.

Christian looked hard and listened long. He saw as Cotton. Nothing. There were no wolves. No little girl in need of rescue. There was only the wind and the black forest. "How?" he asked aloud, a dazed look overcoming his features. "How?"

Cotton's eyes bore hard into Christian on the darkened roadway. This was who Stemmons had entrusted with the salvation of Britain? This frightened little boy who saw things that were not real? There were wolves, but out deep in the forest. And there was no lost little girl. How could he continue, how could he expect success with such an apprehensive half-wit?

"Come along now," he soothed. "There's not a thing ye can do now." He grimaced as he lied to appease Christian's perplexity, "The bloody beasts have her."

Christian did not respond to Cotton's pacifications, opting instead to ignore him and continue searching for the girl. He scoured the pitch forest with his eyes, exerting them to the point of blindness. He saw nothing.

As his look of desperation dissolved into resignation, Cotton gently took him by the arm and led him back to the coach. Continually looking over his shoulder and into the woods, Christian gave the appearance of one who had lost his mind. If asked, he could not tell his name, his business, or his beliefs. The only matter he would address was that of the vanished girl. "But ... but how?" he begged no one for an answer. "I saw the pack, the child ..." Halfway into the cab he grabbed Cotton by his jacket's lapels. "They were eating someone!" he insisted. Seeing in Cotton's face the look of disbelief, he slumped down into the coach, muttering, "There was something ... now nothing ... nothing at all ..."

Looking down at the disheartened young man, the old mercenary was seized with pity, an emotion usually foreign to him. He felt the need to make it right, to console instead of chide. He placed his hand on Christian's shoulder and smiled as he said, "Even if we had been in time, there'd have been nothing we could have done." He felt foolish as the words left his mouth, and with some discomfort chastened Christian, saying, "Come now, bother not with such distress, ye face greater importance."

Christian's eyes rolled up at the big Scot. "Greater importance?" he said, his voice thick with disgust. "More so than the life of a child? I think not!"

He really believes he saw something, Cotton mused. He stared at the ashen face full of indignation before him. Then, with a quick sidestep, he closed the door on his deluded passenger. Shaking his head slowly, he ascended to his lofty and cold seat on high.

Christian stared forlornly out the coach window. He could hear Cotton urging the horses onward outside and feel the sensation of gradual movement in the mollifying lilt of the coach. He could make full use of all his five senses, but his mind would only acknowledge one: his sixth. It was that which told him that what he saw was tangible, that there was a girl. He needed no proof, the hair standing on the back of his neck was proof enough of what he saw. But even with that inner affirmation to bolster his faith, he still longed for the substantial; still searched the darkness for the little, moonlit angel.

"May the good Lord keep and cherish thee," he whispered, blessing himself and holding his crucifix close to his heart.

As the coach wheeled its way down the luminescent road, a buffeting wind eclipsing its noisy carriage, the shrill laughter of a child arose from the woods and was carried on the gusty air.

Not far from where Cotton halted Christian on the roadside there lay a torn and tattered garment enshrouded in leaves. It was all that remained of a huntsman's cap.

# Chapter Three

It seemed like they were traveling the winding forest road forever. Christian kept himself occupied, and from falling asleep, through the forced recitation of biblical quotations and sermons. He whispered them slowly under his breath, his Bible a source of inspiration in his lap.

They had been on the road now for about four hours and their backsides let them know it. Their bodies ached, yearning for sleep. While this was in an odd way pleasurable to Christian (for the soreness warded off comfort, which led to slumber) it was by no means advantageous to Cotton, whose old bones were equally smarting and doubly chilled.

Cotton had the exhilaration of the cold to sustain wakefulness. However hypnotic the ghostly glimmering of the moonlight, the breath of the north wind kept his weariness at bay.

Ruminating about the little girl he had seen, Christian frowned in the darkness of the coach. He had been thinking about her since seeing her, but only now was he cognizant enough to fully ponder her fate and consider her strange behavior. Why did she not fear the wolves? he asked himself. Men equally fear wolves as do women, why not a youthful child? Especially when the bloody beasts were tearing a poor man apart beneath her feet!

He tried to sort out the ridiculous, attempting to believe that she was simply the wolves' next victim, but the entire scene replayed in his head was preposterous. The girl had no fear of the wolves and they took no notice of her, despite being in a voracious feeding frenzy. She even patted a wolf's head and smiled when donning the huntsman's cap. She resembled nothing of a frightened little girl, but rather was most at ease with the predators, treating them more as friends than possible attackers. She giggled and laughed amongst them, making merry their blood-feast. Perhaps, he thought quite irrationally, she was one of those raised in the wild by the wolves, brought into their custody as a babe from one of the neighboring farmhouses and taken into their midst as one of their own.

But she was not dressed as one would be living in the wild. Her white frock was spotless, having not even the faintest discoloration of dirt or marring of blood. She appeared as one so immaculate that dirt and grime cowered from her glorious presence.

Noticing a change in the scenery outside, Christian left his disturbed thoughts as he looked out the window. The forest was thinning into open fields. Gradually the trees retreated into the distance, their twisted, silhouetted shapes writhing in protest at the coach escaping their gnarled, wooden clutches. We must be nearing Bantingham, he noted. Thank God.

Before entering the town, he was to receive further evidence of the necessity of his quest. As they were passing through the outskirts, where farmers have their crops, he noticed several men with lanterns raised. Drawing nearer, he saw that they were laboring in the dark to bury a corpse. Two men held up two lanterns each in order to provide better lighting for those doing the actual work. One man stood alongside the lantern bearers with a shovel resting on his shoulder. Two more men tried to maneuver the body into the grave with long poles.

Smart, observed Christian. They respect contamination and accordingly treat the body at a distance. The men in London should learn from these undertakers.

He had seen the long poles before, put to good use in the south of Wales. They were roughly six feet long and had pointed hooks at their appropriate ends. The poles allowed those disposing the dead to do so, but without the direct contact synonymous with infectious spreading of the disease.

Riding past, he tried to glimpse the body to see if it was male or female, young or old. His eyes were met by the suspicious stares of the men. They looked at him with resentment mixed with fear, a loathing replete with mistrust.

They gaze at me in such manner because they do not know if I carry the Plague, he speculated. The village must be seriously ravaged for them to do such work in the dark dawn before daylight. I hope Rebecca is well.

Rounding a bend, Christian was offered one last look at the buriers. He saw the men with poles tug viciously at the body and it fall ignominiously into place within its hole. Averting his eyes from the sad spectacle, he was once again met by the cold stares of the laborers.

Bantingham, he winced, was not going to be easy.

Traveling most of the night through treacherous woodland, observing things not material, and nearly losing his mind as well as his nerves had Christian scarcely patient for the security of a town. Once inside Bantingham, he and Cotton would procure rooms. The comfort of a locked door and a warm bed only tormented him when he thought of with whom he could be sharing it. Rebecca, his heart lusted, how I long to see you! How I ache for your touch, a womanly touch, a tender touch, a caress I have not felt since your departure. And how I covet your breasts, those two brazen exemplars of womanhood!

The thought of her alone propelled his eagerness to enter Bantingham to an excruciating limit. Fears, questions, and good intentions aside, all he presently wanted to do was bury himself deep within the arms of his estranged lover. All his wants, dreams, desires, and wishes were summed up in the bulge of his crotch. He wanted to share them all with her, to give Rebecca his love, to fill her with his passion.

But was she even alive? his pessimism pushed him into reality. Was she healthy and sound? Perhaps she was not dead but was dying. Or could she not be affianced, perhaps even married, to another?

The suffocating tightness of his ill-fitting shoes added to his bothers; that and the chilliness of the coach annexed his patience. I want liberation from the belly of this cold, fetid, black beast! his mind cried out. I am sick of forest, weary of moonlight, and disgusted with sitting on my ass!

As if on an appeal from Christian's subconscious, Cotton rescued his frantically impatient charge with an abruptness that was music to Christian's itching ears: "We're finally here."

All the resentment at having been interned for so long within the coach melted as ice in fire. Christian's heart soared, lifting him to his feet and carrying him to the all-too-familiar window. With face pressed against the glass, as if in childlike expectation of a second London, he eagerly watched for their long awaited destination.

What rolled into view, engulfing the persistent panorama of woodland, was something of a disappointment even to Christian, who above all others loved this place for the safety it offered and the woman it kept.

The village, if it could be called such, for it was so small, seemed to consist of five major edifices. There was a stable, a tavern, a goods shop, an inn, and a church. All were structured similarly, leading Christian to believe that they were all built by the same people, probably farmers. And from the apparent poor workmanship, he deduced that they were built out of necessity rather than want.

I wonder where she works, he mused. Probably in the goods shop. He could see her assisting old ladies with purchases of lace, her fetching smile broadening at the opening of their purses.

The thought of Rebecca brought a smile to his own lips. He could barely contain his joy at being so close to her. It had been so long, too long. He needed to absolve himself between the beauty of her breasts, to obscure his face in her bosom. He no longer felt the aching of his feet or the numbness of his head. All he felt was the warm giddiness of a lover, a feeling which had been disaffected from him for far too long. The pounding of his heart due to passion, and not fear, was a welcomed return.

He almost choked on his breath when he felt the coach slow to a halt. In his amorous anxiety he had not realized that they were in front of the tavern. Smoothing out his crinkled clothes, he made decent his form. He then wrestled with the coach door, it being difficult to open from the inside due to the fact that it was a processional coach and was made for use with exterior attendants.

Before losing his temper, he was released from his prison of excruciating boredom by Cotton. The old soldier had jumped down from the coach the moment it had rolled to a stop. He too was in need of something, but unlike Christian it was not a woman. His dried throat and shivering bones told him what they required – ale. And in the same frenetic and arduous manner as Christian, he hurried about his business. "We'll rest up here and sup before getting rooms at the inn," he said, helping Christian out of the coach.

Christian nodded in agreement. "I'm just pleased to be free of that monster."

"Aye."

Glancing from the coach to its two wearied steeds Christian asked, "And what of the horses? What will you do with them?"

"I shall take them 'round back to the stables, feed and water them good, then join ye inside."

"Should I not accompany you in your task?"

"Nay, I should think after being on this earth for so long I would know enough how to feed and water horses." He smiled fatherly at Christian, "Thank ye for your generous offer, but I can manage."

"Very well," Christian inhaled the rebuff. "But Cotton," he intoned nervously, "make haste, for I am but a lone stranger 'til you arrive."

"Aye, that I will. And remember, don't tell anyone you're from London. London's plague-city to these folk."

"Alright, I won't."

Christian stood back and watched the nimble old man clamber back up the tilting coach. Once atop it, he gentle prodded the exhausted horses to movement, all the while talking to them. He told them how he was going to care for them, how he was going to rub them down and feed them until their sides split. His voice and the clicking of the carriage wheels grew faint as they turned the tavern's corner and disappeared from Christian's view.

The tavern was as shoddy as the four other structures in the village, if not more so. It was plain in design: a two-story building with two windows on each side, one up and one down. The roof was slanted off-kilter, and suffered from serious rain damage. The building itself was so innocuous that the only part of it which appealed to one's eyes was its signboard. Its carved letters were filled with red paint probably left over from the painting of a barn. It read, The Thirsty Traveler Tavern.

Seconds seemed like years as Christian approached the tavern door. He knew what he was in for, he had known what to expect since seeing those gravediggers on the road. The stares, the fear-hiding anger, the curses issued under breath. In these times people were afraid of strangers, for they did not know who carried the Plague. He had heard of entire towns refusing entry of any visitors, closing themselves off from the rest of the world. New roads had to be created to avoid passing through those belligerent places. Fear of the Plague had caused some townspeople to lose their morals, killing all who happened to wander into their hamlets. Hopefully, he prayed, Bantingham was not one of those villages.

Only when his hand had touched the cold door handle did he realize how frightened he actually was. His fingers quivered like those of a sober drunkard and he required the use of both his hands in grasping the lever. He could die tonight, he grimly realized. He could walk into this tavern and be set upon by frightfully brutal villagers, being torn limb from grisly limb, all his aspirations drowning in a pool of his own blood.

Then he thought otherwise. Someone within may know the whereabouts of Rebecca, or at least what has befallen her. With lust conquering fear, he energetically pulled open the door.

Just remember, he reminded himself, say nothing of London.

To Christian's dismal surprise, the tavern was quite full. It was as if the entire village had decided to spend the night imbibing ale and telling tales. A quick survey of the scene revealed no Rebecca. Just as well, he thought. He wouldn't want her in a place such as this at this time of night. She was probably cuddled up in a warm bed somewhere doing what he could not.

Entering, he closed the door behind him and turned to face a terrifying quiet. Just as in London, all eyes were on him as if attempting to glimpse his soul: their bleak, weather-beaten faces labeling him a foreigner in his own country, each of them assessing his appearance, scrutinizing his health. Was he contaminated? Did he carry the contagion?

Realizing his movements were being examined and deciding that the next best course of action was to sit down, he did so. Those seated at the table to which he sat himself hastily rose and departed, scattering to neighboring tables. They left Christian alone and nervous under the watchful gaze of fellow patrons.

Christian's eyes fidgeted between looking at the tavern's floorboards and into the various faces glaring at him. He played with his hands and restlessly rubbed his shoes together. Droplets of sweat formed on his tense brow and his mouth dried up to the point of making speech difficult, the corners of his lips twitching out of control. He was as a little child in a room full of angry adults.

Observing Christian's distress, and feeling a large part of it herself, was Rebecca Seaton, tavern barmaid. Peeking out from behind the bar, the young woman was careful in avoiding her former lover. He had grown even more handsome, she fancied, her heart pumping with fear and excitement. She wanted to run to him, but the atmosphere in the small tavern would not allow it. Even so, she deliberated, she should let him worry alone. Why should she ease his tension when he had never come to ease hers? She knew that all that was required of her to return the tavern to order was for her to acknowledge his presence through waiting on him. But let him fry, she angrily declared within. Let him sweat it out!

But what if he came here for her? What if he never received her note and had spent all his time looking for her? Undecided in her mind, Rebecca bit her lower lip and waited.

Christian squirmed uncomfortably in his seat. The residents of Bantingham would not avert their eyes! They continued to stare into him. Thoughts fluttered chaotically through his head. Why did they not desist in their gaping? Why did they just sit there and do nothing but observe? Where the hell was Cotton?

For some reason, his attention was drawn from the entire populace of the tavern to just one man. Perhaps it was simply that the man sat directly opposite him. Or maybe it was the leering smirk and overwhelming sense of wickedness that consumed Christian's concentration. Whatever it was, he found he could not take his eyes off the cruel man.

The man opened his chapped smile to reveal an odd assortment of yellow and brown teeth. He wore a dirty, black patch over his right eye and his face was crisscrossed with a combination of wrinkles and scars. A sprinkling of whiskers dotted his jaw line, and his nose hair danced with every wheezy exhalation. His greasy, gray hair was well receded, increasing the size of his vulgar face and falling in clumps on his shoulders. His clothes were tattered and stained, some articles oversized and others under. It was quite obvious to Christian that this was a man who stole from the dead.

The tormenting glint in the man's sole eye prepared Christian for trouble. He watched as the man took a sloppy swig of ale, spilling more on himself than into his gullet. The man then slammed his cup down on the table, catering to the patrons' desire for a confrontation. Here it comes, Christian grimly thought.

The man resumed eye contact with Christian. Then, returning the leer to his vulgar features, said aloud, "Some towns are a-killing strangers."

Christian's eyes darted nervously from face to stony face. It seemed as if time was standing still, as if he was in one of his nightmares. He hoped to God this wasn't really happening, praying for the arrival of the girl in his dreams to show him that all he had to do was awaken and it would be over. But it was no dream. The tavern continued to stare at him, torturing his nerves.

Anxiety wet his flesh, beads of sweat rolling down his forehead. At any moment their fear of me, fear of the Plague, will cause them to rise up and kill me! he woefully lamented. Where in the hell was Cotton, for Christ's sake? He thought of fleeing, but worried that any sudden movement on his part would send the tense crowd into a berserk rage.

Just as the tension reached its highest point, where one could have easily incited those few people of Bantingham to the commission of various acts of brutality, Rebecca rushed to Christian's rescue. "What'll you fancy, sir?" she asked dutifully, putting on an air of dispassion.

He looked up at the bedraggled waitress standing before him. Her hair was a mess, as were her clothes – her general appearance was that of one who worked hard and rested little. In her hands she held a serving tray flat against her abdomen. It was her tired appearance and his uneasy infatuation with her tray that affected his recall. When her voice struck chords of familiarity, he forcefully and most shamefully recognized his lost love. "Rebecca!" he cried out exultantly, rising to his feet.

"Ssssh! Shush!" she admonished him in whisper, "Pipe down, now!" She tried to conceal her frantic gaze, her eyes flying left and right. The patrons seemed acutely suspicious of her relationship to Christian. She decided it would be better to continue in her staged acknowledgment of his anonymity. "What can I get you?"

"You!" he impetuously blurted.

His carefree attitude scraped up the old anger that Rebecca tried to suppress. Looking at him coldly, she replied, "I'm afraid we no longer serve that here."

The glee in Christian's face rapidly melted away. "What in the hell is that supposed to mean?"

"You had your chance and chose Jesus over me."

"I had no choice! To go against the very word of Father Stemmons would have been labeled a heresy. Would you have me ruin all that I toiled for, possibly ending both our lives in the process?"

"Say what you will, Christian, but you and I both know choosing between me and God was easy for you."

He assumed a hurtful countenance. "Your words spear my heart."

"Just as your silence speared mine."

With a curt turn she was gone, abandoning him to the mercy of the crowd. He watched her walk away, her hips swaying an angry farewell. He had hurt her deeply in not responding to her note. Damn! How he wished he had never taught her to write.

Their heated exchange had eased the tension of the tavern customers. The bitterness Rebecca showed Christian seemed to make him more appealing and less alien to the village people. Here was a man beset by the worst plague of all, an affliction with no cure: love.

Taking his seat slowly, Christian sensed little of the anxiety that had harassed him only moments before. He now felt the tinge of red in his face, the warmth of embarrassment flowing through his skin. Looking about, he was pleased to find most of the patrons resuming their original conducts. Some talked amongst themselves, others simply ate and drank. All had turned their concerns from him – they had accepted him as being sound.

With the heavy burden of fear lifted from his shoulders, he let out a sigh of relief and rested his wearied back against the tavern wall. His initial trepidation, coupled with the unpleasant exchange with Rebecca, had made worse his headache. Pain shot through his skull, pulsating throughout his brainpan. He vigorously massaged his forehead, but could do nothing to lessen the misery.

In an attempt at easing his misery by not dwelling on it, he contented himself with the observation of others in the tavern. He let his eyes wander from table to table, occasionally lending his ears to the scrutiny.

The first subjects of his surveillance were a couple of cantankerous old men. They bickered incessantly over all matters, significant or trivial. Their exaggerated and inflated gestures were what initially attracted him to them.

One was larger than the other, although the little one carried more weight. Aside from variances in wrinkles and hair loss, age had made them brothers. They dressed similarly, and while they were not shabby, they were nowhere near elegant.

The tall one seemed to be of a more agreeable nature, speaking in long, drawn out, serene tones. The short one was filled with virulent animosity. He seethed at every disagreement, his irascible temper ruining his legitimacy.

Christian overheard the short old man first, his temper raising his voice slightly above the din of others. He seemed to have caught the men mid-discussion, although that which they were discoursing was soon made evident.

"His head was stuffed with cabbage and served to the blind beggar!" the short one insisted, his greasy jowls flapping in indignation.

"Nay, friend, you are mistaken," soothed the tall man. "The head was placed in a glass canister, filled with ale, and preserved for the princess' personal pleasures."

"It was eaten as a delicacy by a starving beggar!"

"It was not! The princess still has his head to this very hour. His home has become her dresser; she cannot sleep without his face being near. She loved him, you know."

"I know! I know!" cried the pugnacious gnome, attracting everyone's attention. "That is why in rage she fed body to dogs and head to beggar!"

"Nonsense!" the seemingly gentle giant countered with equal venom. "She fucks the head to this hour! It is rumored she smells of a constant brew."

"How does one fuck a head?"

Christian thought it best to terminate his eavesdropping of the old men with that final rhetorical question. He let his eyes dictate where his attention would be drawn next. They led him to a table situated discreetly in a corner. There he saw a young man practicing all his blunted charms on an attractive, but obviously dishonorable, older woman.

The young man was several years Christian's junior, although from his temperament and inflated speech he offered a more aged impression. His pitiful attempts at the braggadocio language of adults were only surpassed in shame by the elaborately sparse threads with which he covered himself. The beautifully mended tears, the eloquently patched holes; surely this man was no ordinary farmer, he was their prince. The mismatch of his dingy vest with that of his dung-stained pants added to his tragically laughable ensemble. His wide-brimmed planter's hat was postured like a crown over his curly blonde hair.

The object of his desire – the older, attractive tart – wore what could be expected. Her extremely deep-plunging neckline allowed for a more than generous view of her bountiful breasts. The faded red of her dress marked her as a scarlet woman, a peculiarity she bore well. To keep warm, she blanketed her pleasantly rounded shoulders with a tattered, gray shawl. It was evident that this shawl was truly black, but repeated washings and the unkind bleaching of the drying sun had drained it of its richness. Her wild, chestnut hair tangled with the shawl, which was deliberately parted so as to not hinder any glimpses of her copious chest.

With a knowing grin, Christian did his best to look unobtrusive. He slyly satiated his inquisitiveness through spying on the odd couple.

He caught the young man at the beginning of a statement swathed in smugness. "I'm hung like a horse, I am," boasted the ridiculous youth, his adolescent voice betraying his postured manhood.

"Really?" replied the tart with mocking sincerity, her laughter barely contained by her speech. She leaned closer to him, furthering the young man's poorly hidden nervousness by the liberal displaying of her cleavage.

"Yes!" ejaculated the youth uncontrollably, his gaze glued to her bosom. Realizing his sudden loss of reserve, he painfully tore himself from her chest and immediately resumed eye contact. Collecting his wits, he responded boastfully, "I used to give rides to little children." He motioned to his crotch, "They'd swing on me pike, you see."

The jesting tart sensuously curved her lips and looked at him most delectably, reacting with a long, drawn out, "Oooooh."

Encouraged by her erotic reaction, the young man found his spirit and displayed his resolution proudly on his face. "So, how 'bout it, eh?" he said with a slight, backward nod of the head.

"How 'bout what?" the tart coyly asked, pursing her lips in a tight smirk.

"How about you and me doin' the act?"

"What act?" she toyed with him. She knew well what he meant.

"You know, the double-backed beast," he replied, slightly agitated. He then raised his eyebrows to further drive home his point.

"What?" she giggled. She enjoyed watching the boy squirm.

The young man's face flushed red. This added anger to his nervous lust and forced him to be blunt. "Let's fuck!"

She leaned closer to him, once again offering her bosom up to his scrutiny.

It was then that Christian saw her hand on the boy's left thigh, slowly moving and massaging its way to his groin. He watched as the young man anxiously looked her in the eye, trying to fathom her sensual silence.

Her hand came to rest on his excited bulge and a smile creased her face, "As big as a horse?"

It was all he could do to nod vigorously – the restlessness of his mounting sexual frustration shriveling his throat.

The tart could contain herself no longer, "I didn't know horses came that small."

The young man's face instantly expressed a crestfallen bewilderment, which in turn exploded into full-blown fury. The red hue of his embarrassed and resentful countenance only mirrored the ire burning within. "Bitch!" he spat out at her, lips curled as if the utterance of the word was revulsion enough. He then collected his things and rose to leave, his frustrated libido making the situation all the worse.

The mean tart waited for the boy to near the door, then before he could escape with what little dignity he had left intact, she called out for all to hear, "Farewell, pony-boy!"

The youth turned wan as the entire tavern erupted in laughter. Christian could see from his vantage point near the tavern door that the boy's eyes began to overflow. He felt for the poor lad. Imagine, he thought, being shamed and dishonored in front of everyone in town.

His sympathy for the boy lingered on even after the embarrassed, overgrown waif exited, running off sobbing into the increasingly cold night. Bury your sorrows in Her darkness, Christian mentally advised the boy. Let Night take your grievances and dissipate with them at the blight of day.

Returning his gaze to the tart, he saw that she was looking at him with pretentious longing. The silly whore, he thought, I would not spend myself a thimble-full with you, woman. I would rather pleasure myself with a hollowed gourd – 'tis cheaper and shan't award my cock the hideous rash.

He couldn't help but smirk at his wicked thoughts, a reaction which he saw as being misinterpreted by the hussy. She returned his foolish smirk with a gestured invitation to join her. At this he turned his face to stone and averted his eyes.

She continued to stare at him for some time, her face displaying her angry hurt at his reserved rebuff, before returning to her drinking.

Christian presently engrossed himself in the assorted edibles those at adjacent tables were consuming. He saw two of the men who had so discourteously risen from their places and absconded to another table when he had entered seated nearby. One of the men was savoring a dish of strong Stilton cheese and a large cup of goat's milk. Dairy products must not be as unavailable here as they are in London, Christian noted, recalling the ludicrous prices London merchants charged for butter, cheese, and milk.

Watching the man eat his Stilton cheese was a thoroughly disgusting experience. Christian had never eaten the cheese, and he certainly didn't enjoy observing others swallow the nasty foodstuff. He cringed as he saw the man scoop out the maggots, which were indigenous to the cheese, with a small spoon and deposit the squirming fly larvae on a deep-dish tray at his side. The man continued feasting on his cheese, and when he was finished, to Christian's horror, he shoveled the wiggling maggots into his mouth!

My God, Christian shuddered, he eats them with great relish!

The man downed the little, opaque-white worms with distinct pleasure. It was as if he had saved the best for last, that he had only purchased the cheese in order to get at the tiny beasties within. Over and over again the man filled his spoon with a heaping helping of writhing life. Occasionally one or two maggots would fall off the spoon and blindly attempt crawling to safety only to be picked up between the greasy fingers of the man and thrown nonchalantly down his gullet. Once, while overtaken by a burst of laughter, the man shot a larva from his stuffed mouth. Christian watched the narrow line of white hurriedly wriggle away as if it knew it had been in the maw of death. The man quickly reached for it, but all his efforts in securing the rampant maggot were futile; the natural oils of the maggot's skin, as well as the man's own slippery saliva and greasy hands, proved to be his hindrance in recapturing the fleeing morsel. In gluttonous anger, he brought his fist down on the meandering maggot, squashing it flat into the wood grain of the table. If it could not join its brothers in serving his barnyard appetite, then it would not live to metamorphose into a pestering fly.

May that which you eat feast upon your innards! Christian declared to himself with much loathing. Any who made merry with such a coarse meal deserved intestinal consumption! How is it that there are those who would choose to gorge themselves on the lowliest form of the most filthy of all God's creatures, when there are more than adequate alternatives? How in the hell does one acquire a liking of such a dish?

The man's friend informed him of Christian's stares, and he turned to Christian with a broad smile. Christian could not look away, for he was trapped by the man's awareness, nor could he speak for if he opened his mouth he feared he would vomit. "You want to know why I indulge in such repast," the gross man stated very pleasantly, "don't you?"

Christian responded with a slight nodding of the head.

"Because I figure I may as well eat as many of them before they eat me!"

When the man saw the blank look on Christian, he could not help but explode into a fit of laughter. His companion, the one who had notified him of Christian's observation, gleefully guffawed as he thrust a ragged piece of neat's tongue into his mouth. The portion of vinegar-soaked cow's tongue frolicked against his palate for all to see, much to Christian's obvious disgust. Does not anyone here, save for myself, abide by accepted dining mannerisms? he wondered in dismay. I know not whether I entered the horses' stable or the pigs' sty, only that I am certainly not in the company of civilized human kind!

Diverting from further spectacles of culinary atrociousness, he spied Rebecca casting him a sidelong glance. He flashed a warm smile that only seemed to make her colder. With a disapproving shaking of her head, and a dour expression, she returned to tending tables.

Christian could do nothing but watch her. He mentally commended her physical attributes; the natural exaggeration of her breasts, the fullness of her lips, the smoothness of her level abdomen, the healthy sheen of her golden hair, and the tender curve of her buttocks. He pictured in his mind his favorite part of her thoroughly luscious body, that which was less obvious than the previously mentioned qualities but in no way less pleasing.

In fact, he had so loved her vagina that although it brought her immense pleasure she had often castigated him for spending too much of his time down there. He leaned back against the hard, wood wall, smiling contentedly as he revived thoughts, never quite dormant, of her taste. He fondly remembered a night long ago when the two of them doused one another in wine. How sweet Rebecca was when she poured the remainder of the wine into herself. Christian nearly burst out in laughter when he recalled what he had said to her after lingering long between her legs, 'I love your drunken cunny.' Cunny, that was what he had called it. He was so enamored of it that he had given it its own name, its own identity.

"Now it's just another cunt," he grumbled discontentedly to himself. Even worse, it could be someone else's cunt. No, he rationalized, the way in which she behaved, her apparent restraint of emotions, seemed to indicate that she was still his goose for the plucking. He looked at her through heavy lids; he was tired, but not exhausted. Tonight, he schemed, I shall reacquaint myself with an old friend.

Satisfied in his resolve, he arched his aching back and stretched in an effort to restore life to his weary bones. His feet were unpleasantly numb, probably due to the constriction placed on them by his masochistic footwear. His headache had not blossomed into the migraine he had feared, although it was by no means a slight annoyance; occasionally sending sudden rushes of pain through his brain. At least my aches keep me from sleep, he consoled himself. But did he really wish to avoid his nocturnal rendezvous? Wasn't there a longing deep within him to succumb to sleep, and to enter once more the arms of his dark beloved?

He shook free of those distressing thoughts, compelling himself to once again spend his idle time in the watching of others and not in the scrutinizing of latent feelings.

Bringing his gaze to bear on the bar in the hopes of yet another glimpse of his fiery barmaid, Christian noticed through the corner of his eye and by the shiver up his spine that he himself was being watched. Without any sudden movements, he slowly closed his eyes and, rolling them underneath the cover of lid, opened them in the watcher's general direction. He thought to take the watcher by surprise, but was in turn unpleasantly surprised himself by the identity of his surveyor.

It was the cruel man, his one, bloodshot eye boring into Christian's ease. This was the man who had greeted him with tidings of death, and by the looks of him still maintained that animosity. Christian shivered, briefly imagining what might have happened to him had Rebecca not come to his aid. It was because of this visualizing that he felt his heart overrun with warmth and passion for his distaff savior. And while staring down that most ugly eye set in a most unsightly facade, his love for her was replenished.

The cruel man removed from his upper coat pocket a young rat and, placing the little ball of fur on the tabletop in front of him, smiled wickedly at Christian. He then proceeded, without taking his eye from Christian, to lift the rat by its tail and place it precariously near the lit candle on his table. The poor rodent let out a piteous screech as the tip of its tail held between the thumb and forefinger of the man entered the cone of the candle flame.

Christian flinched, much to the cruel man's evident delight, and turned his face from the unnecessary barbarity. It was then he noticed that all in the tavern were aware of the rat's plight. Silence, like that which hailed his entrance to the tavern, had fallen once again. He looked from face to passive face, seeking an ally but finding only morbid interest. The old men, the tart, the maggot-eater, and others; none seemed willing to put an end to the abuse.

The pitiful creature by now had most of its tail swallowed by the flame, and the aroma of cooking meat permeated the tavern. Its squeals of fear and pain took on a human tone to Christian, sounding very child-like and furthering his determination to do something. Still, to propel him to act, he needed to find one compassionate face amongst the many dispassionate.

He found the moral support he sought in the face of the woman he lusted after. Rebecca stood tightly twisting a washrag and biting her lower lip. Ah, he noted, how she bites her lip when distressed! It would be wise of me to save this petty rat, he connived, for although I hold no love of rats – if truth be told, I detest them – it would put me in good graces with my lady, as well as comfort my conscience and console my Christian decency.

Rebecca saw Christian look at her, but he had returned his attentions to the man with the rat before she could lock eyes with him. Judging by his face, an expression she had seen before, she knew him to be contemplating some form of action. No, Christian, she pleaded to herself, don't be brash, don't play the hero. I know this one by his deeds and not his name; he is as bad as you'll find, not thinking twice about killing you. I've waited too long to have you die on me now.

She let the dirty little rag fall to her feet, hoping against hope that the sudden movement would attract Christian's notice. It didn't. She was confused, for unlike her Samaritan waiting which had spared Christian possible injury, any move on her part now might be perceived differently, possibly leading to violence. She felt helpless and frightened, and it was through these two emotions that she came to fully realize the love she bore for Christian, which up until now she had either denied or dismissed. She made herself an oath, proclaiming, get through this, Chris, and I swear above all that tonight you'll lie within me.

The cruel man derived great pleasure in watching the assorted reactions he elicited through his torturing of the rat. Most knew him, and fearing him, did nothing. Undressing Rebecca with his eye, the high-pitched squeals of the rat began to annoy even him. He removed what was left of the small beast's tail from the flame and placed the wounded creature gently on the table. It was as if by this simple act the entire tavern had forgiven him, all returning to previous interests. All except one.

He saw the stranger to town return his glacial stare. The cruel man separated his cracked lips to disclose his wretched teeth. He slightly tilted his head in silent salutation to Christian before asking, "What brings you here, and where are you headed?"

Christian looked on the man with unmistakable repulsion. Deciding it best not to answer the question posed him, nor sate the villain's curiosity, he chose instead to put forth a question of his own. Pointing to the traumatized rat still detained within the clutches of the cruel man, he asked, "Must you torture small creatures?"

"Would you prefer I torture you?"

"You have not the will, nor am I a small animal."

At these words, the cruel man's face flushed and he, incensed at Christian's effrontery, lashed out in anger. "I shall cut out your heart and eat it with your balls!"

"A blackheart, coward, shit-stain and a fool, at that," Christian droned mockingly, "Take your place, one eye. Crawl under the dung heap from whence you came."

"I'll kill you where you stand!" the cruel man spat, crushing the poor rat in his hands as he loudly rose from his seat.

Christian looked to see if Rebecca was watching all of this. He lost some of his relaxed demeanor to the sinking feeling in his stomach when he realized that she was not his only spectator, but rather the whole tavern was paying him close attention. Christian, he admonished himself, what has your foolish pride gotten you into now? Instead of pleasing Rebecca with your manliness, you may only anger her with your death.

He returned his eyes to the cruel man standing before him. He saw the crushed rat viciously cradled in the man's right hand. Very well, he decided, I'd have rather not saved the little spawn of Hell. Instantly, as if in justification of his ambivalence, his mind was awash with the scenes of horror he had witnessed in London due to the rodents. You've served your purpose, little rat, now join your brothers in Hades. But fear not, if all goes awry either your tormenter or I shall be there to keep you company.

Seeing how Christian was gazing at the lump of rat in his hand, the cruel man decided he still had a use for the pest, and threw it at him, saying, "You love it so much, take it! I have little need of it now."

Although he tried desperately to avoid the rat's body, Christian was struck by it in the chest. He stood quickly, kicking his chair out from under himself, and looked down at the floor where the rat had landed after striking him. He felt chills race from his spine to the very pits of his stomach: the thing was still alive! Though it only twitched ever so slightly, probably nothing more than nerve spasms, the affect it had on him was startling. He was repulsed by the image of the battered rat; paws uncontrollably shaking and nostrils wildly flaring. He was forced to bring his heel mercifully down on the quaking, little body. Although he had prayed for the death of the entire species of rat in the past, he never liked to kill when he didn't have to. He resented the way in which the man had him finish his dirty work and by how he so dishonored him in front of Rebecca. He would not tolerate any further abuse.

The silence was deafening, a tormenting quietude of ungodly proportions pushing both men beyond reason. It was as if they were actors being forced to perform for the tavern's pleasure. Not an eye stirred from the spectacle, each good Bantingham resident egging the two angry men on over the brink of common sense and decency. There they sat, like cattle chewing their cud, like the foolish farmers they were. Not a single one considered stopping the inevitable violent confrontation, but rather en masse they prayed for its hasty arrival.

Rebecca felt her knees grow weak and used the chair to which she clung as more of a means of support than an object with which she vented her anxiety. She could feel the apprehensively violent nature of the air within the tavern. She looked from Christian to the cruel man and felt queasy. Her protective instincts rising, she sought some instrument nearby that might assist her should she have to come to Christian's rescue; the glint of a steak knife lying carelessly on a vacant table in front of her begged for her attention. She looked on the knife with desperate eyes, holding her breath and praying that she would not be forced into using it.

Prodded on by the abundance of expectant stares, as well as the forceful silence, Christian demanded of the cruel man, "Come now! Or be damned in your cowardice."

With a relieved grin, the cruel man calmly limped toward him. Keeping his eyes locked with Christian's, he let his left hand glide across the tabletops between him and his foe. When his hand had found the familiar shape of a knife handle, it greedily engulfed it.

At seeing the cruel man take up a knife against her former lover, Rebecca startled all with a poorly stifled scream. In that brief instant she had made visual contact with Christian. From across the room his eyes told her she had nothing to fear, but knowing him better than he knew himself she took a step toward the table with the knife.

Christian's face took on a look of apparent aversion. "A knife?"

"I jest not."

"But surely one such as you can do me in without resorting to such brutish vulgarity."

"I'm going to make good my promise, and when I'm done I'll pleasure myself with your little barmaid over there." The cruel man sloppily licked his lips. "I'm going to fuck her on your bloody corpse!"

Although this gibe concerning Rebecca angered Christian, he thought it best to mask his furor from the cruel man, as it was the man's intent to confuse him by making him choleric. Assuming a placid countenance, Christian coolly declared, "Very well, do as you will. You'll have no fear from me, one-eye."

The cruel man took great offense to Christian's trivial quip regarding his disability. The leer was wiped from his lips as he raised the knife high, ready to strike, and proclaimed, "Bravery is a partner in foolishness, 'tis such a waste."

"I should think not," came the gruff sound of Cotton's voice.

The tavern turned in response to the Scottish brogue. Christian looked past the cruel man's shoulder, for he too had turned to face the mysterious Scotsman, and saw his tall guardian leaning against the entrance to the back hallway. He stood slightly behind Rebecca, thick arms folded menacingly across his chest, sporting a look that would put the devil back into Hell.

Rebecca, situated so near the huge stranger, backed quietly away from him. Although she feared him, for he was very imposing, she could not help but feel some affection for him, for he did seem to be coming to Christian's aid, whoever he was.

He must have finished tending the horses and entered through some back door, Christian excitedly thought. Now old one-eye will be put in his proper place, for if he persists against Cotton, he'll shortly know what it was the rat felt!

The cruel man looked on Cotton with restraint. The verbal abuses which had come so easily with Christian had now fallen by the waysides of his mind. Fear, and fear alone, kept him motionless, unable to even blink his single, sorry eye. No matter how hard he tried to scrounge up some courage, he could find little. Just looking at the Scot put the fear of death into his heart. He saw Cotton as he was, a man born of battle: dagger at his hip, infantryman's buff coat upon his chest, and the myriad lines scaring his face and neck. The man was in fact cruel, but not stupid. He knew he could not win, and that frightened him. The knife, which had felt so right in his hand just moments before, now felt heavy and unfamiliar.

Cotton cocked his head back and looked down at the petrified little man who had been so rude as to threaten the life of his ward. Where did this sorry piece of shit get his balls? he marveled. From stabbing defenseless people in the back? He then set his eyes into the man, and assuming an air of strength which he had acquired through numerous similar dealings in the military, spoke in heavy, clear, poison-filled words. "I offer ye a choice: leave or die. For if that boy is harmed in the slightest, ye are tampering with me eternal soul. And for that, cyclops, I shall endeavor to send ye to the grave."

At the completion of his speech, all eyes shifted from Cotton to the cruel man. He himself looked from Cotton to Christian, and deciding it wasn't worth the forfeiture of his life, screamed in frustration, "To Hell with you all!" Grabbing his walking stick, he hobbled out of the tavern slamming the door behind him.

It was as if his departure signaled a return in festivities to the tavern, that at his leaving he took with him the tension and dread so prevalent within the edifice's woodwork.

The people of Bantingham seem much more at ease now without the wolf amongst their flock, Christian noted. He then saw Cotton, his savior in the flesh, approaching in large, boisterous strides.

"Didn't think ye were going to need me, did ye?"

Christian smiled sheepishly, and taking Cotton's broad hand in his, replied, "I shall never doubt your use again, old friend. I humbly thank you."

"Think not of it, for 'tis already done. That filth will never bother ye, nor most likely anyone in this town. His days here are being counted by one with far less patience than you or I, for if he ever angers one who has been witness to his cowardice, he'll be staring the king of terrors – Death himself – in the face with that one bloody eye."

Outside, with the chill of the night vanquishing his angry humiliation, the cruel man staggered from the light of the tavern to the dark of the shadowed stable. He sat down near a skittish horse – its body heat would be of some help to him. He didn't mind the smell, the puddles of urine, or the piles of feces. As long as he was sheltered from the wind, he was pleased. In fact, he rather liked sleeping in stables, preferring a horse's company to that of a man's.

Rubbing his hands to keep them warm, the cruel man felt what his preoccupied indignation and the outside coolness had numbed; a small puncture wound on his right palm. "Damned rat," he grumbled.

Little did he realize that in biting him the rat had gotten its final revenge, for soon he would feel uncomfortably warm, be bathed in his own clammy sweat, and acquire an unquenchable thirst. After a relatively short while, the familiar pustules would take residence on his skin, thus warning everyone he was to be avoided, being claimed by the Plague.

Basking in the warmth of the tavern, as well as in his safety, Christian stretched his extremely weary body. He arched his back and contorted his shape, desperately trying to relax his rigid muscles. The uncomfortable coach ride had put his limbs to sleep and the momentary expectation of violence had shocked his sinews into discomforting contractions. Coupled with his other ailments, one would think him to be rather melancholy, but on the contrary he was quite lighthearted. Being so close to injury, possibly even death, had made him take delight in the simplest of pleasures: living. This joy was only further amplified by his partaking of excessive quantities of ale, which naturally made him feel less worrisome, as well as absolving him of most of his complaints.

His bodyguard had joined him at his table, and the two of them delighted in telling tales while downing drinks. Due to their rejoicing, for they were both pleased that neither of them had come to any harm and that they were no longer traveling the harsh forest trail, the yarns they spun were of a jovial nature.

After contenting themselves for some time in this manner, their empty bellies loudly ordained that they order some supper. Cotton signaled Rebecca to come near, who, with a look of annoyance, complied.

"How may I serve you, sir?" asked Rebecca, avoiding Christian's imploring eyes by addressing only Cotton.

"Ye can start by putting a twinkle in those pretty blue eyes of yours and a smile on those lovely pink lips," Cotton cheerfully advised her. "Come now, ye'll not have me order unless ye show your pearly whites."

Rebecca could not disappoint this most charming gentleman, and with a nervous laugh stretched the corners of her mouth to his fancy.

"There, now that wasn't so difficult, was it?"

"No," she intoned foolishly.

"Good, ye should do it more often, it makes ye look much prettier."

Slightly embarrassed, Rebecca looked to her feet as she felt her cheeks flush. Then, meekly replying through tight lips in an effort to not lose her precious smile, she said, "Is that all that you require of me?"

"What I would require of ye would blacken me good name were I to speak it," countered a mischievous Cotton.

"I am truly sorry, sir, but as I informed this man next to whom you sit, that is no longer on our menu."

Cotton gleefully stamped his feet as he roared in laughter, composing himself long enough to sputter, "Very good, me dear, very good! If we can't have ye we'll have the mutton!"

Rebecca's smile dropped to a cold line when she glanced at Christian before heading for the kitchen. Great, he thought as his eyes hungrily followed her, Cotton will probably have her before I.

"There's one for ye!" his bodyguard bellowed, grabbing him by the shoulder. "There's one ripe for the picking!"

Christian stared icily into his jolly compatriot's moderately drunken face. Blinded by the intoxicating effects of the liquor, he felt as though he had witnessed a particularly sexual exchange and that Cotton had somehow wronged him. How quickly, when concerning carnal lust, did friend become foe and a savior a devil. This is precisely how Christian felt, unjustly sensing betrayal by the one who had so recently been his idol. You think she'll have you, old man? he angrily declared privately, his thinking clouded by his drinking. You think she'll take your saggy prick over mine?

Sensing Christian's displeasure, Cotton drew back, deciding to ask his friend what it was that ailed him. "How is it that I have injured ye, friend? What is it I have done that is so grievous?"

The concern in Cotton's voice, as well as the troubled look he wore on his face, made Christian realize the idiocy of his baseless suspicions. He shed his foolishness with a wry grin, declaring, "The evils of alcohol have momentarily tampered with my reasoning. Believe me, friend, you have done me no wrong. On the contrary – you have saved me from harm."

"Then why do ye cast me such baleful looks?"

For shame, Christian could not answer, but only eye the busily preoccupied Rebecca darting in and out of the kitchen, receiving and delivering orders.

"Ah," said Cotton pleasantly, "ye fancy our waitress. She's a fine lass, Christian. I concur with your wants."

Turning, but maintaining his watch of Rebecca, Christian replied, "'Tis truth she is most pleasing to look at, but a pity that such an ornately wrapped package contains so little."

"Ye know of her?"

"Many a London night I've made my bed her bed, snuggling my heavy head against those two beauteous pillows born unto her."

"Christian, know well that I never intended to offend. Had I known of your acquaintance with the pretty girl, I never would have been so bold to have been so lewd. 'Tis the brew; watch that I don't drink too much, for I myself know not when to stop. I drink not to quench a thirst, for the thirst by which I drink is unquenchable." Taking his mug in his hands and looking at it with disgust, he added, "The contents of this wretched cup are why I am beholden unto ye. Forgive me, Christian, for I have had too much."

Christian took Cotton's calloused and worn hands in his own, and looking him in the eye, said, "Seek not forgiveness, for I choose not to give that which is unnecessary. 'Twas I who acted rashly, and 'tis I who humbly beg you for your pardon."

The graciousness of Christian's entreaty nearly moved the aged mercenary to tears, and he, overcome by emotion, solemnly pledged his allegiance to his ward, swearing, "Above all that is holy, I commit myself unto your service most wholeheartedly."

It was now Christian who felt the humanity of their brotherhood, and through a dry throat managed to utter the only thing his goodwill would allow. "Call me Chris, for that is what all whom I consider friends know me by."

The lateness of the hour had lent itself to the rapidly approaching dawn in many of the villager's heads, and because of this the tavern grew quite bare. Christian and Cotton wearily rested their heads in their hands as they watched each person leave. Neither knew why the other persisted in staying awake when the comfort of their room awaited them so close at hand. Christian maintained his nightly vigil out of fear and Cotton stayed simply because he did not wish to leave without him.

The two old men rose cautiously from their chairs, dropped their tips in a bowl of vinegar, and donning their hats headed for the door. It was clear to Christian that their arguments had been left unresolved by the manner in which they dealt with one another. The tall old man smiled and completely ignored his counterpart, while the little old man looked at no one but the floor, a scowl affixed to his brow.

"Good night, all," announced the tall one as he opened the heavy tavern door and revealed the gusty dark.

"Night, night," grumpily chimed the little one, annoyed at his necessitated farewell.

The few left in the tavern failed to respond as the old men took their leave. As the door shut behind them, effectively silencing the wailing wind, Cotton looked to Christian and remarked, "'Tis a banshee of a wind out there."

Christian merely recognized this remark with a slow nodding of his head. He was tired, but he would be damned if he was going to fall asleep. Besides, he thought, he still had to wait to talk with Rebecca, and he would wait until the first rays of sunlight for that.

Aside from the tavern staff, only the playful tart remained with Christian and Cotton. She finished the last of her drink and cast a forlorn look at Cotton. She saw Cotton acknowledge her stare with an agreeable grin and an inviting raising of his cup, prompting her to open her shawl, expose her fine cleavage, and signal the large Scotsman to join her.

When he had first noticed the alluring looks being hurled at him by a most attractive woman, whom he had taken a marked interest in previously during the night, Cotton was seized by a nervous delight. Once conquering his giddiness, he deemed it proper to raise his cup in salutation to the fair woman. This act seemed to please the lady, and she in turn decided to please him. Her unspoken invitation sent frivolous shivers racing through his bloodstream. His boiling blood rushed to his loins and his mind was made up not with his head, but with his invigorated heart.

"Have ye any pressing or immediate need of me, friend?" he hastily asked of Christian.

Failing to raise his eyes, nor to even wonder why, Christian granted Cotton his leave with a tiresome sweep of the hand.

Cotton sprang from his seat, leaving his fatigue and stress with Christian, and briskly strode the distance between him and his female admirer. Arriving at her table, he cordially greeted her by taking her hand in his and pressing his lips gently against it. Then, in the spirit of a true gentleman, he kindly stood and awaited an invitation to be seated and join her company. He did not have to stand long.

The vivacity with which Cotton had risen had impelled Christian's curiosity. What had put life into those old bones? he marveled, and raising his face saw what he should already have guessed. With a worn smile, he observed Cotton's expertise with the tart, his overwhelming charm and praiseworthy appeals to her virtue. Evidently, Christian lightly mused, liquor is not Cotton's only Achilles' heel.

Wiping down tables with her damp rag and putting displaced chairs proper, Rebecca engrossed herself in work in a futile attempt at driving Christian from her mind. If his proximity made it difficult, then his unrelenting looks of despair made it impossible. Every time she lifted her face he was there, watching her. The unease she experienced made even the simplest of tasks difficult. Gathering trays, stacking plates, collecting silverware, and picking up cups all became chores to which she was strangely unaccustomed. This alienation of daily work was easy even for a fatuous girl like herself to explain: she still loved Christian deeply, and her body conspired with her mind to let her know it.

The man she was desirous of sat drowsily staring at her. Never before had Christian felt so tired, and it was either out of fear or yearning that he kept his eyelids open. The neglect he suffered at the hands of Rebecca was beginning to irritate him. How much longer would he have to wait, he wondered, before she discarded this foolish policy of indifference?

Rebecca glimpsed up from her troubles and caught Christian glaring at her. Perhaps she was being too harsh making him wait, she fretted. But then remembrance brought indignation, and she recollected all the nights spent without him, though not always alone, still longing for his touch. Why should I drop everything to please you when you would not do the same for me? she fumed.

Stepping into Christian's line of vision and obstructing his view of Rebecca was Cotton, bottle in hand and smile plastered stupidly on his face. "Everything is taken care of for tonight. We have a room at the inn ..." he glanced over at Rebecca, "... in case ye need it."

Christian returned his dopey smile and felt guilty afterward.

"Well, that being that, have ye further need of me?"

Christian answered slowly, as though other thoughts preoccupied his mind, "No ... no." He lowered his gaze and stared intently at the wood floor.

Cotton nodded and began to turn away.

"What time shall we leave?" Christian asked without lifting his eyes from the floor.

"Early. 'Twill be a long trip."

"I see."

Seeing Christian so utterly dejected, Cotton thought it best to make light of the matter. "Fear not," he said, smirking, "I shan't forget ye."

This seemed to rouse Christian from his stupor. "Yes," he nodded, looking Cotton in the face, "you may leave, Smith-Patton, but caution."

Cotton studied him for some time before whispering sullenly, "Aye."

The inexplicable strain which Christian had imposed on their conversation made Cotton uneasy. Was the longing of his heart that which rendered him so morose? he asked himself while thoroughly inspecting his detached friend.

The sudden, unexpected sensation of the tart's arm sliding around his waist startled Cotton. Laughing it off with a nervous bellow, he placed his big hand on the small of her back and methodically rubbed. "Ye nearly frightened the spirits out of me!" he whispered into her ear, making her giggle.

The tart looked down on Christian, and seeing him beside himself, felt pity. "Maybe your friend wants to join us," she mentioned to her hoary paramour, but loud enough for Christian to hear.

A tinge of jealousy swept across Cotton's heart. Looking into the tart's face, he replied, "Are ye insinuating that I'm not man enough for ye?"

"Not at all, lovey," she replied innocently, as if taken aback at the prospects of a *ménage a trois*. "It's just that he seems so lonely."

"Don't ye worry none about him. He'll do all right by himself. Ye need to concern yourself with me, or I'll bugger ye fierce."

"You wouldn't!" the tart said excitedly.

Cotton only winked and exposed a crocodile smile. Then turning to Christian, who sat ignorant of their entire exchange, requested, "Pray for me tonight, Chris."

Letting out an exasperated laugh, his ward responded, "That I shall, that I shall."

As the tart led Cotton to the door, he could not take his eyes off his disturbed partner. Even as the door was flung open and the cold nipped him sensible, he looked on his young friend with concern and dismay. Pulling him out into the night and into her arms, the tart effectively drove Christian from his aroused thoughts.

At the slamming of the tavern door, Christian felt the ire burning within him explode. It was as if the sound of the closing door fed more coal into the simmering rage that was his stomach. *How you preach, noble soldier, when there is no whore or bottle to be had! How you offer your fealty when your spirits, as your cock, are low. Good night, good knight!*

The viciousness of his assessment of Cotton shocked him into examining what it was that caused him such smoldering anger. What was it that so agitated him? It did not take him long to realize that it was the import of his mission, the secrecy such a mission entailed, and the gravity of his possible failure that so distressed him. Sitting alone with nothing to do but ponder this, he became quite glum, and so it was that he began to quaff his ale in the hopes of drowning his sorrows. The alcohol, however, served not to appease his anxieties but to amplify them. In his partaking of ale, Christian grew as bitter as that which he imbibed.

This unpleasant condition was only made worse by the whole of the situation. He was so close to Rebecca, and yet so far. And while she remained just out of reach, tantalizingly in sight, she seemed miles from him. He did not feel well enough to play silly games, nor did he have the time or patience. Why did she have to be so pigheaded? he fretted. Why was she always stubborn to the point of exacerbated absurdity? She's erected a fraudulent defense that I surely doubt can withstand one of my offensives. And if it be so, then to hell with her! For I have allowed this siege of lust to last far too long. Composed of forlorn glances and amorous sighs, entreaties to her passion of the most eloquent kind, I have found no success. So when an opportune moment presents itself, I shall arise and seize it wholeheartedly with both hands – as I shall her bosom! And thus proclaiming this to himself, and making up his mind that it was far better to act than to react, he bided his time, waiting for his chance.

He did not have to wait long, for in the process of clearing off tables, Rebecca, clumsy as she was due to his immediate presence, managed to accidentally tip over a pitcher half full of ale. The ale washed across the tabletop and over its edge. Before a single drop had tainted the floor with its wetness, Christian had risen and was marching towards her as if the spilling was some great and dire catastrophe.

Annoyed with herself and with Christian, Rebecca sopped up the ale spread across the tabletop with her rag and then positioned herself on her hands and knees in order to take care of the remaining liquor on the floor. No sooner had she taken her place on her knees then she realized she had taken her place at his feet. Looking up from his shoes, she gave him a spiteful glance and resumed her petty slighting.

He gazed down at her as she scrubbed the floor and momentarily entertained the notion that she was groveling at his feet. Dispensing with his ill-humor, he knelt at her side and, being careful not to stain his fine clothing, reached out and tenderly touched her face.

Rebecca irritatingly recoiled from Christian's fingers. Refusing to speak to her tormentor, she silently twisted and turned her head in avoidance of his weaving, resolute hand. After a minute of this mute sparring, she was compelled to peevishly exhale, "Leave me be," and then tiredly, with a hint of regret and eyes downcast, she pled, "Let me alone, Christian."

Undaunted by her pathetic request, which to him was a plea made amidst a crumbling bastion, he turned the crux of the labored conversation from himself to that of the plain, gold locket overhanging her shirt. "I see you still wear my gift," he said with a soft warmth as he fingered the cheap jewelry.

Rebecca remained tight-lipped.

"Do not shun me, Rebecca," he pleaded, "for 'tis only with love that I speak to you."

"Love?" she retorted with exaggerated preposterousness, her eyes burning into his. "Love for who? Me, or your God?"

"Our God, Rebecca," he corrected her. "Do not lose faith because of me, for if it be so I shan't rest ever."

"Can you ever speak without preaching? For surely you have preached without speaking! If there be a Heaven, you'll burn in Hell for the way you've treated me!"

"Damn it, woman!" he exploded in whisper, "When will you see that I love you equal to God, and that I had no choice long ago?"

"You made your choice—"

"No! I did not. All that I can be accused of, the only crime I can be guilty of, is that of looking ahead to the future; of safeguarding our lives as well as our love."

"... you lie."

Ignoring her remark, which he took in tone to be that of a gradual acceptance, he persisted. "I love you more than life itself – for life is only a gift, and a brief one at that." Touching his breast, he masterfully appealed to her pity, "My heart bleeds for you, it yearns for you." Then, taking her clammy, damp hands in his, he declared, "A man cannot love a woman more than God for the simple sake that to do so would be blasphemous. And not wishing to blaspheme, yet profess my love for thee, let it be known that I put you equal to God in my heart."

Seeing how Rebecca appeared disaffected, and how his equation to God, although very significant to him, moved her little, he decided that the best course of action would be one that petitioned her own selfish, womanly wants. Through the supplication of these wants, he hoped to achieve the added heat and comfort of her company in bed.

Looking deep into her eyes, he spoke frankly and told her what she wanted to hear. "Only the knowledgeable people live well, 'Becca," he whispered as if embarrassed, referring to her by her abbreviated appellation as a means of addressing her affectionate memories. "Only the rich or the clergy acquire knowledge. I was not born into wealth, mine was not a noble birth." He paused and looked down ashamedly, "I am not rich, and the Church is the only option for one such as I to gain true knowledge. With knowledge I hope to amass wealth, and then and only then will I be able to live content … to be happy … with you … forever."

When finished, he peered up at her with a look that might have convinced God to spare His only Son. He was proud of himself; he knew it would only be a matter of time now. He could always tap her emotions, and it was only with slight annoyance that he noted it had taken him so long to confront her. Perhaps he did love her, he mused, but he would have time to consider that in detail later. As for now, all he wanted to do was sample the girl kneeling before him.

Rebecca was astonished. All the pent-up anger and disfavor she held against him dissipated like dew. She looked upon him with renewed love and an awe that could not keep her from dropping her jaw and spilling her eyes. "Oh, Chris," she gasped, fighting against the tide of emotions overtaking her, "why have you never told me this?"

Rubbing the backs of her hands he thought quick, "Because I never wanted you to think I was misusing my religious convictions, that I was pimping my inclinations to mother Church." Dramatically shifting his now teary eyes, he resumed, "I wanted you only to respect me … but now I care not!" He removed his hands from hers and held them lovingly against her face while reverting to gazing into her watery eyes. "I will do anything for you," he declared in a voice full of righteousness. "Anything." Squeezing her cheeks in a gentle physical display attesting to the veracity of his words, he toiled on. "I want you, I desire you 'til the flesh rots off my bones and worms have my innards. There be not a bone under this flesh that does not hunger for your love, your affection, your touch … for you."

The graphic depictions employed by Christian were the final volley he needed to overtake Rebecca. In uncontrollable tears, the simple girl cried, "I love you. I've never stopped loving you!"

Christian took her into his arms and held her tight. He felt her body convulse to the rhythmic onslaught of her insurgent tears, and joined her in weeping. He wept not out of joy that he would have her, but rather out of pity for himself and for her. He really cared for Rebecca, and would probably one day marry her. This in itself brought tears to his eyes for to do so would mean having to settle for an ignorant farm girl, to bid farewell to his ambitions and true desires. But whereas the grim thought of forgoing his dreams brought tears to his eyes, the shame of belittling Rebecca carried them cascading down his cheeks. Although he tried to deny it, there was something about Rebecca that he loved. And although her stupidity tarnished that love, it did not extinguish it, but rather, as love is wont to do, added to its charm.

Feeling this love in his heart descend into his groin, he sought her lips and there planted a kiss. Then, wiping the tears from her eyes, he sowed a whole garden of kisses upon her lips, cheeks, eyes, forehead, and nose. This being done, he rose with her and helped hasten her tidying. When all was as it should be, the two lovers, reunited in spirit as well as in each other's arms, darted hand in hand down the tavern's back hall and up the narrow stairs. There, Rebecca led Christian to her quarters.

Rebecca's room was partial payment, the other being food, for her services at the tavern. Opening her door and escorting Christian in, she proudly exhibited her quaint little domicile. It was very small, and hardly furnished, with only one window. She walked over to it and opened one side. The cool night breeze that entered the little room didn't lessen their warmth as much as it heightened their anxious arousal. Like a ghost, the opaque-white curtains fluttered and flitted through the connivances of the incoming wind, throwing strange distortions of moonlight against the dark bedroom walls.

With the wind mildly tossing her flaxen mane, Rebecca turned to Christian and beckoned him with a look that needed no wordy clarification. Her soft eyes and parted lips, the way she toyed with her rippling hair, it was as if her every pore sensuously sought to signal her intentions. The awkwardness of a spoken invitation would only serve to harm the eroticism of the encounter.

The moon being the room's only light source, an eerie yet beauteous blueness illuminated all in the path of the partly opened window. Rebecca glowed in it, everything about her was a varying shade of blue: her dress, her blouse, her skin, her hair, her eyes. The bed immediately behind her also appeared incandescent, its proportions perfectly and neatly within the streak of blue. Indeed, all that was visible in the room was lapped in light; Rebecca, the bed, and the wall against which the headboard of the bed rested. The polarity between the extremely bright moonlight and the shadowed room made only that which was illumined visible, the radiance of the moon causing the eyes to darken what was already dark.

Christian slowly emerged from the darkness and immersed himself in light. Taking Rebecca into his arms, he felt chords of familiarity being struck within him – a familiarity not necessarily fostered through his embracing of Rebecca, but rather through the aspect of the room. He had seen a similar darkness broken by a beam of moonlight, but where? In his dreams? His nightmares? Wherever it was he cared not, for all that concerned him now was that which he held tightly in his arms.

The moonlit lovers carefully tore into each other's clothing, removing garment after garment rapidly but gingerly. Both realized the shortness of time they had to reassert their love, that with the advent of the first rays of sunlight

their lovemaking must be complete. Already the harsh moonshine had begun
to pale and certain birds were singing.

Discarding the last vestiges of cloth from their bodies, they stood naked;
toe to toe, eye to eye, hand in hand. They let their eyes swallow the imperfect
nudity of their forms, ingesting every inch of exposed flesh. Mentally they
admired one another's figure; she the ripple of Christian's muscle, particularly
the elongated one between his legs, and he the heaving of her erect breasts.
When this period of intimate familiarization was through, Rebecca laid back
on her cool, crisp bed and pulled Christian down upon her.

The moment their bodies made contact, the instant their flesh touched,
they hungrily began to devour one another. Their mouths became one, their
tongues twisted in knots. Nowhere during their lovemaking was there an area
on their bodies left untouched. They massaged and caressed, hugging and
kissing as if morning brought with it the end of the world. All the longings
and yearnings with which they had lusted for each other had to be fulfilled.
Tonight they had to do more than make love, so much more. They had to seek
solace for their sanity, their sense of self-worth. In embracing each other, they
held tightly to their need of being wanted, of being loved.

Christian licentiously maneuvered his hips between Rebecca's legs,
vehemently attempting to enter her. His excitement and alcohol-induced
arousal rendered him virtually incapable of rational thought, so he continued
to poke blindly for a pleasure which was well lit by the peeping moon.

"Help me," he managed to gasp in between suffocating kisses, "Help
me!"

Rebecca slid her hands from the amorous caressing of his taut back to
the steamy warmth of her groin. Her fingers then, as if possessing a mind of
their own, frantically groped for his penis.

Their frenzied encounter was constantly growing more and more strained
with each passing second in which they did not consummate their lust. Rebecca
felt as though she was melting from a fire inside her, a fire only Christian could
douse. Christian, on the other hand, ached from his swollen erection, which
seemed on the verge of cracking if it was not to be relieved soon.

Fortunately for both of them, Rebecca found her prize. Taking Christian's
attentive penis roughly in her left palm, she forcefully led him into her anxious
cavern.

As he slid into her incredible warmth, he gazed into her eyes. He loved to
stare at her face from the moment he penetrated her to the instant he came to
rest fully within her. He delighted in seeing her blissful expression; the ecstatic
flinching of her eyes, the way in which her mouth quivered in expectant glee.

He exulted in her furrowed brow, caused when he exerted his manhood aptly or when he thrust it in too far.

It also pleased Christian when Rebecca made uncontrollable, guttural grunts or similar noises in response to his prodding. On occasion he was even able to induce her to cry out aloud, uncontrollably ejaculating either in respect to his name or in deference to God's. He fondly remembered waking the neighbors one night long ago after an especially energetic boudoir performance.

Let's see if we can wake us some neighbors tonight, he devilishly thought as he proceeded to move himself in and out of Rebecca.

The thrusting of Christian's penis began to slowly and methodically pick up speed. The desire of both parties to enhance their pleasurable experience led them to hasten their exertions in unison. The natural rhythm of their lovemaking, intrinsic in all beasts, began to take shape. Together they worked, keeping time with one another, rapidly and uncontrollably catering to their passion.

The antique wooden bed, shabbily assembled years ago, could testify to many a lovers' tryst, but never in its history to one bearing such intensity as that of this night. As Rebecca and Christian vigorously pursued their selfish wants, it expressed its disapproval through reproving creaks, castigating groans, and other similar articulations afforded stressed works of carpentry.

Rebecca listened to the creaking of the bed. Every blessed push by Christian was duly answered, as if they had a set cadence by which their tempo increased. She marveled to herself amidst a mind clouded with pleasure that it was as if she had an elfin drummer boy behind her headboard, beating on his little drum; in, out, in, out, in, out. And although she had performed many a night with many a partner, never had her petite friend pounded so fiercely or so often.

As the love they made reached its climax, Rebecca followed suit with a crescendo of erotic moans and sighs. Grabbing the back of Christian's sweaty head, she ceased her amorous invocations long enough to look him in the eye and whisper with a sentimental longing, "If only this were for all time … forever …"

Either out of profound love for what he had just heard, for the woman who spoke it, or simply to silence her and continue in his ravishing, Christian assailed her with even more vigor. Taking her hands in his and holding them in place above her head, he asserted himself like never before, entering her with such violent force that he made it quite apparent he held his own gratification above that of his mistress.

Closing his eyes, he fancied it was not Rebecca with whom he was making love, but rather the dark woman of his dreams. The mere thought of being in her darkness caused him even greater delight than that which he was currently experiencing. With her in mind, he kept his eyes firmly shut and continued in his brutal sex.

If one was not learned in the ways of love, or what lovers do in the sanctified privacy of their bedrooms, one would think Christian to be afflicting some great bodily harm upon Rebecca, for not only could her happy cries be misconstrued as those of a more grievous nature, but if one were to behold the actual act they would surely perceive Christian to be guilty of committing some form of barbarism.

The wind outside rarely drowned out Rebecca's orgasmic declarations, for the most part preferring to orchestrate to her midnight solos rather than obscuring them. It also influenced the shadows that entered on moonbeam and mottled a portion of the wall, the bed, and the bed's nude occupants.

Christian glanced over Rebecca's dappled body, observing the beauty of the dancing shadows as they capered all about her breasts. It was then that a soft twinkle caught his eye and he saw between her bosom the silver pewter of his crucifix, reposing face down against her warm flesh. It hung from his neck and came to rest upon her chest amidst twin Golgothas in a valley of shame. He was angry with himself for allowing his desire to so belittle his cherished cross, irately throwing the effigy over his naked shoulder. He thought that if he rendered it out of sight it would be out of mind, and in so believing this, treated his God with an even greater dishonor. But the cold pewter crucifix continued to harass his conscience as it burned like a brand into his warm back. Such was the nature of his faith and the degree to which he let it bother him.

Rebecca began to shudder under his relentless pounding, uncontrollably gasping, "Oh, God ... yes! Oh, Jesus ..."

Christian could not help but smile, thinking, *I knew I could put the name of God upon your atheist lips, woman!*

As he spent himself inside Rebecca, so too did she orgasm, clenching her captive hands into fists and loudly proclaiming one final, "Dear God!" before releasing a contented sigh and letting her body go limp.

Christian rolled off her sweaty body the moment he had finished with her. The bed was not wide enough to provide him with the distance he would have preferred, so he was obliged to place his arm around Rebecca and cuddle.

"I had almost forgotten how good it was," she whispered to him, her face shining in the moonlight.

But I did not, he silently seethed, wondering whether or not to confront her on her relations with other men. Never had she been so loose, he lamented. She must be pleasing herself with every stiff prick, barnyard animals included!

She peered at him shyly, a perplexing look considering what they had just been through, and he knew at once what was to come next.

"I ... I ..." she giggled nervously at her stutter, "I ... I love you, Chris." She then raised her eyes, child-like, and pleadingly looked into his face, anticipating his due response.

"Shut the window," he cruelly replied, ashamedly averting his eyes. "I grow cold."

The familiar ire he expected never arose, the inflamed hue of indignation failed to taint her pretty face or rumple her brow. Instead she bowed her head in silent disgrace and obediently rose and latched the window shut. Instantly the outside wind was stifled, leaving them to only contemplate one another.

He knows, Rebecca painfully realized, that I have lain with others in his stead. As she softly returned to the shallow comforts of a dampened bed no longer in light but in darkness, her heart weighed heavy in her chest. She bore her sorrow as does a beast of burden, covering her dirty body with a thin blanket. Biting into her pillow and choking back tears, she cursed her way with men.

Christian felt foolish for exercising such animosity towards the woman who had been so kind as to let him have her, deploring himself for being so ham-handed with her feelings. Perhaps he was angered by her actions because he truly loved her, because he had been faithful whereas she had not. Or maybe it was that he was not angry with Rebecca, but with himself for loving her. Love could cause one to do rash, foolish things. It was historically the ruin of great and powerful men, the notorious destroyer of destiny, leading men from high standing to the lowly plowing of fields. Some would even die for love. Would he? Would he sacrifice his God-given life in this world for a woman? He thought for a moment, glanced over at Rebecca's back, and decided that no, he would not die for any woman, and certainly not for Rebecca.

Hypnotized by the full and enormous moon outside, Christian stared at its brightness; its white blazing in the dark, early morning sky as if it were a second sun, a twin Apollo. The harsh contrast between the gilded orb that hung low in the sky and the darkness in which it was set served only to enhance its appeal. He could see why heathen peoples deified the moon, calling her Hecate, Astarte, Diana, and Luna – sacrificing life in her light, spilling blood in her name.

As his eyes grew conditioned to the brilliant queen of night, so they began to tire. The strain of staring into her perfect glory, particularly after being accustomed to the darkened room, compelled his lids to close. Had he not engaged in such rigorous folly beforehand, he would have been able to stave off her inducement to sleep. But being as equal in his comfort as he was in his fatigue, he had no recourse but to succumb to what he feared. He closed his eyes, tilted his head against the pillow, and fell into deep slumber.

As he began to dream, his groggy mind tried valiantly to rouse him. His body gave rise to occasional spasms and jerks and his reposing face often flinched uncontrollably, as if in response to some unseen terror. Stay awake, he vainly implored himself. Stay cognizant! But it was to no avail.

In tonight's vision he was not in a crypt or a vault, but rather a domed and archaic cathedral. He found himself standing amongst rotten and worm-ridden pews arranged haphazardly in the semblance of ordered rows. The dust that covered the pews had caked to the point that one could not separate the squalid powder from that of the natural wood grain. The Gothic architecture of the gray structure told of a medieval birth, of a time of genuine worship.

As he examined the cathedral, Christian made note of the most peculiar fact that all objects of an explicitly religious nature — statues and paintings paying homage to the Savior, His apostles, the Virgin, and requisite saints — were absent. Their places were either vacant — with naked pedestals and empty picture frames attesting to their past adornment — or they were replaced by grotesque effigies brazenly depicting various lesser and greater demons. Even the stone cherubs innate to the once-grand cathedral took the form of gargoyles, leering down at him with corrupted faces of former piousness.

Specifically disturbing anomalies of this nature were the caryatid support columns: ten pillars in all, each one featuring a more fiendishly suggestive female. This is a queer cathedral indeed, he privately critiqued. All true icons of proper worship have been removed and supplanted in their places were sacrilegious idols preaching carnality and hatred.

He slowly walked to the dimly lit dais, being careful not to trip on the cracked, brick floor. All around him the air was made heavy by the prevalent dust. He saw it in swirling beams of light and tasted it with every breath he took. As he drew nearer to the raised, masonry platform he saw hidden in the poor light several marble sarcophagi. Unlike the stone caskets in his previous dream, which were crude and inconspicuous, these three monuments were the epitome of grandiose and majestic interment.

Ornately embellished with fanciful scrolling and flowery detail, it was obvious to him that these were the resting places of a most noble family. Of the three, the one drawing much of Christian's attention was the only one to have a sculpture of the deceased crowning its thick lid.

Anxious to discover the name of this stately family, whose residence in such a disheveled place nagged at his dreamy conscience, Christian sought an epitaph. The inscription, carved deeply into the sarcophagus' side, was in a language foreign to him. It appeared to be of a symbolic nature, and he therefore guessed it to be Greek.

Moving closer, he saw that the black marble figure was that of a restful lady in repose. Whoever had chiseled such a masterpiece had certainly bestowed a great honor upon the dead woman, for her likeness in stone was only shown false through the dark coloration of her marble. Her gown rippled with creases and folds which would never be undone, nor would her hem fray. Her hair would forever be fixed perfectly, never a strand out of place. Never. Her countenance would for eternity be one of peace, that of a calm sleep. Her face would no longer be savaged by anger, jealousy, anguish, or fear. Frowns and crinkled noses, grimaces and watery eyes, and other similarly degrading expressions would no longer detract from the perfect beauty of this placid queen. None of the exquisite rings enhancing her delicate, little hands would be taken from her fingers. The soles of her shoes would never wear, nor would they be adulterated by the dusty floor.

Dust, he thought in his dream, all around I am surrounded by objects blanketed in dust. The damned stuff is everywhere – on the furnishings, the walls. It's so thick beneath my feet that I tread on stone and make no sound. Even in the air, it coats my gullet. And yet this marble likeness is as immaculate as the day it was carved. Not a particle of dust defiling her image.

Bending forward and placing his face very near that of the black lady's, he looked hard at her gentle, although cold, features. Her cheeks did not flush red at his incessant staring, nor did her eyes open to meet his scrutiny. She simply was not real, he painfully had to understand. Though delicate in every detail, she was merely the evidence of some unknown sculptor's brilliance with stone. Her true form lay beneath this heavy and extravagant lid: a moldy, decayed corpse, if there was anything left besides dust and bone.

Still, her immortal perfection so captivated him that he found himself remarking that if she were made flesh and blood he would fall at her feet in worship; renouncing his God and following her to the ends of the earth. He would forsake all to be with her, including his life, which he would with monastic zeal devote to the gratification of her every desire.

He could not resist touching her, and let his hand pathetically stroke her stony cheek. How frigid his goddess was! How she coveted his warmth, how she yearned for his love. He increased the vigor of his caresses, hoping against hope that his amorous rubbing would somehow instill some life into her ageless marble form.

After some time, he bitterly became aware that he was no alchemist of love. He could not raise this most perfect woman from her stone slab. Forever would her back be concealed, being one with the sarcophagus' lid. The sorrow he felt could not possibly be imagined, for not only did he grieve for that which he could never have, he also lamented the twist cruel Fate had played on him; for had he been born several centuries prior, he would have enjoyed her company and the warmth her long-cold arms once offered. As it was, he was permitted only to gaze upon an image of what once was and could never be. It was torture to his romantic heart, for here lay a woman he loved and yet never knew. Never had he seen her tilt her head back in laughter, or look starry-eyed into the night. Never did he comfort her when she sorrowed, or raise her up when she rejoiced. Never did he utter one word to her in conversation, nor cast her a pleasing smile. Never, never, never.

He bowed his head against her hard breast and sobbed. Never would he feel her passionate embrace, the tender touch of her lips on his. Oh! he mourned, to be embraced in those arms! To die a most happy death pressed to her chest, to be held hostage to her heart! What a joyous man he would be if he were to make her resting place his own! How fortunate he would be to depart from this world stretched across her dark figure, to die contemplating the excellence of her face!

But this was not to be. Just as he was born too late to tread in her shadow and bask in her sunlight, so it was that he could not will himself to perish. He would never have what he truly desired, for the summation of his desires lay rotted beneath him. She was all he had ever wanted, all he had ever dreamed of wanting. He knew her, somehow, to be a lady of intellect, one well-versed in letters and language. He knew her to be the keeper of knowledge as well as beauty, and whereas beauty fades with age, knowledge lasts forever. But she would never be his, never could be his. Never for ever.

In bitter resignation he slowed his caressing, spilling tears all over her unflinching stone face. He watched his teardrops bead upon her polished features and it made him cry all the more. Feeling the warm water trickle down his puffy cheeks only furthered his misery. He had been depressed before, depression being a constant in his life, but never like this. Never had he experienced such pathos from anyone, let alone an inanimate effigy. Being so utterly dejected, all he could allow himself to do was to continue gazing through watery eyes at the marble representation of a sleeping woman who, although dead for centuries, still captivated him.

As his tears showered down on her perfect face, discoloring her dark, stone flesh, he noticed something unusual in the corner of the statue's shut left eye. Apparently, a liquid of darker coloring and thicker composition had accumulated there. Drying his weeping eyes on his shirtsleeves in order to better analyze this strange condensation, he leaned closer.

It seemed to be a teardrop of blood, which rolled down her marble cheek and formed a small puddle where her hair and the stone slab became as one. Imperceptible at first, due in part to her equally dark complexion, the deep red line caused Christian no great panic. Rather than being considerably disturbed and upset over the inexplicable scene before him – that of a stone effigy shedding drops of blood – he rejoiced in finding that his lifeless lady shared in his deep melancholy of unrequited love.

Taking the thumb of his left hand, he softly wiped the tear from her cheek. He then raised his bloody thumb closer to his eyes and inspected the wet red on its tip.

Her blood had filled the ridges and whirls of the pad of his thumb. The excess remainder of it meandered slowly down his thumb and past his palm to his wrist, where it stained his cuff.

Admiring the hue of her blood and the marked contrast it brought to his own white skin, he took it to be quite beautiful, both in tone and texture. Registering this personal commentary in his love-laden head, it suddenly dawned on him that of course her blood should be fine, for it was her blood. And that being it was a part of her, of which he could not possess the whole, he had to take what she would grant him: that is, her blood. This firmly set in his depraved mind and compounded with his stringent desire to love her as best he possibly could, Christian lifted the thumb to his dry lips and wet them.

Her blood warmed his cold lips, lending its rich coloration to his pale mouth. The foretaste he received from his lips compelled him to suck his bloody thumb as if he were a babe. Inside his mouth, his tongue greedily rolled over his thumb, forcing him to suck back his secreting saliva. The bitter, salty flavor of her blood made him thirst for more.

How she must love me! he joyously decided. For rather than shedding a common tear, which most women do every day for the simplest of reasons, as if seeking only an excuse and not a cause to weep, she has cried blood for me – blood, that most precious fluid which flows through our veins, which causes such fear and woe when spilled. She has given up a drop of such freely, to me! That which is of far more worth to prince and pauper alike than all the gold, and all the riches, and all the pleasures in all the world!

He removed his thumb from his mouth and examined it. Most of her blood had been licked clean, and excepting a few places where blood and saliva mixed, only that thin line which had run down from his palm to his shirt sleeve remained a vivid red. Looking at his thumb, he saw how his spittle gleamed and how white his flesh there had become due to the force of his uncontrollable sucking. My God, he distastefully realized, what has become of me? Have I become so base as to disgust even myself, drinking blood as if it were Florentine wine? Self-pity overcoming him, he hunched his shoulders in disgrace and began to weep for his own woes.

In his despair he lost all control and let himself fall sobbing across his stone queen. Quivering like a frightened child he could do little but occupy his time with tears. He was incapable of coherent speech, being only able to wail like a hungry babe or whimper like a dog in pain. Lying on her form did him no good either, causing him to revive the unnatural passion he reserved for her.

"My love, my love," he wept, pressed against her hard breast, mourning as if she were newly dead, "why hast thou forsaken me?"

He looked to the other sarcophagi orderly aligned nearby. These two had nowhere near the elaborate ornamentation of his lady's, and although by no means less than splendid, were rather plain in comparison. No effigies topped their lids, and flowery reliefs were kept to a minimum. These two were obviously not of the same stature as my lady, he proudly noted. Perhaps they were her servants.

The far sarcophagus was shrouded in shadow and mystery, for Christian could not read its obscured epitaph and therefore did not know who reposed therein. All he could glean from where he stood, for he did not wish to leave the side of his beloved, was that a bouquet of withered roses rested atop the stone casket. The dried and desiccated flowers had been there for some time and yet they, too, collected no dust. Their once bright-red hue had now darkened to a purplish, almost black, discoloration. It reminded him of a wine sipped at midnight long ago.

The nearer sarcophagus lay before his eyes unobstructed. Similar in its decor, or lack thereof, to that of its distant sister burial case, this one was seemingly new in appearance. Not a single particle of dust rested on its smooth, plain surface. Everything about this grave marked it a recent burial. Even the deeply etched inscription, written in common English, was clearly legible. Out of curiosity, Christian read the epitaph in order to gain insight as to what noble family was interred here. What he read made his knees wobble and his stomach weak, his head spin and his heart slow. There, engraved in distinct, incontrovertible stone, was his name: COLESWITTEN.

Fear engulfed his body as do flames a straw man. He wanted to run, to flee this unholy cathedral! But he stood firm. He could not, as much as he feared for his life, leave his dark lady.

Trembling and weeping, Christian was a miserable sight to behold. He clung to his lady's effigy as does a frightened child hide in the folds of his mother's dress. He needed her. He needed her to erase his name from the side of that detestable box, to lead him away from all these hellish relics and constricting dust. He wanted her to soothe him, to hold him in her arms and tell him there was nothing to fear. He needed to hear her voice, her certainly sweet voice. He needed to touch her flesh, to embrace that which was living and not stone.

Crying, sniffling, and uttering nonsense in a pathetic dilution of character, he hugged his cruel lady and talked to her as if she could hear him.

"Why won't you help me? Why won't you speak to me?" he asked with injured disbelief. "Why won't you love me?"

Moving his hands frantically over her form, he reopened the wound he had received from the dangerous gate outside Father Stemmons' pub. Experiencing the prickly pain on his right forefinger, he lifted his hand to his puffy face and stopped his bawling long enough to allow for a brief inspection of the cut finger.

Holding the injured hand carefully within his left palm, he watched almost in reverential awe the blood of his person stealing slowly from the narrow confines of his gashed flesh. Trickling down his finger to the heel of his palm, the crimson droplets rolled from his hand to the black marble below.

Like a spring offering forth life rather than water, so it was that Christian's blood fell upon the unsmiling lips of his stone lady. And just as natural spring water brings about a joyous rejuvenation in a well-parched traveler, so, too, was it that this blood, absorbed through his lady's lips, affected a change in her midnight complexion. Gradually noticeable, her harsh color began to lighten. Her stone flesh became a pale white, as if of alabaster. Her hair and eyebrows maintained their lustrous black, everything else turning a light pallor. Even the gown adorning her elegant figure was of a snowy silk.

Christian stared in amazement, his heart racing with his thoughts. What was happening? By what unnatural means did this bizarre transformation occur? His mind was deluged with the unexplainable, so he was forced to forgo reason and follow his hasty heart. Abstaining from further contemplation, he took a few steps back and watched with rising delight the metamorphosis of rock to flesh.

Her black gone to white, it was now her solidity which softened. No longer did her skin appear as polished stone, taking on the dullness and apparent malleability associated with human skin. She was now a sleeping woman, not merely the crafted, lifeless representation of such. Her bosom delicately heaved with her every breath, for she that was once stone was now alive.

Ecstatic desire surmounting residual fear of the unknown, Christian hesitantly returned to the side of his dark beloved. He marveled at the change that his blood had wrought in her and could barely refrain from taking her into his arms. How lovely she is! he rejoiced. How heavenly exquisite! This whiteness suits her, multiplying her beauty a thousand-fold and affecting in her the aspect of a dear, porcelain doll.

As he admired her faultless form in worshipful silence, he thought he detected on her face the drowsy wincing one associates with wakening after a long and restful slumber. Stooping forward, he placed his face inches above her own and sought some similar indication that she was about to awake.

Alarm began to grow in him. He started to worry that as was her nature, Fate would subject him to the butt of some cruel joke, granting him his lover in the flesh but never rousing her. He would be in constant torment as the love of his life remained comatose for the duration of his lifetime.

Beholding her halcyon face, unmoving as if still composed of stone, he yearned for the color of her eyes. When will she open those well-rested lids? he suffered. When will I see her complete, her gaze perceiving her most ardent admirer of any century?

Yielding to his wish that he should see her eyes, he resolved to wake her peacefully with a kiss. Bending lower, careful not to touch her anywhere but on her rosy lips, he there placed an eminently righteous and lovingly tender kiss.

No sooner had he pulled away, disheartened with her unresponsiveness, than her eyes opened wide.

Momentarily stunned, all Christian could do was smile. Seconds later, tears of delight rolled forth in a caravan down his already water-stained cheeks. He looked into her coal black eyes, finding them absent of passion yet famished with desire. She is alive! his mind reeled. Thanks be to God, she is alive!

Looking him up and down, the resurrected woman smiled her approval. I satisfy her! he celebrated. I please my ivory lady! He then fondled her cheek and petted her hair, all the while with tears streaming down his face.

Reaching up from her firm mattress, the lady fondly caressed his left cheek, outlining his lips with her thumb. Her touch was almost as ice, but enamored, Christian felt only her gesture. She then slid her cold hand to the back of his neck, sending shivers up his spine, and with a remarkable amount of force not found in most women, pulled his head down to her and pressed his willing lips on hers.

She kissed him with wanton lust, smearing clammy saliva all over his cheeks and chin. Her tongue dove deep into his mouth, entwining with his in a pitched battle of sensual gratification. Not allowing him time to catch his breath nor calm his pounding heart, she held him in place with the strength of her hunger.

Christian knew he could not break from her iron grasp, even though he dared not try. And although he found it nearly impossible to breathe, he kept on kissing her. He had waited years for this moment, spent a lifetime of anguished dreams just to touch these lips. He was not going to stop now; he was not about to let a tedious and trivial process such as breathing pare seconds away from her lips. He would rather die than stop his loving, rather fall dead upon her breasts than break off this long-awaited intimacy. In short, he wished to prove his love by permitting her openly and freely to render him as she was. He wanted to love her forever.

Leaving off her amorous onslaught, the lady so saved his life. As Christian gasped deep breaths, she rose to a sitting position and perched herself beside him. Blithely kicking her legs out, as do little children when they are happily satisfied, she playfully twisted his long hair with her slender fingers. Smiling coyly and tilting her head against his shoulder, she rolled her big, black eyes up at his drained face. Never had he seen such sable eyes. She gazed at him through polished onyx. He had seen all manner of eyes before; blue ones, brown ones, hazel ones, green ones, gray ones – he'd even seen an albino's pink ones once while visiting Canterbury – but never had he seen black. And it was not only that they were black that so captivated him, it was the shade of black: darker than the deepest pitch, dim as the grave.

Sliding her head across his chest, she listened with obvious delight to the beating of his happy heart. She then took his quaking hands and calmed him by placing them within her own soothing palms. Gently rubbing her thumbs over the backs of his hands, she stared erotically into his pleased face. Then, slipping from her perch, she touched the dusty ground and stood before him.

His hands still held in hers, she raised them up and affixed them to her liberal bosom. Holding them there, as if fearing he would actually withdraw them from their paradise, she began pressing them into her breasts, massaging them in slow, circular motions. Seductively contorting her face with closed eyes and an open mouth, she aptly demonstrated how well she enjoyed his touch.

Glancing down at her chest, the lady peeled him from her. Underneath his right hand, on the cloth covering her left breast, there was the rusty smear of blood. Letting his left hand fall free from her grasp she took his right hand and studied it.

Tracing the blood on her dress to that on his palm, she followed with her eyes the red trail as it led to his wounded forefinger. Then, conducting his forefinger into her gaping mouth, she sucked the wound clean. When she could get no more from his finger, she lapped up the blood that had run down his palm to his wrist, even sucking to some extent clean the bloodstain on his shirtsleeve. While she performed in this peculiar way, she maintained eye contact with her giving lover, looking at him as if she were engaged in devoted fellatio and not the gruesome transfusion of blood.

When finished, she licked her lips tidy with her teasing tongue. She then took up both Christian's hands and pulled him from the sarcophagus. Laughing merrily, she led him from the dais – away from the cathedral and all its accursed images, away from all tokens of death and decay. Hand in hand, together they ran from the peering artifacts, fleeing to the privacy of a room hidden behind a rotted confessional.

The room was medium sized, a square five yards by five yards, and was from floor to ceiling brick. Totally absent of furnishings or tapestries of any kind, its only feature was a sunken, circular depression in its center. Measuring three yards in radius and a half yard in depth, and possessing two drainage pipes on opposite sides, the stone basin was a pool without water.

A baptistery, Christian decided. The drainage pipes led to the rooftop, where water collected after a rain and was channeled into the pool from piping encased in the walls, he noted, marveling at the ingenuity of some long dead architect.

The lady escorted him down into the center of the font. Stepping out of her gown, she removed the dainty slippers shrouding her feet and stood before him naked in the flesh.

She permitted Christian to contemplate her full, stark beauty. Unadulterated by clothes, exposed in glorious nudity, her brilliance caused him to squint his eyes. How could he ever physically love her? How could he have even kissed her? For her excellence so shone forth in his eyes that to love her would be to love the sun. And should she go often without dress, he being forced to look upon her glory, his vision would blacken and he would live out his days in darkness.

Before he could further mentally expound her many bare virtues, she threw herself against him. Like an animal she tore at his clothing, throwing the scraps out of the font with forceful verve. Piece by piece his fine threads were torn apart and discarded. Even his leather shoes were shredded beyond repair. When she was through, she had fashioned him like her.

Naked, together they embraced with both arms and lips. Moving their hands over one another with dynamic energy, they left no skin untouched. As she entwined her fingers in his hair, he kneaded her buttocks, often rubbing his fingers between her cheeks. She employed every part of her body in an effort to satisfy him; her legs brushed against his, her tongue tickled his throat, her breasts teasingly pressed into his nipples, and her pubic hair temptingly tickled his burgeoning penis.

Christian neither knew if he were experiencing a taste of Heaven or of Hell. For although she pleased him unlike any woman ever had or ever could, there was something not right about her sensuality, something false about her love. It was as if she were in some way mocking him by loving him; drolly laughing with every snide kiss.

With a hungry look she drew him down to the bottom of the empty pool. There they lay, stretched out across the floor with only the hard, cold brick for a mattress. It didn't matter to either of them, their arousal more than compensating for the chill of the stone basin. As he rolled atop her he heard a sudden groaning and creaking emanating from the walls.

Frightened by the mysterious noise, for if anyone should discover them to be making love in a church they would be in dire straits, Christian looked nervously around.

Trying to return him to his previous endeavors, his lady stroked his hair and patted his face, all the while gently cooing to soothe his alarm.

But not even she could dissuade him from his fear. What was it? he demanded. What was it that so shook the walls as if Judgment were upon us? The only answer he received was a sputtering, gurgling noise coming from the pool's water pipes.

Glancing from one pipe to the other, his anxiety mounted. What was it? What was it coming through the pipes? Somehow he knew it not to be water.

As his eyes focused on the opening of one of the pipes, he became petrified. Looking down that rusted pipe, into an inky darkness from which anything could emerge, Christian felt one fear rise prominent above the rest: rats.

He could hear it now, whatever it was, to be close. By the sloshing inflection issuing forth from the pipes, he calculated they did not have long to wait. He was correct.

Flowing out of both pipes with a sickening abundance was blood: thick, syrupy, sticky, smelly, red blood. It poured into the pool, quickly covering the dry bottom. Christian tried to flee, but was held firmly in place by his lady love. There she kept him, despite his rigorous protestations, until the pool was filled to the brim with the dreaded crimson stuff.

The blood washed across their naked, white bodies, staining them a deep pink. Their every pore was inundated in the bitter liquid, submerged in a deep scarlet sea that warmed them. Lapping up against the shoreline of their skin, the dense broth clung to them in a frothy, sanguine foam.

Christian's earlier fear and disgust gave way to the pleasing warmth which enveloped him. That, and the barrage of kisses planted all over his face by the woman beneath him, convinced him to no longer seek flight, but to stay and submit to her desires.

So it was that they made their love bathed in a baptism of blood. Christian made waves as he thrust himself into his lady, causing blood to spill over the lip of the font and stream across the brick floor. For a moment he watched the odious liquid as it ran into the cracks between the bricks, speeding on its way within new found canals.

Either due to his excitement at having a fantasy fulfilled, or the prowess of his bloody lady, in no time at all Christian was ejaculating like a madman. Collapsing onto her chest, he struggled for his second wind against the reek of blood.

Long after their robust lovemaking had ended, they remained in the red; basking in its heat, relaxing in its abundance. The lady rested her soft back against the poolside and Christian reclined in her arms. Lovingly, she massaged the drying blood into his skin, as if it would somehow rejuvenate his drained libido. In response to her caresses, he turned his head and smiled wearily at her. She smiled back at him, and then spoke for the first time.

"Drink ..."

Her tone was not exactly that of a command, and neither was it an offering, but rather somewhere in between. Staring into those cold, charcoal eyes, Christian sought some glean of light, some compassion. He found only greater darkness.

Feeling a growing horror in the pit of his stomach, the smile on his face froze. He feared what this woman was capable of, and of what she had made him capable of. Already he was experiencing disgust over having engaged in such gross, carnal lunacy, over allowing himself to be coated in foul-smelling blood of unknown origin. And now she demanded of him to drink of the blood in which they had just consummated intercourse.

He could not bring himself to look her in the eye as he refused.

Instantly her massaging ceased. He glanced down at her hands lying upon his chest and noted how the ruby of one of her rings matched the color of the blood. She will not make me drink, he thought. I shall not imbibe an ounce of the salty stuff!

From over his right shoulder, very near to his ear, came the unmistakable directive, "Drink!"

The verbal strength with which she asserted her order forced him to look up at her face. No longer was she the placid beauty who had so captured his heart while sleeping. Indeed, that appeared to have been a ruse employed to hide her true guise – that of a demon from Hell.

With her jaw firmly set and her cruel eyes fixed into his, her nostrils flared as she viciously spat, "Drink!"

Christian tried to wriggle free from her grasp, but found that aside from her strong clutches, the blood in which he sat had coagulated and so conspired with her to trap him. As if caught in tar, he twisted and turned and succeeded in only wasting energy. *She had me*, he grieved, *like the spider to the fly she held me in her bloody web!*

Hearing her cackle, he once again braved looking into her face.

Smiling as does the gloating hunter to the frightened fox, she betrayed her nefarious teeth as she leaned forward, whispering, "Taste me …"

Rising suddenly, she moved in front of him, the gelatinous blood tilled by her feet. She stood as the conqueror, with Christian helplessly recumbent between her legs. "Taste me …" she demanded of him once more, grasping the back of his damp head and thrusting his face fully into her vagina.

Christian gagged as fetid menstrual discharge flowed down his throat and filled his stomach. Unable to break free from the hold her thighs had on him, he could do nothing but swallow.

"Taste me …" she sighed triumphantly as she continued to straddle his pleading face. "Taste me …"

He awoke to darkness; choking, shaking, and sopping wet. He was angry with himself for having fallen asleep. The moon had moved past the window, retreating in the face of an advancing dawn, and no longer filled the room with its lustrous light. Though the morning rapidly approached, the cock had yet to crow. So it was that the room was darker in the early morn than it had been that previous night.

He rose quietly from his bedside – dampened by his cold perspiration, it no longer held any comfort for him. *Comfort*, he thought, *one thing I do not need more of is comfort. It was because of a cozy bed that I now quake and shiver beyond my control.*

He saw Rebecca lying huddled against her pillow on her side of the small bed. *If she only knew of the plague inside my head, of the other woman who sought to take me from her. God, how I have wronged her, how I have treated her so badly.*

A cold wind sneaking in through a space in the windowsill made him realize how frigid the tiny room was. His sweat only contributed to his shivers, most of which were not caused by any coolness, but by the aftershocks of fear still rippling throughout his shaking body. He moved to one side of the window and away from the draft.

Looking out of the window's dirty glass, he saw that although the sky remained mostly dark, a faint hue of light highlighted the horizon, which was jagged and torn with the silhouettes of forest trees.

Turning his attention to the large oak just outside the window, he admired its aged and weathered appearance; the wrinkled bark and thick, sturdy boughs. He looked to the clustered leaves, tossing in the early wind. How they were all connected, he reflected, how they were all joined: the leaves, the boughs, the bark, all springing forth from roots planted deep into the earth. How the leaves receive nourishment from the roots, which suck the water from the soil. And as the tree grows, its roots fat with water, so its leaves multiply.

He had been trying to occupy his mind with other thoughts, admiring aspects of God's nature in an attempt at avoiding thinking of her, but he could not. *She is like the tree, and I am as a leaf upon her branch.*

When the sun finally broke from the binds of the earth, Christian was there to greet it. He watched the darkness turn to light and could not help but feel a sense of ease. It was daylight, he calmed himself. She cannot molest me now.

But for how long would he be safe? Until the sky grew red with the farewell of a departing sun, when the moon ascended in all her glory to take up the heavenly scepter in a nightly deposing? When shadows stretched long and daylight grew weak and evening was upon him; that was the time he dreaded, that was what he feared most.

Rebecca woke to find herself alone in bed. Frightened he had left her, she sat up and instantly noticed him standing against the wall, looking out the window. *I disgust him so much that he would rather stand than lie with me,* she grieved. *I can remember when he would always make me his valentine, always bring me trinkets to show his love for me.* Her left index finger outlined the locket around her neck. *Now he hates me,* she thought, her eyes brimming with tears. *Now he is sickened by the sight of me!*

From the window, Christian saw Cotton lead the hitched horses to just beneath him in front of the tavern. Watching him give the horses a final rubdown, he smiled at the great care with which the Scot treated the animals. He probably respects them more than people, he wryly mused. Opening the window, he leaned out and grinned a toothy grin in welcome.

On hearing the window's yawn, Cotton looked up and, recognizing Christian, called out to him. "Well, halloo there! Rest ye well?"

"Indeed, my friend. And you?"

"As a babe."

They broke into hearty laughter, for both knew that neither of them managed much sleep. After regaining control of themselves, they faced the issue before them of getting to Manasseh.

"Almost ready?" Christian queried, pointing to the fitted horses.

"Aye. Hurry or we'll lose daylight."

"Let me be dressed and make my farewells."

"Do as ye wish, but hasten, for the roads are wicked."

Nodding his compliance, Christian ducked back into the room. Turning to look for his clothes, he saw Rebecca staring at him. She seems as though mourning me, he perceived, as if by her love she had died. Avoiding her melancholy gaze, he found his white shirt and covered himself.

Either out of guilt over the unkind way in which he had treated her, or his inability to ignore her imploring, tear-blurred eyes, he spoke to her with a slightly annoyed entreaty, "'Becca, please."

Rising out of bed, she let her covers fall, exposing her attractive form, revealing her body in an effort at tempting him to stay. She ran her left hand across her stomach and toyed with her navel while casting him an alluring glance. "Don't go, Christian," she pled. "Stay with me here. Stemmons can't get you here, it's safe … we are safe."

Fumbling with his stockings, he tried to make light the situation by saying with a broad smile, "Lustful women take delight in kissing the Devil's rectum." On seeing her unmoved by his jest, he promised, "When I am done with what is required of me, I shall return. 'Tis my will that moves me and no other's."

Walking to him, she replied in a voice replete with regrettable disillusion, "If you find what you seek you shall never return."

Stepping into his breeches, he knew she was right, but could not bear to hurt her anymore, so he lied. "Yes, I shall return. I lost you once, I shan't lose you again … no matter what the cost." He took his crucifix from around his neck. "Here, hold and cherish this until my return."

He held the necklace out, holding it open for her. She moved closer, but before putting her head through the chain, removed her own locket. "You gave this to me long ago. Just as I shall wear your cross, so too must you wear my locket."

And with that, she placed the little locket over his head and around his neck. He did the same, afterwards planting a kiss on her fair forehead. He then resumed his dressing, tucking in his shirt and putting on his shoes. When he was finished, he picked up his jacket and slung it across his forearm.

Striding to the door, he was intercepted by his unyielding lover, who barricaded herself between him and his exit. Pressed against the wooden door, she would not let him leave without one final embrace.

Taking her into his arms, he let his hands feel her every part, permitting himself a last touch. He kissed her long and hard, playing on her belief that he would return. But he could tell in her overly zealous tongue and water-dammed eyes that she knew the truth. She knew he would never return.

Maneuvering her to the side, he opened the door and gave her a reassuring grin. Then he let her go and left the room, closing the door behind him.

She stared at her door for some time, all the while rubbing the crucifix that hung around her neck. He would return, she decided, if not for me then for his mother's cross. Standing naked and alone, she had already begun to miss him.

Christian exited the tavern with a bundle of prepared foods and a cask of ale in his overburdened arms. Smiling, he held them up for Cotton to see. "I took what I thought necessary for the trip."

Cotton looked down at him from his seat on the coach. "I'll relieve ye of some of your trouble," he said, and leaned over and took the cask from Christian's hands.

Upset over Cotton's predictable preference, Christian sullenly walked to the side of the coach, opened the door, and placed the food on one of the interior seats. Then he climbed up next to Cotton.

"Would ye not rather be inside? The sun may scald ye," said Cotton in a voice full of genuine concern.

"Nay, 'tis far too cramped in there. I would venture it to get equally hot, if not more so, for 'tis a stifling box with wheels. It shall do me good to ride here, for not only shall we converse, which is always good for the health, but the fair country air refreshes and invigorates me to the point of distraction."

"As ye like it, so shall it be."

Cotton shook the reins, cracked the whip, and set the horses in motion. Trotting at a leisurely pace, they pulled the coach at such a speed that it seemed as though Bantingham had grown during the night. Christian and Cotton looked at the deserted road and still structures and surmised that during the day the farmers were in their fields and Bantingham was reduced to little more than a ghost town.

With so little to contemplate, Christian felt the lack of weight around his neck and remembered exchanging his crucifix for Rebecca's locket. That was my mother's crucifix, he lamented, how could I have been so foolish as to part with that? Glancing back over his shoulder, he saw why.

Standing outside the tavern, clad only in her blanket, stood Rebecca.

They stared at one another for some time, then sunlight struck the metal of his crucifix, mockingly causing it to glisten on her chest. He turned away.

"He'll come back," she whispered, trying to convince herself. "He'll come back."

As the departing coach gradually became a shrinking black dot, a farmer emerged from the roadside underbrush. With great effort, he dragged a fatted pig he had just slaughtered onto the roadway as swarms of flies announced his arrival. Its throat slit wide, the bloated, black pig left a bloody trail, turning the dirt into muddied patches of maroon. The farmer's hounds ran behind him, eagerly lapping up the spilt blood with ravenous delight.

# Chapter Four

In time the forest only grew darker and less friendly. From what Cotton could glean from occasional glimpses of the sun through sparse treetops, it was late in the evening. The feeble orange light that did filter past the concealing trees mixed with the browns of the wood to create a very autumnal scene. Rotting, mildewed leaves filled their nostrils with a pungent odor. The only way in which Cotton discerned the trail, for the leaves indiscriminately blanketed the road, was the obvious lack of trees before them.

"No one's been up this way for a very long time," mentioned Cotton, gesturing with his whip to the undisturbed, thick layering of leaves cloaking the trail. "'Tis so heavy with leaf that the horses labor along."

Christian watched the horses' hooves as they plowed through the dead vegetation. The churning of black and orange leaves, with the occasional pale yellow or brown, combined in a somber color scheme devoid of any greens or vibrancy. Actually it was so with the entire forest, for everything was dead. No wild flowers lightened the depressing earth tones, no animals pranced or birds sang, nor was there any robust shrubbery to ease the mark of Death. Sunlight, that by which all things are nurtured and grown, was even barred from this place; tall boughs and thick, bony branches blocked the light from the sky. Indeed, if ever there was a place that so displayed the briefness of life and the harsh constancy of death, this was it. This was Death's forest.

The decaying leaves littering the forest floor and camouflaging the rarely trodden trail reminded Christian, *I am as the leaf.*

Shifting uncomfortably in his seat and donning his blue jacket, he rubbed his hands together. The sun is nearly set, he thought, it no longer offers us its heat. He wondered if this place had ever known the warm rays of sunlight, and decided that it had not. Warmth was not all the waning sun provided; security, a feeling of safety, lay within its beams. The sun made visible things that darkness obscured. It shortened shadows and restricted the movements of those cowardly criminals and abhorrent creatures of the night whose hearts mirrored the color of their skies.

By the way in which Christian and Cotton looked with sadness on the concluding daylight, one would fancy them to be pagan sun worshipers, bidding silent farewells to mighty Sol Invictus, rather than God-fearing Christians.

They traveled through the weighted silence in silence. Sitting in resignation to the descending truth above them; they would not make Manasseh before dark.

Eventually they emerged from the oppressive woods to find to their happy surprise the sun still hanging in the sky. They beheld the orange orb with a mutual joy, for its eclipsing by the high forest trees had led them to believe it was later in the day, and now they saw that this was not so. Unable to contain their delight, foolish smiles modified their gaping mouths.

"I'll wager 'tis not past five in the evening," said Cotton, looking at the sun.

"That would mean that our journey is nearly complete!" added Christian, overly enthused.

"If I've taken the trail correct, and not been misled by these damned leaves, we should be off our asses shortly and resting with some ale."

"Then sing for joy, my friend, for we are out of the woods and the sun is still nigh!"

"What is it ye would have me sing?"

"Whatever brings pleasure to your heart and to my ears."

"Very well, then! A Scottish ditty it shall be!" Clearing his throat and putting his voice in order, Cotton soon began a lively rendition of an improvised ballad:

"A bonny lass Lord Ruthven took
To be his lawful wife,
Impassioned on his wedding night,
For love he took her life.
Then out and came the thick, thick, blood,
Then out and came the thin,
Then out and came the bonny heart's blood,
Where all the life lay in.
So he ordered the grave to be opened wide,
And the shroud to be turned down;
And there he kissed her clay cold lips
'Til the tears came trickling down,
'Til the tears came trickling down, down, down."

Finished, he smiled gently at Christian, who had a strange look upon his face. "Have I displeased ye with my song?" he asked.

"Nay," replied Christian distractedly, "'tis merely the lyrics striking strange chords within me."

"'Tis only a song."

"I know, I know. A better recited ballad I have not heard."

"And ye never will," said Cotton in a self-mocking tone, his broadening smile wrinkling his face. Returning his eyes to the trail, he saw a small town through the thinning forest. "We're here," he sighed with relief. "There is Manasseh."

From what Christian could make of the town of Manasseh, he saw that its inhabitants practiced little upkeep. The place was so run down and overgrown with vegetation that they had not noticed it until they were upon it. Stunted saplings stood in the middle of the road, withered grass crept to the doorways of houses, and rot and pestilence had diminished many of the homes' attractiveness.

The horses drawing the coach abruptly stopped and nervously began braying.

"Why have you halted us here?" Christian asked.

"I did nothing of the sort," answered a peevish Cotton. "These infernal beasts have gained a mind of their own." Slapping the leather reins against their bare backs, he exhorted the horses onward. "Come now, ye wretched beasts, pull only a little farther!"

They responded with several neighs, forcefully shaking their heads in dissension.

"If that's how ye'll have it," growled Cotton, unfurling his whip, "then here's how I'll have it!"

Cracking the whip several times directly above the horses' heads finally prompted them forward.

These animals are frightened, thought Christian. They endured several snaps of the whip before moving. Something in this unkempt town terrifies them.

He tried to remember what he could of stories told of the sixth sense of animals, but was only able to recall one, that of a dog being used to identify a murderer. And just as that dog arched its back in fear and ruffled its fur when placed before the killer, so did these horses trot rigid and unsure, their heads hung low in either sad resignation or deference to their terror.

Entering the quiet town, the two men were equally struck by the appearance of the windows of the houses, all of which were boarded up with thick, wooden planks. No light could penetrate even the smallest of homes.

Disturbed by the condition of the town, as well as by the eerie silence, they gave each other somber looks. It seemed as though the people of Manasseh had picked up their things and left, leaving only the cheerless shells of worn-out houses.

Cotton steered the horses to the center of the town, carefully maneuvering them past blackberry brambles and ruts in the road. The roadway had gotten so bad through weathering and neglect that, with the dead leaves and grass, it gave the town an appearance of simply being built in the middle of an uncleared wood. Dilapidated houses blended with the forest scenery, a few even sporting trees growing through their roofs and roots upsetting their foundations.

Once they had come to the town square, or what remained of it, they descended from their uncomfortable seats atop the coach and stretched their knotted muscles and stiff joints.

Looking at the lifeless rows of houses, Christian sourly quipped, "Perhaps there are no recorded deaths because there is nothing to record."

"Aye," agreed Cotton, "'tis a bit weird." Staring harshly into the moldered timber and displaced stone face, he added, "Come, let's explore," and then headed off toward the nearest of the homes.

Christian felt a strange chill rattle his bones as he watched the giant Scot walk away from him, and was prompted to whisper to himself, "Manasseh ... is dead."

The two of them checked every standing structure for signs of life, but found nothing. In places where they could enter they found only dust, dirt, and the remnants of a prior occupation. Many of the houses would offer them no entry — either being solidly barred from the inside, or having nails driven through their doorframes. When they came to these secured domiciles, they resorted to crying out to any who might be inside to come down and open up. Every time they did this, they were greeted by silence.

Cotton, frustrated after having gone door to door for naught, grabbed Christian by the nape of his neck as he was leaving the last house and whirled him around. "See there," he said, pointing to an expansive, two-story building set apart from the erratically lined homes. "The inn. If any man is here, there he'll be." He brushed past Christian as he set out for the town watering hole.

Damn this place! Christian cursed. Damn those who have abandoned my dreams! He glanced down at his fine outfit. I have worn my best dress, and for what? The pleasure of forest creatures? My feet swell and bleed in shoes too small, and none are here to behold their bloody, shiny buckles? To hell with all past residents of this grave town!

A sudden gust of wind stopped him in his tracks. Blowing through the withered trees, it scattered dust and tossed his hair. It brought with it a strange foreboding, an almost lucid premonition that cavorted inside his head. It was brief, lasting only as long as the gust, but it would chill him for some time. For in that instant he felt what it was like to be dead.

"What's the matter?"

It was Cotton, calling to him from just outside the inn. He seemed a bit annoyed with his charge, signaling Christian closer with exaggerated movements of his arms.

Regaining his composure, Christian took a deep breath and proceeded to where Cotton impatiently stood. He found as he drew nearer to the inn that he could not meet the old soldier's stern gaze, opting instead to study his sore feet.

"Are ye well?" Cotton gruffly inquired.

"Yes, I ... I am well," replied Christian.

"Ye seem as pale as a ghost. Verily, I can almost see through your head."

"Surely you make merry. 'Tis no ailment of the physical that yields me so, but that of the mind."

"Of what foolery is this ye speak?"

"This place is so swathed in death that by merely treading upon its soil I have felt what it is to be snug in the hole."

"If I have been injurious to ye in some way, please, I beg of ye, tell so that I may make amends. But do not pull an old man's leg with so cruel a revenge as fear."

Christian was shocked that under the circumstances Cotton was not receptive to his senses. He became angered when he was accused of attempting to scare him, as if he were in a mood for folly. "How could you imagine that I would frolic and play in a graveyard?" he incredulously asked. "I feel ... uncomfortable here. I don't like it here."

"Then that makes two of us," Cotton admitted. "I apologize for me disrespect. 'Twas not intended."

"It never is between friends," Christian said, feigning a smile.

"I wished only to deny what I myself have felt upon entering the confines of this pitiable lot."

"Then you have felt it, too?"

"Aye."

They stared at each other, refusing to acknowledge the rising wind nipping at their cheeks. In the pits of their stomachs they somehow knew what was in store for them. Cotton was first to break the quiet.

"I say we get out of this fiendish wind." He pointed with his thumb over his shoulder at the inn behind him. "Seek shelter and persons within."

"Agreed," responded Christian as he huddled in his poorly insulated jacket. "Boreas takes not kindly to us today."

Jointly they removed the fixed boards from the doorframe, discarding the wood to one side. As Christian tossed a board aside into the high grass encircling the inn, he heard it clatter, as if striking something other than overgrowth. Curiosity aroused, he ceased assisting Cotton in the removal of the boards long enough to investigate. Bending at the waist, he parted the profuse grass with both hands. The dry yellow cracked and splintered under the force of his arms, sending many spindly blades twisting and turning in the cold wind.

There, obscured under a patchwork of dead grass and pressed leaves, lay the placard to the inn.

Cotton, engrossed in pulling free the nailed boards, saw that his friend had found something. "What's that there that ye've come across?" he inquired.

"It appears to be the inn sign."

"How does it read?"

Brushing away some of the grime from the sign's face, Christian found the lightly carved letters to be easier read maintaining the dirt they held. Shaking the filth from his hands as he rose, he answered. "It reads, Inn of the Dell."

He did not mention, however, that the word 'Dell' had been corrupted. Someone had taken the time to disfigure the 'D', cutting deeper into the wood than the original carving. Adding a sloppy bisecting line from left to right and extending the letter's vertical lines, whoever had done it had made a 'D' into an 'H'. Christian also noticed how faint the 'of the' part of the sign was in comparison with the other words. It was as if someone had attempted to diminish its distinctness by milling it away. Read properly, the sign would read, 'Inn Hell'.

He could feel traces of that chill again — faint tremblings of that same coldness which had numbed him only moments before. There is something definitely not right with this place, he decided.

While he pondered the state of Manasseh and how its apparent vacancy had left his ambitions as lifeless as the town itself, Cotton succeeded in removing the final board impeding their entry into the inn.

"There we go," he huffed as he flung the last board aside. "Now, in we go." With unmerited caution, he gradually applied pressure to the old door. The brown hinges creaked and groaned the misery of rust. The sound of splintering, deteriorated wood begged to stay shut and open no further, but to no avail. From deep within came the scurrying sounds of rats and roaches fleeing the incoming light.

Not without fair trepidation did Christian follow Cotton into the darkened interior of the inn.

The first of many things to greet them was the stale, dank smell of the place. Lacking any ventilation due to the shut windows and doors, the inn reeked of dust and mildew. The simple act of cracking open the door caused a flurry of dust and light debris, swirling like airborne whirlpools across the filthy floor. Dust and mildewed wood were not all that assailed their nostrils. An overpowering odor of fleshly decay joined their noses and their hearts in horror. Beneath the staid aromas common to aging there lay an underlying pungency, a smell all too familiar to them from the streets of London: that of putrefaction.

Instinctively the two threw their hands to their faces, covering their noses and mouths. Cotton moved from his place in the doorway and permitted Christian an unobstructed view of the foul room. It did him little good, for his eyes had yet to adjust to the darkened interior and the evening sky outside afforded scant light through the open doorway.

Stumbling in the dark, Cotton blindly labored to find the boarded windows from the inside of the inn. Locating what he sought, he peeled the planks from their mountings.

Instantly, one side of the room was made visible. Christian could see tables and chairs arranged as if it were only an hour since they were last used, although the velour of dust said otherwise. He saw dining utensils, mugs, pitchers, and plates all set upon the naturally clothed tabletop. Not in any particular order, but rather varying in placement, the dinnerware seemed to have been in use when this place was deserted. Taking no time to put things in order but rather forsaking them to nature, much like a few of the houses they were able to enter, whoever had resided here had left in a hurry, and with little care for material possessions.

Cotton busied himself with the removal of all the boards on the remaining windows, of which there were four. In no time at all the place was somewhat brighter, but no less dismal.

After dislodging all hindrances of the late evening light, Cotton felt secure enough basking in the dying beams to call out to anyone who might still be residing in this cobwebbed filth. Although he doubted, and in a way hoped, that there was no one living here, he was obliged to yell out. "Is anyone here? Ho! I say, is anyone here?"

From the swirling shadows came no reply but the howl of the rising wind.

Detached, looking stupidly at a small rat eating a large cockroach in a corner, Christian mumbled, "Like the grave."

Bullied on by his unease and propelled by his adventurous heart, Cotton assaulted the inn's crude, warped, wooden stairs. "Let's have a look up here," he puffed as the deteriorating stairs moaned under his weight.

As Cotton disappeared up the unsure steps into the darkened hallway of the second floor, Christian moved closer to one of the abandoned tables.

He saw the dirty plates and the remains of rotted and molded food. Brain-like fungi spilled from one saucepan to the next, eventually clustering on a large portion of the tabletop and trickling down a leg. The mugs and pitchers were still full of what used to be ale, which by now had degenerated into a foul-smelling brew not even the most desperate drunk would imbibe. Peering into a pitcher, Christian saw several little bubbles percolate to the top of the oily, black quagmire. He shuddered at the thought that something had made its home the bottom of the vessel.

Feeling queasy, he removed his gaze from that particular pitcher to another of the same kind, only empty. Picking it up, he brushed away some of the gathered dust to reveal fine engraving underneath. Impressed with his find, its discovery posed new questions for him: Why would simple country folk have need of elegant goblets, and why would they leave them behind?

Lifting the pitcher to his nose, he inhaled and made a sour face. God, he thought in amazement, how long has this dwelling been left unattended that even the faint smell of ale has turned rank?

Putting the pitcher back in its place, he was horrified to see a large black beetle crawl out of it and perch precariously on its rim. As he eyed the slimy black bug, its antennae twitching inquisitively back and forth, he was repulsed not only at the sight of it, but also because he had just held the pitcher under his nose.

Turning to seek Cotton, something he previously had not noticed caught his eye. A small cup, unlike any at the inn, sat near the end of the table.

The cup seemed new, or at least newer than its companions, and perhaps it was that and not its relative size which drew Christian to study it. Before lifting it, he took note of the marks in the dust surrounding the cup; proof of it being moved only recently. He had not touched it, and neither had Cotton. Then who had?

Raising the cup slightly off the table, he turned it over and tapped its bottom so that if there were any beetles within they would tumble out. Beetles did not fall out, but rather rust-colored flakes. Perplexed, Christian calmed his worried mind by assuring himself that the flakes were either the dried curd of some soup or the caked spices of some sauce.

Cotton suddenly reappeared at the hallway entrance at the top of the stairs, giving Christian a start. He quietly motioned his friend up the stairs and then disappeared once again into the darkened hall.

Returning the little cup perfectly to its spot in the dust, Christian walked briskly to the foot of the small stairs. Pausing long enough to prepare himself for whatever it was Cotton had to show him, he took in a deep breath and ascended the noisy steps as silently as he knew how.

Once reaching the top, he could see in the incredible dimness Cotton standing outside the first door on the left. Walking to him, Christian whispered in strained agitation, "What?"

"Sssh!" Cotton hushed him. "Quiet down!" Excitedly pointing to the door, he added, "There's someone in there, I heard the bugger!"

Christian looked dumbfounded at the plain, wooden door. He took hold of its brass latch, only to discover it locked. Giving Cotton a questioning glance, he proceeded to rap lightly against the door. "Sir," he said softly, full of hope and fear, "might we gain entry? We have need of you ... to answer some questions."

No response was forthcoming from behind the locked door.

"Are you certain you heard not rats, or the settling of the inn?" he asked Cotton.

Angered by Christian's disbelief, Cotton pushed him aside and began hitting his fists into the door, causing the ancient hinges to rattle and the door to clatter in its frame. "Open up in there!" he shouted above the din of his pounding, "Or I shall batter down this door!" Stopping long enough to catch his breath and listen, Cotton heard muffled sounds from within. "There!" he rejoiced, "Do ye hear him?"

Christian nodded his agreement. He was speechless at the prospect of someone actually living here, in this town, let alone this ruined inn.

The noise they heard grew louder as the person within approached. It was a shuffling, shifting noise, with a gentle creaking accompaniment that announced the innkeeper's arrival. Then, from behind the door, came his lethargic whisper. "You have been prepared for ..."

Cotton furrowed his brow and threw Christian a look of bewilderment. "What was that ye said?"

Again there was no response from the unseen innkeeper.

Christian pulled Cotton away from the door and whispered into his ear, "We were expected? They knew and anticipated our arrival?"

Stunned at the implications of Christian's revelation, Cotton stuttered, "No ... no, they did not."

Momentarily dazed, he stood in thought. *Who told them of our arrival, and what had we been 'prepared for'?* Unable to come up with a sufficient answer, he allowed himself to surrender to his frustration and indignantly returned to the innkeeper's door, raining down more forceful blows upon its fragile wood. "Innkeeper!" he shouted, "Show yourself! Why do ye hide from us? Why do ye treat your guests so poorly, let your inn fall to pieces? What is wrong with this town?"

Barely audible, and in disregard to Cotton's queries, the innkeeper monotonously murmured, "Your rooms are the last two on the right ..."

Both men peered down the shadowy hallway at the last two rooms on the right-hand side of the hall. "What is going on here?" Cotton said, more to himself than to the innkeeper or Christian.

"I do not know," his young friend sighed, "but fear we shall find out soon enough."

Out of desperation, Cotton struck once more at the beaten door. "Open up, old fool! Why do ye not face us?"

Silence was the innkeeper's reply.

Undaunted, Cotton continued, "Why does no one greet us?"

It became apparent that the innkeeper had either fallen asleep or he liked his mute response.

Christian peeled Cotton from the proprietor's door. Pulling him by the arm, he appealed to Cotton's sense of reason. "Come," he soothed, "leave him, let us tend to our accommodations."

Cotton agreed and the two walked to their rooms. As they neared the last couple of doors on the right, a feeling of dread overtook them. What lay behind those doors? They both expected to find rooms suitable to a hostel such as the one in which they were in, with curtains of cobweb, sheets of dust, and vermin for company.

Separating, each staked claim to his own room; Cotton taking the nearest, and Christian the farthest. They looked at each other before opening their doors. At the very least both were pleasantly surprised.

The rooms had been recently cleaned and dusted, looking out of place in such a place. The beds were large and made, with cotton blankets and down pillows and sturdy wooden frames. Each room had a single window that allowed for a panoramic view of the entire town. Nearby was a small table with a full pitcher of water and a washbasin.

Christian strode over to the washbasin, and in disbelief examined his full pitcher. The water was clear and clean, with not even a particle of dust besmirching it. Tipping it over in the basin, he permitted a few drops to spill forth. He dabbed his fingers and touched them to his tongue. It was deliciously sweet – the finest water ever entertained on his palate. Glancing up from the basin, he noticed his window was not boarded as the others downstairs had been.

Cotton framed himself in Christian's doorway, watching with interest his young companion's reaction to the immaculate room. Catching him in the corner of his eye, Christian turned and exchanged a look of perplexity with the old man. Then, in quiet accord, as if sharing one mind, both of them re-entered the hallway and flung open all other doors save the innkeeper's, which was locked.

Every single room opened was as musty, dusty, filthy, and infested as the rest of the inn. Beds had been transformed into rat havens, the floor moved with insect life, and sunlight was excluded by the familiar boarded windows.

On the opening of the last room, Christian moved behind Cotton and whispered, "What in the name of God is going on here?"

Turning in profile, Cotton answered him in a voice suffused with dire resignation. "It appears that not only are we expected, we are known to be only two in number."

The weight of his words added to the already burdensome quiet, and the plain truth behind them served only to heighten their fear and concern over the inconceivable implications their tidy accommodations offered.

Reentering his quarters, Cotton submerged his weathered hands into the cool washbowl water, cupping them to bring the invigorating liquid to his face. He felt his weariness dissipate as he rubbed the water into his pores, returning to the basin to pour a handful down the back of his neck.

He heard the wood creak behind him and knew without raising his head that Christian stood in his doorway. "Yes?" he asked, as he dried his hands on his shirt.

Christian leaned against the doorframe, transferring much of his weight from his legs to the wooden jamb. "I'm going for a look about before we lose the sun completely."

Cotton turned and faced him with a serious demeanor. "Use caution, common sense, and do not wander off. I'll fetch our belongings from the coach."

Christian nodded and left. He wanted to walk around mainly because if he had gotten comfortable in his room he would have fallen asleep, his drained body being no match for the cozy bedding. He did not wish to fall into slumber solely that he might dream, but also because he was suspicious of the innkeeper and of the inn he kept.

As he carefully descended the noisy stair, he could not help but wish that Cotton was accompanying him. He had told Cotton of his walk certain of the soldier's compliance with his suggestion, but was astonished when the old man offered only words of advice.

Stepping amongst the scattered tables and strewn chairs across the front room, he kept his eyes on the pale orange light outlining the open doorway, and avoided observing the offal-covered tabletops and corners piled with rat excrement.

Emerging from the inn, he stretched, yawned, and gave thanks for the crisp breeze that enlivened him. Looking up and down the road, he saw nothing but occasional dust devils. Moving from the inn, he eyed the empty houses all in a row. The sun, touching the horizon in its fall from glory, set the houses afire in a faint golden-orange, reminiscent of the inn's illumined doorway. Houses the color of flame, Christian reflected. How suitable for Hell.

Continuing to distance himself from the inn, he caught a glimmer of sunlight reflected off one of the houses' obscured windowpanes. There must be a slight space between the boards, he thought, and a beam found its mark. Watching the twinkle of the faraway glass, it seemed to him that the house was not, in fact, vacant. Perhaps everyone in this village is as the innkeeper, he speculated, and in truth there are more persons here than are outwardly apparent. The idea sent shivers down his spine and forced him to move on.

Treading on a gravel path, he deserted the main road and ventured down a shallow embankment. After a short while, he found himself in a small thicket. Perusing the astoundingly lush vegetation, he discovered it to be an overgrown orchard. A lone apple tree was all that would bear fruit in the thicket, and so it was that he reached up and plucked himself a shiny, red apple from one of its healthy green boughs. It seemed odd to him that a tree would be offering ripe fruit in such a season, but he was no horticulturist, he was simply hungry.

With care he turned the piece of fruit over in his hands. He found it hard to believe that there were no blemishes, spoiling, or worms on the apple, especially in this place. I guess the bugs here prefer to make themselves snug in houses and not apples, he mused.

The apple was the reddest he had ever seen, its richness in color probably preparing the consumer for its richness in taste. His mouth watered at the sight of it, and his palms delighted in its handling. He raised it to his nose and was pleased to find that its aroma was consistent with all previous virtues.

Just as he was about to sate his whetted appetite on the ruby apple, from behind him came the snap of a broken twig. He froze, staring blankly at the apple just in front of his mouth. Please, God, his mind pled, let that be Cotton behind me. Gathering his courage, he swiftly pivoted and raised the apple as if it were a weapon. What he saw instantly reduced him to a fool, not merely because he defended himself with fruit, but rather the stature of his intended foe.

Sitting knees bound by arms against her chest, the little girl laughed at Christian's panicked posturing. The vanishing sun gave her white, toga-like garment an orange cast and colored her platinum blonde locks strawberry.

Christian lowered the apple but did not lower his guard, for he knew this to be the same child he had seen only last night surrounded by vicious wolves. Peering suspiciously about, he coldly asked, "Who are you, child?"

The girl stood and dramatically cast out her arms. "The cure that is worse than the disease!"

"What speak you about a cure? Whatever do you mean?"

The little girl giggled and gave him a fawning look.

He had no idea how the girl had arrived in Manasseh without the aid of a means of transportation, nor did he know why she hinted of a "cure", the very reason for his being here. All he knew was that he was going to get nowhere with this little creature unless he danced to her tune. This was no child, he decided, but it affected the likeness of one. And so it was to this image, this semblance of a little girl, that he had to confer his inquiries. His face assumed the kindest guise and he tenderly opened his arms. "Where are your parents, little one?"

The girl pointed to a tiny, ancient graveyard just beyond the thicket. "Sleeping."

"I am sorry about your mother and father," Christian said as he approached her, "I was not aware of a cemetery being there. Tell me their names and I shall put a garland upon their graves."

The girl shook her frilly locks in playful refusal.

"Here," he countered, drawing her attention to the apple in his hand, "take what I can give and enjoy."

She took the apple from him, and smiling gleefully pronounced, "You are truly worthy of my love."

Christian stroked her head and asked, "Have you any guardians to which I may speak?"

Taking a loud, juicy bite out of the apple, she replied past a mouthful, "The Baron cares for me ... the Baron cares for us all."

"And where does this Baron live, sweetness?"

"He doesn't," she responded sarcastically nonchalant.

Annoyed with this prolonged charade, Christian vented. "Let us put an end to this foolishness, child, wood nymph, or whatever you are! 'Tis important I find someone willing to address me in an adult fashion. My mission is of the gravest necessity, and many lives are at stake. Now, where might I find that which I seek?"

Placing her hand in his, the little girl led him to a clearing in the thicket, the village cemetery, a point where one acquired a view of a hillside obscured by the forest. There she pointed to a large castle resting atop the hill. "There is where you'll find the Baron," she quipped cheerfully. "He will be more than happy to address you ..."

Christian removed his eyes from the child just long enough to glance up at the castle. "I thought you said he was dead?"

When he received no answer, he looked down to discover the little girl had vanished, and that rather than her hand, he held his apple.

In daunted silence, he stared at the apple. Was it all an hallucination, a tired mind aimlessly remembering what he had thought he had seen a night ago? Turning the apple over in his hand, his heart skipped a beat. He could feel that deathly chill overcoming him, the dryness of his mouth and leaden belly presaging its arrival. His hands shook, his knees quaked, and his nerve buckled.

There, in the red, red apple, were the tooth marks of a little girl, the missing chunk gaping white amidst an orb of crimson.

Darting his head left and right, he tried to catch the child, but saw nothing. Not even her feet had left prints upon the dirty ground. All he was left with was an apple and an added burden to tax his stressed mind. Standing in a cemetery looking out at an ominous castle was too much for him to bear. Panicking, he dropped the precious fruit and ran.

Chasing him on the wind was the mirthful laughter of an unseen child.

Stumbling in his wicked shoes to get away from the evil thicket, Christian looked to the inn, that place of former repulsion, as a sanctuary. For there was where Cotton was, and though he was an old man, the sight of his imposing figure would lessen much of Christian's fear.

Holding no regard for the brambles and thorn bushes that grabbed at his clothing, he ran with a wild fervor. In his mind he saw the entire thicket coming to life, trying to snatch him back to the graveyard where a sunken grave was reserved for him.

Slipping on the loose gravel trail, he spilled out onto the main road. As the displaced dust blew from him, he could see the inn about thirty yards away. The fading sunlight struck only the angular roof, as if a beacon showing him the way. He rose to his feet in continuing flight and soon reached the inn's dark doorway.

Rushing inside, he was momentarily taken aback at its dimly lit interior. But before he could wonder who it was that had set out lighted wax candles on every table, his mind reeled. The inn was full!

Not a chair was left unoccupied. There must have been well over twenty townspeople; some seated, others leaning feebly against a table for support. With drawn faces they stared at Christian.

He returned their stares, noting nervously their pale, cankered skin and their hollow and distant eyes. These people resemble those suffering from the sickness rather than those spared from it, he thought. And from whence did they all come?

Frantically he started for the stairs. He had to find Cotton! Why do they persist in gawking at me? his mind screamed. Why do they look at me so? Keeping as far from the occupied tables as possible, he hurried past them. Before he could set one foot upon the bottom step, he heard someone whisper his name.

"Christian."

Following the sound, he traced it to a table which had been set apart from the rest to his right. The scrape marks on the dusty floor attested to its having been moved only recently. There, with his back to the wall, sat Smith-Patton.

Hastening to him, Christian stopped in front of the table and leaned across. "There's nothing holy here!" he gasped loudly, out of breath. "This town is cursed by the Devil!"

"Shut up and be seated!" hissed Cotton forcefully, his eyes darting nervously in his head.

Adamant, Christian stood his ground. "Do you hear me?"

Grabbing him by the cuff, Cotton pulled Christian down into the seat next to him. "Look, listen, and learn, Christian. I've no time to mother ye." He nodded his head at the queer patrons. "Observe the company we presently keep."

Christian slowly glanced behind, allowing only his eyes to peek over his shoulder. He saw them, in huddled little groups whispering amongst each other, their eyeballs glued to him.

"Note how pale they are," Cotton continued, "and how they greet us with hungry looks."

Christian saw that everything the Scot said was true. The eyes of the people of Manasseh were full of a craving he dared not suppose.

"And from whence do they come?" Cotton added to his confused misery.

Catching an evil gleam in the eye of one of the townsfolk, Christian shuddered and turned away.

Cotton leaned forward in his chair, intent on filling Christian in. "They came shortly after I returned with our bags from the coach. I heard them wander in and thought ye had returned with people ye had found on your walk. When I saw 'twas not so, I took a table and awaited your return. I'd not let ye walk through that door alone into this den of wolves." Taking a swig from the cask of ale Christian had brought from Bantingham, he went on. "Not one has indulged me in conversation to seek out me business here. It's as if they know ... they know why we are here."

"We are in agreement," Christian interrupted. "I myself have just had a most strange encounter of which I shall tell you later. But please, go on, what more do you imply?"

"That someone is expecting us. I don't know who or why, but someone has gone to the trouble of preparing our rooms in anticipation of our visit." He scratched his head, grasping at straws, "Perhaps Stemmons notified someone here, although he never told me so he may have forgotten."

"He would not inform the people of our coming!" protested Christian. "I have the authority to steal if necessary, and I —"

"Steal?"

"Yes," Christian replied, with a modicum of shame.

"Do ye have the authority to kill?"

"What?" he blurted, mortified.

"To kill," Cotton repeated coolly. He then surveyed the throng with unsubtle distaste and remarked, "I have seen starving dogs in unchristian lands with less hunger in their eyes for roast mutton."

At Christian's urging, for he could not bear the weight of the stares any longer, they withdrew to the privacy of his room.

Cotton transferred what little baggage he had into Christian's room. Sitting on Christian's bed, he undid a leather wrap and produced a medium-sized hatchet. The axe was roughly two-thirds of a yard in length, and crowned with a mean hook. Wielding it in his right hand, he proudly claimed, "Lochaber. The best hand weapon any man could ask for. Many have I felled with this same axe."

He handed it to Christian, who hefted it admiringly in the candlelight. "Not heavy. I would venture five pounds," said Christian.

"That would be correct. I cut down the handle so it could be stowed." Cotton took it from him as if he were only a boy and replaced it in its bag. "How is it outside?" he asked, pointing to the window. "Do we have a good moon?"

Christian arose to look out the window. When he turned his back to Cotton, the sly soldier removed the long dagger from his belt and buried it deep within one of Christian's many bags. He then sat back and acted as if nothing were peculiar.

"Looks as though we may be in for rain," Christian sighed as he watched the night clouds roll above as if the sky were one, big, dark unruly sea. Turning to Cotton, he added almost sadly, "I see no moon."

"Very well," Cotton smiled as he reclined comfortably across the bed. "Now, come here."

Christian left the window and sat down next to Cotton's legs.

"I have shown ye the axe so that if the need arises and I am unable to reach me bag ye may do so," he patted the bundled leather.

"I pray it doesn't come to that," Christian said, shaking his head.

"Aye, but I fear it might."

Changing the unpleasant subject, Christian pointed to the large scar marring Cotton's forehead and asked, "Where did you get that?"

"Germany. 'Tis where I got most of me wounds."

"The Thirty Years War."

"Ye know your history well."

"I escape by reading. More often than not I wish I were a part of something monumental. It seems I am destined to live out a life of unexceptional stock."

"Everyone has their place in history," Cotton assured him, "ye will find yours, for better or worse." The mention of history brought Cotton to remember his own military exploits, the most painful coming to mind first. "When I fought at Preston, I had me fill of history. Historians tell only of the nobility or chivalry of such adventures, never do they speak of the horrors involved." His face flinched in bitter reflection. "The people of Preston treated we Scots as scoundrels, not liberators. The entire battle was a wet, bloody mess. What little powder we had was damp, and the men were fatigued with disillusion. 'Twas a total rout, a dishonorable surrender which even today I have trouble addressing."

"Did you never see the good General Monck?"

"I met with him once after I had turned me loyalties from Parliament to the king. We Scots had no business in your civil wars, although I was deeply saddened upon hearing of the king's execution."

"Tell me of your other expeditions, ones concerning voyages outside of England."

Cotton sat up and removed his protective coat. Standing, he set it near Christian, who touched its thick leather with awe.

"What is this article of dress you wear?" he asked.

"'Tis me buff coat, issued to me near twenty years ago," Cotton said as he pulled his shirt from his trousers. "It can withstand a pike thrust, and protects the wearer from a musket ball at fifty yards."

"Amazing."

"Aye, I know from experience it works well." He began unbuttoning his shirt and then stopped, asking, "Ye still wish to hear of me adventures in distant lands and exotic places?"

"Oh, yes," said Christian, looking up, perplexed at Cotton's undressing.

Seeing Christian's confused appearance, Cotton quickly explained. "The story of me life is written in the scarring of me skin; when age has made the mind forgetful, 'tis often helpful to have physical reminders." He finished unbuttoning his shirt and threw it to Christian.

Christian caught the shirt and laid it atop the heavy buff coat. On seeing Cotton bare-chested, he was startled. He was not sure whether it was due to the surprisingly firm, athletic build of the old man, or if it were the numerous scars lining his torso. Like cracks in a statue, he thought as he examined every fissure, however minute, on the broad chest and thick arms of the Scotsman.

Gazing down his abdomen, Cotton gingerly traced his lined blemishes until he came to the one he so desired. A long, straight scar, deeper than most and horizontally segmenting his bellybutton, it ran the expanse of his slight paunch. He could not refrain from grinning as he softly fingered it. "This one was given to me by an enraged Turk. 'Twas during one of me more exotic missions." The sharply etched wrinkles of his grin grew faint as he had a more sobering recollection. "Had I not taken evasive action, I would have suffered a gelding's fate."

"Why would a Turk wish to castrate you?"

"He caught me with his woman."

The lighthearted way in which Cotton replied compelled both men to nervous laughter.

"Ah, she was well worth it, though!" swore Cotton as he came out of his bout of laughter. Rubbing his forehead, he felt the deforming line engraved across his brow and instantly grew cold. It was as if the sudden remembrance of the scar, or rather how he had received it, triggered some inner anguish which expelled the spirit of hilarity from his body. Angrily stroking it as if to wipe it from his flesh, he looked at Christian in all seriousness, and coldly advised, "Never trust a woman, Christian. 'Twill be your undoing."

His recollection-induced gravity caused their minds to once again examine their present plight, that of being in a town peopled by weird looking and queer acting persons. They uneasily noticed how during the entire duration of their conversation they heard not a single noise from below. It was as if they were the only people inhabiting the inn, despite the hungry crowd downstairs.

Cotton sunk down next to Christian on the bed and picked up his shirt. Putting it on, he asked, "What was it ye wanted to tell me before?"

Thinking of the strange little girl and not wanting to cause Cotton further worry, he replied with postured indifference, "Oh, that was nothing. I simply came across an old castle on a hill north of here."

"Was it abandoned?"

"I believe it to be so, for when it was revealed to me it appeared in ruins."

"In this place that could mean it's inhabited by the Duke of York himself."

"From the people I have seen, I'd venture Cromwell to be prince of these lands."

Cotton nodded at Christian's dry wit, but could find no proper response and so sat in thought.

Christian, pressured by fear to continue his discourse, abruptly turned to the essence of their journey. "Why do you believe this place to be free of the Reaper?"

"I do not."

"But none have died for many a year."

"See ye these people here?" Cotton pointed to the floor. "They do not avoid Death, but rather walk hand in hand with him."

"Regardless of how they look, they live! We must find the cure and remedy the ills of England."

Cotton stared blankly at the window. "Some have claimed to have seen between the early hours of one and three, the souls of people ascending to Heaven from the ravages of London ... a great many souls there were."

Christian perceived sadness in Cotton's voice. He was so moved by this that he had to inquire why Cotton so cared for the good of England. "How come you to reside in London," he asked, "center of a nation which abhors both your nationality and your chosen religion?"

"I know of no other home," the tragic Scot answered, for the first time sounding like the tired, old man he was. "Me family speaks in the tongue of Luther, if I were to return I would not last long."

"Then why not Ireland? Why not live there?"

"Perhaps," he said, arching his brow and concealing his scar in wrinkles, "but that is later."

The misery in the man's voice was so strong that it affected Christian as well. Lacking the comforts and joys of a family he sired, never to know what has become of his clan, Cotton sacrificed all for what he believed to be the true religion. Could I make that sacrifice? Christian asked himself. Deciding it best to depart from the melancholy matter, Christian put on his best smile and playfully mocked, "Father Stemmons claims you are the blackest sheep in all of the Lord's flock."

"Stemmons is a fool and a lecher!" a moody Cotton flared. "Do ye really believe we are here for the benefit of the Church and for the health of the country? Ha! I doubt anyone knows even of our existence!"

"But Father Stemmons informed the Pope …"

"The Pope! Is that what he told ye? Christ, and I thought I was a-goin' to Hell! The man will burn for being a lousy liar!" He stood and stretched to ease his frustration. He could see he had to calm down in order to get through to him. He knew Christian knew he was right, but didn't want to accept that the trip was all for naught. "Christian," he softly chided, "don't be so naive. He wants whatever 'tis we find for himself. He'll probably only offer it to those who can pay."

Christian saw that he should have left the irate soldier to his lamenting rather than inciting him to argument. He knew Cotton to be correct, but as was his nature, he could not let a dispute go without exploring all its advocacies. "How can you say such things against the honor of a man who has devoted his life to God?"

"Because 'tis the truth."

"One cannot consider himself good simply by pointing to the misdeeds of others."

"I do nothing of the kind. I am a soldier by trade, not a priest. The only hypocrisy I can be accused of is treason. The soul I damn is me own. What of our Father? Who pays for his hypocrisies?"

"If you feel so, then why do you serve him, traversing hard forest road in cold, windy night for what? Who be the hypocrite here?"

"I am doing me penance."

"You give penance to a man you despise?"

"I give penance to a God I love! A God I have forsaken all I cherish for! Stemmons be not of one farthing value to me! 'Tis God I serve, sir. Who is it that is your master?"

The savagery of Cotton's reply tore into Christian with all its simplicity. He not only believes in God but loves Him as well, Christian noted. I find it difficult to do one or the other, let alone both.

Draped in silence, the room became almost unbearable, and if it were not for their fear they would have left each other's company at once. As it was, they sat mutely and avoided eye contact. After several minutes, Cotton finally spoke.

"Tell me, Christian," he uttered in a half-whisper, "why do ye serve this lecher?"

"I seek only to serve our Lord."

Cotton saw right through his fiction. Staging an outrage he cried, "That is a bold-faced lie! Liar! Liar! Ye blacken His name! Ye seek only to take what the Church offers; education, a better life, but seek not to return." With thick disgust, he concluded, "I've seen your kind before, am I not mistaken?"

Troubled in his confrontation with the truth, Christian bowed his head in shame and sighed, "Yes, 'tis valid what you claim."

"Then be wary, me friend, for those who misuse the tools of the Lord shall come to no good end."

Cotton saw how he had disgraced and worried his friend, and although it hurt him, he knew it to be for the boy's good. Rising, he walked to the window and looked out over the dark town. Not a light could be seen in either window or doorway. Peering up at the rapidly approaching storm clouds, he sought the moon. Without moonlight they might as well have been in an abyss, for the roiling night sky made it difficult to see not more than three yards in the dark.

As the black clouds spread themselves across the sky, foreboding the severity of the storm to come, a momentary lull caused an opening through which the serene moon peeked. For a few moments the immediate countryside was illumined, and Cotton took advantage of this good fortune. Casting his gaze back to the town, he saw every detail; rooftops reflected the blue-white moonlight and every minute, overgrown dirt road was aglow. So well could he see by the light of the moon that even the planks boarding all of the windows and doors were discernible.

Then he saw something in those few, scant rays of moonbeam that made his blood run cold and forced him to throw open the window in order to obtain a better view.

"No!" he screamed above the howling wind. "No!"

Christian rose from his seat on the bed, concerned over the way Cotton reacted. He could see the man's hands tightly gripping the windowsill in anguished frustration as he thrust his body halfway out the window and into the night, his white hair flailing in the unkind wind. What now? Christian wondered, never really wishing to find out what it was that had made his brave soldier friend such a miserable wreck. As the frigid wind flooded into the room and chilled his already shaking frame, he rushed to Cotton's side. "What is it?" he demanded above the din of the wind. "What is the matter?"

"No!" Cotton repeated over and over again. "No!"

Grabbing his shoulder and pulling him back into the room, Christian shouted, "What? In God's name, whatever is it that you deny?"

"The coach!" he cried, seizing Christian in his arms as a raging gale buffeted both of them. "The horses! They are gone!"

The words tumbling from Cotton's mouth shivered Christian more so than any tempest ever could. Without the coach, without the horses, they were trapped here, in this wretched, isolated place. He could feel the bile welling up in his throat and the nervous pangs of nausea twisting in his stomach. My God, he prayed, to be trapped anywhere but here!

"We left the horses in the square when we searched the town, remember?" Cotton reminded him.

All Christian could manage was a nod in agreement.

"When I went back for our items, I thought it best not to retrieve the horses," the Scot explained, "for the square was the best place for them to graze and there wasn't a soul about to molest them." He took a deep breath, "Finding the inn full upon returning, I feared leaving to get them in the event ye needed me and I was gone from the only place ye knew me to be."

"Perhaps they wandered off," said Christian, his eyes painfully straining in the dimming moonshine to see some movement, anything that might reassure him of the horses' whereabouts. He saw nothing. The cruel clouds had hid the moon once again, plunging the town into an even greater darkness and frustrating Christian to the point of madness. "I can't see a damned thing!" he complained. "Cotton, let's go look for them."

"Nay."

"Nay? Nay? My God, man! Do you not realize that without those beasts we are incapable of leaving here? That we are trapped?"

"Aye," said Cotton dejectedly, "whoever has anticipated our arrival has conspired against us. We'll not find those horses, for they've been taken from us. They'd not walk off on their own." He sat himself down in a corner and popped the cork out of his keg of ale.

When Christian saw what he was about to do, he flew into a rage. "I'll not have you drink yourself into a stupor now!" he blared as he sailed from the window. "You'll not drown your sorrows here!" He tore the keg from Cotton's hands as precious alcohol spilled out onto the floor.

"Give it back to me, Christian," Cotton demanded, getting up from his corner with a malicious glint in his eyes.

"No. I will not!" said Christian, nervously backing towards the window.

"Give it here!"

"Bugger off!"

Christian felt the billowing wind and saw that he was next to the open window. Returning his eyes to Cotton, he could not help but smile.

"No!" Cotton cried in desperation. "Don't ye do it!"

"To hell with you!" Christian yelled as he threw the wooden keg out the window and into the darkness.

Cotton lunged at him and gripped his arms, forcing them to his side. He then hurled him against the wall, pushing him back up before he could fall down. Holding Christian by the throat, he muttered, "Don't ye ever do that to me again."

Christian looked the sorry drunk in the eye. "Do what?" he asked angrily. "Prevent you from endangering our lives? Have you forgotten where we are?"

He could see the anger bleed from Cotton's face, replaced by intense shame. Redirecting his eyes, Christian wished the old man would redirect his breath, which so reeked of alcohol that he nearly gagged.

"I'm sorry, Christian," Cotton said sadly as he removed his hand from his ward's throat. "'Tis not me, 'tis the brew."

"'Tis all right, Cotton," Christian mumbled as he fixed his collar, "just do not let it happen again."

As Christian started to move past him, the elder man reached out and touched his arm. "I swear I'll not swallow another drop for as long as we're here," he assured him, eyes clouding.

Christian studied him with contempt, but his heart was so moved by Cotton's tears of pity that he forgave him. "Very good, my friend," he consoled, taking the blacksmith's rough hands in his own. "Very good."

Gradually rising above the noisy wind was a familiar, methodic click-clocking. Brought into the room on the violent breeze, the distant sound grew nearer.

Cocking their ears, the men's hearts leapt with joy; it was the horses! They had returned to their masters!

As this realization dawned on them, all former complaints between the two vanished. Smiling at each other, irrespective of the dispute that had nearly forced them to blows only a moment before, they sprang to the open window. It was a while before their eyes adjusted to the pitch dark outside, the moon being of no help to them. They could hear, but not see, that the horse-drawn coach was somewhere below them.

"Would to God if I could only see those valiant steeds!" Christian exclaimed happily.

Cotton patted him on the back in concurrence.

"We'll be able to leave here, Cotton. We'll be able to go."

"That we will," added Cotton, drying his eyes with his shirt sleeves, "and I'll never let those horses from me sight!"

Feeling carefree and that all was right with their world, they laughed long and hard.

"Come," said Cotton, motioning to the door, "let us retrieve our horses before they pass us by!"

He started for the door, but Christian reached out and took hold of his arm. "Wait," he cautioned, "something is not as it should be." He craned his neck and stuck his head out the window. "The horses have stopped."

"What?"

"They no longer move. Listen."

Cotton stepped closer to the window and listened hard. "Right ye are! The bonny beasts must be a-waiting for us downstairs. Let's go." Turning from the window, he proceeded to the door, but before he could lay a hand on it, Christian called out again.

"Hold!"

"What is it now?" Cotton groaned.

Providence had decided that the moon should once more illuminate their view, and just as it had done the first time what was revealed to them withered their spirits.

There, in the fleeting light, below him to the right, Christian saw the coach. Its horses brayed nervous, visible breaths and shook their black manes restlessly. He also saw a figure mounted atop, a thin silhouette of a man in whose hands rested a long straight whip. The horses did not come here of their own accord, he thought, they were driven by some strange individual.

Before Cotton could return to the window, the vision was gone, smothered once more by the darkness.

Christian, aware now of the cold, ducked his head back into the room and shut the window. The sound of the wind was instantly cut off and the unpleasant silence returned.

"What's wrong with ye?" asked Cotton, somewhat nervous.

"I believe I know why the horses have returned the coach to us."

"And why is that?"

"Because someone has driven them to it."

Cotton's eyes widened in disbelief. "What? Someone rides the coach?"

"Yes. I caught a glimpse of someone ... a man, seated at your place, the driver's place."

Shifting his eyes to his feet, Cotton rubbed his chin in demonstration of silent thought.

"He had in his hands a long whip ..." Christian went on, attempting to somehow influence his experienced companion's decision.

"Ye are certain that the coach is ours?" Cotton abruptly queried, without lifting his gaze.

"Oh, yes. Quite sure."

"Then it seems," he ruminated aloud, "that our unseen patron has sent for us. Having no coach of his own with which to usher us to his lodgings, he commandeered ours and placed upon it his own man."

Christian gave Cotton a long, hard look. He knew that what he had said was more than likely true, only he didn't want it to be. For it only confirmed what he himself already knew; that someone held complete control over them.

Walking closer to him and peering out the window, Cotton muttered, "If only we knew where his lodgings were we would know where we were about to be taken."

"I believe I know where he who has expected us resides," Christian whispered, as though he were in church. He then slowly raised his eyes to the far wall of the room as if he could see beyond the wood and masonry, through the line of forest trees, to the steeply sloped hill and the castle that sat upon it.

Descending the warped and rotten wooden stairs, Christian and Cotton re-entered the large front room of the inn. To their unpleasant dismay, they discovered that the inn was still packed with townsfolk. Because they had heard no noise while in their rooms, they had thought, or rather hoped, that the strange people had left. Avoiding the ravenous looks that were cast their way, the two briskly headed for the doorway. Nagging at their conscience was that even now, visibly seeing the mass of ill patrons, they still did not hear anything save for the blustering wind outside.

*All they do is stare at us,* Christian mentally complained, *look at us with famished derangement.*

Pulling open the inn door, Cotton allowed the displeasing wind entrance into the room. He turned to Christian, but saw beyond him that not one of the townspeople even shuddered. *We are wrapped in our coats and our bones clatter,* he thought, *but they wear little and do not even flinch!*

With this in mind, he quickly ushered his friend out the inn and followed, slamming the door behind them.

Outside, the wind was merciless in its pounding. The cold tore through their bodies, frosting the very skeletons supporting them. Huddling together, the pair made their way slowly to where they had seen the coach.

"Why is it so much colder here than in London?" Christian chattered.

"I suspect 'tis because of the storm clouds. They're bloated with water," shouted Cotton above a gale's shriek.

Turning a corner, they came upon the coach. Their coach. There was no doubt about it in either of their minds, whoever it was that had sent for them had been responsible for the abduction of their ride. The familiar black mares fidgeted uneasily in their leather binds.

They did not notice him at first — that is the coachman. He was not seated in a position at the helm, but rather stood alongside the horses. He was so tall and thin that he was eclipsed by the vehicle, appearing at first as only a shadow or trick of veiled moonlight. He let his presence be known by opening the coach door.

To Christian and Cotton, the opening of the door first appeared to be the work of the wind, for the coachman was still invisible to their eyes. They soon perceived, however, the shape of the tall man, and it frightened them that they had been so close to him and had not seen him.

Once he was recognized by the men, he became more clear in their minds. He wore a high-crowned hat with a wide brim pulled low and an oversized riding coat with the collar raised. The low brim and raised collar hid well the man's face, and the complete black of his attire shrouded the proportions of his body in the darkness of the night.

"You have come for us?" Christian yelled at the tall man not more than two yards away.

The man did not answer, but rather chose to let the wind speak for him.

Cotton traded looks with his younger companion, then bellowed, "Where is it ye are to take us?"

Again the tall man did not interrupt the oratorio of the air. He simply stood before them, his eyes fixed on some distant point above their heads, and patiently held the door.

Christian turned to Cotton and cupped his hands to the old man's ear, whispering, "What is it we shall do?"

Whether prodded by curiosity, some element of possible danger, or the natural desire to get out of the cold, Cotton answered his friend by entering the swallowing dark of the coach's interior.

For a moment Christian was dazed. How could he so freely enter destined for where he knew not? he sourly wondered. Only a simpleton would behave in such a way! He then felt a sharp gust numb his back, and hurriedly rejoined his friend inside.

Their mute coachman closed the door and limped to the front of the coach, where he climbed up onto his seat. With a snap of the reins and a crack of the whip, they were soon off.

Inside, seated against the cab wall nearest the front, Christian let his trepidations pour forth. "What are we doing? Why are we allowing the wind to forsake our better judgment and go willingly wherever 'tis this man is taking us?"

"Curiosity," said Cotton dryly as he looked him wearily in the eye. He was tired of the youth's incessant queries, tired of the annoying fear he so often displayed. For one so smart he should be able to figure a few things out by himself, he thought with exasperation.

He doesn't understand! Christian realized, looking at the worn old man. He cannot fathom the dread evil at which I blanch. I know where we are going! I don't know how, but somehow I do. We are running blindly to that castle upon the hill, that place to which the wicked child pointed and laughed. I cannot begin to imagine, for fear, who or what dwells there.

Glancing out the window, the same window through which he had seen the girl and her wolves, he could not help but feel a sense of loss, as if in bereavement. What is it that causes me such grief? he thought, sifting through his tumbling emotions. Is it for us that I so lament? He sought the quick comfort of his Bible, but to his horror found it not where he had left it.

His view offered him little, for the moon shyly kept behind her clouds, but what he could see was typical to the area. Withered shrubs, diseased and gnarled trees, and a general lack of vegetative prosperity vitiated the encompassing landscape. To come to terms with Death here was unavoidable, he thought, for evidence of his work was everywhere.

For a moment he lost his train of thought as the coach violently tossed and turned over a particularly rough spot in the poor road. Shielding himself from battery, he leaned against the coach's interior. He soon regained his wits, and with renewed indignation yelled at Cotton above the noise of the rocking coach. "What of our baggage? What of that which is our only safeguard?"

Cotton slid across from his seat to one beside Christian. He was infuriated that the foolish boy should make known his axe and was intent on that reference never leaving the walls of this coach. "Christian," he assertively whispered, "if ye make mention of those bags, or of what they contain, I shall give ye a good smacking!" He could see anger flush red Christian's face. The boy is not afraid of me, he thought. Good.

Christian wanted to scream out, he wanted to chastise the dimwitted old man, but instead held back. With a temperate tone he enunciated his words clearly: "Why did we not simply leave with our bags as opposed to leaving without them?"

Disgusted, Cotton moved away, muttering, "Shut up about the bags … ye think too much." He sat his tired bones down on the cushioned seat opposite Christian and looked blearily out his window. He was getting too old. *The anger I showed the boy was me vain, old pride,* he reflected. *'Twas I who neglected the horses – I, who in a state of excitement, forgot the bags.* He glanced out of the corners of his eyes and beheld his troubled companion. *Christian cannot be held to account for any of our mishaps, for he has placed his trust in me and 'tis I who continually fail.* The argument over the ale back at the inn flashed inside his head and he closed his eyes in self-loathing. *I must be strong for Christian,* he encouraged himself. *I shall never let him down again. Never!*

The black horses drew the coach up a steep slope, causing the cab to tilt backward. Unable to maintain his seat at such an angle, Christian plopped down next to Cotton. Casting his neighbor a look of aversion, he channeled his attention outside the cab. *Where was the castle?* he thought. *Where was it?*

He did not have to wait long for an answer. A few, short moments later and they could feel the coach leveling. The pace slowed and it seemed almost as if they were coasting.

Christian strained his eyesight, attempting to see out his window into the moonless night. He saw nothing, but the sluggish trot of the horses said otherwise. Pressing his face against the cold window glass, he strained all the harder.

Then suddenly it was upon him.

The castle walls loomed from out of the darkness like rising tombstones to dwarf the approaching coach. The weathered brick seemed to grow as the horses pulled them near, almost as if it was inflating itself in expectation of visitors.

From his seat at the window, Christian saw that although in serious disrepair, the castle was crafted expertly. Every brick was perfectly matched with an equal, culminating in a grand motif of eight sides. The castle's octagonal design was mimicked in its towers, which bloated at every corner in a most exquisite fashion.

Between two of the foremost towers he spied a portcullis gate. Its resemblance to an open mouth with sharp, pointed teeth could not escape Christian's active imagination. *So,* he joylessly mused as the coach neared the entrance, *we pass into the maw of Death.*

Arrow loop embrasures looked down on him like hungry eyes. The contrast of their shadowed recesses on the light gray brick captured his attention and drew his gaze upwards, above the broad gateway. There his eyes read in horror a crudely carved motto as his lips whispered in dire affirmation, *"Lasciate ogne speranza voi ch'intrate."*

"What was that?" asked Cotton, leaning closer to his companion. "What was it ye just said?

*"Lasciate ogne speranza voi ch'intrate,"* repeated Christian. "'Tis Italian, meaning: Abandon every hope all those who enter here."

Cotton sat bewildered. What is the meaning of this? he questioned his failing reason. How is it that we are confounded at every turn of events?

The words soon disappeared from their line of vision, gone from their eyes but seared into their brains, as they were drawn into the castle's gateway portal. The gate being raised, the little coach was soon devoured by the mammoth of brick and mortar.

Once he had passed through the archway, Christian was seized by an attack of the shivers. He felt as he had earlier in the town – as if his soul had left him, as if he had given up the ghost. This sensation terrified him, but he kept it from Cotton for he did not wish to add further vinegar to the old man's open nerves. There he sat, huddled like a mouse before a playful cat, unable to cease his quaking and barely able to hide it in the darkened cab.

He was going to die, he painfully acknowledged. Here he would meet his death.

After what only amounted to a few seconds, but seemed an eternity and a half, the coach emerged from the gateway and entered a fairly large courtyard.

Here were the castle grounds: an expanse of dead grass and withered trees surpassing even the town in dilapidated rot. Christian could hardly believe his eyes, for although he had not expected much better than what he had already seen below, he did not imagine it could be any worse.

His eyes narrowed at the waste – the jaundiced grass and anemic shrubbery, the sickly oaks and peaked elms with their roots exposed and their leaves turned to mulch on the branch. Even the soil seemed somehow sapped, as if the castle was a great cancer upon the land which sucked the very vitality from the surrounding countryside, enfeebling Mother Nature herself.

While Christian was distracted by the forsaken surroundings, Cotton took note of the sound structure of the castle. Admiring the battlements as only a former soldier could, his eyes stopped at their parapets. Squinting in disbelief, he saw there that several corpses were impaled through the chest, hanging from iron shafts in a blatant display of perversity. Occasionally one would twist in the teasing wind, its ragged clothing losing a few more strips to the weather. There were many of them that he could see, and many more that he assumed he could not – for they were not restricted to lining the interior parapets, but extended to surrounding the upper level of the castle itself. These guests that would never leave would provide a gruesome view to anyone looking out of a second floor window. The shafts were fixed in an orderly way, directly above the thin ledge underlining the windows.

It did not shock Cotton, for in his many campaigns he had seen worse. What did alarm him, however, was that this inhumanity was committed during a time of peace and not of war, and that there were so large a number of them. It could be said that there was an impaled man for every side of every one of the towers.

The coach came to a slow stop, and Cotton opened his door and leapt out. Following, Christian stood beside him before being gently nudged and shown the impaled corpses. Christian was at first horrified, and then angered, that someone would so treat a person's remains. Pointing at the grisly parapets, he accosted their coachman, "Does your master always treat his guests in such fashion?"

The only reply offered by the coachman was the crackle of his whip as he directed the horses away.

Watching their transport leave through the gateway from whence it had just come, Cotton quipped, "He must be related to the innkeeper."

Christian returned his eyes to the wind-battered cadavers weaving overhead. How many there are, he noted as he turned his head to see them all. I wonder how long they have been up there?

Glimpsing Cotton abandoning him, he shifted his eyes from their grim feast and watched where his tall friend was going. He saw him approach a large, ornate doorway housing a broad wooden door. He hadn't seen the beautiful doorway before because of his preoccupation with the courtyard and the dead swinging high above them.

Flanked by thick pilasters topped by Corinthian capitals, the white marble doorway was surmounted by a rounded pediment. Obviously not indigenous to the castle, Christian noted as he slowly walked closer, probably of Italian design.

Above this ingeniously crafted portal was a mullioned stained glass window depicting the fall of Lucifer. The light from within the castle illuminated the red of the Devil's skin, making beauteous that which was so hideous.

Enclosing the intricately assembled glass was an angular arch that recalled the architecture of antiquity. Looking at it in the context of a stone frame for the biblically inspired window, Christian took it to be symbolic of the Trinity. How the power of a religious piece is reduced to mere art when set in the confines of this keep, he grimly judged.

Reaching Cotton's side and standing slightly behind him to the left, he looked on as the wide hand of the Scot reached up and took a firm hold of the big, brass, demon's head knocker centered high on the oak door.

Glancing over his shoulder at his nervous companion, Cotton affected a smile and announced, "Let us see who is home." He then raised the knocker and let it fall three times.

All at once, from deep within the castle, came a rising tide of sound. A huge outpouring of intense emotion, of elation at the prospects of having visitors, was vocalized in many feminine tongues from inside. Joyous whispers and excited giggles merged to form one, all-woman choir that loudly heralded the arrival of the cold and weary Londoners.

Looking to one another for support in their confusion, Christian took a step back and Cotton gently reached out and clasped his shoulder, giving it a light squeeze and holding him in place.

Then, as abruptly as it had begun, the intense cacophony ceased.

As it often had, the quiet which followed was far more agonizing.

The sound of bolts being eased back and of locks being turned echoed throughout the courtyard and imbued the air with an unpleasant anticipation.

Christian's eyes bore hard into the door, as did Cotton's. Any moment now that door would swing wide and reveal the fiend responsible for all their present miseries.

Creaking ever so lightly, the heavy door was slowly pulled open to expose the outline of a woman clothed in a white nightgown. The light pouring from behind her made her face indiscernible but her gown transparent, unveiling a figure unrivaled in all the sculptures of ancient Rome.

Abashed, Cotton diverted his gaze. Christian could not, however, take his eyes from the perfection before him. Seeing only her shape and not her face, he had the strange sensation that he knew her from somewhere before.

The woman drew a fine, three-pronged candelabrum from behind the door, the added candlelight returning the cloaking of her gown. Holding it near her cheek, she displayed to the men a face that would cause fair Helen jealousy.

Stunned by her beauty, the two stood in awed silence. It was as if she were Medusa, and had rendered them to stone not through her foulness, but through her excellence.

With a slight smile, as if mildly embarrassed at the unspoken tribute being paid her, the ravishing lady greeted them with a voice sweeter than that of Philomel the nightingale.

"Welcome to Castel de Mormeau — our home." Her eyes seductively fell upon Christian and she sighed, "I am sure you will enjoy your stay ..."

# Chapter Five

Christian kept his eyes on their handsome lady as he followed Cotton past her and into the wide anteroom of the castle. How fine she is! his heart rejoiced. How she intoxicates all who look upon her with love.

Cotton was also pleased with their hostess. He wore a doting smile, although his eyes betrayed a less than fatherly affection.

Closing the door and barring it, the lady turned to them. Behind her a lit torch lent its light to Christian's biased imagination, forming a halo about her pretty head.

Christian nearly swooned. *The radiance of her beauty shines forth like rays from Heaven! Indeed, how she looks most angelic, how very tender and womanly her form! Her nose is a dainty bit centered squarely on her rounded, but not too rounded, face. Her hair is as the raven in color and falls to about the mid of her back: as dark and as long as the night itself. Worn loose and flowing, it gives her the contradictory appearance of a wanton angel. Her eyes are darker even than her midnight hair, but gentle and loving. Her eyebrows are full and thick, being separate and not bushy, but smooth and well formed. Her mouth is neither big nor small, but of a perfect pout. And her lips! Oh, to plant a kiss upon those velvet pillows! Of such a healthy red hue they are that they invite kisses without even her voiced inducement. Her skin is of the purest snow, she being whiter than her own gown, and her copious breasts a certain delight to suckling babes. Indeed, I swear that I have never seen beauty so bestowed upon an individual! She is the loveliest creature I have ever laid eyes on! What I would not do to lie in those arms, to kiss those lips, to—*

A frightful notion popped into his head, one that would return him to his adherence of caution. What if this woman was the dark lady of his dreams? He had never been able to remember much of the lady after he had awoken, only that she was irresistibly attractive – not unlike his present hostess.

'Tis only a dream, he assured himself, a figment of my lustful imagination. But try as he could to convince himself of this, he remained uneasy in her presence.

For the moment being disenchanted with her excellence, he looked over the anteroom. A raised ceiling and a spiraling stone staircase marked this otherwise plain room. Several torches lined the brick walls and he noticed two doorways: one directly opposite the front door, and the other on the wall adjacent to it. He saw through these doorways that the rest of the castle was not as well lit as the room in which they were. He also marked how dusty everything was, not unlike the inn. Glancing up at the high ceiling, he caught sight of cobwebs dangling from the rafters. How could anyone live in this place? he marveled.

Their feminine attendant moved between them to the stairs. As she climbed the impressive staircase, she charmingly commanded, "Follow me."

"Why have we been brought here?" Christian asked, more than a little anger coloring his words.

With a winsome smile, she replied, "Because the Baron wishes it."

"And where is this Baron?"

"The Baron will see you shortly," she said nonchalantly. "I will show you to your rooms. From now on, you will be staying here."

Fear flashed across the faces of the men simultaneously. They were to stay here for how long? Forever?

"Fear not," said she, "Horst, our coachman, shall bring you your belongings from the inn."

Both men thought the same thing, but dared not ask it. How did she know they had any baggage at all? It could be mere conjecture on her part, but her tone betrayed her certainty of their having luggage. Trading cold glances, they silently understood each other's suspicions.

Looking up at the woman on the stairs, Christian's heart was once again moved by her beauty. God's own handmaiden stands before us, he mused, and yet I must not be swayed by her sight. Sometimes the most dangerous animals in the world are its most beautiful.

He watched as she turned from him with a smile, and with one hand pulling up her hem, restarted her climb. He could not help but inquire as to what her name was, reasoning that that which brings one so much pleasure should not go unknown. "May I ask our gracious peeress for a name?"

She countered with an obviously mocked suspicion, showing pleasure rather than annoyance at his request. "And who is it that wishes to know?"

"Christian Coleswitten, my Lady," he responded with heartfelt solemnity, crossing his legs and bowing to her. Then rising, he pointed to Cotton. "This is my friend, the smith Cotton Smith-Patton."

Cotton duly paid her his homage as Christian had done before.

Continuing, Christian added, "We are but weary travelers from London who seek only a warm meal and a place to rest."

"London?" said the lady in astonishment. "Whatever is it that has brought you from that most dear city to our little hamlet?"

"A matter of great urgency and import, of which I shall discuss with your Baron when 'tis suitable to do so."

"And how is lovely London with its rolling Thames?"

"My Lady," said Christian with much regret, "London is no longer a metropolis, but subsists as a necropolis; a city in which the dead far outnumber the living – a city of the dead."

"Ah, yes," she responded sorrowfully, "the Plague."

Christian wanted to question her as to why no one here had become infected with the sickness, but hastily decided it would be better to take up such a subject with the Baron and not this gentle woman.

After a few seconds of awkward silence, as if in remembrance of all those dead of the Plague, she began to walk once more up the stone steps.

"My Lady," Christian called after her, "I beg of you, torture me no longer. Reveal to me that by which beauty is defined."

With a happily embarrassed expression and a grin that could not be restrained, she answered, "I am known by many names, but you shall call me Cassandra."

Paying no attention to her puzzling response, Christian delightedly repeated her name inside his head. Cassandra! he clamored, now I know how to describe the virtues of a summer sunset, with its multi-colored hues of magenta, fuchsia, and azure. Or the reflection of a harvest moon upon the serene sea, a pearl in a bed of aqua. *From now 'til forevermore they shall be Cassandra to me, as will all things of an excellence beyond wordy description and mortal thought.*

Proceeding up the stairs alone, their hostess chided them nicely. "Come along now, gentlemen. I must finish attending to you quickly, for the night is ever so short and the Baron has much to ask of you."

Cotton followed Christian to the staircase and the two of them pursued their perfect lady up the stepped incline. The upper level being without torches, they had only her candlelight to guide them through the darkness.

At the top of the stairs, Cassandra turned left down a hallway. There were only two doors in this part of the castle, the nearest being on the right hand wall and the other at the end of the hall. Stopping in front of the first door, Cassandra produced a skeleton key from one of the many folds of her gown. She unlocked it.

The men watched as she entered what was obviously a servant's quarters, and lit with her candelabrum a similar candleholder situated on a tiny wooden table. Standing in the doorway, they gave the room and its accommodations a brief inspection.

Roughly three by three square yards in size, the little chamber was furnished with only the barest of necessities. A table, wash basin, and bed embodied all of the room's charm. Not even a single window with which to allow the occupant a view of the rotten courtyard below broke the pattern of gray brick.

Moving aside, they allowed Cassandra to leave the miniscule quarters and re-enter the hall. "This will be your room, sir," she said, addressing Cotton. "I trust you find it suitable?"

Cotton once again peered into the small, austere room. Curling his nose at the petite bed which was to support his long and heavy body, he could not help but lie in response to her query. "Why, yes," he said, grinning. "'Twill do fine, thank ye."

"Good," she said, taking Christian by the arm and leading him further down the hall. "If you need anything, just call out."

Cotton looked with some dismay at his friend as he watched him being led away. "But I thought I would share a room, perhaps, with him …" he pointed pathetically to Christian as if afraid of her response.

"No," their hostess replied politely, "that is not necessary, we have many rooms here."

Not liking the idea of being separated from his penance, Cotton maintained a troubled look.

"If you would rather be together …" Cassandra offered with a raised brow, insinuating homosexuality, "I am sure it can be arranged."

"No," blurted Cotton, annoyed at her little innuendo, "that will not be necessary. This will do, thank ye." Nodding to Christian, he backed into his tiny room.

"Fear not, noble warrior," she soothed as she pointed to the door at the end of the hall, "your friend shall be close at hand."

Bowing to her, but unable to manage a smile, Cotton eased his door closed and left Christian with Cassandra in the shadowy hallway.

Alone before such an attractive and mysterious woman, Christian could not gather enough courage to look her in the eye. His gaze fixed to Cotton's shut door, he hoped his friend would emerge to save him. Unable to resist admiring her excellence, he compulsively glanced over at her, only to find her staring at him with an equal, if not exceeding, fascination.

"Come," she implored him as she held out her hand, her voice ringing like church bells in his ears, "I will show you to our room."

Momentarily seduced by her dark eyes and the promise they held, he took a step towards her before recanting his brash action. Reason tempering his lust, his mind dissected her words. "Our room?" he questioned, his nervous tone exposing his mistrust. "What mean you by 'our room'? Explain yourself, woman."

Withdrawing her refused hand, she attempted to conceal her chagrin with a twitchy smile. "The Baron goes to great pains to ensure his guests' comfort …"

I bet he does, Christian's mind interrupted, flashing images of the impaled inside his head.

"Your friend shall be looked after," she continued following an embarrassed pause, "just as I shall look after you."

"And what if I don't want you to look after me? What then?" he indignantly shot back. "Have I no choice?"

"Yes," she replied through pursed lips, as if trying to contain a smile, "but when dealing with me, choices are merely limitations, which, like life, expire rapidly." Then, in a much more directing tone, she added, "What I want is the only choice you have. I want you, and shall have you …" Allowing her smile to break through the seriousness of her words and allay Christian of any of his fears, she pleasantly sighed, "Patience is not one of my virtues."

Less concerned with her veiled words than with her beauty, which grew in his estimation at every glance, Christian controlled his lust by channeling it against the one whom he so dearly desired. Acting as if taking offense to her flippant denial of his free will, he spat, "Show me to my room, woman, and make arrangements to sleep elsewhere tonight."

He could see her facial muscles tense at his refusal, but she collected herself well. "As you wish, Christian," she coolly responded, "but I shan't sleep tonight."

Reaching the far door, Cassandra yielded the same key she had used previously and opened wide the entrance to what was to be Christian's quarters. Moving aside, she allowed her guest to enter, dutifully handing him her candelabrum.

Christian was astounded by his room. He did not expect much more than what Cotton had received, and yet stood in an expansive suite fit for a king. Polygonal in design, the chamber was obviously situated in one of the towers. It could swallow up ten of Cotton's rooms and still have space for furniture. And whereas Cotton had not a single window with which to observe the outside world, Christian had six large French windows lining his far wall. They permitted the now visible moon to lend her rays in lightening the darkness so prevalent in what he had seen of the rest of the castle, making this the best lit of all the rooms he had beheld.

The furniture did not detract from the room's glory, but served only to enhance it even more. A large dresser lined one wall, while a standing closet distinguished another. A broad and lengthy table stood nearest the center of the room, accompanied by several chairs, and a magnificent queen-sized bed had its headboard flush with the wall directly opposite the French windows.

"What is this?" he asked, motioning to the lodgings as he set the candelabrum on the table.

Leaning alluringly in the doorway, Cassandra frustratedly sighed, "This is our— *your* room."

"Why do I receive such a room and Cotton a servant's quarters?"

"Is he not your servant?"

"He is my friend," Christian proudly declared, "and deserves equal."

Looking away, Cassandra somewhat sadly remarked, "That is for the Baron to decide."

"And why does your Baron have such an affinity for me when we have never met?"

Returning her sad eyes to Christian, Cassandra shrugged and said, "The Baron's reasons are his own. I do not question."

"I see," replied Christian, while in deep thought. Contemplating his reflection on the polished wood grain of the table, he streaked his fingers across it, and upon examining them found no residuals of dust. *As clean as our rooms back at the inn,* he noted. Glancing up, he allowed himself a smile. "I will have many questions for the Baron when I meet him."

Suddenly delighted at seeing Christian smiling at her, Cassandra straightened and quickly added, "Then your questions will be answered shortly. The Baron will see you within the hour."

Slowly walking towards the wondrous female framed by his doorway, he nodded, "Very well."

As he approached, Cassandra smoothed out her gown like some nervous schoolgirl anxious for a first kiss. With sensuous hope she asked him, "Have you further need of me?"

"No, that will be all," he said, as he began to ease the door closed.

Holding her hand against the door in an effort to prevent him from shutting her out, she solicited, "Do you not find me beautiful?"

"Yes," he readily agreed, "most certainly so. You are very attractive."

"Then why do you treat me so?"

"I have a woman," he said, more as an excuse to get her to leave him alone than out of any loyalty to Rebecca. "I love only her."

Moving closer to him in the narrowing doorway, locking her eyes on his, she confidently asserted, "You will love me, too."

Powerless to move, to close the door on her angelic face, a dismayed Christian sputtered, "But ... I hardly know you."

Closing on his flushed face, her lips almost touching his, she whispered, "You know me better than you think ..."

Breaking the trance her beauty had put him under and tearing his eyes from her hypnotic gaze, he breathlessly exhaled, "No ... I mustn't!" before slamming the door on her temptation.

Breathing heavy, with his back to the door to further protect against her entrance, Christian nervously quaked in his shoes. It was the most difficult thing he had ever done in his life, turning away such beauty. How he wanted to take her into his arms, into his room, into his bed. To love her would exceed anything a man could ever hope to accomplish, and to be loved by her would surpass all ambitions in all of God's creation! She had almost had him, almost caused him to overlook his suspicions and concerns and to take her into his heart. She put him at odds with his rationale, causing him to wage war with reason and tempting him to throw caution to the wind. She almost had him. Almost.

It was the way in which her eyes reflected the moonlight that reinstated his guard, compelling him to shut his door and bar her from his sight. They were not glossy, as are a living being's eyes, but instead were quite dull. Recalling to his mind the anguished eyes of the dead of London, lust turned to loathing, and his fire being quenched, he was emboldened to shut her out into the hall.

Standing by his windows, Christian overlooked the blue courtyard. The inconstant moon had pushed her way through the ill-bred storm clouds for about a half an hour now. Under her beams the entire spoiled landscape below became even more grotesque.

"Whatever 'tis I seek, surely 'tis not here," he uttered to himself in a moment of uncontrollable aversion. How can anything situated in a place so foul as this be of any use to anyone? he thought. What good could come of this land? Certainly not something that would prolong the life, buttress one's health, or avert the merciless grasp of the Great Plague. He mumbled a favorite expression of his father's. "Farmers do not till graveyards." Somehow, it seemed appropriate.

As he was about to pull away from the depressing sight, something caught his eye. Entering the courtyard through the gateway was the coach. Piloted by the same thin man, he followed the coach to just under his room. There, outside the castle's elaborate doorway, it drew to a halt.

He watched as the tall man descended from his carriage with all their baggage in his hands. "He's quite strong," Christian remarked to himself, "for one so slender." Observing him in relation to the horses by the auspicious moonlight, he was in awe at his apparent size. My God, his mind blasphemed, the man's a giant!

He saw him walk to the door and then enter, disappearing into the castle. I suppose we'll be receiving our bags shortly, he reflected.

Pressing his face against the cold glass, Christian examined with distaste one of the impaled corpses that hung just outside his window. In all, there were three he could see that were aligned with the thin ledge under his windows. Following the ledge around the interior of the courtyard, he could see many more. Shedding his fear, he inspected the corpse closest to him.

Its skin tanned a rich brown from its years of hanging in the rays of the embalming sun, the sorry semblance of a man gently rocked at the mercy of the wind. His eyes were but open sockets – holes which displayed the emptiness of his head. His ears and nose had been ravaged by decay, the elements and birds being of no help to his features. The mouth gaped open, as if in an eternal, silent scream. His shrieking face gave the appearance that even death offered this poor soul no release, that even in death his anguish knew no bounds. His contorted body was naked, his threads long deserting his frame. Certain parts of his physique were more skeletal than others. His hands were long and bony, missing several of their digits, and his feet were mutilated beyond recognition. His emaciated build revealed every rib, chest bone and rung of his spinal column.

He gazed in horror at the hard instrument of death which supported the cadaver. The long, black, rusted iron shaft penetrated the corpse through its anus, exiting through its broken chest. "Lord God," Christian murmured. The pain these pitiful men must have suffered! Pierced through the rectum, they impaled themselves on their own body's weight. Death could be agonizingly slow, perhaps taking hours. He shook his head in shocked disbelief at the barbarism before him. Whoever has done this, he seethed, is unworthy even of Hell.

Recoiling from the ghastly sight, his hand instinctively flew to his chest, seeking his crucifix. Finding Rebecca's locket in its place, he angrily remembered their exchange in Bantingham. "Silly girl," he complained, "your feminine wiles have charmed me of the one thing that could bring me consolation in such a place as this."

Before he had time to increase his indignation against his distant lover, a rapping on his door roused him from the furtherance of such thoughts.

On his way to respond he was assailed by more knocks. "I'm coming," he yelled in annoyance, "I'm coming!" Upon reaching the door, Christian grew cautious. Addressing whomever desired entry, he prudently asked, "Who's there?"

"'Tis me, ye slow boy! Cast down your caution and throw open your door!"

Without further hesitation Christian permitted the excited Scot into his room.

Breezing past him, Cotton had his arms full with baggage. Seeking the nearest surface on which he could unburden himself, he headed for Christian's bed. "I've brought your things. They were just delivered unto me—" He stopped in his tracks just as he had in his speech. Looking about in amazement at the size of Christian's room, he remarked, "The Baron must really like ye."

"Yes, mustn't he," said Christian suspiciously as he closed his door.

Cotton busied himself with laying Christian's belongings out on the bed in an orderly fashion. Standing back, he eyed each bag until deciding on one in particular. "'Tis this one, I believe," he said as he picked it up.

"Whatever are you doing?" asked Christian, mildly concerned that Cotton was handling a piece of his luggage.

"Back at the inn, when ye wasn't looking, I hid me dirk amongst your effects. This bag," he said, holding it up for emphasis. "I feared me bags would be searched if we were separated from them."

"And were your fears justified?"

"Aye, me battle-axe is missing."

Christian remained silent as Cotton opened the satchel and fumbled for his weapon. He prayed the soldier would find his steel; at least they would have some means of a defense should the worst possible situation occur.

Uncomfortable with the quiet, Cotton felt obliged to speak. "I shan't bring the incident up with the Baron, I do not wish to arouse his suspicions." There was a moment of tenseness before he joyously exclaimed, "Hah! Here 'tis!"

He pulled out the dirk and Christian swore to himself that it was the second most beautiful thing he had ever seen. The knife's blade reflected the blue moonlight, glowing as if it had a life all its own. Holding it raised above his head, Cotton appeared a hero worthy of Homer.

"Why did you suspect my baggage not to be searched?" a curious Christian asked.

"Who fears a priest's apprentice?" Cotton replied a tad too nonchalantly.

"That shall be his undoing," Christian muttered to himself.

"Aye," Cotton agreed, overhearing his companion's angry utterance. "Regard this Baron with treachery. Question his every move, suspect his every word. Never trust one who would have ye disarmed."

"Indeed. I feel as though we have entered into a sepulcher of the most unholy kind." Then, as if contemplating what he had just said, Christian asked, "Have you a crucifix?"

"I possess a cross."

Christian looked at him hopefully. "Might I wear it for a while? It puts my mind at rest."

Cotton shook his snowy locks. "'Tis left in London. I feared highwaymen would covet it should we be stopped."

"Oh, I see," said the young man, full of disappointment.

An abrupt knocking startled both of them.

"Who's that?" Cotton forcefully whispered.

"How the hell should I know?" said Christian irately as he moved to answer the door.

"Wait!" implored the old mercenary in a hushed tone. He hurriedly replaced the dirk in its bag, set it amongst the others on the bed, and hastily assembled the baggage so that it looked innocuous. When he was done, he turned to Christian, who patiently waited near the door, and nodded his approval.

Christian nodded in return, then carefully opened the door a crack. His heart leapt as his spirit sank.

It was her! his heart reveled. Beauty personified! No longer was she in a simple white frock, which in no way had detracted from her looks previously, she now appeared before him in an elegant purple ball gown. Frilled with black lace at the hem and cuffs, the gown was made remarkable by its low-cut bodice, which allowed for a more than generous perusal of her two greatest assets.

Her hair was worn up, with wisps of bangs covering her forehead. Not unlike how his mother used to wear her hair, he thought fondly. She wore little jewelry and that also pleased him for he never could tolerate the flaunting of one's wealth. Her ear lobes held simple earrings of polished onyx, and on her hand she wore a single ruby ring.

Standing still, she granted him his examination with much pleasure. After looking her over in awed silence, Christian caught sight of the delighted smirk thinning her lips. Straightening, he appropriated an air of indifference.

"Yes?" he asked peevishly.

Blinking her large, dark eyes in dismay at his vexed manner, she looked as if she were about to cry as she expressed in a wavering voice, "The Baron will see you now. Both of you are requested to join us for supper, as I am sure you are famished due to your long journey ..."

How he wished to dry those teary eyes! How he loathed himself for being the cause of her distress! And yet for all his yearning he managed to stand firm in the face of his goddess. "Very well," he conceded, "we shall join you shortly."

A teardrop rolling down her silky cheek was the last he saw of her as he closed the door. Turning more so from himself than from their shut-out hostess, he cast Cotton a weary look of despair.

"Never have I gazed upon such timeless beauty," the Scotsman avowed, "and I have attended many a court." Seeing how his praise seemed only to reduce his companion into a further state of despondency, Cotton quickly amended himself. "Ah, but women!" he sighed distastefully. "They'll smother ye as a blanket does a fire, snuffing out your life, yet keeping ye warm so as ye should not feel the icy fingers of Death."

Christian nodded dumbly to what Cotton said. He glanced over at him as he wandered to the windows with an engrossed look plastered to his face. "What is it that so captivates you?"

"Them," answered Cotton, motioning to the corpses. "Do they not beckon to ye?"

"Yes, in fact they do."

Cotton turned from the view in disgust. "I'm glad I have no windows in me room."

Christian felt compelled to issue his friend a warning. "Just remember," he cautioned, looking him in the eye, "not everything is as it seems, in reality or in dreams." Then, as if struck by a sudden realization, he became blank, and with a trace of paranoia whispered, "I fear we are trapped between both … in that nether-region named nightmare."

Staring at him with some concern, Cotton responded with a suggestion. "Perhaps ye could do with some rest."

Christian looked dumbfounded at him. He's allowing his stubborn rationale to blind him from his fears, he frightfully realized. A typical soldier's reaction, believing he is invincible in the face of present danger. I will have to look out for the both of us. Shaking himself free of his bewildered appearance, he clapped his hands together and smiled broadly. "Come," he commanded, "let us go and meet this Baron." Then, gesturing with open arms to his accommodations, he added, "This Baron who so treats his guests with such charity." Casting Cotton an angry glance, he thrust his arm out at the corpses hanging just outside his room, shouting, "*All* his guests!"

Cotton saw what he meant and instantly felt foolish for masking his concern from Christian. He was afraid. He felt the fear that so permeated every brick in this edifice, from the foundation on up. But how could he apologize for simply trying to put on a brave front? He could not, and therefore bowed his head and followed his furious friend out of the room.

Throwing open his door, Christian was surprised to see Cassandra patiently waiting for him in the hallway. His astonishment turned to guilt when he realized he should have invited her in rather than shut her out. *My complaint is with the Baron,* he reminded himself, *not with this most excellent Lady.* But something deep inside, that part of him perpetually captivated by the dark paramour of his dreams, told him to treat her with as much caution as he did courtesy. "Had I known you were to wait on us, I would have allowed you entry into my quarters," he apologized.

"The wait was not long," she assured him. "Besides, I do not mind waiting for that which gives me so much pleasure."

"You are too kind."

"Kindness has nothing to do with it. Love is my malady."

Taken aback at her amorous assertion, Christian was at a loss for words and promptly grew red in the face.

On seeing his embarrassment, she drew her hands to her mouth and let out a girlish giggle. "I've rarely seen anything so red," she attested between breaths, "but I'm certain you have something of a darker hue ..." Her eyes finished her sentence as they fell to his crotch.

Offended by her overtly sexual suggestion, Christian let the abashed grin on his face drop. *Not very lady-like,* he judged. Still, there was something about her he liked, something compelling in her ways.

Peeking out from behind Christian, Cotton's face lit up when he saw Cassandra. Bowing his head slightly, he greeted her.

"Ah, my courteous soldier," she sighed happily, "how good 'tis to see you once again."

Before Cotton could repay her in reply, Christian, envious of the way in which she hailed his older companion, called her to account. "How come you to know his former occupation?"

Looking quite confused, she answered, "I should think it obvious by his facial scarring what manner of work was his choosing." Then, as if to increase Christian's jealousy, she added while looking directly at Cotton, "In no way do they detract from your appeal, sir. On the contrary, I've always found men of combat rather intriguing."

Bucking up in his boots, Cotton conceded her another bow, this time in appreciation for her kind words. "Never in me life, Lady," he alleged, "have I been the subject of such fair flattery. Ye do me a great honor simply because 'tis praise from the mouth of beauty herself."

Cassandra awarded him a curtsy for his compliments. As soon as she had completed her gesture of thanks, she returned her attention to Christian, who stood smoldering.

How soon Cotton retires his ward for the smile of a pretty girl, he righteously thought. I can only pray that wine is not served with our meal.

"Come with me," Cassandra politely ordered them, "I shall take you to the dining room."

She turned from them and began walking away. Following her, Christian noted that she seemed to be moving on air rather than the ground. Her feet not visible because of the shrouding of her purple gown, she appeared to be gliding along with little of the bob and sway usually associated with a walking person.

Cotton closed Christian's door and hurriedly caught up with his companions at the stairs. As they began their descent together, he could not abstain from inquiring about others residing in the castle. "Where are the rest of the ladies of the house?" he asked their beautiful guide.

"Why, I do not know what you imply," she softly protested, "I am the only woman here."

"But we heard the laughter of many a woman when first we approached your door."

"I am afraid you must be mistaken," consoled Cassandra. "Perhaps 'twas nothing more than a blustering gale."

"'Twas no blustering gale!" Cotton vigorously objected. "I know the sound of excited females when I hear it!"

Looking back at him, brandishing a smug grin on her face, she replied, "I'm sure you do."

Ignoring her remark, he appealed to his young friend. "Christian, tell her what I say is true! Tell her that ye heard, as I, the laughter of several women!"

Cassandra eyed Christian with playful concern. "Is this so, Christian?" she asked him. "Am I to be made a fool of in my own house?"

Halting in his steps, Christian looked deep into her uniquely attractive, but lusterless eyes. *What secrets hide you behind those curtained windows?* he pondered. *What would I lose should I render you a liar here on your own steps? What would I gain if I dallied here with you? To side against you would be to tell my sincere belief that we did in truth hear other women. To side with you would be to forsake the trust of my friend.* After a brief deliberation, he spoke.

"'Tis my right, proper opinion that Cotton and I did truthfully believe to have heard the merry voices of women, but on your assurances otherwise I must therefore conclude otherwise. For you are the Lady of this castle, and surely you would not seek to deceive your guests."

This answer seemed to please both feuding parties, although it was Cassandra who recognized the diplomacy in Christian's response. As they neared the end of the staircase, she leaned next to his ear and whispered, "You must be careful of what you say … and what you believe. I am pleased to have such a worthy visitor under my roof. Perhaps we can … talk later."

The moment's hesitation she took in phrasing her invitation told Christian she had something more in mind than harmless conversation.

The three of them continued on in silence. It was not long after descending from the stairs that they went through a narrow doorway and emerged into a well-lit dining room. Larger in length than in width, its two main attributes were a fireplace and a long, oaken dining table.

The fireplace crackled and snapped with heat-giving flame, its orange illumination painting everything in a warm, healthy glow. The hearth itself was quite large, although plain, having no mantel upon which to rest things or ornamental decor enhancing its appeal. It was a brick structure of the barest necessity, a hole in the wall in which fire was kept.

In contrast, the dining table was a magnificent work of art, a true testament to the beauty of human engineering and design. Stained a dark mahogany, the table was roughly four yards in length and stood a full yard high. Its construction appeared sturdy, as did its accompanying chairs. The real distinction of the table was not in its size or length, but in the painstakingly detailed carvings it bore. Depicting scenes of varying carnality, the artist was very graphic, and very knowledgeable in his subject.

The erotic table was set to seat four for dinner. A chair was at either end of the long table, two more at precisely its midsection. Dining utensils had been laid out in advance of the meal, as had fine crystal glasses, large cloth napkins, and two wine decanters, one for each end of the elongated table.

Moving nearer to the table than her two guests, Cassandra began her explanation of the seating arrangements. "Here is where we shall dine this evening. I trust the table does not offend?"

"Not in the least," replied Cotton, looking past the carved images of sex and eyeing only the decanters.

"Good," smiled Cassandra. Becoming serious, she gestured to the chair at the far end of the table. "The Baron will sit there, at the head of the table. I shall sit there," she added, pointing at one of the middle chairs, "to his left." Looking at Cotton, she touched the end chair nearest them, "You, sir, shall dine here."

"If the Baron is the head, what am I?" he jested, seating himself.

"The ass," offered Christian grumpily.

Laughing lightly, Cassandra motioned to the last chair. "Chris, you are to sit there."

Noticing that his chair was one of the middle chairs, and that he would not only be near the Baron but dine directly across from Cassandra, he asked of her, "Who is it that wants me near? You? Or the Baron?"

With a mischievous grin, she responded as she sat herself, "Perhaps 'tis the both of us."

Pouring himself some wine, Cotton declared, "I would be honored to dine across such beauty. I am certain to do so would add spice to any dish."

In a display of gratitude, Cassandra tilted her head and said, "You, sir, are a gentleman."

"Only when I wish to be," he chuckled before sampling the wine. As the red liquid rolled over his palate and down his gullet he nearly cried out in joy. This was the finest wine he had ever tasted, surely the best claret ever brewed. His tongue quavered in anticipation of his next gulp; before long, he would have to refill his glass.

Christian took his place at the table, but remained standing. He was concerned at the lax atmosphere being presented, as if no one here knew of the pitiful state of the town or, even worse, of its inhabitants. It seemed as though great trouble and expense had gone into the preparations for their visit, and yet none had been notified of their coming. And he could not reconcile the eerie feeling Cassandra's smug certitude left him.

"Do you dine standing, sir?"

It was Cassandra, in a tone mocking formality, batting her long lashes at him.

Slowly sliding into his chair, he refused to take his eyes from her, regarding her as if she were poison.

"Fear not, Chris," she playfully threatened, "I do not bite."

Outside the walls of the castle, the brewing storm erupted in exploding clashes accentuated by bright flashes of pale blue light. The brilliance of the sudden volley of thunder and lightning interrupted the ongoing conversation between the hostess and her guests. Sitting still, they listened with dread to the fierce cataclysm raging in the black sky above.

"We're in for a bad one," muttered Cotton, cutting through the prevalent apprehension.

"I love a good storm," Cassandra stated. "'Tis as if there were a war in Heaven."

"And that pleases you?" Christian asked, appalled.

Pounding his heavy fist into the table, a slightly intoxicated Cotton admonished him. "Christian!" he hollered, "Stop jumping all over her! 'Twas merely an expression, nothing more."

"Yes, Chris," pled Cassandra, "I would never mean to offend you."

Feeling her long leg slowly caress his inner thighs under the table, he stared into her lovely face and irately confided, "You offend me even now."

Dismissing his angry comment with a light, rhapsodic chuckle, she assured him, "Not offend, Chris . . . arouse." Her foot reached his crotch and delicately began to tease him.

Shifting uncomfortably in his chair, Christian offered her a look of embarrassment. He did not, however, remove her offending foot from his groin. "Tell me of yourself," he asked the woman who so titillated him.

"There is not much to tell," she modestly replied.

"Come now, you have demonstrated your humility, now enlighten me as to the possessor of such beauty."

"You flatter me."

"'Tis impossible, my Lady," he seriously protested. "One cannot flatter perfection, for everything one says is not adulation but truth."

"Even in your denial you offer me praise. What is it you wish to know?"

"Anything and everything."

"You like to speak vaguely, don't you?" she merrily reproved him, all the while intensifying her massaging in display of her fondness.

He could only smile, for the magic she worked had him ready to explode. With his left hand he eased her foot from his stimulated crotch. He would not fall prey to her charms, no matter how good they felt.

Giving him a toying pout, as if his refusal of her caress had wounded her pride, she succeeded in arousing him more so than in actually touching him.

Those lips! he thought. Oh, to have them planted upon my shaft would be tantamount to pure bliss! Do not, countered his sanity, be swayed by her allure. Forget not the circumstances which brought you here, nor the queer behavior you have witnessed. What have I to fear from a woman? his desire reasoned. What have I to dread from Cassandra? From the back of his mind came reason's chilling reply: everything.

The rumble of thunder underscored the sudden chill of the talk. It echoed the turbulence of Christian's indecision: should he fear her, or love her?

"Are you feeling well?" Cassandra asked him, her brow wrinkled in concern.

She must have seen uncertainty on my face, he thought. It would be best not to raise her suspicions or concerns, whichever her feelings may be.

"I simply crave a little rest, my Lady," he said as he flashed her a weary smile. "The trip was long and arduous."

"I can imagine," she concurred sympathetically. "I myself have undertaken many a taxing journey in my time. I promise you, all the rest you could ever ask for shall be yours after supper."

"That seems to be the greatest charity I could ever hope to have promised me," he said in all seriousness, thinking of how he had never really known true sleep. The dark rings under his eyes were a testament to the fact that his dark lady granted him only a few necessary hours every night.

"Do not consider it charity," she cheerfully scolded, "think of it as ... a gift."

"And I thought we had three months 'til Christmas," he jested.

The mention of that holy holiday stirred something within his lovely hostess. She looked down sadly at the ground and whispered in a trembling voice, "Christmas. I remember Christmas."

"Does not the Baron celebrate the birth of our Lord?"

Shaken from her moment of sorrowful reflection, she glanced up at him and smiled a foolish smile. Looking past her masquerading lips, Christian saw that her eyes were no longer of a dull nature, but instead glistened and glimmered. Tears, he realized, she is holding back tears.

"I apologize for my lack of composure. I realize 'tis unfitting for a host to behave in such a way," she said as she wiped the tears from her eyes. "In response to your question, as you shall see, the Baron has little devotion to the holy days. Once again," she bowed in disgrace, "forgive my sentimentality."

Christian shook his head in protest. "My dear Lady," he offered his assurance, "'tis no crime to cry. I have not even met your Baron and already I find I have somewhat of a dislike for him — not recognizing holidays and demanding such fortitude from a tender woman! A woman should never be ashamed to shed tears, as 'tis her nature to do so."

Gazing at him with deep admiration, she revealed her awe. "You are a most tender man, a true champion of the virtue of all women."

Feeling a bit parched, Christian lifted the decanter that sat between them and poured himself some wine. As he eyed the churning red filling his chalice, he became appalled at his blatant gaffe: he had not offered her any!

Quickly correcting himself, he stopped his pouring forthwith and, holding the decanter up, provided her with a belated offering. "My most sincere apologies, Madam. In my haste to slake my thirst I have forsaken my manners. Would you care for some wine?"

"You owe me no apologies, for you are but a guest in my house. 'Tis I who has erred in not filling your glass."

"But etiquette dictates that the stronger sex should defer in all social settings."

"Are you so certain that you are the stronger sex?"

"I am a man."

"And I am a woman."

It was then that he sensed her power, the iron will within her that made him love her more. However, he was not blind in seeing that she had successfully changed the subject from his offer of a glass of wine to one of sexual dominance.

"Do you or don't you desire wine?" he asked rather crossly, as though he were offended by the calling into question of male superiority, particularly his.

"I find wine to be disagreeable, it being too sweet."

"And what do you find agreeable?"

"You."

Caught by surprise at her praise, Christian could do nothing more than place the decanter on the table and stare into her mysterious black eyes. With a gentle sweep of his hand, he moved the obstructing decanter to his right so as to minimize the amount of objects set between him and his dark angel.

Having finished his own, Cotton leaned over and grabbed Christian's discarded decanter and began replenishing his cup. Taken by Cassandra's beauty, Christian failed to notice the theft.

"How long have you resided in Manasseh?" Christian queried Cassandra before taking a sip of wine. The beverage was masterfully aged.

"For some time now," she replied with much ambiguity.

"And do you not find the townspeople a bit odd?"

"I lead a very sheltered existence, Chris. What little contact I do have with the people of Manasseh is usually not in the form of conversation."

"But do they not seem strange ... sickly, perhaps?"

Her eyes widened in fear. "You are not intimating the Plague? Surely, this cannot be so!"

"I meant nothing of the kind," he calmed her. "'Tis just that they do not act as decent persons should. They seem as though their strength has been collectively sapped, their will broken, their souls stolen."

Cassandra put her hand to her mouth and attempted to suppress her laughter in a lady-like manner. "Ah, Christian," she sighed between chuckles, "you certainly have an active imagination. You possess even the talent to translate it into words."

Beaming in response to her acclaim, much like a schoolboy encouraged by a teacher's inspiring plaudits, he proudly divulged to her his true intentions.

"I do love to write," he confessed. "I seek to enhance my writings through the accumulation of knowledge. Only through the classics will my genius be released."

"How you shed your humility like the lamb its wool."

"Madam," with a smile he duly informed her, "in the service of God I am a humble man. I seek nothing more than an entrance into Heaven at the end of a weary life. However, there are three aspects of my persona to which I cannot practice modesty. One concerns my intellect, the other my physique."

"And the third?"

"That is for you to find out," he hinted with a devilish grin.

"I presume I shall when you are not in the service of God."

He was not sure how to take her remark. Was she simply being coy, or was she snide in mocking his seemingly lackadaisical worship of God? Her tone of voice offered him no solution, so he was obliged to choose. He decided she was being true to her coquettish nature.

"Is there no one here for me?"

It was Cotton. On the verge of drunkenness, he felt wounded at his exclusion from the conversation.

"Why, whatever do you mean, righteous knight?" asked Cassandra in her most innocent way.

"He has ye, and ye have him." He flailed his arms in a pathetic pointing gesture. "I have no one."

"I am sure we can find you a worthy lady willing to lend you her ear."

"'Tis not her ear I want!"

"Cotton!" spat a horrified Christian, "Watch your tongue!"

"Have no anger, Chris," placated Cassandra, "I've heard worse spoken in my presence." Casting Cotton a sidelong glance, she smiled wisely. "You desire a companion, and 'tis my duty as a proper hostess to find you one. 'Twas my vanity in believing I was good enough for the both of you."

"But ... but ..." mumbled Cotton feebly, "I thought ye said there were no other women here?"

"That is so."

"Well I'll not take one of those rotting townsfolk!" he unreasonably cried. "I'd get something far worse than the itch from one o' them!"

"Cotton!" Christian sputtered in disbelief.

"Christian," Cassandra assured him, "'tis quite all right." Then, looking Cotton directly in his bloodshot eyes, she whispered softly, "You will be taken care of ... I promise."

This seemed to appease Cotton's lustful inquiries. Satisfied, he fell back into his state of quiet drinking.

"I must apologize, my Lady," confided Christian in a low voice so as to not be overheard by Cotton, "for this dreadful behavior is totally unbecoming of his character. Judge him not by his actions at this table, for to do so would be a great injustice to the man I know. Free from the evil grasp of liquor, Cotton Smith-Patton can be one of the most able, courteous, and generous men you could ever hope to find. He is as pure in spirit as his flesh is blemished by scarring."

Holding Christian's hands, Cassandra nodded and said, "I believe what you say is true, for I recall the man he was not more than an hour ago. But put away your concern. I could never dislike one who demanded so much of your praise."

Lovingly, he gave her grasp a little squeeze. "Who are you?" he emphatically asked. "Who is this embodiment of bodily grace in whose hands I am held?"

"I am nothing more than a pretty face."

"Acting demure does not sit well with you."

"Oh? And why is that?"

"Because it renders you a liar." He saw her flinch uncomfortably and begin to draw away from him. Tightening his grip on her hands, he held her in place. "Do not shirk from me," he pled. "Drive modesty from the table and tell me of your exploits. I seek not to debase you but to respect and admire you more."

Eyes downcast, she sighed, "If there is one thing I should not inspire within you, that is admiration."

"Lady, please! Enough humility."

"Ah, my precious Christian," she spoke sadly, "I was not being humble."

What sounded like a terrible cannonade overhead reminded the little group of the bitter storm outside. Flickers of lightning cast darkened parts of the castle in harsh blue light with greater frequency. The howl of the fierce wind occasionally rattled the windows in their frames, threatening to blow in without an open invitation.

The calm within seems in stark contrast to the chaos without, Christian noted. Perhaps there is more of a similarity between the two environs than presently presented here. Cloaked beneath cordiality, and under the warm glow of candlelight, perhaps lie our souls, twisting in the wind like the leaves on a tree or the dried-out shells lined above us.

"Where is the Baron?" he asked Cassandra, watching while she fingered the stem of her empty wineglass.

"He is attending to some business. He will not be much longer. Are you hungry?"

Choosing to ignore her inquiry into his appetite, he pressed her further on the subject of the absent nobleman. "What manner of business could be so vital at this late hour?"

"Very important business."

'Twas funny she should point out my own vagueness, he lamented, when she is steeped in it herself.

Perhaps realizing her truncated replies to his questions left him dissatisfied, or seeing the suspicious look forming on his face, Cassandra elaborated on her earlier response. "The Baron is planning a trip," she said with a slight smile. "He has gone to great lengths to ensure its success."

"And where will you be traveling?"

"Whatever gave you the impression that I was to accompany him?"

"Is it not customary for a mistress to follow her master?"

"I am slave to only one master," she bitterly retorted, "and 'tis not the Baron Mormeau."

"Who, then, is your master?"

"The one who captures my heart."

"Then your heart is presently free?"

"No, master," she smiled strangely, "you hold my heart."

Despite all disbelief that she could have fallen in love with him in a matter of hours, Christian's spirits leapt for joy. His passion pressed him to find out more about her. "Of what nationality are you, my dear Lady? Are you French like your Baron?"

"I am of many nationalities," she said shyly. "I have resided in many countries, all of which I call my home, for I have left a little of me wherever I have gone."

"Oh," sighed Christian, "please, tell me of your foreign lands. I have never seen past the Channel."

"I shall do so later, as an incentive for us to be alone."

Christian was of the belief that she was a native Briton, for when she spoke she did so in flawless English. It was her exotic looks which suggested a foreign birth. "Do you like living in the country?" he asked in a pathetic attempt at small talk.

"It does have its advantages," she replied. "The remoteness of it all makes virtually anything possible."

"I should think it paradise being so far from London – away from all the noise, filth, and people."

"Oh, but that is what I miss most about this isolation: the swirling mass of humanity, the hubbub and commotion of city life, the smell of cooking food and latent fear."

"How long has it been since you've visited London?"

"Far too long," she sighed.

"Be thankful you are not there now."

"I am only thankful that you are not there now."

Again her open affection for him left him speechless. His only response was to turn beet red.

"Stop turning crimson," she playfully chastised him, "you're making me hungry!"

"Aye," blurted Cotton loudly from his place of neglect, "when shall we eat?"

Cassandra pleasantly talked down to him as if he were a stupid child. "We have only to await the arrival of the Baron, my dear Smith-Patton."

"Where is this Frenchman?" he asked, with some degree of distaste.

"She has already said he is tending to some important business," Christian snapped. "Had you been sober, you would have remembered."

"I ... I shall drink no more," he stammered in his slurred brogue.

"That is because there is no more to be drunk," Christian shot back, pointing to the empty decanters. "You drank it all."

Unable to respond, Cotton looked to his friend for leniency. He found none. Once more bowing his head in shame, he sat with eyes downcast. The euphoria of his drinking soured into a depressive remorse.

Christian turned from his alcoholic companion in disgust only to find Cassandra sensually stroking the table's erotic carvings. Glancing down at the carved scenes before him, he took in various depictions of buggery, fellatio, and sadomasochism. Returning to Cassandra's snaking fingers, he saw that she was fondling the small, wooden breasts of a bound girl. He watched as her fingertips rolled over the mounds of meticulous detail. Raising his gaze to her face, he was caught by her enticing smirk.

She always returns to sex, he thought in mild despair, as if she thinks that is all which concerns me. Still, to have her would be to taste Heaven. But would it be wise to experience such pleasure when ultimately she could not be his? Despite her objections to the contrary, she would always be the Baron's mistress, the Lady of his castle. Her love for me is merely the perverted hospitality of a Frenchman; nothing more. Or is it? Perhaps she does find me to her fancy, most likely being closer to her own age than the as-yet-unseen Baron. Does she or doesn't she care for me? His mind reeled in uncertainty.

Cotton cleared his throat and ventured, "Might I tell a tale?"

"Why of course," a delighted Cassandra encouraged him. "Tell us of the grandeur of battle, the thrill of the kill, and the pretty ladies that follow."

Cotton looked to Christian for a personal consent. With a light nod, Christian signaled him to begin. Being careful in his wording, for the wine had loosened his tongue, the Scotsman commenced in relating to them his story.

"Once, long ago," he opened, "there lived a young knight who sought to enter into the service of some noblemen. As providence would have it, an ongoing war had tapped the kingdom of its men and had created many openings for an ambitious man to fill. He soon found himself fighting under a good, Christian prince in the north of Europe.

"One day, during a long battle, this knight was separated from his fellow soldiers. Behind enemy lines, he carefully tried to make his way back to his compatriots. Nearing dusk, he decided it would be worth the risk to seek refuge from the cold in a barn by a farmhouse nearby. Having been wounded in combat, the knight was in dire need of warmth and rest. Entering the barn, this good knight made the hay his bed and spent the night huddling with animals.

"Come morning, the weary knight failed to awaken, and instead lay stretched out on his straw bedding. It so happened that the farmer's daughter, her duties being the care of the livestock, entered into the barn and discovered the late sleeper.

"Seeing that he bore the coat of arms of the enemy of her country and religion, she was at first frightened. But after studying the gentle features of the sleeper, she took him to be a good and noble man, regardless of whomever he fought for. At that moment she decided not to tell her father of her knight, for her father would surely kill him.

"And so 'twas that when the knight awoke he found fresh milk and cheese awaiting him — a gift from his farm girl. Hungry from his long walk the day before, the knight hastily devoured the food. And so it went on like this for several days and nights; the girl not revealing to her father that there was an enemy soldier resting in their barn, and the knight waking to find a more than generous supply of food and water.

"One morning, the knight, curious as to who the Samaritan was who had been leaving him this food, pretended to be asleep when in fact he was not. He lay still as he heard the barn door open and little footsteps approach. When the girl was right upon him, he opened his eyes to catch her, but instead was captured by her.

"She was so lovely. With long, flowing red hair and the bluest of eyes, she dazzled him silly. Roughly equal in age, she, too, had felt the same feelings of love for her knight, which is why she never told her father of him.

"When the gentlemanly knight attempted to bow to his lady, he exerted himself with great pain, for his wounds were as yet unhealed. In truth, had his open wounds been left unattended much longer he would surely have died of infection.

"Seeing that her knight was injured brought the girl much anguish. She tore up her best dress and wrapped his wounds in the clean cloth. Often she would change the wrappings herself, in no way shying from the cleansing of his ghastly wounds.

"At first their love was impeded by language: he knowing very little of hers and she none of his. Gradually, over the following months, they came to comprehend one another by speaking in broken bits and pieces of each other's tongue. Before long they were able to profess their love for one another, and as soon as his injuries were well enough healed, they demonstrated the truth of their love on the warm straw.

"It so happened that one day the girl came to her knight with a mark upon her cheek. When the knight asked her where she had received such a mark, or who 'twas that had given it to her, she shied away and refused to tell him.

"So it went on like this for some time; the girl coming to him with a new welt or bruise somewhere upon her person. Always she would tell him she had gotten them from being clumsy, or from slipping and falling. But the knight had seen many such injuries to know that they were inflicted upon her. One day, on finding a particularly bad bruise about her thighs, the knight could remain silent no longer. ''Tis your father who has done this to ye!' he angrily yelled at her. ''Tis he who has been injuring ye!'

"Unable to deny it any longer, the girl hid her face and began to cry. 'Yes,' she said through her tears, ''tis true what ye say.' She then went on to explain how her father had been beating her for neglecting her chores.

"Feeling great anger that his lover was being abused, as well as some guilt, for 'twas because of him her chores were neglected, the knight resolved to free his maiden from the clutches of her cruel and torturous father. Come the next day, he would confront the brutish man about his daughter.

"Rising early, the knight collected up his things and walked toward the farmhouse. He would sleep with the animals no longer. When he had reached the door of the little cottage, he pounded his fist harshly against it, demanding the farmer show himself.

"What his lover had failed to tell him was that she was not merely the daughter of the farmer, but sister to his three sons as well. All four of the bad men came out of the cottage, brandishing sharp weapons, and set upon the sole knight. With no great difficulty the knight slew them all, dispatching their souls to Hell in a hurry.

"When he was through with the men, he saw that his fair maiden had been witness to it all and was most displeased. 'Leave this place!' she cried. 'Return to your battles instead of having your battles returned to ye!'

"He was most upset with her attitude, for he had fought for her freedom. 'Me Love,' he objected, 'I did it all for ye.'

"'Did what?' she cried again, 'murder me entire family? Kill me only remaining kin?'

"'But they abused ye,' said the confused knight.

"'And in saving me ye have done far worse!' cried she. 'I would have run away with ye! I was only waiting for the proper time! But now, now I can never be with ye, for ye have murdered me blood. How can I give me love to one who has rendered me an orphan?'

"Before the knight could answer her, she chased him from her land and bade him never to return nor seek her forgiveness. And so the knight did as his lady commanded, eventually leaving her country and never returning. In time, he heard rumors that his Greta had fallen to a strange type of sleeping sickness and that her life seemed to ebb away at every passing day. Though wishing to see her one last time, he maintained her last request and stayed his distance. For the rest of his life the knight would never forget his little farm girl. And although he would in time marry, she was never far from his thoughts."

"How very sad," Cassandra wept. "Most tragic."

"Me dear, dear Lady," Cotton hastily responded, "'twas not me intent to make ye cry."

Drying her eyes on her napkin, Cassandra flashed him a melancholy grin and said, "A lady can control her emotions only so far. Any more and I would be nothing more than some powder and a dress." She straightened, took in a deep breath, and added, "Whether you have made me cry or made me laugh, made me sad or made me happy, you have moved me. That, sir, is a commendable deed in itself and should not require your apology. On the contrary, I should like to thank you for your entertaining tale."

Cotton absorbed her words with unsubtle pride. Still inebriated, her praise had a kind of sobering affect on him, however slight.

Christian watched Cotton rise in his chair and attempt to put on an air of sobriety. *If only he tried to please me as much as he pathetically tries to please her,* he thought with more than a modicum of ire.

"'Tis a pity his tale held no happy ending," he critiqued, his jealousy coloring his bias.

"True," Cassandra granted, "however, other than in fairy tales there can be no such thing as an actual 'happy ending.'"

"And why is that?"

"Because of the inevitability of death," she stated unequivocally. "How can any ending be truly happy when 'tis nothing more than a moldy corpse in a rotting coffin?"

Christian found it difficult to refute so strongly worded an argument, something to which he was unaccustomed. Usually he could scrounge up the last word in any exchange, but with her he was befuddled. Her intensity, the revulsion in her expression at the mere mention of corpse, sent his innards quivering. He had finally met his equal, if not his superior, and rather than feel envy felt only admiration.

Thunder and lightning exploded outside like never before. The wind howled and screamed as if in terror of its own ferocity, and the loud patter of raindrops began to beat down upon the framed windows. Turning — as if by some strange foreknowledge — Christian looked to his left, toward the far entrance into the dining room. There, amidst dazzling flashes of electric sapphire light and clamorous fits of thunder, suddenly and most peculiarly appeared the silhouette of a man.

It was as if the turbulence outside heralded the arrival of the Baron Philippus Mormeau. Stepping forward into the light, his whisper cut through the air. "The night has been unruly."

# Chapter Six

All heads angled toward the man framed in the entranceway. Christian was stunned as to how he could suddenly appear between spontaneous flashes of lightning. It was as if one moment he wasn't there, and the next he was. He sought mutual surprise from his comrades at the dinner table; Cassandra revealed a somewhat annoyed expression, while Cotton's rumpled brow and angry stare told Christian that he was not alone in his confusion.

The Baron Mormeau took to his chair like a fox on the prowl. Dressed entirely in scarlet, from the red bows on his shoes to the auburn locks upon his head, he gave the appearance of one accustomed to the finer things in life. Even the double collar of fine lace about his neck was dyed a deep crimson. His stockings were red, as were the garters holding his breeches at the knees. His doublet, without waist-seams and worn open from mid-chest, revealed a red shirt underneath. Nothing on the man's person was any color other than a shade of red, save for his black shoes and the gold metal of his rings. Concerning his jewelry – while the rings were gold, the stones seated in them were rubies. From his hair to his ankles he was a scarlet man, save for his hands and face, which were as alabaster as Cassandra's pale beauty. Draped over his back, he wore a half-cape that perfectly matched the ensemble of his dress.

Christian, barely overcoming his astonishment, managed to utter only the obvious, "You are the Baron."

"I am the Host," said the red man in injured English, betraying his French descent.

Sitting in the glow of the candlelight, the Baron's features gained a distinctness to Christian's sharp eyes. It was quite obvious to him that the man's hair was not his own, but rather a fanciful periwig. His eyebrows had been plucked into thin little arches, contributing a very feminine look to his overall facial appearance; and his nose was long and thin, its ridge looking capable of cutting. His pointed nostrils served only to further the menacing aspect of his proboscis, and his thin lips seemed curled in a constant sneer. Gaunt was probably the best definition for the Baron's emaciated physique, his cheeks sunken and eyes set deep within their sockets.

His eyes, Christian could not help but note, were the same dull coals possessed by the Lady Cassandra. Could their similar complexions and unique eyes connote a shared ancestry?

"I trust Cassandra has offered you good care," said Mormeau as he cast Christian a wink.

"Yes," Christian replied while looking at Cassandra, "she has been most courteous."

"I am sure she has." The Frenchman oozed smugness.

"Baron," Cassandra interrupted, "do you not wish to know who 'tis you are to dine with?"

"Eh?"

Christian saw her shoot Mormeau an irate look.

"Oh, yes," the Baron nodded foolishly, "yes, yes! Introduce me, my love."

"The handsome gentleman across from me is a Mister Christian Coleswitten," she told him. "Across from you is the Master Cotton Smith-Patton. They hail from London."

"London," Mormeau repeated with clear dislike, "how very interesting." He then proceeded to withdraw from his inside breast pocket a small, bronze bell. Giving the bell a light shake, he summoned forth the giant German manservant.

Coming from the same entrance into the room that the Baron had just used, the large man approached the table.

"Horst," the Baron ordered him, "build up the fire. Our guests must be freezing." Seeing the empty decanters, he added, "And fetch us more wine! Should our guests die of thirst?"

Horst acknowledged his master's command with a slight bow and then advanced to the fireplace. As he passed by, Christian was shocked to see the man's face; divested of its high collar and the cover of darkness its gross mutilation was exposed for all to see. The entire left side of the man's face was literally gone. Skeletal in appearance, nothing more than muscle and bone, it looked as though the skin had been scraped from him. His left eye stared out emotionlessly from its socket: no ridge of flesh existed to hold it in place or lend it character. Both his cheeks had holes in them – the left cheek having the bigger of the two, which permitted one a partial view of his cheekbone, as well as the inside of his mouth. Christian's jaw slackened in horror at the sight of Horst's teeth through the hole. The two rows of yellowed and blackened pegs stood out in stark contrast to the dirty white of his ruined flesh. My God, Christian thought, how does he eat? How does he drink without his beverage spilling from his open cheeks? How does he live?

As Horst neared the fireplace, Christian perceived he walked with a slight limp. Favoring his right leg, the mutilated man bent at the waist and began picking up firewood. As he lifted one log, a small rat ran out of the woodpile. Before Christian could even recognize the rodent, Horst gave it a light blow with a log. Stunned but still living, the rat offered no resistance as he took it up and placed it inside his pocket. He then went about his business, dispensing wood to feed the fire as if nothing abnormal had occurred.

"Your manservant has a strange predilection for rodents," Christian whispered to Mormeau.

"Yes," he responded, "Horst has a dreadful fear of them. He has had bad experiences with the petite creatures."

"I find them rather cute," chimed Cassandra. "I like little, furry things."

Cotton leaned forward, suddenly interested. "Have ye ever eaten one?"

She ignored his remark, though the Baron found it amusing.

Waiting until after Horst had finished his chore and taken his leave of them, Christian asked the Baron, "What of him? What woe befell his face and body?"

"Leprosy."

He recoiled visibly from the remark, causing Mormeau to break into laughter.

"No, no, no, no!" their host waved his hands and shook his head in frantic assurance. "It was fire, not disease, that so spoiled handsome Horst. You have nothing to fear from him save for those damnable rats."

Christian remained uneasy. The Baron's poor humor served only to escalate the discomfort he felt in the presence of these bizarre people. He thought it necessary to inquire as to the total number of household staff. "If I may be so bold," he asked politely, "who else is in your employ?"

Mormeau threw Cassandra a quick glance, then said, "No one but Horst."

"One man does all the work about this place?" Christian asked skeptically.

"Yes."

Although he found it hard to believe, Christian could see that it might be possible. The castle was not in the best of shape, he thought, but one servant for all their needs? And to a baron, no less? The more he ruminated upon it, the more he felt he was being deceived.

"Outwardly, Horst may look monstrous," conceded Cassandra, "but inside him beats a most gentle heart."

"If he is German then he has no heart," Cotton stated sagaciously from the far end of the table.

"Enough of this prattle!" roared the Baron, throwing his hands up into the air. "We have more important things to discuss," he turned to Christian, "such as why you are here."

Feigning innocence, Christian pled, "Why, Baron, only you know why we are here."

Shaking his long, curly hair, Mormeau smiled, "No, you misunderstand. Why have you come to Manasseh?"

Not wishing to reveal at this time his true reasons for visiting this dreadful place, and also desiring to gain some insight as to why Mormeau brought them into his castle, Christian replied with a veiled accusation. Looking the Baron straight in those limpid, black eyes of his he accused, "I believe you know why we have come to Manasseh as well."

Sliding back into his chair, Baron Mormeau could not repress a pleasant giggle. "Ah!" he sighed, "I see we have a guest suspicious of his host. Why do you greet me with such resentment?"

Before Christian could reply, Cotton answered for him. "One must always be suspect of the kind ways of strangers."

Unable to contain what had been bothering him for much of the conversation, Christian blurted, "Especially those who adorn their battlements with impaled corpses."

Smiling, the Baron leaned forward in his seat, placed his elbows on the tabletop, and supported his head lazily in his palms.

Christian could see by Mormeau's smile that the man's gentle features were made fierce by the peculiar elongation of his canines. Appearing abnormal, it made the Baron look rather bestial. His fingertips were also somewhat savage, being crowned by nails superior in length to Cassandra's. Painted red, Christian had not noticed them before because they had blended in with the totality of the Baron's crimson garments. Mormeau's defense of his actions ended Christian's scrutiny.

"My friends," he appealed, "I will have you know that I invite all strangers to town into my abode. And while it may seem humanitarian of me, it is in truth rather selfish. I long to hear of tales from the outside world, the real world, not the superstitious prattle of small-town gossip. I look forward to guests and treat them accordingly in the hopes of seeing them again." He motioned to the outside. "As for the impaled remains, they were in place long before I purchased this castle and serve mainly as atmospheric ornaments."

"Ornaments?" Christian ridiculed. "How could you so treat the former containers of life? Should they not be let down and given Christian burials?"

Mormeau grew rather cross. "They are corpses of heathens and are undeserving of any burial, let alone a Christian one."

"When I pass from this life," Cotton broke in, "I do not ask for a wake or an elaborate funeral. I do not even wish to be remembered, but rather to be forgotten, never to have my moniker associated with such a malignant world or despicable people."

"But remembrance allows one to live on after he has departed," Christian tried to enlighten his associate. "The gravestone offers us all our earthly immortality after we have attained our rightful places in Heaven."

"There are ways other than the gravestone that tender immortality, my boy," suggested Mormeau, "but explain to me how we 'attain rightful places in Heaven'."

"To attain one's rightful place in Heaven, one must complete a journey fraught with pain, replete with sorrow, rife with anguish and unremitting death. 'Tis a journey of persistent disasters and continuing mishaps, an adventure of little joy and much malice ..."

"'Tis life," said Cassandra in blunt summation.

"Yes," Christian smiled, "how very perceptive you are."

His Lady blushed and averted her eyes, whispering in deference to him, "I only said what you said without want of elegant speech."

Before Christian could offer her his assurances that this was not so, and in so doing restore her pride, he was halted by the Baron's crafty accusation. "By your definition, you care little for life."

"Not so, Baron. I see the lives we lead as the keys with which to open wide the doors of Heaven."

"If Heaven is a heaven, then why need it be locked at all?"

"To keep out the serpents," Christian coolly replied. Then, looking over the Baron's apparel, he added, "And all the red devils in Hell."

Disregarding Christian's quite blatant insinuation, the Baron verbally deduced, "If the life one leads is the key, then why fuss over the empty baggage left behind?"

"Again you return to the subject of a cadaver's sanctity."

"Oh, I hold in the sanctity of nothing. Living or dead, nothing is sacred to me, especially not those rotting wretches above us."

"By what rights judge you these men?"

"By the rights vested in me when I wore the collar, or yoke, if you prefer."

Christian's heart skipped a beat. "You're a priest?"

"I was a priest," Mormeau said in all nonchalance, "but gave it up. It was a fruitless occupation."

"A 'fruitless occupation'?" Christian cried. "How can you call the saving of souls a '*fruitless occupation*'?"

"Because, my naive friend," Mormeau stated as if it were an accepted fact, "there is no God."

"There is no God? There is no God? If you believed that, then why justify not burying those corpses with the excuse that they are undeserving of burial?"

"If I believe it, then why even bury them at all? Ah, Horst has returned with more wine."

Christian had been so shocked by the Baron's atheism that he had not even noticed the mutilated giant enter. Placing two full decanters on the table and removing the empty ones, Horst looked to the Baron for further instruction. With a backward flip of his hand, Mormeau dismissed his mute servant. Bowing, Horst left as silently as he had arrived.

Studying the decanters before him, the Baron gazed past them at Cotton, who stared thirstily at the wine. Taking one of the decanters, he slid it across the table surface to the alcoholic.

Stopping just in front of him, the red wine tempted Cotton like no woman ever could. He forced his eyes away long enough to glance at Christian. Eyeing him with contempt, his ward offered him little support. Beads of sweat formed over Cotton's skin as he returned to the solitary glass decanter within his immediate reach. *What curse has befallen me which so renders the decision to drink or not to drink an agony?* he bitterly asked his drunken self. *What do I care if Coleswitten agrees or disagrees? He is nothing more than a bloody Englishman who perhaps likes nothing better than the English domination of Scotland.* Taking the wine into his hands, he poured himself a drink and thought with unreasonable malice, *I'll toast to his displeasure.*

At seeing his friend fall to the alcohol, Christian shook his head in disgust. *What remained of a once-great man was to be found at the bottom of a bottle,* he sadly noted.

"There is one religion all men bow to, Monsieur Coleswitten," Mormeau's voice boomed, "and that lies between a woman's legs. That is where life comes forth. That is your Garden of Eden."

Christian was outraged that the Baron would say such a thing in the presence of a Lady. He looked with some dismay at Cassandra, who lowered her head in embarrassment: an open invitation for him to champion her cause. "Why, Baron Mormeau," he said, minding Cassandra, "how can you say such vulgarities when there is a Lady present? Do not tarnish this good Lady with your miscreant theological views; the honor of all women is at stake when even one is impugned."

"But women have no honor," Mormeau insisted. "How can they that allow themselves to be governed by passion rather than reason be deserving of any honor?" Addressing Cassandra, he asked, "What did the lonely Greek women do with themselves when all their men had left them for the Trojan Lady?"

Cassandra forced her lips into a smile, but Christian could see by her eyes that she was most upset with him. "How should I know, my Baron?" She acted unaffected. "I was not there."

"But you continue to practice in their ways."

"To you I would prefer anything."

"Then why not Horst? Or a townsperson, perhaps?"

"We all must have our standards, Baron, save for you."

Christian dared not interrupt their conversation. Aside from it being obviously personal, he did not know to what it was they referred.

Removing his little bell again, the Baron once more summoned Horst. Like the obedient creature he was, the manservant was waiting on Mormeau's bidding in no time at all. "Horst, bring us their sup," ordered Mormeau. The ghastly gaunt man lumbered off, presumably to the kitchen.

Christian was more than a little queasy at the thought of that "walking rot" handling, or perhaps preparing, his meal. Seeking some comfort, his eyes descended on the Venus sitting across from him.

Cassandra saw that her admirer was once more admiring, and bequeathed him a smile. As her full lips parted to reveal her teeth, Christian felt as though his heart was pierced; not by another of Cupid's arrow, but by his own horror.

Perhaps it was because he had only recently observed the Baron's feral grin, or because the Lady's possession of a haunting allure similar to that of the woman of his nightmares forced him to see what he did not see before, or rather, what he had chosen not to see.

What has her beauty, and elegant ways, hidden from me? he lamented as he looked on her pointedly accentuated canines. Paleness of skin and darkness of eye aside, apparently she was related to the Baron through the teeth.

"So, Christian," Mormeau called for his attention, "tell us of yourself."

"What is it you wish to know, Baron?"

"I do not know, you tell me."

"Only on the condition that you return the favor."

"You have my word," Mormeau nodded. "I shall answer any question you pose me."

"Then so shall it be," Christian agreed. After clearing first his throat then taking a sip of wine, he launched into a greatly condensed version of his life.

Spending little time conversing about his family, as it was still too difficult for him to do so, he dealt mainly with his goals and aspirations. He spoke of his desires to enter into a cloister or monastery, of his unquenchable passion for knowledge, and of his attempts at apprenticeship. The Baron ignored most of what Christian said, however, when Christian spoke of seeking to apprentice under a wealthy or noble man, he instantly perked up.

"Look no farther," he said as he grabbed hold of Christian's hand, "for your noble patronage lies the length of my arm! I have been in dire need of one such as yourself: strong, young, intelligent, and ambitious. Allow me the honor of being your tutor, benefactor, and friend!"

Pulling his hand from the Baron's cold, clammy grasp, Christian looked at Mormeau as if he were quite odd. "I have been in your castle for no more than two hours, in your presence far less, all that you know of me has come out of mine own lips, and yet you tender such a generous offer?" Hearing the validity of his own spoken words made him grow cross. "Come now, sir," he boldly charged, "speak true. What need have you for me?"

Ignoring Christian's question, the Baron shook his head. "Suspicion clouds your reasoning," he said sadly, pointing to his temple, "I offer you here and now what you claim to desire, and yet, through either your fear of French customs or your fear of reality, you shun my proposal."

"I have done nothing of the sort, I only question your motives."

"Would you additionally deny yourself the continued company of the good Lady?" Mormeau pushed onward, gesturing to a disturbed Cassandra.

Christian looked at her. "I would never wish to deny her company—"

"Then why do you not accept my offer?"

"I have not decided one way or the other!" Christian shouted. "I seek only to find out more about your offer before I commit myself unto your service!"

"Baron!" Cassandra admonished, coming to Christian's aid, "see how you have aggrieved our guest; how the blood has flowed unhealthily to his face?" Rising from her seat, she continued to reprove his horrendous behavior. "I shall not sit silently by and watch you offend my London friend! If you persist, I shall be forced to dine elsewhere tonight!"

Christian saw that the glare she gave Mormeau seemed to almost frighten him. Forsaking his relaxed demeanor, Mormeau pled with her to be still. "Please," he implored, "be seated. I did not mean—"

"Oh, but you did, my Baron," she coldly corrected him. "You did."

"Stay for supper. Do not go."

"Show Mister Coleswitten and Master Smith-Patton the courtesy and respect I have shown you, and I will be content."

"That I will, my love, that I will."

Lady Cassandra took to her seat, satisfied. Christian glanced over at her and smiled a thank you.

"I did not mean to cause you any distress," Mormeau apologized in a tone lacking sincerity. "Please, Christian, accept my regrets."

"Accepted," the Englishman readily granted.

Mormeau smiled and glanced at the tabletop. "Now that we are finished with that, tell me, good Christian ... tell me what you think of one who hast fallen to temptation."

"Are you referring to yourself?"

"Perhaps."

"The loss of one's soul is the single most contemptible deed one can so accomplish," said Christian without thinking. "'Tis so very easy to do: succumbing to every desire, fulfilling that which is forbidden by Divine laws and accordances. One must keep in mind that we exist merely for the preservation of our souls, for life as we know it is short, but the fires of Hell are everlasting."

"You actually believe that a life is lived solely for the observance of God? That one must be pure, chaste, and virginal to the extent that he shall avoid even the taint of rot in his grave?"

"Once again you claim I say what I do not. I believe that our Creator knows well humanity's frailties. Need I not say that to err is human? I do believe, however, that God must be given His due. Is it so much to ask for one Sunday every week? To fast on certain days, and avoid certain foods on others? Our Lord sacrificed Himself to a horrible death so that we could gain entrance into Paradise. I should think a decent individual could be mindful of that, respect God's laws, and live a full and happy life without being a dullard. So long as one loves Jesus and rejects evil he shall be more than compensated for his troubles in the Hereafter."

"And what is evil?"

Christian felt the strong desire to answer "You!", but instead thought for a moment before replying, "I believe evil exists in all forms: man, animal, conscious and unconscious. And while Satan is the summation of all evil, the embodiment of sin and antithesis to all that is holy, I do not believe evil to be beyond mortal comprehension, relegated only to devils and demons. The supernatural, after all, is nothing more than the extension of the natural."

"Interesting, if not intense," the Baron conceded. "However, I feel you have done evil an unnecessary injustice."

"Really? How so?"

"Why, how can you criticize that which you have never fully experienced?"

"I am sure all of us in this room have committed some sin at sometime in their life."

"But to commit those sins without guilt, to be free of groveling for forgiveness in a Sunday confessional: that is true freedom, that is living life well."

Christian shook his head in disbelief. "A remorseless conscience – there is the root of true evil. Within us all lies this weed which must be kept under control. A lifelong battle between good and evil rages beneath our breasts, pitting sanity against insanity. Constantly, day in and day out, this vile weed sucks at our souls; as we age our resistance weakens. Fear of death and sickness offer the weed its nourishment, seeding doubt and bitterness. The weed of wickedness can only be plucked from us by God's own hand."

"You speak like a Calvinist," Mormeau observed with some disfavor. "Do you not know that the weed must be allowed to grow before it can be plucked?"

Christian chose to concern himself with the Baron's initial remark, which bothered him greatly, rather than address the question posed him. "I offer you my assurances, Baron," he spoke with grave earnestness, "that I do not, nor have I ever, nor will I ever, espouse or embrace the Protestant doctrine." Satisfied that he had refuted Mormeau's allegation, he took another sip of wine.

Horst limped into the dining room, holding a large covered tray in his hands. Setting the tray down on the table near Christian, he removed the lid and exposed two hot bowls of stew and two small loaves of bread. Taking a bowl from the tray, he placed it before Christian, he then handed him one of the loaves.

Christian took the loaf from Horst's rancid hand and set it next to his bowl. He was starving, but could not bring himself to partake of the stew while Horst was so near. The stench of him overpowers the delicious smell of the food, he disgustedly noted. And his looks! How could anyone eat when served by him?

Horst moved on to Cotton. When he was through serving the guests, he tucked the tray under his arm, dutifully bowed to the Lady and her Baron, and pivoted, leaving them the way in which he had come.

Christian looked with mistrust at the stew before him: chunks of beef sitting in a thick, obscuring, brown gravy. He picked up his spoon and began to cautiously stir in the hopes of dredging up something foul so he would have an excuse not to eat it. Although ravenous, his good sense would not allow his appetite to dictate his actions. He poked and prodded the beef several times with the tip of his spoon before deciding it to be to his satisfaction. Glancing up to see why it had become so quiet, he found Cassandra and Mormeau watching him with great concern.

"Is it not to your liking?" a caring Cassandra asked.

"Oh, yes, my Lady," he assured her, "I am just waiting for it to cool."

Mormeau smiled at him and mumbled something in French to Cassandra, who furiously answered him in a barrage of unpleasant sounding garble. All Christian could make of her indignant response was the last word: "*stupide!*"

Pressured by their stares and emboldened by her inquiry, Christian dipped his spoon once more into the dark broth and raised it to his lips. As the hot liquid ran down his throat and coated his hungry belly, it instilled in him a sense of rejuvenation. Warmed by the stew inside him, as well as delighted with its rich taste, he hastily spooned some more into his open mouth. Scooping up a large morsel of meat, Christian delivered it past his lips and chewed with pleasure the tender beef. I have never in all my years, he thought, sampled such a divine stew. So soft is the meat, so heavy the sauce, so robust the flavor! If this be my last meal then there be no complaints from me!

"You like?"

He raised his eyes in response to Cassandra's query. "That I do!" he exclaimed. "'Tis most excellent."

"I am content you are enjoying yourself." She flashed that familiar, sad smile and watched him eat with what appeared to be a curious longing.

Wishing to see how his friend was faring, Christian threw Cotton a quick glance. On doing so, he at once regretted his inquisitive nature.

Cotton sat playing with his food. So drunk was he that he had somehow managed to spill his stew on himself. The large stain spreading from his buff coat to his shirt attested to his inebriation, as did the puddle of sauce on the table before him. He seemed incapable of operating a spoon, opting to use his fingers instead. The only success he could manage was dipping his bread into the sauce puddle and pouring himself more wine. Christian forced himself back to his meal in a subdued rage.

Breaking a small piece of bread from his loaf, he dunked it in his wine and placed it on his tongue. Swallowing, he gestured to Mormeau and asked, "Why do you not dine, Baron?"

Grinning, Mormeau glanced sidelong at Cassandra and replied, "The meal to which we are accustomed takes a little longer in preparation. I did not wish to spoil your appetite."

"You are so gracious a host," taunted Christian in caustic praise.

"That I am, sir, but you are no good guest."

"And how is it that I am the villain?" Christian asked as he sipped the last of his stew.

"You have eluded my questions pertaining to your presence here. I house you, feed you, and endeavor to please you and yet you choose to reward me with avoidance."

Resting his spoon against the side of his empty bowl and clasping his hands together, Christian looked on Mormeau in all seriousness. "Before I reveal to you the circumstances which have brought me here, fulfill that which you have promised me. Tell me of yourself, as I have told you of myself. I have never heard of a Baron Mormeau, and am interested."

"Are you really?" an amused Mormeau asked in disbelief.

"Yes, I am."

"Excellent!" He clapped his hands together in an exuberant show of elation. "Simply excellent!" So thrilled was the Baron in Christian's interest that he talked rapidly, his mediocre English pronunciation suffering because of it. "I shall not bore you with details of my obscure youth, but begin at the beginning of my rise to power. Many years ago in my native France I pledged myself body and soul to the Catholic regime. I was young and foolish and hot for the blood of Huguenots. My cruelty toward them knew no bounds, and as such I rose rapidly in stature, eventually attaining a cardinalship."

Christian had been aghast at finding Mormeau to have been a common lay priest, he now sat dumbstruck at the news of his having attained the rank of cardinalate.

"Ah! I see that you are shocked," Mormeau noted with distinct delight. "Do not be, it was another life."

"I see now why you have maintained your anonymity here in England," Christian managed to utter. "Being a known persecutor of Protestants in a country of Anglican worship can be very disadvantageous to one's health."

"Exactly! And as Cardinal, I presided over the deaths of several hundred people." Taking on an air of pride, he added, "I personally attended every execution I ordered."

Seeing how this troubled Christian a great deal, Cassandra squinted her eyes and keenly observed, "You, too, are Catholic."

"That I am," he responded arrogantly. "The foundations of the Anglican church are built upon the lecheries and greed of a glutton."

"Christianity as a whole is founded on the precepts of deluded Jews and a false Messiah," Mormeau sought to correct him.

"So says the venerable Baron Mormeau," ridiculed Christian in a tone laden with contempt.

"You speak truer than you know," Mormeau informed him, "truer than your ambitious little mind could possibly know."

"Gentlemen, please," interjected a distressed Cassandra, "can we not speak of something less volatile?"

Both men showered her with their apologies. When they had gone past the point of reasonable requests for forgiveness, she directed them to silence and bade only Christian speak, much to the displeasure of the Baron.

"Continue with your tale," he instructed Mormeau. "Tell me more of your life so that I may glean a better understanding of your heathen ways and beliefs."

Mormeau swallowed hard and looked to his Lady as if asking for her clemency. When he did not receive anything more than a spiteful grin, he recommenced his tale. "In 1534, when I was not more than seven years of age, anti-Catholic posters appeared all over Paris. It was because of this and the Council of Trent a decade later that I came to so loathe the Protestants of my country. I was there when the villages were torched and eight hundred of the heretics were put to the sword. I helped stoke the coals of the Chambre Ardente, the place where many were burned for witchcraft, and mine own hands assisted in the placement of decapitated Huguenot heads on the iron spikes of the Chateau D'Amboise. My true day of glory, however, was not to be for sometime."

"The Saint Bartholomew's Day Massacre?" Christian offered in an attempt at ridicule.

"Precisely. I myself was one of Catherine De Medici's personal advisors. I counseled her in the Tuileries Garden that fateful Saturday afternoon." Mormeau's eyes sparkled as he recited the Queen's virtues. "Ah, Madame Catherine, never was there a better defender of the Faith. Her beauty and intelligence were exceeded only by her cunning manipulations. France will never see her kind again!"

"She's well past any worth, even for the worms," quipped Cassandra, seemingly envious of the Baron's praise for his former employer.

Mormeau chose to ignore her remark and went on in the relating of his recollections. "Once the Queen was satisfied with the design of the total annihilation of Protestant France, she convened the advisory until later that night. Oh, but how the Louvre was active that hot, August night! How the French and Swiss guards were giddy with excitement, as were we all! All court ladies gathered into the Queen's bed chamber, giggles and gossip mingled with celebrating toasts of wine."

"And you expect me to believe that you attended this tasteless party?" Christian questioned his host's sanity.

"Attended it?" cried Mormeau as if insulted, "My dear boy, I'll have you know that without my direct intervention there might not have been a celebration!" He calmed down and explained himself. "The Queen had become most troubled, threatening to perhaps call the entire action off. It was none but I, possessor of the silvery tongue, who persuaded her not to. Taking her aside, I asked of her how all of Paris could forgive those who had twice besieged us to the point of starvation, brought foreign mercenaries into our land to rape, murder, and pillage, and who forced us to look with hungry eyes on the dog, the cat, and the rat. Once I was finished, she ordered the tocsin to be sounded at once, an hour and a half earlier than scheduled. The big bell of Saint-Germain-L'Auxerrois was rung and the city militia signaled to arms."

"And you were there?" Christian asked skeptically, "In fifteen hundred and seventy-two?"

"Yes."

"Impossible."

"Let me finish in the recounting of my life and I will better explain myself later."

Christian yielded to this request with a curt nod.

"Now, where was I?" Mormeau happily asked himself. "Oh, yes, the Louvre." He shifted excitedly in his chair. "At the Louvre, Protestant pigs were lined up and systematically executed by the royal guards. From the comforts of inside, we Catholics watched as rows upon rows of the heretics were slain. Hors d'oeuvres were served, as was an exquisite sherry. We feasted and laughed as the corpse heap in the courtyard outside grew in size. All had a splendid time, save for Queen Marguerite and the King's foppish younger brother Alencon." Mormeau's face was sapped of its glee as he remembered their reactions, "Marguerite was quite upset, the little whore – she locked herself in her room and would not come out. And Alencon, he would rather speak of humanity and brotherly love as an excuse not to take to the streets. He probably feared the sight of his own blood."

"And what of you, Baron?" asked Christian, "Did you not take to the streets?"

Mormeau took offense at his guest's suggestion that he was a coward. "Sir," he angrily defended himself, "I will have you know that I did in fact take to the streets." Bragging, he added, "I rode in the company of the noble Guise, and saw with mine own eyes that snake Coligny taken of his head, flesh, and balls!"

"Baron, please!" Cassandra protested. "Can we not avoid such talk at the dinner table?"

"History is not pretty, my dear."

"The attractiveness of history depends less on actual events and more on the historian."

"You trap me with your speech."

"I simply ask of you to use words more palatable."

"Palatable?" he asked in irritated confusion.

"Acceptable, Baron." Exasperated, she tried to explain herself better, "Words more suitable at this discourse."

"Woman," he properly admonished her, "let me finish my tale without further interruption."

Christian saw the Lady's face softly darken. He was not certain whether it was due to embarrassment or anger.

Mormeau persisted in his account. "The carnage continued on through the hot night. The next day, Sunday, was the Feast of Saint Bartholomew. The day was spent in ridding the city of remaining dissenters and Calvinist corpses." He shut his eyes and took in a deep breath, as if he were still there. "Even now I can smell their bodies. My ears hear their scraping as they are dragged to the Seine and tossed in." He opened his eyes and grinned pleasantly at Christian. "I saw the bloodthirsty mob further mutilate the broken remains of Admiral Coligny. In their hands he fell all to pieces ..."

"An interesting story, Baron," derided Christian.

"You do not believe me."

"To do so would be to insult both our intellects. The wars against the Huguenots ended nearly a century ago."

Mormeau fumed in agreement: "The damned Edict of Nantes."

"You could not possibly have survived those wars and look your present age," Christian continued.

"You have a flair for history," Mormeau chuckled. "Good." He then leaned closer to his doubting acquaintance and asked, "How old do you reckon me to be, Christian? Eh? How old?"

Christian thought for a moment, then answered, "About the mid-forties, I should think."

"Forty-five, to be exact," Mormeau nodded, "however, in all actuality I am aged over three times that amount."

Christian laughed. "Come now, Baron Mormeau," he begged him, "surely this farce has gone on long enough. No one can seriously claim to be one hundred and thirty-five years old."

"One hundred and thirty-eight," Mormeau said, dead serious.

Seeking some explanation, Christian turned to Cassandra, who provided him with nothing more than a spiritless stare. Receiving no assistance from her with his perplexed state, he faced a patient Mormeau and collected himself. He knew, somehow, that if he asked, what would be revealed to him would not only be true, but horrid as well. Clenching his jaw and closing his eyes, he prepared himself for the dark secret that had so suffused itself into the very air of Manasseh. Steeled in his resolve, he opened his eyes and gave in to the Baron's wishes. "Explain yourself."

Satisfied that he held Christian's curiosity, Mormeau rocked back against his chair and picked up where his story left off. "It was in the immediate weeks following the massacre that an unsuccessful assassination attempt was launched against me. Being known to the Calvinist underground as one of the Queen's most trusted advisors, I was targeted for death. They blamed me, and rightly so, for the instigation of the massacre. They claimed my pulpit sermons stirred up the Catholics against them, and that I was the power behind Richelieu as well as behind the throne. They called me *Le Sanguinaire*, and *Le Diable Rouge*."

"And how did these Calvinists try to assassinate you?" asked Christian, absent of any derision.

"They ambushed my entourage on the road into Paris. From the bushes they charged, at least ten of them, armed with swords and muskets. They decimated the entirety of my riding companions while I managed to escape on horseback into the woods with only a flesh wound upon my thigh. It was then that I realized how fleeting life was, how so soon it could all end. It could have been me lying in my own blood on that country road that day, and the fear of death crept into my thoughts like never before. I was obsessed with cheating the Reaper – never would I allow this body to be defiled by the teeth of worm nor would I allow it the cruel ravages of time. Having enjoyed too much the pleasures living offered to forsake it all for a shallow possibility, I sought means which would ward off Death's sharp sickle ..."

"You were unsuccessful, of course."

"No." He cast a quick glance at Cassandra and smiled. "I found what I desired in the orifice of a woman."

The Baron's shrouded references served only to add to Christian's confusion. Seeking some clarity on the subject, he asked, "Elaborate, if you would be so kind, as to the nature of this woman."

Mormeau fidgeted with his long nails, picking the dirt out from under them. "It was a gypsy girl that so granted my wishes, taking me to a quiet, little village where a strange woman lived."

"And what was so strange about this woman?"

"It was rumored she had lived for many centuries."

"And she passed her secret on to you."

"She passed more on to me than a secret — she gave me a new perspective on the way I took life."

"What befell this witch?"

"She was no witch," Mormeau corrected him. "I had burned enough to know."

"Then if not by sorcery, how did she enable you to be as you are today?"

Once more Mormeau responded in riddle. "She gave me life by taking my life."

"What?" spat Christian in irritation.

"She brought about my immortality through the realization of my mortality."

Angered by his addled state, Christian denounced the Baron's intentional ambiguity. "What game do you play with my mind? How can you expect me to believe, much less fathom, what 'tis you claim?"

"I should think it far easier to comprehend and accept my words than those found on the pages of the Bible!"

Christian shook his head in disgust. "What manner of man are you?"

Turning grave, Mormeau's eyes twinkled like ice as he uttered, "I am one who is neither living nor dead, but am living in death."

"Baron," the Lady Cassandra threatened, "if you do not cease in the annoyance of our guest I fear I shall be forced to depart."

"*Mon amie*," Mormeau acted innocently, "what have I done?"

"You know very well what you have done," she said as she rose to leave.

Christian could not let her go. He could not bear to be left alone at the table with the Baron. Cotton was of no help to him in the state he was in, and Cassandra was the only aspect of this whole place that he liked. Before she could move away from her chair, he stood. "Please, Madam," he begged her, "do not be guilty of that by which you charge the Baron and appear so discourteous as to leave the company of your guest."

"If you like, you can come with me," she offered in a tone full of hope.

He was tempted to go with her, to leave this base table to its wretched masters and vanish into a dark corridor or up a winding stone stair with the woman who was capturing his heart by the seconds. But looking to Cotton, who could not even raise food successfully to his mouth due to his drunkenness, he knew he could not abandon his friend in such a state in such a place as this. "I cannot be so callous as to desert my companion," he gestured limply to Smith-Patton. "Were he cognizant, I should think he would not desert me."

"But he already has!" Mormeau laughed as if Christian were a fool.

"Baron!" Cassandra cried.

"Take to your seat and be silent!" the Frenchman roared.

Although directed at Cassandra, Christian promptly sat himself. If Mormeau's words were not enough to compel one to sit, his wrathful countenance was.

And yet the Lady Cassandra still stood!

Christian sat in awe of her. In the face of this vicious beast, he thought with admiration, whose eyes reflected rage and promised punishment, she stood firm and unyielding, not even blinking in acquiescence to his facial conveyance of displeasure.

The Baron sighed a contrite plea. "Please, my dear," he mumbled, "be seated and I shall talk no more of it."

Cassandra took to her chair, but leveled a glacial stare at Mormeau, who did his best to avoid it.

Tugging Christian gently by his shirtsleeve, Mormeau grinned and asked, "You wish to know how I received my baronage, eh?"

Christian removed his arm from the Baron's touch and looked uncomfortably at Cassandra. He was stunned to find his Lady seething. Though covered by her red lips, by her jaw line he saw she clenched her teeth in anger. So enraged was she that on realizing he was watching her she could not even offer him the sad smile he had become accustomed to. She cast her eyes from him and gazed with mute fury at the castle wall.

With Mormeau waiting on his reply, Christian managed to tear his concerned eyes from Cassandra and nervously respond. "Yes," his voice quavered, "pray tell." His fear mounted to an almost unbearable pitch. The room had gotten so cold, and yet sweat dotted his face. For the first time he actually felt alone. Cotton wasn't with him, and for the time being, neither was Cassandra. The Baron was certainly not with him — if anything, he was against him. He was alone, in this archaic, decrepit castle with these peculiar people. What troubled him further was the hidden secret to which the Baron alluded, much to his Lady's displeasure. What was the dark secret of Manasseh? Of the castle? Of Baron Mormeau? What was it about this place that so smelled of evil?

"I obtained my title through the careful manipulation of an influential aristocrat," Mormeau boasted. His beady eyes rolled to Cassandra. "It seemed I had something he was willing to barter for."

"And what purposes were achieved in your acquisition of a noble ranking?"

"It permitted me to live in the way in which I had become accustomed. By being a baron, my purse strings grew thick off the populace and offered me the privacy I so needed in going about my business."

"And the aristocrat who granted you your title, what of him?"

Mormeau smiled as his hand ducked inside his vest and reemerged with Horst's bell. Ringing it twice, their gruesome waiter limped into the dining room.

"Horst, bring the Lady and I our sup." ordered Mormeau.

"I am not hungry, my Baron," Cassandra demurred.

"Are you not dining tonight, my dear?"

She shook her head. "No, I do not feel well."

Shrugging, Mormeau seemingly took no offense. "Very well, then," he sighed, "I shall join Christian and—" he stopped before referring to Cotton when he saw the Scot groggily fight to stay awake. "Ha! Ha!" he laughed, "Your friend seems to prefer the wine to the food!"

"So I noticed," Christian coldly responded as he angrily glared at Cotton.

"Now, Christian," the Baron instructed him, "every man has his vices."

"But few overindulge in them."

"That is not so, and you know it." Looking at him with those little, black eyes, Mormeau added, "And what is it in which you overindulge, Christian? Eh?"

"That is none of your business, Baron. If you would please, keep your prying insinuations to yourself."

"I am only curious as to who it is I am feeding," Mormeau spoke defensively. "I have fulfilled my part of our bargain, now you fulfill yours."

"You wish to know why I am here."

"Yes, and spare me the accusations."

Christian leaned close to the Baron, as if to exclude Cassandra and Cotton from his revelation. "The intent of my mission is to either retrieve or ascertain a cure for the Great Plague. As I am sure, you are well aware of the ruination of London, and of the poor state of most of the counties of England, I humbly ask for your assistance."

"But why should I wish to aid the enemies of my people?"

"Have you any common decency, sir? Do you call innocent women and children your foes?"

"I love children — they fill my heart with delight!"

"Then will you not help me?"

"That I will, but I do not see how I can be of any help to you."

"This town has had not one case of the Plague, nor death for that matter, in over twenty years. How is this so, Baron?"

Mormeau moved from Christian. Seemingly troubled, he asked, "How is it that you have this information?"

"Taxation census."

The Baron flashed Cassandra a nervous look, but seemed to gain strength from her stony countenance. "I think you will find this town to be unlike any you have ever witnessed," he smiled. "It holds what it is you seek."

Christian sat up excitedly. "Where? Where can I find such a remedy?"

The Baron only grinned, his peculiar teeth apparently being answer enough.

"Cast aside your petty patriotism, Baron," Christian pled. "That may have worked for you in France, but not here."

"Why should I care if all of England dies? The world will only be rid of a vulgar people, not to mention many Protestants!"

"There is a point where religious differences mean nothing, where common decency must reign supreme! I do not proscribe to the view that this disease is from the hand of God. I believe it to be a natural occurrence, a natural disaster."

"How typical," said Mormeau smugly, "how you choose only miracles to be from Heaven, and disasters from nature. Can you not see that they are one in the same?"

"Now you play the pagan. Can you not make up your mind as to what 'tis you do or do not believe in?"

"I believe God to be nothing more than a man's desire."

"Desire for what?"

"Desire to explain what cannot be explained, the desire to believe there is something more to life than simply living: to believe that there is an afterlife, a palatial estate in the sky."

"And you are so certain this is so?"

Without a moment's delay, the Baron answered, "Yes."

"And the risen Christ?"

Mormeau's forehead wrinkled in annoyance. "Christ never rose!" he indignantly insisted. "He is nothing more than dust and bone, while I am flesh and blood! I walk as He does not, yet I am not elevated to godhood!"

"How can you make such a blasphemous charge?"

"How can it be blasphemous if I do not believe?"

"Gentlemen, please!" Cassandra implored them, "Desist in this arguing!"

In accordance with the Lady's strained request, the dining room fell silent. All that could be heard were the staggered steps of Horst, resounding throughout the castle as he strove to bring the Baron his meal.

Turning in expectancy to the room's most used entranceway, Christian patiently awaited the manservant's emergence. The uneven tones of his footfalls played havoc with Christian's nerves.

The rest of the dinner party sat oblivious to Horst's approach. Mormeau examined his long nails, often holding them up to the candlelight. Cassandra was content with studying Christian's angular features, removing her hands from the table to the secluded warmth of her lap. Cotton propped his heavy head up with one hand. Having finished all the wine set before him, he could do nothing more but contemplate his misery.

Horst entered the dining room carrying a large, covered pewter tray. He held it out in front of him like a good waiter, though his broken gait wrecked any poise or fluidity of movement. Walking to the left of the Baron, he stood at attention between Mormeau and his Lady.

Ignoring him, Mormeau ceased in the picking of his nails and leaned towards Christian. "I ask you once more," he said earnestly, "will you not come under my wing? Will you not join me?"

Looking from Mormeau to Cassandra, Christian shook his head. "I cannot accept your gracious offer, Baron, for I must complete that for which I was sent here. I have been entrusted to find a cure, so 'tis that which I must first do."

Falling back into his chair, Mormeau muttered, "So it shall be." He then motioned with a violent waving of his hand for Horst to set the tray before him. Tying a white napkin around his neck, he rubbed his hands vigorously together and proclaimed, "Let us see what Horst has whipped up for me tonight." Licking his lips, he winked at Cassandra, who closed her eyes in disgust.

Lifting the cover from the tray, Horst revealed the Baron's supper, to the obvious delight of his master. "Ah, Horst," Mormeau clasped his hands, "my favorite!"

Christian's eyes widened in shock – there on the cold metal tray, lying before the hungry red devil, was a newly-born child!

The infant gazed up at the Baron in wonder. He smiled innocently as Mormeau rubbed knife and fork together over him as if about to carve a roast pheasant, and tried to grab at the entwining utensils.

"Surely you jest, sir," Christian managed through a dry throat. His eyes darted back and forth between the baby, the knife and fork, the smirking Baron, and Cassandra, who could not raise her eyes to his. In fearful bewilderment, he even looked to Cotton, who stared stupidly as if through a haze at the spectacle across the table from him.    Returning to the Baron, Christian nervously gripped at the arms of his chair and watched in silent horror. He hesitated to stop Mormeau, for if it were a mockery he would appear a fool before the good Lady, yet if he intervened he might spare the life of a small child. His mind kept repeating over and over again, *this cannot be possible, the Baron is toying with me!* Yet for all his intellect, his instincts told him different.

Melodramatically looking over the knife and fork in his hands, Mormeau shook his head and asked, "What need have I for these?" He then tossed them into the air behind him.

Letting out a slow sigh of relief, Christian eased back into his seat. 'Twas nothing more than a game, his mind silently rejoiced, a sick, sick game.

The clatter of the knife and fork striking the stone floor prompted Cotton to confusedly sputter, "What manner of trickery is this?"

Without batting an eye, in a tone of voice thick with absurdity, Mormeau replied, "It is no trickery ... it is supper." Then, in a flash, he bared his vicious teeth and fell upon the hapless babe.

Christian jumped up in horror at the sight, knocking his chair to the floor. "Monster!" he screamed breathlessly, "Monster!" The piercing cry of the little newborn and the image of it impotently pushing at the Baron's ugly red head stirred him from his momentary lapse of reasoning and inability to act in the defense of the babe.    Overcoming the restraint of his paralyzing disbelief and revulsion, he lunged at Mormeau in a mad rage, but was held firmly in place by Horst.

While Christian's attention had been captivated by the bizarre and grotesque display before him, the foul manservant had maneuvered behind him, readily catching him when he attempted to save the baby.

Desperately fighting against the vice-like grip of Horst, who embraced him tightly across the midsection, Christian felt compelled to threaten the Baron. "You bastard!" he spat, "You bloody French bastard! I'll see you dead!"

In response to his guest's threat, Mormeau lifted his face from the child's neck. Christian recoiled in terror, instantly ceasing his attempts at wrestling his freedom from the strong German and actually finding comfort in the restraint of his rotting arms. Mormeau's eyes blazed like they were aflame, the blood of the newborn smeared all over the lower portion of his face and his canines as pronounced as ever. "How can you kill what is already dead?" asked Mormeau, with obvious pleasure.

On seeing the Baron's face dripping full with the babe's blood, Cotton sank from his chair to the floor. There he assumed a crouched posture on his hands and knees and vomited uncontrollably.

After responding to Christian's threat to his satisfaction, the Baron Mormeau returned to his most unholy meal. The harsh sound of his sucking choked the grimly silent room and was lowly accompanied by the pathetic gurgling murmurs of the dying child.

What manner of beast is this, Christian wondered, that so sucks the blood of an infant? That so uses the life force of a baby as nothing more than a beverage with which to fill his moldering belly? He had heard tales of such creatures when young — tales from the very heart of the Continent, of demons in human form that roamed the night in search of blood, that in death rose from their graves to harm the living. As he grew older he had dismissed such stories as successful attempts by malicious adults to frighten a bothersome child, but now in the face of such gruesome evidence, he was not so sure.

The stench of Horst was enough to make him sick, but coupled with the gory injustice before him and the sounds of Cotton retching forth the contents of his stomach, Christian had to gulp down the nauseous feeling welling up inside him. In a frantic attempt at regaining his freedom, he exhausted himself to the point of collapse, but it was to no use. For all his efforts Horst held him like an unyielding rock.

"I'll kill you dead!" Christian cried, nearly out of breath. Raising his eyes once more to the babe's face, he saw that there was no longer any life to be spared. "God," he sobbed, "my God!" and then fell into a fit of weeping. He wept for the soul of a child who would never fully know life, a child who had scarcely suckled off of its own mother. His mind gave Last Rites, for his trembling lips could not. He vented his anguish and frustration through lamenting wails. *A newborn has just been executed before mine own eyes, and I stood and watched, powerless to act on its behalf! I should have never hesitated, but seized the Baron by the throat and choked him 'til dead. Now a baby is gone to Limbo, and I am in a castle of death! Woe is me, dear God, I beg of You to let me avenge the murder of this little one! I desire nothing more than to rid the earth of this hell-spawned nobleman!*

Horst let him fall weakly to the floor. Crumpled there, Christian covered his face with his hands and continued mourning a tot whose name he did not even know.

Finished with the toddler, which looked so shrunken and shriveled from its original size that it seemed as though drained of its very last drop of blood, Mormeau pushed the tray from him and sat back contentedly licking his lips clean. Wiping his bloodstained face with his napkin, he began to methodically pick at his teeth. "God will not save your soul, my young Christian," he sighed. "You are lucky I was not famished, for I would have devoured the whole suckling."

Christian rose feebly from his place at Horst's feet to a sitting position and wiped the tears from his eyes. His grieving was over; it was this emotional frailty which had allowed the child to die. Now, as he dried his cheeks with his sleeves, he strengthened his resolve.

"All blood does not taste the same," Mormeau educated him. "I prefer the blood of small children. Babes are best — they being most pure — having little time to become tainted by the ills and ailments of the body."

"Unclean beast!" shouted Christian with newfound vigor. "Nothing is so vile as that which takes the life of a child."

Astonished, the Baron reprimanded Christian for taking such a tone with him. "I invite you into my home, treat you as I would royalty, and this is how you thank me? With threats against my life and vilifications slung at my name? It is you who is most inhospitable! It is you who offends."

The unbelievably chastising manner in which Mormeau spoke to him infuriated Christian. After committing a murder so atrocious, the Baron found his guest to be offensive? He glanced up at the table from his seat on the floor and spied the handle of his dinner knife overhanging the table's ledge. Without a second thought, he sprung to his feet and grabbed the knife from the table. Allowing no time for Horst to stop him, he lunged at the Baron and attempted to drive his blade deep into that smug, white face.

Just as the knife neared its mark, Mormeau calmly grasped his attacker's hand, twisted the knife free, and then threw Christian, with one arm, into the stone fireplace.

Christian impacted against the unmoving stone and slid semi-conscious to the floor. A gentle trickle of blood flowed from his forehead as he looked up in dazed confusion at the Baron. *How is it possible,* he pondered with great difficulty, *that he tosses me with the strength of ten men? He looks in no shape to do me such damage, let alone to even breathe. And yet the power of his single arm has lifted me off my feet and planted me here, a goodly three yards hence!*

"I be not a kindly host any longer," said Mormeau, in no way masking his irritation. "Horst, escort Christian and his drunken friend to their rooms."

Horst bent down and seized Christian by the collar. Raising him to his feet, he then proceeded to Cotton with Christian in tow.

Christian, dragged by Horst although his exhausted and injured body offered little resistance, managed to present to the Baron one final threat. "Through me the way into the suffering city," he rasped against Horst's bony knuckles that gripped him by the collar as if he were a dog. "Through me the way to the eternal pain, through me the way that runs among the lost ..." He said it off the top of his head, perhaps being in some way influenced by the motto he had read earlier in the evening above the entrance to the castle.

"You quote Dante," Mormeau smiled perceptively, "however, there are no three blessed ladies praying for you in the court of Heaven, and Virgil will not come to deliver you from the maw of Hell."

Christian was yanked back before he could reply as Horst reached down to pick up Cotton. He felt as though his larynx was being crushed by the dumb German.

Cotton was pulled to his feet with seemingly as little effort as Christian had been. Appearing more aware of what was happening around him, he wiped the vomit from his mouth and asked anyone, "What is to be done with us?"

"You shall be confined to quarters until you are reasonable enough for conversation," the Baron informed him. "Away with you!"

Wrinkling his face in disgust, Cotton proclaimed, "Undead and French, a truly revolting combination." He then spat on the shiny wooden tabletop before being brutally pulled away by the scruff of the neck.

Mormeau raised an eyebrow at the insult as the two men were drawn from the dining room into the shadowed anteroom.

Striding as if unaffected by the weight of the men in his hands, Horst limped up the staircase, hauling them behind him. Several times Christian had to kick out his already bothersome feet in order to gain footing as Horst rapidly ascended to the upper level of the castle. Cotton feared choking to death in Horst's fingers as his neck often painfully stretched under stress from his own dragging body weight. After what seemed like an hour of torture, they were at the top of the stairs.

Turning left down the dark corridor, they soon came to Cotton's room. Horst let Christian drop to his knees as he began to open Cotton's door. Christian immediately massaged his swollen neck. As his fingers slid across his throat, he could feel the impression of Horst's knuckles.

Once Horst had gotten Cotton's door open, he discourteously threw the old Scotsman in as if he were nothing more than a sack of rubbish. He then shut the door and locked it from outside with a key he produced from his waistcoat.

"Ye fucking German pig!" Christian heard Cotton growl from the other side of the closed door. "I've killed many of your kind before! Many a German I've sent to Hell! Ye won't be the first!"

If Horst was angered by Cotton's threat, he showed no reaction. His face remained as hideously expressionless as it had while he acted the part of waiter at dinner. He calmly reached down and took Christian by the collar once more, pulling him to just outside of his own door.

Christian could still hear Cotton ranting down the hall, though could no longer make out what it was he was saying. He stood straight as his door was opened and forcibly removed Horst's skeletal hand from his person, saying, "You do not have to toss me in, brute, I can walk of my own accord." He then drew closer to Horst as he passed into his doorway, adding maliciously, "I can walk of my own accord on mine own two good legs." He punctuated his derisive comment by spitting into Horst's torn face and slamming the door. Once inside, he could hear the lock being turned and any pleasure he had derived from his wasted spittle quickly dwindled into a familiar despair. He was trapped in a castle formed of nightmares, and he could not help but feel as a fatted pig awaiting slaughter. Did he glimpse his own death in the death of the child?

He moved away from the door and to the large French windows. Looking out into the turbulent night, he rested his weary head against the cold glass and listened to the pitter-patter of the rain. Alone, he was left only with his thoughts, which turned to the babe. He could still see the child, the large hole in its tender neck, as vividly as if it were before him. Closing his eyes only made it seem more real. He shuddered, gazed out into the storm, and thought of Cassandra. She is as the Baron, he sadly acknowledged, she sucks the blood of babies and renders the living dead. Tears stung his eyes and rolled down his puffy cheeks. How he had wanted her, and how he wanted her still! Her dark beauty was incapable of being surpassed by anyone or anything, even the angels looked upon her with a jealous eye. Yet she made a meal of life, if she was as the Baron Mormeau, of which he had no doubt. Her reactions at the dinner table told him, as did her resemblance to the Baron in paleness of flesh and sharpness of tooth. His heart ached to ponder on it and he raised his eyes into the darkness outside. He looked for Manasseh, that damnable town which had brought him here, but could see nothing. "Not a single bloody candlelight," he whispered aloud. "I imagine the entire town has been these demons' sustenance." He rubbed his neck and stretched his bruised and battered body. And where was dawn? he asked himself. Where hid the calming light of day? Oh, Eos! Pray for me, for I fear I shall never see your splendor again. Eos and Eros, he gloomily reflected, only a letter difference betwixt the two.

He caught sight of the narrow ledge just below his window and pressed his face to the glass to see where it led. It ran around the entire exterior of the castle, being roughly a yard below the upper floor windows. He could see that it was this ledge to which the impaled corpses were secured, and that one could successfully maneuver upon it to where the high defensive wall met with the castle. Once there, all a person had to do was climb over the wall and he was a free man.

Excited at this prospect, he furiously tried to open his windows, but found that despite his efforts they would not budge in the slightest. Rust and debris had sealed the hinges tight, and a force far more powerful than anything Christian could muster was required to pry them open. *I am trapped*, he sadly repeated his previous mental acknowledgement. *I am trapped in Death's fortress.*

It was then, in the midst of his dark despair, that his mind formed an idea so necessary that it was imperative he act on it at once. He rushed to his baggage and hastened to find the one that contained his writing materials. Once he had found what it was he was searching for – a quill pen, an inkwell, and several sheets of paper – he quickly strode to the table in the middle of his room and arranged these articles in an efficient fashion upon its surface. Pulling up a chair, he drew the candelabrum closer and popped open the inkwell. Examining the tip of his quill to make sure it was not bent, he dipped it into the inkwell and began to write upon the clean, white face of the pressed paper.

He wrote with purpose, not unlike those divine few who set to posterity the Word of God many centuries prior. He did not stop to compose his thoughts, nor did he halt his scribbling to rest his arm. What he committed to those sheets of paper was important to him. It outlined the entire course of events that had befallen him in a condensed manner. Briefly describing the purposes of his mission and naming the characters and location involved, his tale ended as it had up until now – with his imprisonment and writing of the letter. He told of Mormeau and Cassandra, of Horst and the unfortunate babe. In his composition he affirmed his hatred for the Baron and stated clearly his intentions to do him in. He wrote for no particular person and addressed it as such, the sole purpose of describing what had transpired in the past few hours was to educate whoever found this last testament. He made it known that he was a Catholic in the event that should his body be discovered it would be given a proper burial. When finished, he folded the account neatly and tucked it into the inside pocket of his jacket. If his body was to be found, so would his final words, which would warn others of the dead that still walked. All he could hope for now, besides some miraculous rescue, was that if he were to die he could exact some form of revenge from beyond. He was quite clear in explaining who and what the Baron was, where he lived, and what he had done to the infant. Whoever was to come across it would be compelled to act, the wording used being very inflammatory and descriptive.

It was a faint hope that should he be killed someone would even discover his body, let alone his information. Shivering as he looked up at the corpse outside his window, Christian knew that if he was to die most likely he would join those poor souls' impaled display. The sun would tan his body black, the humidity and weather would spoil his flesh to bone, and the birds and vermin would feast on whatever was left of him. He would hang there forever, forever to be looked on in horror by others who would be unfortunate enough to stay at the Castel de Mormeau, others who would eventually join him in rot. And the thing that bothered his heavy heart more than this, more so than even death, was that the Lady Cassandra would gaze upon his bloated carcass as his features became unrecognizable and the maggot nibbled him identical to the others speared in place by the iron shafts. How could she continue to look at me with those tender black eyes when they are filled with a putrid horror? he lamented. How could she even persist in the love of my memory when confronted daily with the stink of my decay and the sight of my putrescence?

He rose from the table and collected the implements of his composition. Placing them back into their proper bag, he lifted the candelabrum from the tabletop and carried it with him to his bed. Removing his baggage from the bedspread to the floor, he set the candelabrum on the bookshelf to the right of the headboard and reclined on the abundant mattress.

It was his intention to rest his exhausted self, but as he assumed a comfortable position, his eyes caught the presence of another in his room near the door, and he leapt to his feet at once.

"Greetings, Christian. I did not intend to frighten you."

It was the Lady Cassandra, looking demurely beautiful in her purple gown.

# *Chapter Seven*

How the Lady Cassandra had entered his room without attracting his immediate attention astounded Christian. He did not see nor even hear the creaking of his door as she invaded his privacy. It was as if she were suddenly there, as if forming from nothing at all.

"Stay away, woman-thing!" he madly shouted as he pointed at her. "Come no closer!"

Cassandra looked genuinely hurt by his guarded attitude. Her creased brow and pouting lips conveyed an unwanted confusion. "Why ... I mean you no harm, Chris, I ... I only wanted to see if you were well." She gestured to his head wound in a feeble attempt at reconciliation.

"And I should let you tend to my wounds?" he said incredulously, "You who would be nurse and mortician in one, who would treat my malady and relieve my pain by relieving me of my life?"

"You think me like the Baron. I am not."

"Oh? Then perhaps I should fear you more! He prefers children; I assume you like your meals aged a little longer!"

"The child was taken from a neighboring town without my knowledge. I would never condone such a thing, nor would I seek to harm you."

"Liar! You want my blood!"

"I want you."

"Yes," he shook his head fiercely, "for the Baron."

"No," she whispered with unmistakable exactness, "for myself."

His response was to stare at her. He desired it to be true, all that she said, but felt betrayed. He wanted so much to look away, but fearing it to be a sign of weakness, of acceptance, his eyes stayed firm on her flawed perfection.

Moving towards him cautiously, as if fearful of causing him further distress, Cassandra continued to speak to him. "I have never met a man like you, Chris. You awaken in me feelings I have not felt in so long a time ... a lifetime. Feelings I thought were dead."

"Like you? Why torment me? I've given you no reason to care for me."

"But I do."

Those words nearly rent Christian's heart apart. How he had wanted her to proclaim her love for him, to admit to caring for him! He was thankful she had not actually stated she loved him, but only that she cared, for he felt he would die of bliss were it otherwise. So happy would he be at hearing her say the very word "love" in relation to him that should he not be given sufficient warning he would probably fall at her feet and offer up his ghost.

And yet, underneath this wellspring of joy bubbling within him, lay a deep sadness. His rationale, that torturer and savior within all decent men, that which destroys pillars of fancy and plays pessimist to wishful thinking, reared its ugly, bloated head. She is a demon! his mind screamed over the excited and happy beating of his heart. A succubus of the flesh! Was not Lilith beautiful, was she not exquisite even as she stole the souls of little Jewish children? Indeed, that may be into whose unholy eyes I am gazing! his thoughts turned to irrational paranoia. He felt hurt, painfully so, as if finding a loved one to be dead. That was it, wasn't it? he ruefully asked himself. I have fallen in love with a talking corpse: a murderous denizen of the night, a bloodthirsty cadaver that was a most heinous thief, stealing the very life from man.

"Christian," she called for his attention, "let me prove my love to you."

"Be you as immoral as the whore-queen Semiramis?" he accused her, taking her offering to be that of a carnal nature. "Be you a Jezebel?"

Shaking her head sadly, she whispered, "My love for you is all that I have which is pure. I have saved it for you, and now freely give it, thereby dispensing of my redemption."

"You are undead," said Christian, as if what she had told him was preposterous. "You are incapable of love. You willingly forfeited that right when you chose to become what you now are."

"I never chose!" Cassandra screamed in indignation and frustration. "The Baron wanted me and took me!" Then, as if in painful recollection, she turned away. "My life was stolen from me, Christian," she spoke in a slow, hushed tone. "He came to me in the cover of night, that early hour before the dawn, when resistance is at its lowest ebb and sleep smothers one in forbidden dreams." Raising her face to his, she implored him, "Hate me for what I am, but not for what I once was, and in heart, still am."

Not knowing how to respond to her passionate entreaty, Christian allowed his suspicions to guide him. "How do I know you are not lying? The Baron could have put you up to this."

"The Baron forbade me to see you."

"I wish he could forbid my mind from seeing him," he said as he shifted his gaze to the floor. "A thousand years I could live and never forget that man's name, nor the hideous semblance of his face."

"You have only to remember! Confronted with him daily, I can never forget." Cassandra tried to lighten her words with a smile, but failed.

"So you are forbidden to visit me?" Christian returned to the initial subject of their talk.

"Yes," she nodded earnestly, "Philippus is extremely jealous, and although he has many women, I am his favorite."

"Then why do you risk coming here?"

"To talk with you, listen to you ... touch you."

Christian could not suppress a smile. "Come now, my Lady," he said tiredly, "playing the part of strumpet does not suit you."

"I will be whatever you want me to be, Christian. I will do whatever you have me, so long as you have me."

Christian was forced to sit uncomfortably on his bed when Cassandra's remarks unexpectedly inflated his passion. He crossed his legs and looked up at her, hoping she was ignorant of his erection. "I'll talk with you," he proposed in an effort at avoiding an embarrassing silence, "but only on one condition."

"Ask and it shall be so."

He swallowed hard before speaking, not knowing how she would take his request. "Provide me with ample means of an escape."

"If I do this," she said, drawing closer to his bed, "you will tell me all I wish to know?"

"Yes, only if you agree to help me out of this place."

She smiled. "Granted."

Somewhat surprised at how easy it had been to make her an accomplice in his flight, Christian leaned back on his mattress and sighed, "All right, where shall I begin?"

Walking briskly past him and around to the other side of the bed, Cassandra delightedly ordered him to begin, "From the beginning, the very beginning." Climbing onto the mattress next to him, she merrily added, "And don't skip!" Her face beamed with excitement. "I want to know everything about you." Her sable eyes locked onto his and intimated far more than words. "Everything ..."

Cotton groggily woke from his uncomfortable and cold sleep on the stone floor. Shortly after realizing that shouting at Horst through his door would get him nowhere, the inebriated Scot had passed out where he sat. Now he painfully lifted himself to a sitting position and assessed his damages. The hard floor had given his old body aches, and its low temperature had revived the rheumatism in his right elbow. His head spun and his throat still throbbed from Horst's hand.

"The bloody German," he muttered, making a face. He then grew fearful for his ward and began shouting, "Christian? Christian, can ye hear me? Are ye there?" After listening for some form of response and receiving nothing, he groped to his feet and staggered to the door.

Trying the latch, he found it to be locked. Feeling impotent, he put his back to the thick door and slid to his knees. What have I done? he shamefully thought, what have I allowed to happen? He felt anger at falling prey to his vice. All I had to do was protect Christian, and I have failed! I do not know what has become of him, or what is to become of me, but please, dear Lord, grant me requital!

Under the commanding influence of the alcohol still washing through his veins, he had to valiantly fight back tears of disgrace and self-pity.

It was then that he heard a light scuffling in the hallway just outside his door. It sounded like hushed female voices.

"Ho, there!" he called out through the space between the door and floor, pressing his cheek to the cold masonry. "Can ye hear me?"

The whispering stopped at once and Cotton knew that they, whoever they were, heard his cry for attention.

"Come here and let me out," he quickly asked of them, afraid of losing his opportunity at freedom. "I implore ye, whoever ye may be, out of the goodness of your heart let me out of this room at once!"

The soft footsteps of a woman drew near. Rising in hopeful expectation, he put his ear to the door and waited.

From out of the taut silence came a whisper laced in French pronunciation. "Will you play with us?"

Despite the accent, the request was so clear to Cotton's ear that it was as if whispered in his very head rather than through a wide oak door. It was the odd nature of the solicitation, not that he did not hear it, which caused him to ask, "What's that? Come again?"

In the same deliberately sensual slowness, from the darkness behind his door, came the reply, "Will you play with us?"

Seeing this bizarre demand to be a chance at acquiring his release, Cotton hastened to consent to his unknown friend's wish. "Yes," he tendered his assurances, "yes, I will play with ye, but ye must first unlock this door and let me out."

The silence that followed seemed to last forever as his ears labored to hear some response, but heard only the inspired beating of his heart. Then, a light giggling rippled through to him as the door's lock was noisily turned.

Cotton stood as best he could, balancing himself with one hand against the wall, and awaited his door's opening. Nothing further happened. It was as if all his friend had done was unlocked the door for him; he would be required to open it himself. Hesitant, he put his right hand to the wood of the door and gently pushed. The door maliciously creaked a long farewell as it opened on the dark hall.

From his doorway he saw no one. Venturing warily out into the hall, he looked first to his left as his eyes were drawn to the solitary figure of a woman standing at the head of the staircase.

Clothed in a simple white night gown, much like the one Cassandra had worn when she first greeted them, the fair-haired woman poised herself on the stair and beckoned to him. "Come," she whispered in awkward English, "come play ..." The light of a dying torch on the wall behind her rendered her gown opaque and her words more suggestive.

Cotton threw a backwards glance at Christian's door just down the hall to his right. He was free, and could probably set his friend free as well, yet something prevented him from acting. The same sick desire which had sopped his tongue in wine now worked its black arts on his libido. He looked nervously from Christian's inanimate, faceless, wooden door to the lively and lusty young girl inviting him to dally in some dark part of the castle. How could he choose? His yearning affected his thinking. How could he when there was no choice? To rescue Christian would mean to refuse the invitation being extended him: to turn away such beauty, such seemingly unspoiled youth. He was a man who had seen his best years pass him by while on some faraway battlefield. The wars had not only scarred him physically, but left him mentally repulsive to the opposite sex as well. It had always amazed him that he had ever found a wife, a woman who had overlooked all his flaws save for religious conversion. Since leaving his family behind in Scotland he had become a consumer of whores and a lover of sluts. He had slept with women he detested, women he found repellent. And now, here before his very eyes, was this lovely young creature, this beautiful flower in so black and withered a meadow. How could he, a worn-out old soldier with no wars left to fight, not partake of her fleshly delight? What had been unfairly denied him in his youth was now his to indulge.

His thoughts did manage to return to Christian's plight, as well as his own. Dare he forsake any chance at escape from this hell for simple sexual gratification? Dare he risk Christian's life for nothing more than a brief folly? And what if this was some form of trap? The Lady Cassandra had assured him of her being the only female; if this was so, then what so filled his eyes?

And what if this woman shared the Baron's taste for blood? What if she, too, wished to drain him of his essence?

Caught in a moment of indecision, his mind was made up for him with help from the woman on the stairs. "Come play …" she sighed as if her voice were the morning's breath, "come …"

His feet moved in her direction without being told to do so by his mind. It seemed as though he was powerless to avoid her, as if she were his destiny embodied – a destiny he could no longer avoid.

As he neared the staircase, the object of beauty which had so enticed him began to walk further down the stairs, and for a time disappeared from view. Upon reaching the head of the stairs, he looked down to discover an agreeable surprise. At the midpoint of the staircase stood his impatient French belle, but at the base loitered yet another stunningly beautiful girl.

Dressed in the same white gown as her friend, a plain but revealing piece of attire, this woman, whose hair was of a chestnut hue in rather dark contrast to the first female's golden-blonde, looked up at him with a pearly smile.

Steadying himself against the staircase's supporting wall, Cotton cautiously descended, all the while wondering where it was they were taking him. It appeared now the Lady Cassandra was twice a liar, he more than happily noted as he watched the two young women gather at the landing and await his arrival.

Cotton was about to ask them where and what they were going to play when he was silenced before even opening his mouth. "Sssh," the blonde whispered to him, her long finger placed sensually across her lips, "do not speak, follow …" They took him by the arms and led him from the staircase in hushed ecstasy.

Surprising even himself, Cotton allowed them to direct his person wherever it was they so wished. He felt their giddiness, their frivolous sexuality mooring to his heart, grafting to his roused flesh. From the nervous knotting of his insurgent stomach to the sheen of anxious sweat covering his scarred face like a veil, he experienced more than lust, far more than bare desire. The blood coursing through his timeworn veins and the adrenaline whirlpooling inside his gray head told him he felt more than a base yearning. He felt their youth! As if injected with life while still living, as if passing from winter into spring, he felt reborn! His muscles no longer ached, his rheumatism vanished, and his spirits soared. He could care less if they were guiding him to the very gates of Hell; as long as their libidinous attentions induced such renewal within him, such revitalization, he would readily face the eternal flames armed with nothing more than his whiskers.

They passed quietly from the anteroom into the dining room, and from there to the hallway from which Horst had constantly re-emerged during that miserable supper. It was in this hallway that the girls, as if unable to control their patience, broke from Cotton and delicately danced ahead of him.

He followed them into what appeared to be the kitchen and almost instantaneously, despite the present state of euphoria he was experiencing, grew ill. The meal which he and Christian had eaten had been prepared here? he thought as his stomach seized up on him. He had to fight not to vomit. The place was as filthy as the rest of the castle, if not more so. Dust was in abundance, as were insect-laden spider-webs. The kitchen looked more like a dungeon, and a rank and horrid one at that, than a place where food was to be fixed.

As his shocked eyes penetrated the dimness of the room, they came to rest upon an oversized meat cleaver that was set in a thick wooden chopping block. He slowed his pace and permitted his two female guides to gaily pass on into the next room without him. When he was satisfied that they had been too wrapped up in their own happiness to notice he was missing from their company, he acted quick and moved to the cleaver.

Hesitating before the massive meat axe, he stood at odds with himself. One part of him, that part containing his lust, derided him for even thinking about taking the cleaver. What had he to fear from a pair of simple girls? he reasoned. Everything! his warrior instincts rallied as he recalled an old maxim: never go into the company of strangers unarmed. His fingers traced the deep scar across his forehead and his mind was made clear. Plucking the large, rusty cleaver from its perch and slipping it behind him into his belt and beneath the cover of his shirt, he continued on after the cavorting girls with a feeling of added security resting against the small of his back.

"Do you like the moon?"

Christian looked from Cassandra to the pattern of moonlight his windows threw across the floor. "Yes," he answered her, as if just realizing it himself, "I favor its rays to those of the sun."

"'Tis my sun," said Cassandra rather regrettably, "by its cold rays I am warmed."

Returning his eyes to her splendor, Christian stared at her melancholy features for some time in silence. In the past hour they had grown fairly close through conversation, and now sat facing each other with less than half a yard between them. He wanted so much to reach out and touch the soft slope of her cheek, to slip his hand to the back of her long neck and pull her to his lips. It took much of his gentlemanly skills to quell the desire to do so, and in an effort to conceal from her his private war, he asked, "You no longer see the world of the day?"

"I choose not to. The light of day causes me to recall my prior existence, and in so doing brings me much grief. I have not seen, nor felt the warmth, of the sun's rays for many, many a year."

"What are you?" he asked with profound concern. "All that I know is composed of fairy tales and the like, supplemented by the incomprehensible witticisms of the Baron."

The Lady swallowed hard in preparation for what she was about to tell him. "What I impart unto to you," she spoke clearly, stressing the importance of every word, "is of the utmost secrecy. You must swear to me that you will never reveal to anyone what I now reveal to you."

"I swear it!" said Christian hastily, eager to find out more about his strange hosts. "Upon my life I hereby swear to you that I shall reveal nothing!"

She impulsively extended her hand to the side of his face and tearfully commanded, "Oh, Christian, my good Christian, do not loathe me for what I have been made! As I have told you before, I had no hand in my corruption. I fear that the secret I disclose to you – that of my existence – will compel you to shun me, to revile me, and to hate me to no end."

"My dearest Lady," he comforted her, moving her hand from his face to his chest, "I swear upon my heart's blood that nothing could ever cause me to find you loathsome, or unattractive. To me you are the sum of all things beautiful, beauty itself personified, and I could never feel malice towards that which continuously gifts my eyes with such unyielding pleasure."

"You are too kind to me."

"And are you undeserving of my kindness?"

"I am, as you already know, one of the living dead." Once these words had passed her lips, she turned away in shame. "I subsist by feeding off the lifeblood of man. I am that which you heard of when you were a boy, that which you dismissed as fiction when you became a man. I am one who has no other hunger but a craving for that which runs through your veins."

"If you are as you say," said Christian as he took her hand in his, "and you feel such aversion for the life you lead, then why not end it?"

Pulling her hand from his she began to slide away from him. "I knew it!" she cried. "I knew you would hate me if you heard mine own lips affirm that which you yourself tried to deny!"

"Nay! My Lady," he tried convincing her this was not so, "I did not mean any offense. I only suggested—"

"What?" she shot back angrily, "That I take delight in taking lives? That since I do not end my own life I am wicked? Is it not your own Church that moralizes against the taking of one's own life?"

"Please, please, my Lady," he soothed as he held out his open hand, "do not go. Stay, and I promise you we shall talk no more of it."

She glared at him for a moment, treating him with guarded suspicion. "You promise?"

"I promise."

Once he had assented, a change came over her entire demeanor. No longer was she the vexed, defensive woman that stood before him with a fire in her eyes. There had been a return in her to the Cassandra of old, the sweet and caring Cassandra to which Christian had lost his heart.

He did not know what to make of her tantrum, but then again he did not know what to make of her. Was she the innocent corrupted as she so staunchly contended, or was she no more than a liar, a trickster trying to con him out of his blood. He tended to put more weight on her corruption due to the quite reasonable fact that if she were only concerned with his blood, she should most likely find no difficulty in taking it from him by force. Judging by the inhuman strength of Baron Mormeau, this seemingly frail flower could very well break him in half.

He found it quite odd to have fallen in love with a monster. He did love her, he realized, despite her immense flaws, the fact that she was dead being chief amongst them. It was her unpredictable personality: generally polite and not overly condescending, although subject to sudden bouts of anger, depression, and sexual innuendo, which held his praise. He enjoyed entertaining the prospect of conversing with a refined Lady who he knew, just as she bested him in intellectual matters, could best a whore in bed. That was the main attraction he felt towards her, the indefatigable magnetism which pulled him to her. Her beauty was merely an added incentive, the icing on the cake. What he really loved was that she was, in one physical body, all that he loved. Intelligence, wisdom, humor, etiquette, and passion all invested in a figure which could never lose his interest.

*Rebecca has not one percent of her charm,* he almost comically compared the two, *and yet 'tis she that lives.*

He had touched on the one obstacle standing between him and undiluted bliss; despite all of Cassandra's attributes, all of her wit and virtue, she was at root nothing more than a murderess corpse. *How many lives have been sacrificed to that mouth?* he bitterly wondered as he gazed on her full, red lips. *And how many more shall be?* Yet, his passion protested, what a way to go: to die in her arms, proffering your life to serve nothing more than slaking her unholy thirst. To do so would be the ultimate demonstration of love, the uttermost act of giving. Bizarrely enough, he found in himself a slight tinge of jealousy for those who had contented her appetite in the past.

"You expressed an interest earlier to my Baron of a profound desire to know much."

Cassandra's observation roused Christian from his troubling reflections. "Why, yes," he mumbled, caught off guard by the sudden change in subject, "I wish to study the classics."

"I studied under many of the greatest teachers," she stated proudly, "attending the best of schools throughout all of Europe." Smiling at him, she sighed, "That is one of the pleasant perks of a noble ancestry."

"And what did you study?" Christian asked excitedly, making no attempt to hide his interest in any information that would make him love her more, if that was indeed possible.

"Theology, philosophy, mathematics, languages—"

"Languages?" he interrupted.

"Yes."

"What languages?" he nearly pled. "I wish to know in what tongues you are conversant."

"I am fluent in many tongues," she spoke dryly. "English, French, Spanish, Portuguese, Italian, Greek, German, and Latin."

"Fascinating," he breathed in awe. "I know only of my native tongue, and can read a little Latin, thereby ascertaining some parts of the Romance languages."

"If you wish I can teach you all that I know, or whatever 'tis you desire to know."

"I would like that." Turning inquisitive, he asked, "And which is your favorite tongue?"

Shyly tilting her head away from him, she coyly responded, "Although I have had no experience with it, I am sure my favorite tongue shall be yours."

Christian could feel the heat of his blushing and hid his face in his hands. 'Twas going to be a long night, he mused. Then, abruptly turning serious, he eased his hands from his face and thought of Cotton. He prayed he fared well.

Shortly after exiting the kitchen, Cotton rejoined his two comely companions in a narrow corridor which meandered down a flight of crudely carved stairs. In keeping with the castle's ambiance, the lighting here was quite poor, consisting only of two low-burning torches strategically placed opposite one another in rusted wall brackets. Even in the scant torchlight, and possessing little knowledge of the craft of architecture, Cotton could see there was a great disparity between the masonry of this lower level and that of the upper level from which he had been conducted.

"What's this?" he asked them as he gestured with open arms to the new surroundings.

"Come, oh noble Pentheus," said the brunette in what sounded like English lightly seasoned with Slavic, "follow down these stairs and into our anxious hearts."

He was unfamiliar with the name by which the brunette had referred to him, but did what was asked and pursued the two women down the short flight of stairs.

As he lifted himself off the last stone step and onto the cracked and uneven clay ground, the women surrounded him, one on each side, once more taking up his arms in theirs.

"Look, love," the Frenchwoman whispered in his right ear, turning his face with a clammy hand to the wall before them. "You see before you two doors …"

Cotton squinted hard in the dim corridor to find that there were in fact two poorly constructed and badly rotted wooden doors facing them. Set roughly two yards apart, the doors appeared identical in all respects save for variances in water damage and natural deterioration. Large, rusted iron rings served as door latches, and what looked like carpenter nails performed the task of hinges.

Again the blonde spoke in a hushed, drawn-out whisper. "Behind one of these doors lie immeasurable pleasures of the flesh." She removed her cold hand from his face and pointed to the portals. "Choose the correct door and we shall be yours, handsome Orpheus …"

Cotton did not know what to make of the strange names they were calling him, but it concerned him little. He glanced happily from door to door and smiled.

"If you choose incorrectly," warned the Slav in a voice absent of any alarm, "immeasurable pain shall be inflicted upon your body …" Her left hand playfully curled Cotton's hair between her fingers as she sighed restlessly, "Choose carefully …"

They backed away and permitted Cotton time to think by himself without their immediate presence affecting his decision making.

The smile on Cotton's face waned as he faced the perplexing conundrum being posed him. No longer was this some simple game, he thought, as the brunette had added an element of danger to it. He scratched his head and toyed with his beard. What should he do? he endeavored to reason. Should he end this game here and now, before selecting a door, or should he cast his fate to the wind and pick? The prospects of some form of pain being implemented against him should he fail to choose correctly caused him no fear, for as a career soldier he was used to all manner of misery. What did cause him worry was that should he decide incorrectly he would not get to romance the ladies. His eyes darted from door to unrevealing door in the hopes that one would offer some indication as to which he should favor. He saw nothing of relevance but two wooden doors.

"We are impatient, love ..." said the brunette from behind him.

He turned from the damned doors to find the girls whispering to each other constantly and giggling occasionally. They saw him looking at them and began to rub against one another, kissing long and often as their fondling hands disappeared beneath the scant cover of their white gowns. The sexual energy they held was so overpowering that they could not wait for Cotton, and had to expend some of it on each other.

As he watched the women reciprocate their love, he could feel his own desire overtaking him. What had previously been not much more than a state of high arousal became an uncontrollable passion as he saw their velvety tongues slide in and out of each other's mouths and their gliding hands cup erect breasts.

Once their lusty fondness for each other abated, they returned to Cotton. The Slavic brunette pressed her ripe bosom into his side and softly stroked his face as the French blonde caressed his chest vigorously. Both were careful not to injure him with their extremely long nails, which were painted black and assumed the appearance of feline claws.

The brunette's breath raised the hair on the back of his neck as she effectively murmured, "Choose now ..."

Following a moment's delay in which he made a last-minute deliberation, Cotton blurted, "That one." He pointed limply to the right-hand door.

He glanced nervously at his companions to try to ascertain in their pale, pretty faces whether or not he had chosen wisely. The women assumed a look of teasing disappointment before breaking into mutual grins.

"Very well chosen ..." said the blonde as she traced his lips with her fingertip.

Each took turns planting kisses upon his face and mouth as they guided him to the selected door. Their damp kisses ran tingles up and down his spine, and as he looked past their red, red lips to the alabaster of their teeth, he saw that they, too, had the pearly points of Cassandra in their mouth.

The Frenchwoman opened the door, pulling Cotton eagerly into the darkness within as the brunette pushed from behind. A blast of cold air hit him as he stepped forward, and for a brief second he smelled not the inebriating perfume of his lady friends, but rank decay. It was so strong, in fact, that he likened it to the stench of rot common to fields the day after battle. Peering into the gloomy room, his old eyes adjusted to the dark and saw that the walls were lined with barely lit torches. He had just begun to make out something large in the middle of the room when the door was closed behind him and the sound of female giggling filled his ears.

In the dark he felt a growing regret, for the giggling he heard came from more than two women. Much more.

"Would a rose by any other name smell as sweet?" Cassandra put Christian's Shakespeare to the test.

"Yes," he responded quite definitely, much to the Lady's surprise.

"How so?"

"If 'twas christened Cassandra."

His compliment did not go unnoticed by his attractive companion, who forgot herself with an open smile.

"Have you any family?" Christian innocently pried.

"None still living," she saddened, "no."

"I am sorry—"

"Do not be," she wiped her eyes. "I do not miss them much, save for my sister."

He could see a certain sparkle in her dull eyes and sensed that her response had touched her in some way. He quickly decided to explore this, requesting, "Tell me of your sibling."

"My sister," she boasted, "was far my superior in every way. She could do everything better than I." Then, as it had often, her mood turned lamentable. "I loved her ... far more than is possible ... far more than a sister should." With a forlorn gaze she glanced out the window and sighed.

"You miss her greatly." He noted the obvious.

"Yes," she shuddered as a tear glistened off her cheek, "I miss the joy she brought my afflicted heart, and the love she gave me freely."

"I, too, miss my father," said Christian, trying to pool their grief and thereby put an end to it.

"And not your mother?" she asked him rather incredulously.

"I did not know my mother," he explained, "she died in childbirth."

"How tragic," she whispered as her fingers offered him comfort by moving his hair from his face.

"Yes," he agreed, taking pity on himself. "All that I do know of her consists of my father's recollections, and stories good neighbor women have told me. She has been dead for over twenty years and still they remark of her beauty and virtuous deeds." He took her hand in his and massaged it fondly with his thumb. "No, I never laid eyes upon my poor mother, nor did she ever hold me in her loving arms and suckle me, but I love her just the same. I love her as much as any child can love his mother."

"And your father?" Cassandra continued in her pleasant interrogation.

"My father was a carpenter by trade, although he did a little shipbuilding occasionally. I can still remember him bragging to me of the work he had done on several galleons." He smiled fondly, "He returned one night with an exact miniature of the ships he had been repairing. He had carved it for me."

"How precious," she remarked. "And you have it still?"

"Yes," his smile melted as he turned from her to conceal his tears. "It carries much significance, for not only was it carved by my father, but 'twas presented to me on the last night of his life."

"'Twas his last gift to you."

"Yes." He felt the warmth of his tears spilling down his cheek and wiped at his face angrily. "That was the last time I ever saw my father alive. Come morning, he breathed not."

"And you cherish his galleon."

"I both adore and despise it," he spat emotionally, "for although 'tis a gift of my departed father, 'tis representative of the very thing that killed him! Working on those ships strained his ailing heart to the point of death!" He gulped down the torrents of sadness rising in him and fought to control his feelings while under the mindful eye of Cassandra. "Paradise aside," he swore, "just seeing him again is reason enough to gain entrance into Heaven."

She gently forced his face to confront her and dried his cheeks with the soft material of her sleeve. Looking down on him much the way he imagined a mother would, she tenderly asked, "How did he die?"

"The Lord was merciful," he muttered. "'Twas while he slept."

"That is the best way."

He could sense he was losing the suppression of his emotions, and shook his head violently in disgust.

"What, Christian?" she asked him softly.

He answered her with another head shaking.

Cassandra's eyes narrowed to slits as she voiced her evident concern for what troubled him. "What is it, Chris, that so mutes your tongue and diverts your eyes?"

Rather than shake his head again, he simply ignored her.

"Chris, please!"

How could he ever disobey so lovely a mistress, so enticing a goddess? Swallowing hard, he vented the rage he had harbored under his breast for so long. "If there is one thing I cannot stand about God," he cried, "'tis that He takes those close to us away. I despise death! It seems such a pitiful demonstration of godly powers."

Cassandra let her thin finger trail the slope of his nose, offering, "There are ways of avoiding death ..."

Instinctively he moved from her, recoiling from her touch. "Avoiding death by causing death?" he shouted down her monstrous proposition. "Never! I could never do as you." He planted his aching feet firmly on the merciless stone floor and stood with the assistance of a bedpost. "I would embrace Death as if it were my lover," he continued, "warmed by the knowledge that I took no lives and comforted in the dreams of an eternal paradise."

"But what if there is no Heaven?"

Her blunt handling of such a sensitive question struck him dumb. He searched for some assistance in her eyes, but found none. "There must be a Heaven," he declared with all the confidence of a child.

"And why is that?" Cassandra increased the difficulty of his defense, seemingly aloof to the anguish she was causing him.

"There must be a Heaven," he whispered with an almost zealous blindness, "because goodness must be rewarded."

Cassandra raised her pretty self to her knees and hobbled to him from across the bedspread. Sensitively prying his hand from the bedpost, she pulled him onto the mattress. "I love the way you are so committed." She showered him with adulation as if a peasant girl dreaming of her knight. "I've not known many men, but there is something you do to me, something I cannot describe, only that 'tis good."

To please her was to make himself content. Lying beside her, he gently smiled his gratitude as her soft, cool hands stroked his warm cheeks.

She mimicked his previous statement in a low, husky whisper, in so doing adding a twist of carnality and earthiness to it. "Goodness must be rewarded ..."

Even down in the bowels of the castle, Cotton could hear the faint roll of thunder. Despite the harshness of the autumn storm, he would have preferred to be outside right now, with the fresh inundation of wind bearing down upon him. The air inside the ancient room was stale and dry, and caused him to breathe with a more than usual amount of effort.

As his guides led him to the center of the room, the large object he had first spied there began to take on a more familiar form. He could see now that it was a large bed, incredibly oversized as if to accommodate some king or queen and fully bedecked with all the necessary bedding amenities.

"A bed fit for a company," he spontaneously remarked, though his mistresses paid him no attention.

They sat him at the foot of the considerable bed and knelt before him. Each taking one of his hands in their own, they stared at him with sharp grins and eyes darker than the dark of the room.

"Look about you," whispered the blonde with a sense of urgency. "Look at the work of man, see his failings ..."

The dying torches began to brighten in their rusted wall brackets, their light moderately increasing until the only darkness in the room was the shadows they cast.

Cotton blinked his eyes at the strange magic. How had they made the torches burn bright? he marveled. And how had they done so by no more than the spoken word?

His thoughts on the matter dissipated as he took in the age-encrusted construction of the room. The low ceiling and narrow length was all but unfamiliar to him with the exception that it brought to mind a few of the older buildings he had visited when in Brittany, those built by the venerable Romans during their European occupation.

The ceiling itself, seemingly composed of hardened red clay which flaked bare in certain areas, was supported by a double line of rounded stone pillars. From his place on the bed looking out towards where he had entered, Cotton sat precisely between the row of columns. To his right there was a line of four supports, and to his left there was an equal number. They converged upon the bed, making it the focus of the room.

"We are representative of the defiance to man and all his mundane creations," the brunette supplemented her friend's earlier statement. "We are that which one only dreams about, and dares not speak of ..."

As her voice trailed off into silence, something at the far end of the room caught Cotton's eye. From behind the last pillar on his left, before the doorway, appeared another female. She walked towards him with a methodic slowness, as if a snake slithering to its prey, her white gown aligning her with the two women kneeling at his feet.

As she drew close, a second woman appeared from behind the last pillar to his right. She, too, was dressed the same as her sisters, and walked with a similar gait.

And then another woman emerged from the shadow of a pillar, and then another, and another. Cotton looked nervously from his left to his right as the females, each new one more exceedingly beautiful than the last, materialized from behind their own stone support as if abdicating caryatids.

The first woman to have issued from the pillars approached him, kissed him on the lips, and then sat herself on the bed behind him, setting a precedent by which the others readily adhered.

And so one after the other they kissed him and took their places on the bed. The last woman to do so was a flaming redhead with Nordic features. Upon seeing her, Cotton gasped, "You!" before being silenced by her lips.

In all there were eight of them, one for each of the room's pillars. Added with the beauties at his feet, Cotton was in the presence of ten incredible women, all of whom were sexually aroused. There were light and dark-haired ones, tall and short ones, women for every desire and preference – it was a sampling of Europe's delights, and all for him to enjoy!

"I've never seen so much white," he happily remarked in reference to their garb as well as their pallor. "'Tis as if I were in a blizzard of love."

The women giggled their approval of his observation, then began disrobing one another.

Heaven can't be much better than this, he thought as he watched them reveal themselves to him.

The well-rounded curves and firm hints of muscle, the variance in shapes and sizes of breasts and buttocks, all titillated his old eyes. The sight of their nakedness combined; girl stretched erotically across girl, hands massaging and grasping in an orgy of forbidden delight.

He almost felt the urge to not join them, to not ruin their beautiful lovemaking with the intrusion of his rough and unsightly male body, to do nothing more than watch.

As if reading his thoughts, the blonde at his side solicited, "Will you not indulge us?"

He managed to tear his eyes from the writhing mass of female bodies strewn over the bed to see his guides, as naked as their sisters, peering at him.

"I am afraid to intervene where I am not needed," he spoke weakly.

"Oh, but how you are needed far more than you realize ..." the brunette implied with a telling grin.

"Who are ye lasses?" Cotton asked in awe of their forwardness.

"Freedom," the blonde said simply as she crouched and removed the boots from his feet.

"Freedom?"

"Yes," she sighed contentedly, as her friend released her from the removal of his stockings, "we represent freedom from all life's concerns ... freedom from life itself. We are your freedom, graybeard."

Her words struck a chord of fear within him and he voiced a half-hearted attempt at clarification. "What exactly do ye mean by that?"

"Relax, lover," said the brunette as she softly, yet forcefully, pushed him down upon the bed. "We are all alike here." She began fumbling with his belt buckle. "We, like you, are servants of Bacchus ..."

She exchanged a secretive glance with the blonde and both broke into a hearty laughter.

Lying on a comfortable bed and surrounded by gorgeous nude women, Cotton could not help but feel dubious. Something obviously was not as it seemed with his lady friends. He was smart enough to know that they could not possibly find him attractive – at least, not all of them. And what of the foreign names they constantly called him? he silently complained. Were they being insulting without him even recognizing it?

All about him he could hear the soft moans and sweet groans of female pleasure. The walls reverberated with their sighs and hollow invocations to God, the juicy sounds of their erotic frolicking. It was almost more than he could bear just listening! What would he do when forced to participate? How could he make love to such abundant excellence?

The removal of his belt returned him to a reality he suddenly wanted to flee. Somehow he felt in the pit of his stomach a feeling he had only experienced on nights before battle, that of noxious dread, a foreboding of death.

The reassuring discomfort of the hard meat cleaver pressed against his tailbone alleviated some of his angst, but not all.

Looking into the coal-black eyes and salivating mouths of his stunning lovers, he could not help but wonder if he were in Heaven or Hell.

Cassandra removed Christian's shoes carefully and set them quietly on the floor. How pleasant it was to be free from them, to have his poor feet breathe, he thought with much satisfaction. She was so kind as to take them off herself, to not trouble her loving guest with such an embarrassment. Indeed, she seemed to sense his discomfort, and, like the good hostess, sought to relieve it at once.

The bottoms of his stockings were stained with the blood of his blistered soles, and she hesitated before peeling the silk from him. Examining his bare feet with great interest, she asked almost as an afterthought to the curious poking of her fingers, "Why did you place your feet in such torturous shoes?"

"Because I had no better to compliment my suit." He flinched as she touched the torn remains of a blister under his big toe.

"I am so ... sorry," she offered lamely, oddly preoccupied with his bloodied feet. "Let me cleanse them for you."

Placing a bowl under his feet, she undertook to washing the rusty red from his flesh. Pouring cold water from a porcelain pitcher over his swollen skin, she scrupulously washed him clean. The water stung at first, but then lapped away the pain he had come to grudgingly accept as a consequence of his fashionableness.

"See how the purity of the water bathes away the hurt?" she asked astutely. "See how the crimson stain of misery is effected soluble by the untainted clarity of the water?" She fastened her eyes on him, adding, "'Tis much like love."

The icy water slipped between his toes and into the bowl below, taking with it his diluted blood. Lifting his feet and pointing to the pink water contained within the bowl, he told her, "Look there, see how even purity is polluted? See how pain exists in all things corporeal? Even love?"

Her face turned to stone as she rose without a sound and removed the bowl from its place on the bedspread to the table in the center of the room. Standing with her back to him, she stared down at the defiled water and silently cried.

My haughtiness has wounded her heart, he berated himself while regarding her slender back, I had best make amends. "Lady, please," he beseeched her, "do not take offense at the arrogance of my fatuous tongue."

Without turning, she asked, "Do I not please you?"

"Yes, that you do," he readily acquiesced. "You are unlike any woman I have thus far encountered. So knowledgeable, so courteous and lady-like." He smiled his admiration, "So perfect in every way."

Leaving her place at the table and gliding back to the bed, she smiled brightly through her tears. "I am the woman of your dreams, and Lilith to your fantasies ... you cannot resist me."

"If only you were not—"

"Dead?" she finished his sentence with a note of absurdity. "But am I? Am I not one of the living? Do I not breathe, and walk, and talk, and see? Have I no compassion? Am I incapable of love?" She reclaimed her place next to him on the bed and impulsively ran her fingers through his hair. "I am as alive as you."

"But different," he said as he lifted her hands from his head. "You are aged beyond your years, an old woman's wisdom in a young woman's bosom."

"Perhaps I was always meant for you," she proposed, placing his wounded head upon her lap, "destined to live beyond my years so that I could spend an eternal bliss within your arms."

"You wish me to become as you."

"'Tis the only way we can be together, for I cannot change what I am."

He looked up at her from the soft pillows of her thighs. "Understand, that against all reason and sense, I do love you. However, why indulge in a brief traipse through Heaven when if I refuse your generous offer I shall reside there for all eternity."

"But it can be eternal!" she insisted fiercely, thereby exhibiting her deep affection for him. "You and I can partake of a heaven here on earth."

"That, my Lady," he said philosophically, "is a contradiction in terms."

A disturbing quiet hung between them for some time before a rippling blast of thunder instigated a continuation in their conversation.

"I know that God exists ..." conceded Cassandra.

"How is that?" he asked out of mild curiosity.

She leaned over him, her hands sliding down his chest and her face hovering just above his, her long hair draping intimately the sides of his head. "I know that He exists, because He answered my prayers." She gave the tip of his nose a teasing kiss and straightened herself back into a sitting position.

Troubled by the abrupt insertion of the Lord into her speech, Christian revolted against that part of him which allowed him to lie at her knees like a lamb before the lioness. Rising, he directed her to "Speak not of Him," as if by doing so she had committed the gravest of heresies.

"Would you have me be so evil as to deny the Christ?" she spoke in an even, almost mocking tone.

"Surely one such as you cannot—"

"And why can I not?" she asked peevishly. "Because I do not live as you? That in forfeiting my life I also forfeited my beliefs and faiths?"

He found himself unable to properly respond to her, and therefore sank into an embarrassed muteness.

"Oh, Christian," she sighed pleasantly at his chagrin, "my good, little Christian. Rest your befuddled head in my lap." She then pulled him gently back down into a prone posture.

He offered her no resistance, for something indescribable had affected him when she laid her hands upon his shoulders. He could not explain it, nor could he readily dismiss it, only that he knew that he felt more than love for this incredible woman. He had become engaged in far more than the sweet beginnings of a simple love affair, far more than even love itself.

Smiling mischievously while stroking his long hair, she whispered confidentially, "Tell me of your woman, Chris. What is she like? I wish to know."

The comfort her lap afforded his throbbing and confused head made him drowsy. Half awake, he responded without reflection. "She is a beauty, but flaws herself with her temper and ignorance."

"And where does your princess reside?" she asked innocuously.

"In Bantingham, at an old tavern there."

Her soft smile breaking into a grin, Cassandra raised her eyes from her hopeless paramour and out into the night. "How lovely ..."

Cotton sat up to aid the women in his undressing. His belt had been taken from him and his pants stayed in place only by the assistance of his protruding belly. All of the ladies had a hand in his disrobing, and eagerly undid whatever it was they could undo upon his body. His buckles were thrown open and his buttons popped, his laces untied and his ribbons loosened. It was around the time the women had begun to remove his leather buff coat that he noticed something which had previously escaped him.

Looking past the nude shoulders and bare necks of his milky lovers, Cotton saw that the two doors from which he was ordered to select actually opened into the same room. He could not contain his laughter, nor could he his perception, when he loudly declared, "Why, there's no way I could have failed, clever girls! Both doors lead to the same room—"

In mid-sentence he realized the implications of what he said, and felt the bottom of his stomach drop away. If both doors were of the same room, then he should not only experience pleasure, but pain as well. Frantically glancing from face to face of the pretty horde surrounding him, he saw that they denoted a hunger or thirst, not sexual lust.

He was stricken with such an overwhelming sense of horror at arriving at the treacherous truth that it took all of his stamina to stave off the paralyzing effects of his fear.

Frantic, he moved his head about wildly from side to side in order to eye all those around him. This frightened response elicited a sneering laughter from the women, who now did nothing to hide their true intent.

"Look at him," one giggled, "he's as meek as a mouse!"

"Is this what age has left us?" another derided. "Is this a soldier, or an Italian's lackey?"

The laughter increased in a sinister unison.

"Sisters, sisters, please!" the Frenchwoman came to his defense. "Are not the best wines those that have matured?"

"If that be the case," a cockney voice retorted, "then this one here be more vinegar than grape!"

Cotton saw faces that had before held so much love and desirous affection now brandished hatred and an appalling longing. Perhaps they had always looked at him in such a way, that it was fear that had removed the blindfold lust placed over his eyes. How they gaze at me as if I were nothing but a meal, his thoughts panicked, nothing but a spitted lamb!

Before his terrified sight, they changed. As everything before, their transformation was synchronous: all metamorphosing into lurid beasts with sharp fangs and glowing eyes. The similarity to anything human ended with their general physique, in all other respects they appeared as demons in the flesh.

Their eyes! his mind cried out in alarm. Look at their eyes! The black of the women's eyes seemed to burn brighter than the torches that hung in place along the walls – brighter in radiance, but not in tonality, for they raged a blood-red rather than fiery orange. Once their stare had been dull, literally lifeless, but now their gaze seethed with an inner force, as if all of Hell were contained in their glare.

He arose at once, barefoot with little protection save for his loosened buff coat. "What manner of creatures in God's good earth are ye?" he gasped in dismay.

They answered him with a shrill laughter that reverberated throughout the narrow room.

Inching his way gingerly from the bed and towards the door, Cotton saw that they had him surrounded like a pack of rabid wolves. When he could move no further in the direction of his freedom, he stopped and scrutinized his encircling hostiles.

They were close to him. Very close. He could reach out and tweak their noses, but dared not. In their expressions he saw a spite and maliciousness he had never beheld in any of the many faces of his foes. There was such an ineffable cruelty about them, an unspeakable evil written in the crinkle of their brow and the curl of their lip. They were an aggregate reality formed from the varied parts of his worst nightmares.

The women goaded him, cursed and berated him as if he were a simpleton deserving of their wrath. They spat at him, coating him with a hail of foul smelling, brown saliva.

All the while Cotton did nothing but watch them. He eyed them with contempt as he took in their hatred and received their ignominious behavior. Such a reaction warmed and readied his own viciousness, steeled his nerves in preparation for what must be done. The excitement and youthful elation they had so ardently dispensed to him previously now would act against them. The resurgence of his heartiness by their passionate attentions brought about a renewal of the warrior he once was. The power coursing through his veins, that which had been raised on the expectations of sex, was now channeled to buttress his instincts of self-preservation. What had been stirred for making love was now provoked into making war.

As his hand flew beneath his shirt and latched onto the large, wood handle of the meat cleaver, he fully realized this would be his final stand. To die in combat, he thought with a relish that surprised him, to die with honor. He then uttered a silent prayer against such ungodly enemies.

As the women descended upon him, pouncing like wild animals, he withdrew the cleaver and with a wide arc brought it to a halt in one of the nearest females' faces. The keen blade bisected her face into nearly perfect halves, from the crown of her brow to the split of her lips. She screamed in agony as he pulled the cleaver from her ruined countenance and released a deluge of bloody gore that oozed from the wicked gash.

Frantically fingering the crevice that ran vertically through the remnants of her nose and ruptured lips, she cried hysterically, "See what he hast done to me! My face! My face! He hast destroyed my beauty!"

The women delayed their attack while listening to their wounded comrade. It seemed they might be on the verge of calling off their murderous intentions, as if weighing the value of Cotton's blood with the risk he posed to their appearance. Then, in a move which dispatched Cotton's hope of their abatement, the Frenchwoman shrieked, "Kill him!"

They tore at him with their long nails and bit him with their sharp teeth. On every available piece of his flesh they carved. He would have died instantly were it not for his buff coat, which shielded him from the full viciousness of their inhuman blows. As it was, he was badly bled in areas left unprotected. His arms and legs were ripped, as was his noble face, which looked as if composed of raw meat. Despite all of the wounds the women had inflicted upon him, he fought on. Summoning from his very essence all that he possessed, he slashed, hacked and screamed back at the bloodthirsty horde.

"You bastard!" the Slavic brunette screeched as he relieved her of her right hand.

Cotton replied in laughter. He threw punches with his left hand and wielded the cleaver with his right. He tossed, kicked, pummeled, and cut the vengeful women over and over again, and still they returned for more. No woman went untouched by either his blade, foot, or fist. Indeed, many bore the stains of their own blood upon their white skin. Many also were besmirched with the blood of Cotton, who fared far worse. In the short space of time that had elapsed since the melee began, the women had given him more wounds and pierced flesh than he had earned in his entire career as a soldier.

Although he fought bravely, the loss of blood pouring from his opened veins weakened him. He tried valiantly to keep his balance, pushing off a pillar and landing with his back against the hard wall. There he rested, panting like a cornered dog as the mob moved cautiously closer. They had rightly acquired a fear of him, and stayed a healthy distance from his butcher's blade.

He wiped salty blood from his eyes and took in a deep, strained breath of stale air. "Ye want me blood?" he asked in a hoarse voice punctuated by disgust. "Ye'll have to earn it first. I know what ye be, and what ye be be legend no longer!"

From the heart of the thirsty throng came the woman whose face he had first cleaved. Pushing past her sisters, she rushed at him with a blind rage and an unintelligible scream.

Cotton, as if expecting such an action, calmly reached up and removed one of the torches from its brown iron wall bracket and touched it to her flesh. The flame caught instantly, taking to her like she was no more than a bundle of dry hay, rendering her a shrieking ball of fire. Even in this incendiary state she attempted to clutch him in her arms and burn him with her. He batted her to the ground, using the torch as a club until she moved no more.

As he straightened his pain-wracked body from the burning corpse, the Slav jumped onto his back and buried her teeth into the unshielded portion of his neck. Grunting more out of anger than pain, Cotton dropped his weapons and grabbed her by the arms, plucking her from him. Raising her above his head he flipped her, hissing, into the fiery body of her friend. Landing atop the snapping flames of the unceremonious funeral pyre, she, too, exploded in a blaze of orange and screams.

The sickly-sweet smell of cooking flesh made Cotton slightly nauseous, although he was revived somewhat by the pleasant crackle of his ally, the fire. The popping of fissured flesh and sizzle of bodily fluids produced a delight in him that made such crass sounds akin to even the prettiest of chamber music. "Come on, bitches!" he snarled, standing with his back to the wall, "I'll give it to ye good!" Taking up the cleaver in his right hand and the torch in his left, he added maliciously, "Let me hack them pretty little faces of yours!"

Rather than attack, the women retreated as the torch light of the room diminished to a mere blush.

As the darkness multiplied the only source of light for Cotton was the two blazing bodies nearby. With his elbow he steadied himself against the wall and limped closer to the fire.

The fire was both a blessing and a curse, for while it provided him with some protection against the assuredly lethal dark, it cast wavering and shifting shadows which played havoc with his nervous eyes.

Where are they? his mind ranted, where were their bloody hides?

He caught a shimmer of reflected orange from the firelight and then a shape thrust itself at him from out of the darkness.

The female that assailed Cotton flew at him not figuratively, but literally. Much to his terror, she floated towards him, her bloodstained hands outstretched and grasping for his neck.

Throwing all of his weight to his left side, he slid against the wall and avoided her brutal claws. As she hovered above him in a scant moment of surprise at his continued energy despite his severe blood loss, he straightened himself and, inverting the dying torch, speared her through her rotted heart with its pointed end.

Parting with a befuddled gasp and an outpouring of a thick, syrupy solution that splattered down the length of the protruding torch, the woman – or rather, what was left of a woman – dropped to the floor like a sack of rocks. At Cotton's feet she lay, ultimately discharged of her immoral similitude of life.

As he looked down with satisfaction at the motionless dead, he could not arrest the peculiar fit of laughter brewing within his belly. "Ye foolish wenches," he wheezed between painful bouts of chortling, "know ye never to meddle with a man of Highlander stock, a man of Celtic blood!"

Barely had he finished with his brief but noble soliloquy when yet another of the ghastly females beset him. Ripping at him with her keen, black nails in a hectic manner, she managed to shred the few remaining leather ties of his buff coat. Absent of any suitable binding, the coat fell to his ankles, as useless to him now as the cow whose flesh had made it.

A lull ensued in the fighting as the female traded stares with Cotton. They both knew that at his feet lay his only protection from the death he had so long eluded, that without the buff coat he would be open to the full damage their bizarre strength could wreak upon his already critical figure. But whereas this knowledge caused the woman to gloat, it prompted Cotton to act.

Employing the only weapon he had left in his possession, the gore-caked meat cleaver, he assailed her neck with a rabid fury usually reserved for desperate or insane men. Chopping into her thin, white throat with a merciless overkill, Cotton labored to sever her head from its body. Sprawling onto the floor with his gagging victim, he struck again and again at her mutilated neck. The spray of her pierced jugular wet his tense face a brackish red, and the pathetic gurgling she had been making ceased as another blow destroyed her voice box.

"Bitch!" he cursed between his butchery. "Good-for-nothing cock whore!"

The extent of his violent aggression did not seem to bother him, although the product of his rage took much of his desire to fight away. He knelt above the tattered remains of a beautiful woman, her struggling having subsided some time before he halted his carnage. Looking into her untouched face, the face of a sleeping innocent, he experienced remorse rather than contentment. True, she was no ingenue, for she had endeavored to take his life; but was he any different? For years he had fought in campaigns, waged wars for nothing more than idiotic ideals or to line his purse. Gazing into her open throat, looking on her severed neck bone, he could not avoid the realization that he was no better than she, perhaps even worse. Divested of her life, this poor creature resorted to a base animal hunger for blood in order to survive. He had killed in order to live, too, but his was a profession, not an inescapable lifestyle. He could have made his living as a carpenter, or fisherman, but chose instead to take men of their lives. This pale child was undeserving of any of his hate, he thought ruefully, this piteous girl, this—

His wandering mind returned with a force that nearly blinded him. *What form of evil is so alluring that even in death, in true death, am I captivated by its charms?* He gave her one final blow, shattering the last pieces of flesh attaching her head to her neck, and rose to a standing position with her head in his big left hand.

Looking out into the flickering dark with a newfound repugnance for his rivals, Cotton lifted the decapitated head and waved it in taunt. "Come join your sisters," he offered pleasantly, "come join them in death!"

A sudden aberration to his left compelled him to turn and face the emergence from the shadows of a tall, obviously Danish, beauty.

Coincident to her materialization was a queer sensation which ran the length of Cotton's spine to the bottom of his belly. It was his sixth sense, honed from years of dangerous living and instructing him to turn around at once.

Without delay he obeyed his feelings and whirled about to discover one of the fiends suspended upon the wall like a cat about to pounce on an unsuspecting and preoccupied prey.

Sparing not even a moment of thought, he struck her across the eyes with his cleaver. She tumbled to the ground with his only weapon lodged firmly in her skull. Writhing in an agony caused by the mere ruination of her visage, she cried shrilly, "He has blinded me! He has robbed me of my sight!" Latching on to the cleaver with her quaking hands, she sobbed, "I am blind for all time!

Never to see forever!" The blood streaming from her gashed eye sockets added a grotesque twist in that it appeared as though she were crying.

Before he could retrieve his sole defense from her broken countenance, the Dane rushed at him, her long strides bearing her quickly towards him.

Employing all that he had left, Cotton threw with what little strength his haggard sinews could offer the severed head he held in his hand.

The head whirled through the heavy air like a missile launched from some powerful catapult, finding its mark square in the face of the oncoming Dane. On striking her, it bounced high then rolled off into the overpowering shadows of the room. The Dane's legs crumpled under her and she toppled to the rough ground. Touching tenderly her flattened nose, she wailed as she came to terms with her ruin. The clotted blood and mucus which poured forth from her broken proboscis intermixed into an appallingly tar-like black. Her teeth clattered to the floor as she opened her mouth in bewilderment and induced a new bout of self-mourning.

Channeling his attention from the Danish woman, who engaged in nothing but the collection of pitiful pieces of teeth scattered about the floor, Cotton's eyes came to dwell upon the tempting form of the redhead.

Standing directly before him and assuming no menacing posture, the swaying light of the fire seemed only to perfect her lovely figure. She looked precisely as she had the last time he saw her. The long legs, full hips, and mellow breasts held him enthralled. How many nights had he been denied them? his heart spoke. How countless were the years?

She slipped through the curtain of brown smoke wafting up from the cooking bodies, nearing him wearing only a grin that intimated either familiarity or certainty.

He let her come within arm's reach of him. If he still had any weapons, he would not even think of using them against her. She was to him what Cassandra was to Christian, only that he had loved her long before Christian was even born.

He did not struggle or put up a fight as she slid her arms around his neck and drew him to her for a kiss. He did not even flinch as her ruby lips touched his and he sadly realized how mistaken he had been to think her the same girl he had loved amongst the animals; the same lively, energetic, and robust farm girl who had once taken his heart and now tried to wheedle away his life. Her cold, dead lips afforded him no pleasure. On the contrary, in such an amorous pose his heart was burdened like never before. He was profoundly grief-stricken by what had become of his young love, his first love. Seeing beyond her beauty and into the heartless, icy glare of her eyes, he knew she was not Greta, but rather a thing; a bloodthirsty, non-living entity which bore none of the affection he had come to associate with her burning red hair while she lived.

Parting gently from her lips, he felt his heart forsaking him and knew he would have to act quickly. He could not die and leave her this rank creature, his overbearing love would not allow it. As salty tears burned into the open wounds on his cheeks, he moved his lips down to her bare neck and placed another kiss just over her carotid artery. He forced his eyes closed and uttered a personal prayer before opening his jaws as wide as could be managed and closing them on her throat.

Her body went rigid as his teeth ripped through her pallid flesh and unleashed a shower of dark red blood which coated him from head to foot. She pushed him away, standing before him with a hurt look plastered to her face. Her hands did little to hinder the generous flowing of her swarthy blood, the gaping bite resembling a second mouth upon her neck.

As the blood fled from her weakening corpse in a shocking display of arterial spray, Cotton thought, or perhaps hoped, he saw a flicker of appreciation in her dry eyes. She still loved me, he insisted as he cried tears of pain. She never ceased in her affection. Even after becoming a beast, after losing her life, her love for me was maintained, though kept dormant. Her love was unbound by death. True death.

Her red eyes rolled back into her head and she collapsed with a sickening thud onto the harsh floor. It was an unfitting end to such a moving moment for the Scotsman.

Peering down through his tears at her legitimately deceased body, he felt numb. He could taste her foul blood on his lips and feel the shreds of her throat's flesh caught between his teeth. He no longer felt much pain from his wounds, but from the wound he inflicted. His gradual paralysis of sensation was not due chiefly to blood loss, but rather a state of bereavement. His heart had been broken by her years and years ago, yet had never mended. Seeing her lying motionless, a ghastly expression upon her dead face, caused his heart to bleed once more for the German girl. That, and the fact that he had been the instrument of her demise, cruelly tore at his reasoning. True, he had freed her from the wretched existence to which she had been chained, but at what price to his mental and emotional states? The very thought of her toasting over the blood of a baby, of her brutally leeching the life from someone, made him ill. He no longer wished to live in such a world where fear, sickness, and death reigned supreme, where nothing more than a conflict in beliefs, even when concerning the Word of God, would be enough to cause mass tortures and wars. A world in which evil flourished, historically recording one atrocity after another, one genocide serving only to birth a greater carnage. He rescinded all claims he held to his mismanaged life and to the world into which he was born without choice. Quitting all that he possessed in this plane, he placed himself firmly in the realm of the next. Committing all that he had left, his very soul, into the hands of Christ, he offered one final prayer for his family and for Christian, then prepared himself for a rendezvous he had put off for some time. A rendezvous with Death.

Sensing the loss of aggression and peaceful resolve in his demeanor, the remaining women broke from the reveling shadows and fell upon him like frenzied animals. Nails tore and teeth gouged into the old man's flesh. His body was battered about to foster a more generous blood flow, and his hair was ripped in great clumps from his head and beard. The crowning, and oddly merciful, death blow was delivered by the French blonde. Grabbing him from behind, she plucked open his neck with her long, sharp claws.

Somehow breaking from them, more dead than alive, Cotton stumbled towards the doorways clasping his rent neck in his bloodstained hands. As the blood drained profusely from his weary and pummeled bulk, he was pursued in a maliciously slow fashion by the few females left. In response to the abuse they slung at him, he released a woeful scream that seemed to shake the very castle to its foundations.

Christian sat up startled, "What in God's name was that?"

Cassandra tried to ease him back into her lap but found he would not budge. "I heard nothing."

"Surely you heard someone scream!" he insisted.

"I heard only the soft laughter of the wind and the mournful cry of the storm ..."

Shuffling with great exertion, Cotton dragged his tattered self closer to the room's exits. Impotent of all defenses and powerless in the midst of his acceded death, his unsound mind, through loss of blood and oxygen, called upon the one person who should be kept from such danger.

Whether due to an innate fear of a solitary demise, or a last minute effort in seeking forgiveness, Cotton cried out with his hands still clamped firmly around his open neck, "Christian! Christian!"

Nearing a door, he let his left hand fall from his neck and into the ancient wood with all his body weight. He collapsed forward as the door swung wide to an empty hallway. Leaning his bruised back against the doorway, he glanced from the dark hall to the women, who crept closer with each passing second. More than any other part of their form, he could see their glowing red eyes; peering at him full of burning ire and an obscene yearning.

Turning his head limply to the hallway, he winced in pain as he again called out, "Christian!"

Musing tragically at the parody he had become, he noted how the guardian now sought the ward for protection.

Sensing the proximity of the women, he cleared his throat of blood and cried out once more, "Christian!"

A placidity in the storm outside produced a quiet in the castle that was not unlike that of the grave. Perched at the foot of his bed, Christian sat head cocked listening for further confirmation of the scream he had heard. He was about to dismiss the entire event as a defect of his ears and bow to the Lady Cassandra's reasonable explanation when he clearly ascertained, although quite distant and muffled, his name being called.

"'Tis Cotton!" he breathed in horror as he jumped to his feet. "Good Lord, 'tis Cotton!"

He bound to his door and struggled to open it. Discovering it to be locked, he attacked it vigorously, striving to rattle it from its ancient hinges. This being to no avail, he turned a desperate and angry eye to Cassandra. "If you have any of the humanity left in you, any of the love you so openly profess, then for Christ's sake let me out!"

Rising with concern she protested, "But you may be harmed!"

"You let me out or I shall despise you to no end," he promised coldly, seeking his quickest release by threatening that which he assumed she most feared.

His assumption proved correct; she carried herself from the bed to his side at the door. Placing her hands on the latch, she hesitated before turning it. Keeping her eyes on the large brass handle, she whispered weakly, "Chris—"

"Be done with it!" he yelled into her ear, causing her to flinch and successfully quelling any further delays.

To his astonishment, without producing any form of key whatsoever, she gave the latch a downward twist, unlocking the door instantly. Stepping aside, she dropped her hands and permitted the door to swing slightly open.

Casting her a look of profound awe, Christian slipped past her and through the doorway. Rushing down the hall, he stopped only to give Cotton's room a hurried examination. Finding the door open and no evidence of the Scot's presence, he continued onward.

"Christian!"

He heard it more clearly now, although still distant, as he approached the top of the stairs. Running barefoot down the cold and uneven stone blocks was murder on his tenderized feet. He dared not think of what he was doing to his blistered and bloodied soles, let alone the possibility for infection all the dust and grime scattered about the floor allowed. All he concerned himself with was the condition of his friend. In what dire state was Cotton placed which would make the burly Scot cry for him like a babe for its mother? The mere thought of Smith-Patton asking for anybody's help, let alone his, troubled him greatly.

Flying from the staircase before touching every step, Christian slowed his pace and listened. He did not know from whence the cries originated, and had to abide by his ears rather than eyes in plotting his course. Coming almost to a standstill, he whispered helplessly to himself, "Cotton, please, call my name once more and I shall be there ..."

As if heard by the Highlander himself, from the dining room came another familiar solicitation.

"Christian!"

Dashing into the room, he followed the departing cry's echo to the kitchen. Here, he too paused when confronted with the filth Cotton had seen earlier. He felt his stomach seized by something other than the nervous fear that so gripped him, something akin to nausea. Stumbling in haste, he quit the kitchen by way of a narrow hall.

Down uneven steps, the foundations of the castle becoming a ceiling, he was met by such pure and brutal violence as he had never witnessed in any of his days in London. Until now, Christian would have thought such barbarities to be only practiced in the domain of nightmares.

He saw Baron Mormeau viciously tear to pieces a quivering nude woman. In one instant she was whole, in the next his harsh nails had reduced her to nothing but ragged bits of flesh and splints of broken bone.

Upon dispatching the woman, the Baron proceeded to his next victim, a tall blonde lacking any form of clothing who maintained her composure as he taunted her with French insults.

As Mormeau shouted at the woman, Christian glanced down to see near his feet the remains of what appeared to be three to four other women. He could not make a decisive determination for they were so ravaged that their bodily parts intermingled in one great mass of blood and innards.

Diverting his eyes from such an unpleasant spectacle, he was moderately startled to find the blonde woman responding to Mormeau indignantly. Whatever it was she said, it so angered Mormeau that he ripped her limbs from their sockets and beat her about the head with them. While in the act of clubbing her with her own arms, he ranted rapidly in his native tongue. The woman, who did nothing to defend herself but watch the blood spurt from her gaping sockets, slid to the floor under the barrage of Mormeau's blows. After a brief minute had transpired, her head caved in and the Baron, apparently satisfied with his handiwork, ceased his bludgeoning.

Dropping her arms, he began to lick the blood from his hands when he noticed Christian standing horror-struck in the mouth of the underground hallway. "Christian!" he uttered in pleasant surprise, totally oblivious to what he had just done. "Where are your shoes?"

Ignoring him, Christian stared at what was left of the blonde. Blood continued to spill from her battered head. Moving closer, carefully past the remains of the other women, he spied bits of brain matter and skull bone being carried by the slowly meandering blood. Her own arms sat crossed in her lap, shielding her lower nudity from his gaze. The gentle slope of her shoulders ended in protruding bone, torn cartilage, and hanging flesh.

Laying his hand on Christian's back, the Baron asked naively, "What troubles you, my son? What is amiss?"

Shrinking vehemently from his touch, he managed to look Mormeau in his emotionless eyes and madly utter, "What ails me? What is wrong with me? 'Tis you, fiend, who has done nothing but perpetrate acts of unthinkable aggression! 'Tis you who has inundated my conscious thoughts with nightmares! Who has displayed only perverse cruelty since our first encounter!"

His thin, purplish lips curled into a smug smile. "Come now," he placidly spoke, "have I not treated you kindly? 'Tis you who does me the dishonor of not accepting all I choose to grant …"

The sly reference to Cassandra did not escape Christian, and he turned from the Baron's hard gaze. Frustrated with Mormeau's total lack of remorse, he looked past the evil Frenchman to Horst, who crouched over something bloody lying half-in and half-out of a doorway. "And what did you do to that poor creature?" he asked with a tilt of his head.

Slowly glancing over, Mormeau's smile lost its potency as he muttered, "I did nothing to that poor creature …" Rolling his wicked eyes back to Christian, he stated with clear delight, "He did it to himself."

Christian's eyes widened in shock and disbelief. *My God!* his mind staggered, *that gory mess is Cotton!*

Just as he realized the condition of his friend, further affirmation of the horrible truth came as Cotton moaned desperately from his place on the floor, "Christian … Christian …!"

Shouldering past Mormeau, Christian rushed to his fallen companion. Enraged at seeing Horst hover over Cotton like some beast that partakes only of carrion, he forcefully shoved the rotting man to the side, exclaiming, "Away from him, you monster!"

Unbalanced, Horst landed upon his backside. With a look that unquestionably summed up his hatred for Christian, he started to move for him. Catching sight of the Baron's displeasure at this reaction, his face resumed its rigid guise and he picked himself up. Moving quietly to the small piles of disassembled bodies, he bent and began picking at the shredded flesh and exposed entrails, as if consuming the choicest cuts of meat.

Ignoring Horst's cannibalism, for he was so taken by the extent of his old friend's injuries, Christian knelt and undertook to tending Cotton's wounds and alleviating his pains. Ripping a strip of shirt already torn and hanging from Cotton's mangled chest, he tied it as a bandage around the dying Scot's bleeding neck. On perceiving this to be a useless gesture, as the quick blood easily bled through the porous fabric of the shirt, he was moved to weep for the fate of his friend and the complete frustration he felt at being unable to help him.

The man was a mess. His face was a crossroads of nail-cleaved streaks and tooth-punctured perforations. One particularly mean slash had robbed him of his right eye. Christian stared into the cavernous pink pit that oozed with blood and the off-white remnants of eyeball. Patches were missing from his beard and mustache; forcefully pulled, the absent hair was replaced by pocked craters that dotted his face. So thick with blood was his visage that what remained of any facial hair was dyed a deep red and nearly blended with the overall hue of crimson.

Shifting watery eyes from the ragged portrait of his friend to that of the mangled rest of him, Christian could look no further than Cotton's stomach. There the man's bowels hung naked, like some hideous parody of a Scotch sporran. The pulpy, pink mass of intestine pressured Christian's eyes shut, and in so doing forced the tears he had been warring against to rain down upon Cotton's open face.

The sting of teardrops cascading onto his chafed and cleaved cheeks inspired Cotton to crack open his one good eye. Gazing up blearily at his weeping friend, he swallowed some of the blood that had collected in his throat and weakly began to exhort Christian to cease his touching display of emotion. "Don't bother," he rasped breathlessly, "I am done for …"

Christian clutched the old warrior's bleeding head and moved to within an inch of the man's shattered features. "Do not speak such things," he sobbed. "There is always hope."

"There is never hope!" the Scot spat bitterly in the face of Death. Then, as if to himself in subdued delirium, he annexed his denouncement, "… Never hope, but always failure …" His own mention of failure seemed to incite a sudden vivacity within his dying breast. Reaching up with his right hand, he grabbed Christian by the shirt collar and pulled him even closer, down upon his blood-streaked face. Shaking with the forcefulness of his conviction, he wailed into his young companion's ear, "I have failed ye! Just as I have failed me family and shamed me God, have I failed ye!" Turning reflective, he whispered sadly, "Succumbing to temptation ... I have failed. I am doomed and deserve damnation dearly."

"You shan't be damned!" insisted Christian in teary protest. "I'll not allow it!" Then, as if a man who has witnessed the fall of his god, he wept, "Oh, Cotton, how could this happen to *you*?"

Mustering from somewhere within his collapsed chest a viciousness so exceeding as to disgrace the dark angel himself, he angrily cursed, "Women!" Upon the passing of such a powerful utterance he began to swoon, his vocal condemnation draining him of what little life he still clung to.

The Baron peeked past Christian at Cotton and saw the vast quantities of blood which had leaked from the latter's body and now ran into the cracks and fissures of the stone floor. His shrewd face gave the impression of a cook who had seen his food go to waste.

Raising a trembling hand barely from the ground, Cotton directed Christian's eyes to the interior of the room. Looking in, Christian saw by torchlight the dismembered and mutilated corpses his friend had fought against. Pieces of flesh and parts of body lay scattered everywhere about the ground. Lakes of blood gathered upon the dust-laden foundation and also lined the walls; gruesome frescoes created by breached arteries and peeled veins. Nearest the wall to his left appeared the charred forms of two women, their blackened skin like coal, blending them visually with the fire-damaged masonry. Sizzling pus still escaped their fractured flesh.

"I got most of 'em," said Cotton, his pride surprisingly still intact. "Them bitches are hard to kill—" a fit of coughing assailed him and he rocked violently in his friend's arms. Blood splashed from his hacking mouth, accompanied by a thick, red froth.

He's hemorrhaging, Christian noted dismally. Having tended to the dying, he knew it would not be long now.

Straining, Cotton gulped down much of the blood pouring from his mouth and managed to express between swallows his ardent beliefs. "The devil is a woman!" he cried. "A cunny whore!"

Christian, unceasing in his tears of devotion, held him as he shook uncontrollably. His own sobs joined Cotton's repetitive coughing, mingling into a strange requiem.

As sudden as the seizure had began, it abruptly ceased. Tightening his grip on Christian, Cotton's sole eye burned with intensity. "Pray for me,

Christian," he spoke gravely, "for I've done many a wrong." Halting only to take a laborious breath, he continued, affecting a more desperate tone. "Do not let them have me remains!" he emphasized strongly, hurting Christian with his grasp. "Do not let them have me body! Do not— oh!" Convulsed once again by Death's spasm, his eye grew cloudy. Amidst incredible pain, his need for absolution dominated his final thoughts. "Forgive me, forgive me, forgive me ..."

The rippling of his throe departed from him by way of his right leg, which quivered long after life had retired. Cotton Smith-Patton, mercenary, blacksmith, and sinner, would be counted among the living no longer.

Christian hugged the lifeless form of his big friend close to him. He wept for the man he would see no more of in this world, he cried at the torturous circumstances of his death, and he lamented his own plight at being orphaned in such an iniquitous place. "No!" he raged against Death, "No!" He then resorted to appealing to the dead man's soul, begging, "Cotton, stay with me! Don't leave me alone, not here!" But the time for prayers had, like the old Scot, already passed.

A cold hand gripped Christian's shoulder and rancid breath tickled his ear. He did not have to glance up to know that it was the Baron Mormeau who so touched him; shivers were sent up his spine and his stomach turned queasy.

"You see the needlessness in death, the waste?" Mormeau spoke softly, respecting the dead through tone, but being depreciating in his choice of words. "It did not have to be this way for your friend, and it does not have to be this way for you. Join us, Christian! 'He who is not with me, is against me.'"

"Scripture quoted from the mouth of the Devil himself," said Christian as he raised his anguished eyes to the entity of his hatred. Too engrossed earlier in the Baron's butchery to notice, he was now startled by Mormeau's appearance – a healthy hue replaced the sickly white pallor and a hint of rose blushed his cheeks. Overcoming his initial shock, he reverted back to the handling of the Baron's entreaty and spitefully dashed any hopes of persuasion held by Mormeau. "Join you? Never!"

The Baron squinted his eyes and rocked gently with a light chuckle. "Surely there is no need for insult."

"You laugh?" Christian spoke in disbelief. "You who takes life so carefree, who because of the natural perversity of his true self is resigned to live out eternity as a leech even amongst demons?"

"You are still upset about the child," Mormeau commented, as if referring to something as light as a spilled cup of tea. "Is not the cat still beloved after it has eaten the bird?"

"How blithely you speak of so grievous a sin!" Christian gazed down at Cotton's torn remains. "This man, this noble soldier—"

"Noble?" retaliated a vexed Mormeau. "Hardly. He was a drunkard, a lecher, and at the very least a poor excuse for a guardian." Signaling the room's two entrances, he added, "He gave in to pleasure, and left through pain."

Christian placed his hand upon Cotton's blood-soaked shirt for added emphasis. "This man wasted his last breaths of life begging for forgiveness for a mere hour of failure. You, sir, have made a failure out of everything and everyone you have ever touched!"

"Hold your tongue or I may forget your importance to me." His face contorting in restrained anger served only to exhibit, rather than hide, his intense reaction to the living man's allegation.

"I shall do nothing of the sort!"

Shaken at Christian's open objection, Mormeau stammered furiously, "Why, I ... I shall destroy you!"

Leaping to his feet, Christian furthered the Baron's dismay by grabbing him savagely by the lapels and shaking him. "I shall destroy you!" he screamed as grief overcame him. "You, who art the ultimate creature of darkness! Of evil incarnate! Lucifer himself be not as wicked as ye, for he was once an angel! You, Frenchman, were always a devil!"

"Enough!" cried Mormeau as he pushed Christian from his breast. "Get your filthy English hands off me!"

Stumbling backward, Christian regained his balance by latching onto the doorway. There he stood, breathing heavily and casting daggers at the Baron with his eyes.

Brushing off the front of his jacket and smoothing out wrinkles formed by Christian's fingers, Mormeau spoke as if truly astonished with the young man's behavior. "I invite you into my home, offer you the comforts of a king, give you my woman, and this is how you treat me? You, sir, are a disgrace."

Mormeau reproaching him for being an ingrate infuriated Christian. In light of all that has passed, he fumed, of all the cruelty and inhumanity practiced by the Baron that I have witnessed, a lifetime of sins committed in the space of a few hours, I am to be taxed for seeming the ungrateful guest? I am to be chastised for upholding the laws of God? For observing decency and goodness am I reviled? I have not taken a single life in all my years and here a murderer many times over criticizes my morality? Oh, you have greatly underestimated me, Baron, for I shall see to it that you kill no more!

With his passions in such a state of burning rebuttal and incredulous anger, Christian jumped at Mormeau, screaming, "You bastard! You sick bastard!"

The boldness of his prior conduct had prepared the Baron for such an action. Allowing the temperamental youth to come within inches of him, he slapped him down with a blow to the head.

Christian fell to his knees under the force of the openhanded smack. His mind whirled and his vision blurred; pain and confusion ruled his jumbled thoughts as he slipped into the escape of unconsciousness and collapsed at the Baron's red feet.

"Horst," Mormeau spoke over his shoulder, "pick up this impudent piece of shit and take him to his room."

The squatting manservant rose from his ghastly meal with more than a little discontent lining what human features he still retained. His pale fingers were colored with blood, as were his lips. In his teeth, which were visible through his cheek, one could see particles of flesh and organ. He lumbered over to Christian and slung the English youth's unresisting body over his shoulder. Horst then withdrew to the upper levels of the castle, leaving the Baron alone with his thoughts and his corpses.

Moving from his place near the doorway, Mormeau stepped over Cotton's lifeless body and entered the room in which Death had been an active visitor.

Congealing blood lay in puddles here and there, the variance in hues easily distinguishing the dead's dark hemoglobin from the living's lighter crimson. On the floor before Mormeau was a severed hand, to his left lay several bodies, two of which were burned to a crisp, and to his right sat a bodiless head. A few other cadavers graced his view of the room's feminine carnage before his placid eyes settled on the immense bed. The sight of such an overwrought luxury appeared to trouble him more so than the women scattered in pieces around him.

Hearing a muffled sobbing, Mormeau walked behind a pillar and there discovered a large blonde shielding her smashed face with her big hands. On seeing him through her fingers, the woman cringed in fear. Seeking to mitigate her fright, Mormeau crouched in front of her and tenderly combed her stringy hair with his fingernails. "Why could you not wait?" he spoke fatherly into her flattened face. "He was promised you after we had the boy. You may have ruined things for us now."

The woman smiled at him in a sorry attempt at pleasing him, her missing teeth only adding to the homeliness of her leveled nose.

Reverting back to his days as a priest, with the gentle sloping smile of a confessor upon his thin purple lips, Mormeau let his hand fall from her head to her throat, ripping out her jugular vein with his claws.

Coated in her reeking blood, the Baron rose as her body fell. Turning, he headed for the room's exit. On reaching the open door, he stood on Cotton and looked down in disgust at the dead's face. "And what shall I do with you, noble idiot?" he hissed before stepping down.

Passing his hand over his face, he smeared sprayed blood into his waxy flesh. Looking from his hand to the stairway, he noticed Cassandra there watching. Tears lined her eyes and trickled down her smooth cheeks.

Mormeau offered her a cold stare and she turned away, disappearing once more into the obscurity of shadow.

Christian awoke slightly dizzy, sprawled out across his bed. The absolute darkness of the room was only thwarted by his friend the moon, whose beams poured in through the window glass. Rising, he felt the rush of blood to his head and sank quickly back into his prone state.

Gazing up at the ceiling, he was overwhelmed with the events that had nearly torn his rationale to shreds. He was in a wicked castle situated in a most inhospitable town, fiendish purveyors of evil served in the capacities of host, and his friend had been bitterly murdered. What was he to do? What was any man to do? It was clear to him that there was no cure to the Plague in Manasseh, only something which he thought was not possible. Something worse.

"The cure that is worse than the disease ..." he mumbled to himself, quoting the strange little child he had encountered only hours ago in the town below.

He knew that if he lay in thought and did not busy himself, despair would soon force him into despondency. He would do nothing but weep for his departed companion and for himself. Fighting against this urge, he slowly lifted himself upon his elbows.

Surveying the still room for any other occupants, a perplexing feeling that he was not alone gave rise to the hackles of his neck. Validating his isolation did little to alleviate him of this fear.

He had just begun to stretch his sleeping back when a low creak caught him in mid arch. The sound was not so peculiar as to instill in him concern, but the location from whence it came terrified him senseless. From across the room, one of the French windows, lodged closed by dirt and neglect, had started to rattle in its rust-soldered hinges.

Following suit, in no time at all the other windows joined in creating quite a racket. Having tried them earlier, Christian knew that they had been fastened firmly by age. Where they would not budge an inch through his exertions, they now shook freely through no force accountable but the wind.

Yet there was little evidence for such a gale. The storm had been in a lull for some time, and the movement of the panes was induced without the necessary howl or shriek associated with high velocity gusts. The only sound was that of the clattering glass and the loud beating of Christian's heart.

In an instant the windows were forced open with such energy that it was strange their glass panes did not shatter. Blown inward, the wooden borders took a beating as they pounded against the stone of the interior wall.

Christian was immediately propped straight by fear, which blew over him on the invading wind, tossing his thoughts as it did his hair. He could see leaves tumbling into his room; brown, dried, and dead, they scattered across his floor and capered about in whirling masses.

In the short space of silence and inactivity that ensued, he heroically tried to recount some prayers that lay in the back of his mind. Try as he might, he could not form even a single word on his trembling lips, for something ghostly white approached his window from the quiet dimness outside.

With heart exploding under his breast and breath bated and strained, he watched with eyes squinted in terror as the form of the seemingly weightless Lady Cassandra wafted into his room.

What is it I am privy to? his mind struggled with bewilderment. What is this that is airborne? Who is this woman aloft, the wind her carriage?

Floating midway between Christian and his windows, Cassandra wore only the flimsy white gown in which she had first introduced herself to him. The dry leaves whirled about her bare feet and heralded her arrival with their rustle. Touching down, the leaves collected at her toes and there remained.

She stood roughly ten paces before him, her nude silhouette cut sharply through a gown made transparent by contrasting moonlight. Then, seemingly with no effort on her part, the gown slid from her shoulders to her ankles and she was in true nakedness, the smirk on her lips being all that she wore.

Christian's heart nearly stopped. She was her! he now readily accepted what before he had so ardently denied. She was the dark lady of his nightmares, that which infested his unconscious thoughts! Seeing her in shadow and similar circumstances as those which had been played through his dreaming head many a night, he realized it could no longer be repudiated! What he had taken to be horrific only in the realm of sleep was now a stark and undeniable reality. He could never refuse her in his dreams, how could he spurn her advances now? And despite all the fear and loathing he presently experienced, a maddening desire, one so strong as to make the most celibate inflamed with passion, gripped him and would not let him go. He shook as if with the fever, for it was a fever which so ailed him; the burning of unreserved and total longing.

"Love me," she begged as she stepped out of her gown and walked toward him, "love me . . ."

He wanted to run; not from her, but from her excellence. She frightened him no more, the peculiar affection he bore her pacifying his restlessness and quelling any thoughts contrary to his loving her. Hers was a beauty unsurpassed, even the Father of all creation would quake at the sight of her. If God would falter, he parodied reason, then man shall surely fall.

His absurd reflections were interrupted as she climbed lioness-like into bed with him. Slithering up to his lips, she presented him with a quick kiss, a tantalizing teaser of what was to come.

His arousal was at such a pitch that he was mindless of the clamminess of her lips or the chill of her touch. His was an attraction that went far beyond the limitations of human sensation.

She tore at his clothing, attacking his dress as if it were her most vile enemy. Plucking off his shirt, she tossed it aside; his breeches she flung behind her. When finished, she examined with pleasure the young man she had denuded.

Taking her forcefully by her left arm and behaving according to his passion, he pulled her to him and beset her face and body with an abundance of kisses.

Pushing him back into a prone position, Cassandra mounted him. Reaching between his legs, she took hold of his erection and thrust it inside her.

Christian, for a fleeting moment jolted by the cold rather than warm feeling of her vagina, looked up into his lover's eyes. The emotionless black coals were as frigid as her nether region, and yet he knew, somehow and in someway, she loved him.

As they progressed in their lovemaking, Cassandra began to acquire some of Christian's intense body heat. Her flesh went from a lukewarm to a warmth nearly approaching that of a living girl.

My God, Christian marveled, she does things to me unlike any other woman I have lain with. Nothing is too vulgar for this patroness of the libido, this elegant Lady from whom a whore could learn a thing or two.

Gradually reaching the pinnacle of their fleshly exertions, Cassandra implored her paramour, whispering with a tinge of sadness rather than elation, "Come into my darkness."

He emptied himself into her. She sapped him of what little strength remained, all of his energy being deposited deep within her, being transferred to her sepulchral womb. Barely able to lift his head, he watched as she got off him.

Perching herself by his side, she made circles on his chest with her fingers. Ceasing her love play, she drew close to his face. "Taste me," she commanded, biting down on the bottom of her lip and planting a bloody kiss upon his open mouth.

He kissed her amorously, thoughtless of the salty, bitter taste of her blood. As she pulled away from him he sucked her lower lip as though it were a teat.

Standing at his bedside, she straightened and pulled back her long raven locks. It was then he discovered she held in her hand Rebecca's locket, stolen from his breast by her encircling fingers. Placing it around her own neck and letting her hair fall free, she looked down on him and smiled slyly. "You are mine now, Christian," he heard her sigh contentedly as he succumbed to sleep, that most tireless of pursuits. "You shall always be mine ..."

# Chapter Eight

Christian's eyes opened onto the patterned brick above him. Lying on his back and gazing up at the ceiling, he snuggled in the warmth of his bed. He could not recall the last time he had slept so soundly. It was as if all his fears were taken from him, all his stress evaporated. He felt renewed as he stretched his well-rested body, giving rise to the long overdue savoring of a complete relaxation. And the dream he had entertained! he thought with pleasure. How lovely it was to conceive of something while asleep which did not startle him awake with the immediacy of a musket shot. If he experienced more dreams like that he should prefer to sleep forever!

The dream, or rather fantasy, seemed so real to him that he had to glance down to see if he was undressed. Finding his clothes in place about his person, he sighed with a tinge of disappointment. If only it were real, he wished as he envisioned a naked Cassandra in his arms, if only it were so.

A heavy rapping at his door propelled him to a sitting position and back into reality.

"Yes?" he called out, his voice quavering. "Who's there?"

A strained silence was all the reply he received.

Rising quickly, he found his stockings and shoes by the guiding light of the moon. He balanced himself precariously, alternating one foot after the other, as he thrust his feet into the hose.

Plopping onto the bed in order to ease his murderous shoes into place, he was struck by the peculiar taste which so filled his mouth. Ignorant of it before, either through the re-examination of his blissful dream or the mistaken attribution by him to a simple case of cottonmouth, he now analyzed the properties of the slightly bitter taste. It was salty and vaguely sour, with an unrelenting aftertaste.

A chill overtook him which he could not shake. It was blood! The taste in his mouth was all the evidence that remained of a most repugnant swallow.

As his mind flashed back to his dream, he remembered having sucked blood from the Lady Cassandra's lips. His heart raced as his hands instantly flew to his chest and searched there for the one item which would verify whether or not he had in fact dreamt anything at all.

It was gone! he thought frantically. The locket was gone!

The emptiness around his neck which Rebecca's locket had once filled now felt heavy and cumbersome. My God! he mentally beseeched. My God! The dream wasn't a dream! All was real!

He shook as if struck by a palsy. He had made love to Cassandra, on the very bed on which he rested he had held paradise! But she was *her*, the woman who had haunted his thoughts, both sleeping and waking, since before he could adequately remember. The woman who he visited in ruined churchyards and loved in desecrated vaults, the very woman he could not resist, who could turn his eyes from the splendor of Christ Himself and whose words intimated far more than the natural. It was Cassandra whose breath reeked of lost souls.

What had he done?

The clicking of his door's locks obliged him to abandon his current horror and prepare for whatever terrors yet awaited. Gazing from his bed, apprehension registering on his face, he watched as his door opened with an excruciating slowness. Has she come to finish me off? his mind fearfully ranted. She has taken my heart, does she come now to relieve me of my blood?

From behind the shadow of the door loomed the sinister specter of Horst. His glacial countenance offered Christian no relief as he motioned him to follow.

Wincing as he squeezed his feet into his shoes, Christian stood erect, and dutifully, although sorely, made his way behind Horst.

The two walked silently down the black hallway, their only conversation being the clacking of their shoes. Christian slowed somewhat as he passed Cotton's open room. Hoping that if his dreams had become reality then his reality might be transferred to dream, he glanced in to see if his old friend was there. Of course, the Scotsman was absent, the hard truth once again burdening Christian's wearisome heart.

They proceeded down the stairway, re-entering the antechamber and moving towards a door set directly across from the dining room. On reaching the door, which was closed, Horst thrust out a bony hand and pulled its rusted latch open.

Christian had to wait until Horst shifted his large frame from the narrow doorway to see inside. Peering in, he was surprised to find the room well lit. A fireplace crackled an invitation as he followed the skeletal servant inward, placing his shoes on a plush maroon carpet.

The overwhelming theme of the small room was the color red. Varying tints and hues served as drapes, rugs, and tapestries. Everything was swathed in a shade of the color — even the furniture was padded in crimson velvet.

The resounding echo of the door closing behind him made Christian uneasy. He felt as if he were in a lion's den, but did not even bother to turn and face Horst, who remained vigilant in front of the door, blocking Christian's only exit.

Maneuvering himself in front of the fireplace, Christian glanced up at a large painting hung just above the mantelpiece. The image coated onto the canvas was that of a cardinal resplendent in scarlet robes. Only hard scrutiny coupled with prior knowledge of the Baron's former occupation allowed him to perceive it as a facsimile of Mormeau.

It was not that the picture was flawed; on the contrary the artist, whoever he was, had done an admirable job. The high cheekbones, arched eyebrows, thin lips, and piercing stare, all traits of the cruel Frenchman, were there, yet there was something captured in the painting which was so overpowering as to make difficult an easy association with Mormeau. Although the Baron's hair was shorter and appeared darker in the rendering, such trivial differences did not hamper immediate identification as would be expected. It was not the fault of the artist, nor was it the style in which Mormeau wore his hair that so perplexed Christian, it was that the painting was of the man before his death. Life flowed in the fullness of the cardinal's cheeks, the glimmer in his eye, and the healthy hue of his lips. His veins were hid under tanned skin and his nails were well-manicured.

Remarkable, Christian thought to himself, how the very essence of life, when in place, transforms one's appearance like no barber or beautician ever could.

The only evident imperfection was a rather large hole torn out of the center of the painting. Judging by its position over the breast of the cardinal, and tracing the little black beads which ran from around Mormeau's neck to the hole, Christian assumed the perforation to have been where a painted cross once lie. It was obvious to him that someone had ruined the portrait in order to deface the depiction of a rosary's crucifix. It was equally apparent to him as to who the vandal was.

"I trust you napped well, my handsome little necro-copulator," the Baron's tired voice croaked thick with sarcasm. "Oh, the blessed hypocrisy."

Christian looked over to his left and saw Mormeau curled up like a cat on one of the padded red chairs. The scarlet of the evil man's robes rendered him near invisible in the big chair. The firelight caught in his cold eyes but did not warm them.

"Was I not a beautiful man?" Mormeau gestured wearily to the portrait, a look of faded pride adorning his sallow face.

"A bit on the portly side, I should say," quipped Christian in response.

"Portly?" asked Mormeau, confusion furrowing his brow.

"Fat," Christian clarified bluntly. "You looked then as the very incarnation of life as you do now the very embodiment of death."

"Seat yourself, please," Mormeau instructed his insolent guest with marked agitation.

Christian did as he was told, easing his body into the chair situated across from the Baron.

"Horst," Mormeau ordered as he rolled his eyes to the ceiling, "pour Christian a drink."

Under the weight of being in the presence of Baron Mormeau, and being in his presence alone, unaided by even the company of Cassandra, Christian ached for the cool comfort of his pewter cross. Damn her! his thoughts turned illogical. Cursed be Rebecca for divesting me of my crucifix. May she wear it falsely when she thinks me untrue, for how can I reclaim it from her neck when I am drained of my blood? The image of Rebecca swearing against him for never returning brought a strange smile to his lips. She will come to believe that I have deserted her once again, when in truth I shall have deserted this very existence.

The soft gurgle of wine being poured into a chalice on the table to his right alerted Christian that Horst was no longer safeguarding the door. Slyly turning his eyes to the unguarded exit, he contemplated fleeing.

As if reading his mind, the Baron purred, "Don't be foolish, child. If you escape my castle, you must then escape my town. If you escape my town, you must then escape my wood. No matter what you do, nor how hard you try, you shan't escape from me. Now, please, drink." He motioned to the chalice which Horst held out to Christian.

Reaching up, he carefully lifted the full chalice from Horst's cadaverous fingers. Once he had done this, Horst resumed his position at the door.

Staring intently at the burgundy liquid in his cup, Christian feared that the red liquor might only look like wine.

"I assure you it is only the very best Bordeaux."

Christian responded to Mormeau's assurance with a suspicious glare. Swirling the drink to check its consistency, and finding it quite watery and not thick or sluggish, he put it to his lips and sipped. It was probably the richest wine he had ever tasted, surpassing even that served at supper.

"You know that I can kill you very easily, don't you?" Mormeau spoke as if it were a well-known fact. "Your life hangs by a thread, and I am as Atropos."

"If you kill me," countered Christian, "my blood will cry aloud for vengeance in Heaven."

"Then your cry shall fall upon deaf ears."

Christian stared at the grinning red man. Even from his near distant place in the crimson cushioned chair he could still make out the pointed fangs glistening at him from the Baron's cracked mouth. The weed must be allowed to grow before it can be pulled, he reflected. So fearful had he become that all his thoughts were now executed in a hushed mental whisper.

"You realize that no matter what," Mormeau hesitated, the pause being to add weight to his already laden words, "tonight is your last night alive."

Sullen, Christian averted his eyes. He had already come to recognize this horrible truth long ago.

"Do not be so dour!" the Baron happily reproved him. "If murder were my foremost intent, you would be in my belly by now!" He let out a sickeningly merry cackle, then instantly turned grave. "I offer you a choice: die a lurid death at my hands, or join me and live on for eternity."

In the face of so blunt a threat, Christian exploded. "Only two things are eternal, Baron! The love of God and the fires of Hell! You, sir, shall know of the latter!"

"I am to infer that you choose death?"

"My God died at the hands of the Romans. I suppose I could manage the same."

"But you are no Christ."

"And you are far from Roman."

Mormeau could not help but laugh at his young guest's incisive repartee. "You mock me double, insulting my nationality and my past vocation."

"To make a mockery of you is not difficult. Your aristocratic airs, powder, and finely tailored clothing do little to mask the deformities caused by the rendering useless of the soul."

"You are snide."

"I am alive."

He could see this response garnered a flush of contained anger within the Baron, and reserved future jabs at the man's non-living nature for later use.

"Yes, you are alive," Mormeau eventually whispered, "but for how long?"

"For as long as my God wishes."

"In that case," said the Baron as he eased back into his chair, "I am your god tonight."

"You couldn't be god to a swine!"

"In saying that you do yourself more injustice than you do me."

Christian tired of the insulting banter, opting to reason with the unreasonable. "You call this living?" he asked, motioning to the heavily draped windows. "Fearing the day, living in seclusion?"

"Yes," sighed Mormeau, as if Christian had just given him a rock upon which to build. "Nothing is worth more in life than in death. I can take my time. I am never rushed by the fear of my inevitable demise, for I am already dead!" He calmed himself and continued. "I have beaten death by becoming Death. That which I was in life, I am in death." Once more he grew ecstatic. "I shall live on forever! Never to grow old! Think of it, Christian! I offer you the same."

Conveying a condescending tone, Christian responded to the Baron's enthusiasm rather dryly. "I am sure your generous offer stands out of the kindness of your overflowing heart."

"You doubt my sincerity?" asked Mormeau, actually looking hurt at his guest's skepticism. "You question your importance to me?"

"And why am I so important, Baron?" provoked Christian. "Is it my unfinished schooling you find so attractive, or perhaps the way in which I wear my hair? Or is it that you cannot release me for fear I may alert others as to your existence?"

Mormeau offered only a cordial smile in response to the Englishman's charge. "Horst," he uttered inattentively, his eyes locked on Christian rather than addressing his servant, "you are dismissed. I wish to converse with Monsieur Coleswitten in private."

Horst did as he was told, exiting the room in a swirl of silence.

"I cannot bear to look upon that thing," griped a disgusted Mormeau. "The sight of him makes me sick!" Smoothing out the curl of his displeased lips, he gazed on Christian with noticeable delectation. "I want you to take Horst's position, to become my apprentice."

Christian shifted uneasily in his seat.

"We shall travel the world together," Mormeau quickly appended, enriching his initial offer, "experiencing life's pleasures, as well as attaining great knowledge. Imagine! The wealth and wisdom you desire can be yours, and you'll have forever to enjoy it!"

Christian shook his head. "I cannot yield my soul for such earthly fancy." He dropped his melancholy gaze to his feet, ashamed that such a proposal could arouse in him such temptation. "I must refuse what you offer."

"Then live out your life, Christian." said the Baron, insulted. "A short life … for a life filled with discontent is best ended swiftly."

"And are you to kill me now?"

"Now? When your face belies that you are far from seduction? Of course not!" Mormeau stood and stretched. "I think that I shall take you on a tour of my castle, it is long overdue."

Christian set his chalice down and rose to his feet. He looked to the Baron, who with an open hand gestured to the doorway, then proceeded to leave the room.

Mormeau, following behind with a lit candelabrum, closed the door to his study and overtook his guest. Acting in the capacity of guide, he began to lead Christian into the darkest and most remote parts of the castle. "You have already seen the turret rooms," his voice boomed with authority, "as it is in them you have been comforted. And you are aware of the dining room and study from whence we came." His purple lips crumpled into a smile. "I wish to take you on a grand tour! I shall show you rooms many guests never had the pleasures of enjoying." Arching his brow and wiggling his fingers in a mock show of fear, he concluded, "First, let us be off to the dungeon!"

Following the man in red as he turned and progressed towards a small door hidden in shadow, Christian could not help but do as he was asked. The Baron was exactly right when he had stated there was no escape for him. Accepting this was the single greatest thing Christian could currently do. And while he may have acceded to the impossibility of his situation, and of his own doom, he reserved for himself a small portion of revenge, for which if the opportunity ever presented itself he would gladly take advantage of such providence and do the bad Baron in. But as things presently stood, he could only watch and wait and follow Baron Mormeau on his excursion into the horrors of Gothic architecture.

The groan of the opening dungeon door was long and labored, probably much like the painful cries which had ceased to echo from below long ago. And although the implements of torture had not been put to use for some time, the very walls attested to their past service. The stale air maintained a hint of misery and the atmosphere held an oppressive gloom about it. Agony, however faded by the washings of time, had etched itself a permanent niche in the concealing dark.

"The foundation of this castle is an old Roman settlement," expounded Mormeau as they descended the winding stone stairs. "The castle itself is obviously of Norman make, being far superior to any Saxon fortress I have yet seen."

"I would not be wrong in assuming this to be among your favorite haunts of the castle?"

In the flickering candlelight, Christian saw the Baron's face twist into a scowl. "Must you think me such a monster?"

"Can I think any different after being privy to the bestial behavior you so wantonly display?"

"I was a patron of the arts once."

"And what were your artists commissioned to depict: scenes of death, brutality, and mutilation?"

Mormeau smiled, his purple lips appearing black in the harsh orange cast of the candles. "You think you know me well?"

"I know only what I have seen, and what you yourself have told me."

The Frenchman put his free hand against Christian's back and spoke as if in confidence. "One should not always believe what one hears, or take to truth that which is spoken. No matter if it is spoken from the mouths of gods ... or goddesses."

The last remaining steps before reaching the floor were spent in silence. Christian pondered the mystery of the Baron's cryptic retort, while Mormeau did nothing more than affix a peculiar smile to his face.

Moving from the foot of the stairs to their left, the two entered into a large, cavernous room. The dungeon was typical of what one would expect to find in the bowels of a medieval castle.

Mormeau left Christian's side and began touching his candelabrum to several of the room's unlit wall torches. As he progressed, the increasing light from the burning torches illuminated the dungeon's treasures.

Torture devices of every size, shape, and function littered the area. Racks and pillories, Iron Maidens, spiked wheels, and less recognizable, though no less terrifying, instruments of pain chilled Christian's eyes. Some were obvious in how they accomplished their cruelty, others were not, but all were crafted meticulously for nothing more than the generation of repeated and prolonged anguish. An added shock was that some still retained the subjects of their misery: the skeletal remnants of long-dead prisoners.

Even now they seem in agony, Christian thought in grim amazement. Despite the lapse of time and life, they still seem to hurt. One particular skeleton, that of a man stretched out across a rack, appeared to be screaming at him for release. Long after the poor soul's skin had left him, his pain had not.

Another of the prisoners who had never found reprieve, who continued to serve out his sentence even in rot, exhibited the potency of the Iron Maiden. The Maiden, looking like some Egyptian sarcophagus and lying half open, had skewered the man in many vital regions, most notably the brainpan. The point of one such spike stuck out of his wasted and empty eye socket, while others piercing his bones served chiefly to keep his corpse forever standing.

Returning to Christian from his brief departure in lighting torches, Mormeau surveyed his dusty apparatuses with manifest pride. "Ah, my playroom," he sighed with a tinge of recollected glee. "You English must have invented the delicate art of torture."

"You French must have perfected it," replied a nauseated Christian, "for surely you are racking my mind."

"We improve," agreed Mormeau, smug in his nonchalance. "Now, here, observe this device." He stepped up to the rack that still retained its captive corpse. Placing his thin hand on the turning handle, he began to apply force to the rack's neglected mechanisms. "I have never seen men broken easier," he whispered almost religiously, "then when in place." The creaking of the turning wood ratchets nearly obscured his hushed voice as the ropes tied to the limbs of the deteriorated man grew taut. "This fellow you see before you — I broke him," Mormeau clenched his teeth and continued to turn the operating handle, "I broke him all to pieces." The stress put on the brittle bones of the ancient dead man by the stretching ropes was too great. What little dried and tattered flesh remained upon his gray form cracked and flaked off as his arms and legs were pulled from their respective sockets. Tendons and cartilage, too shrunken in their disuse to provide any cushioning to the unrelenting pull of the ropes, snapped apart as the entirety of the prisoner's corpse exploded into dust.

Christian shielded his eyes from the particles thrown into the air. His lungs choked on the inhalation of the fine powder that clouded the room as he tried to cough out the dry taste of decay. "These implements are disgusting!" he wheezed between coughs. "Your cruelty knows no bounds! Not even time diminishes your viciousness!" Any further remonstrating words were cut off by a harsh bout of hacking. God, he thought revoltingly, I have the sprinklings of a dead man in me!

"You think these furnishings cruel?" Mormeau asked angrily. "Many here were devised by your own Church!"

"There is," said Christian clearing his throat, "as you well know, evil in the hearts of men, not in the Kingdom of God."

Taking on the posture of a concerned parent, Mormeau contended, "You are too religious for your own good, my friend. Trust me, I know."

"What I do not know is whether or not you are the Devil, but for sure you are the Devil without the 'D'."

"You think me evil? What brings you greater horror, Christian: fear of me, or of your own fallibility? Of your own inclinations towards enticement?"

"I shall not even justify that charge with a response."

"Because it is true? How quick you are to point out my faults, yet when yours are made apparent you flee behind excuses."

Setting his eyes firmly on Mormeau, Christian evenly replied, "And who am I to justify myself to: a man that is not a man, a thing that no longer lives, but exists only to defile the laws of God? Never in my worst moment, multiplied tenfold, could I even come close to the flagrant and abundant infractions you have so callously made common."

"Good and evil are inventions of man," said Mormeau, his demeanor assuming a more scholarly manner. "All faults, or at least those defined by current social morals, are explained away as being the influences of some demonic force. A person's 'good' attributes are inflated to become blessings from Heaven. I am not evil, nor am I good, but simply exist according to how I wish. Governed by my own inclinations and not some invisible potentate's, I act as I desire — hindered not by the shackles of guilt."

"Relinquishing reason and decency for baseless passions you descend into the pit of degeneracy."

"And by what do you judge me, Christian? The Laws of Moses? The worm-ridden words of Christ? The accepted morality of a hypocritical world? Judge me not by those archaic institutions, institutions of brittle foundation. Judge me in context of all things natural and you will find me no different than the leopard or the wolf."

"I'll not argue that, except to say that I liken you more to a fox."

Smiling, Mormeau restated his point. "I am above the laws of God and man."

"Nay, Baron," Christian objected grimly, "you are below them, far below."

Mormeau stared at him intensely for some time before fracturing his lips in grin. "Come!" he spoke with a robust happiness, "let us leave this place of misery for a place of merriment."

Though his mouth curled upward and his tone was kind, the eyes of the Baron bore into Christian like burning coals of hatred.

As both men headed for the stairs, Christian stepped aside so that Mormeau could light the way better with his candelabrum. In moving to his right, he stumbled over something hidden in the darkness.

"Look out!" Mormeau cried, grabbing Christian by one of his arms and pulling him close. "Take care!"

Christian wrung himself free from the Baron. "What in God's name is that?"

"That," replied Mormeau as he aimed his candles at the floor, "is Horst's prison."

Revealed through candlelight, Christian saw that what he had tripped over was nothing more than a large metal grate set poorly in the ground.

"He must have hundreds in there," Mormeau mused from behind.

"Hundreds of what?"

Acting rather than answering, Mormeau moved his candelabrum even closer to the grating.

Within seconds panicked squeals issued from what appeared to be a bottomless black pit. So intense was the clamor that Christian had to shield his ears lest he be stricken deaf.

"Rats," said Mormeau as he removed the light, thereby ending the noisy reaction. "All he has accomplished is breed cannibalistic rats. They must feed upon each other to survive."

"Like you?" Christian responded as he let his hands fall from his ears.

"Perhaps," the red man smiled as he stepped towards the stairs. "Come!"

As he started after the Baron, Christian noticed a door set beneath the staircase. "What lies there?"

"Not what, but who," the Frenchman replied in enigmatic fashion.

"A vault?"

"*Oui.* Therein lie the remains of the most ignoble House of Anglais, original occupants of this place."

"Are they all dead?"

"*Oui,* though some more so than others ..."

For reasons unknown to him, Christian was drawn to the door. He stood there and did nothing but stare at it.

"You wish to enter, eh?" the Baron whispered almost reverently. "You wish to see the fate of all Anglais?"

"Yes," Christian conceded, his eyes shifting to Mormeau. "Yes, I would like that very much."

Mormeau's free hand disappeared into one of his robe's pockets and after a moment of searching re-emerged, clasping a thin bronze key. "As always the good host," he lauded himself, "I shall accommodate." He then walked over to the door, inserted the key, and unlocked the vault.

Despite having been in place for some period of time, the door to the castle burials flew open effortlessly. Entering the once holy chamber Christian blessed himself and the room in general. Mormeau leaned rakishly in the doorway, the candles he held dripping their hot wax all over his insensate hand as he watched his entranced guest wander through the stifling dark.

Moonlight trickled into the vault from a crack in the ceiling above. I must be near one of the outer walls, Christian noted, for the crack exposes the light of the outside moon rather than the floorboards of an inner room.

With what little light was afforded him, he was able to determine the location of marble caskets and that the room had also doubled in the past as a chapel.

"What befell this family?" he queried Mormeau as he tried unsuccessfully to read the caskets' epitaphs. "Why do they all rest here? Are there no survivors?"

"The Anglais were a cruel lot who eventually turned their cruelty from their serfs to themselves." Mormeau placed the candelabrum at his feet and began to methodically peel the drying wax from his hand. "Had you seen some of their extravagances, you would not think me so bad."

"And how is it you witnessed what occurred so long ago when by your own admission you are only three and twenty years an Englishman?"

"I speak only of what I have been told," the Baron said as his eyes squinted, "and never refer to me as an 'Englishman'."

Christian walked carefully in the pathetic light, attempting to determine the number of interred. "How many rest here?" he finally asked Mormeau.

"Twenty-six."

"But I see not so many sarcophagi ..."

"That is because most are interred in the walls, their bones fostering the foundations."

"The marble seems so cold," Christian sadly remarked aloud, "as if no life ever animated that which it encases."

Mormeau stooped down and picked up his candelabrum. Approaching Christian in a huff, he stopped before one of the carved stone rectangles. "You wish to see what life leaves you?" he ranted. "You wish to discover what Death has in store for you? Behold!" With one hand he tore the thick, stone slab from its place atop the sarcophagus, casting it aside in a tumult of splintering rock and debris. "Behold the futility of rot!"

The sight of such desecration, such gratuitous profanation of the inviolability of the grave, appalled Christian. And yet something within him, a curiosity ingrained in all things living, urged him to step forward and look into the casket.

Huddled in the cold, marble cocoon wrapped in molded shrouds lay the shriveled, mummified body of a dead Anglais. The man or woman, difficult to determine due to decomposition and absence of proper dress, glared up at Christian with cavernous eyes and Death's familiar grimace.

"Note how decay reduces all to a comparable likeness," Mormeau commented quietly. "All are destined to deteriorate into the brotherhood of the bone, you are no exception." Slipping his free hand around the back of Christian's neck, he pulled the inquisitive man closer to the corpse. "In those empty eyes you see your own. Where once there was a nose, see yours. The taut grin that so belatedly offers you welcome is reminiscent of your own thin-lipped smile. You see before you yourself, which despite vaulting ambition and grandiose aspirations is ultimately nothing more than a meal for maggots. Kings and paupers are rendered alike in death. Should you choose to continue in your desire to reject me, the same fate awaits you as met your brother centuries prior. There is no Heaven after death, only Hell. And Hell is the grave!"

"Hell is living through murdering, spending one's time in the pursuit of blood and evil deeds."

"Come now, Christian," Mormeau beseeched him, removing his hand from the younger man's neck, "you should know by now that it is not whether one has done good or bad, but whether one has done anything at all."

"Your Philistine philosophy, Baron, not mine."

"Perhaps, but abide by your canons and this is your paradise." Mormeau set the candelabrum down on the ledge of the uncovered sarcophagus. Its proximity to the mummy caused its warm light to become more concentrated and harsh, thereby revealing full the wretchedness of death, furthering the weight of the Baron's argument.

Christian gazed intently, almost hypnotically, at the withered remains. Blackened skin stretched tightly over bone and wrinkles ran into cracks and fissures. Pockmarks that dotted the arid flesh were all the evidence that remained of the past visitations of vermin. However good this person was in life, he observed, he is of no good to even bugs in death. How precious was life when death effected everything worthless?

*My Lord,* he thought in terrible awareness, *I am in agreement with Mormeau!* In an effort to extinguish his escalating acceptance of the Baron's words, Christian launched into a tirade against such notions. "As I am sure you are well conversant in the beliefs of the true Christian Church, Baron, then you very well know that the final resting place of the soul lies not with the rot of the corpse, which is nothing more than a disposable container, but in the airy splendor of Heaven! Did you reach your office without introduction to the Holy Writs? 'And God will open wide the gates of Heaven for you to enter into the Eternal Kingdom of our Lord and Savior Jesus Christ.'"

"Do not quote me what I am already familiar with! A lie is less potent when it is known."

"The only lie is you!"

"This is your lie!" Mormeau screamed as he lifted the frail body from its disturbed rest. "There is no afterlife, only foolish rot for those who choose to fear a vacant Heaven!" He pressed his face close to the shriveled cadaver. "Look well, young Christian, and see that which is the truth – you stare at two dead men, but only one is truly dead. I renounced God and all things holy, now I ask you to do the same. I offer you what He cannot; I offer you life everlasting!"

"Your offer has the hint of a confidence game and the stink of a London sewer. And while I do not doubt that you can, through some form of black arts, sustain me past death, I would by no means be living. For while outwardly I would appear vital and extant, inwardly I will have decayed far worse than that which you so dishonorably hold in your hands."

Coleswitten's stubbornness caused the Baron to erupt. "See you no difference?" he shouted at his resolute guest. "See that I can talk and walk and eat and reason while this piece of dung does nothing but decompose? Do you not see? Are you blind?"

"If I have any difficulty in seeing, 'tis because what I am looking at is so exceedingly repulsive that it transforms the human spoilage in your claw into a resplendent beauty, which like a fine wine is only enhanced through age. The prime pleasure in Paradise must be in the observance of one's earthly dissolution, for through such action are all worldly ties severed."

Mormeau stared at Christian long and hard before abruptly turning and taking a large bite out of the cheek of the mummified man. "I eat of your Paradise," he muttered, barely audible with his mouthful of ancient flesh, "and it offends me." He then spat the petrified chunk at Christian.

The rejected morsel struck Christian on the chin, just below his mouth. Vigorously wiping away the faint traces of Mormeau's saliva, he angrily cried out, "Bastard! You sick, perverted bastard!"

Tipping back his head, the Baron chuckled bitterly. "You are afraid, Christian," he stated joyously. "Like all humanity, you are afraid." Letting the corpse fall from his fingers and drop disrespectfully back into its burial case, he punctuated his dramatic discourse on death with a final dig at his displeased companion. "Christian," he shook his head and spoke in pretend sadness, "my poor, poor, poor Christian. Your own doubts shall be your undoing. Coupled with your internal desires, it shall yield a French victory."

"The only victory you can establish for France," said Christian as he continued to rub his chin red, "is for you to return there and feed off the local peasantry. I am sure the nobility will reward you handsomely for it."

"But why kill Frenchmen when one can kill the enemy?" replied Mormeau evenly. "And English blood is much thicker, the cold making it so."

"Gallic pig."

"Ssssh," Mormeau cautioned, "be mindful of what you say here."

"Oh come now, Baron. Do not ridicule me with your sudden reverence for this once holy place which you yourself have defiled."

"I speak not out of respect for the dead, for being one I have none, but rather for the tender ears of a child."

"And where be this innocent you have so much concern for? In your belly?"

"Not my belly, my walls."

"What?"

"My walls," Mormeau repeated as he took up the candelabrum and stepped away from the stone casket. Heading toward the exit with Christian in tow, he elaborated. "It has been rumored for quite some time that there was once a young girl bricked up behind one of these dungeon walls, and that she remains in haunt."

"And who interred her here?" Christian questioned Mormeau's intimate familiarity with the tale as they emerged into the torture chamber. "You?"

"Christian," the Baron stopped, "you know that I would never do such a thing. I am perhaps cruel, but not wasteful!"

"If not you, then who?"

"Those who built Hadrian's Wall."

"The Romans? Whatever for?"

Resuming his way towards the stairs, Mormeau uttered over his shoulder, "Perhaps to consecrate their fort with a sacrifice to one of their numerous gods."

"Sacrifices were killed, not interred alive," Christian dissented from behind.

"Then perchance she was in violation of some Roman law, or a warning to other Britons who opposed Roman rule in England. I know not, nor care not."

"If you care not, then why make mention of it at all?"

"Because," Mormeau sighed as he began to ascend the stairs, "I sought only to enlighten you as to this structure's long and varied history."

"I believe otherwise," charged Christian as he trailed in the Baron's footsteps. "I believe you made reference to the child in order to cause me further grief. I also think that 'twas you who placed the final stone in place over that girl's screams."

"Think what you will, Christian," Mormeau grumbled wearily, "but as you yourself proclaim, I am not Italian, I am French."

Leaving the dungeon and all its tortures behind them, they resurfaced into the antechamber.

"There is not much more you have not already seen," said Mormeau as he closed the dungeon door. "I live in but a humble fortress; many rooms are the same, many are boring." He thought a moment and then brightened. "Of course! I know of a room you would love to visit! How mindless of me to forget the castle library!"

"Library, you say?" Christian asked with constrained interest.

"*Oui.*"

How you must think me the simpleton, Baron, to play me so openly for a fool! he thought indignantly. You knew upon first meeting me where my passions lie, and only now do you tempt me with a depository of books?

Mormeau stood back and watched Christian struggle with his desire to view the bookroom and his refusal to ask permission. "Would you like to peruse my tomes?" he asked, relieving the Englishman of his internal strain.

"Yes," Christian grudgingly admitted. "Take me to your precious library."

"Then away, this way!" the Baron cried cheerfully, as if an angler who had just ensnared a fish. He then directed his guest to follow him once more into the dining room.

Walking through the dining room, Christian could not refrain from further inquiry concerning the entombed girl, as it bothered his good heart. "Have you ever heard the child's cries?"

"Eh?" said the Baron, his auburn tresses bobbing as he strode.

"I asked if you had ever heard the child whom you claim is behind one of your walls. You did say she haunted this place."

"I have heard her moans," Mormeau agreed. "It was that which first introduced me to the ingenue."

"You've met her?" Christian asked with suspended belief.

"I have seen her shade, yes. Initially I endeavored to capture her, but she always slipped through my fingertips, vanishing."

"A ghost?"

"You seem so ridiculous," said Mormeau through a heavy-lidded stare. "Do you not believe me?"

"At this point I am liable to believe anything," Christian answered innocently.

"Good," the Baron smiled, "good."

Coming to a seemingly ordinary wall opposite the wall which bore the entrance way to the kitchen, Mormeau waited for his guest to catch up with him before pressing on an inconspicuous spot along the wall's surface. On removing his fingers, the wall panel, through some action triggered by Mormeau's touch, slid to the side and revealed an opening.

"A secret passageway," whispered an awe-struck Christian.

"I keep my knowledge as it should be kept," asserted Mormeau. "Well hidden." Affecting manners, he then held out his open hand and gestured for his companion to enter.

Compelled perhaps by the smell of aged paper that greeted his nostrils, Christian unhesitatingly stepped through the wall. There, before his excited eyes, appeared orderly rows of stacked books. He squinted to make out each separate spine in the dim, unlit recess. Although Baron Mormeau's "library" consisted of a single bookcase, its oversized length and width combined with a plenitude of shelves provided a resting place for a considerable quantity of literature. So congested with books, pamphlets and essays was the small room that various writings sat precariously atop one another on the shelves, while others constituted lofty, though uneven, stacks upon the floor.

"You like?"

It was the Baron, entering the cramped bookroom and bringing with him additional light.

So fascinated was Christian by the impressive collection of tomes that Mormeau had accumulated, many being obscure Latin texts which until then he had believed only existed in legend, that he failed to even acknowledge the librarian's existence.

Undaunted by his guest's discourteous behavior, seemingly pleased rather than angered by it, Mormeau dusted off a nearby book and continued talking whether his captivated companion was listening or not. "I see that although you do not respond to me with your voice, you do so with wide eyes and happy ignorance. Any and all books you so desire to read, you can. Any you wish to keep, you may. As you already know, what is mine is yours."

Turning from the crammed shelves, Christian looked to Mormeau with a childlike eagerness. "All, you say?" he asked in delighted disbelief, for the moment forgetting who it was offering such liberal reading rights. "Any I wish?"

The Baron nodded his consent in an ostensibly paternal way.

"Why, it would take forever to peruse all these fine publications!"

"You would have forever to do so," Mormeau reminded him, "should you comply with my wishes ..."

The innuendo played to an empty audience as Christian slighted him once again in favor of the dusty works. Literature of all tastes abounded on the crude shelves. Scientific, mathematical, astronomical, physical, philosophical, and spiritual texts titillated the well-versed young man. Censured books, such as those pertaining to the Greek philosophers, and romance fiction filled his eyes to the point of tears. Volumes on the black arts and necromancy, as well as explicit manuals concerning fornication, danced through his line of vision. All knowledge he could ever desire or need, for so varied was the Baron's collection that it encompassed nearly all styles and subjects of writing, was at his fingertips.

"Do you want this?" Mormeau's voice boomed from somewhere close behind him.

"Yes!" he admitted with unrestrained passion, finding this cache of reading material every bit as tempting to his intellect as Cassandra was to his carnality. "Yes!"

"Then this I give you," said Mormeau with a sweep of his lean hand. "And as an added incentive, to sweeten the deal, no doubt, I also bequeath unto you the hand of the most exquisite Lady, not solely in England, but in all places at all times."

Christian gazed at the Baron with a slack jaw. Perplexed at how fate had turned for him all evening, he now stood poised to inherit all he ever wanted, all he had ever dreamed of attaining.

"Here is the knowledge you seek," whispered Mormeau, as if explaining himself to a child, "and above us awaits that which you have sought. And she has been waiting for you for so long, Christian – longer than is known even to me."

*The books ... the books and Cassandra!* His brain pounded as his stimulated heart pumped blood like lightning through his veins. *All I desire offered by all I detest. How can I accept such offers when they are not gifts but rather merchandise – the price paid being my eternal soul? But to live forever with Cassandra! To have her read to me from some tome foreign to my understanding! To quote to her cherished passages from some poetic text which I would never have access to otherwise, while making love to her moonlight-mottled body! To make my paradise here on earth: surrounded by volumes upon volumes of literature and securely embraced in the arms of one whom I readily love and hold dear to my heart! But to murder most foul for sustenance, and to never see the glorious face of God?*

"What say you, Christian?" Baron Mormeau pushed him further for an answer. "Will you not join me? There is no catch, I wish only to make you immoral– eh, I mean immortal."

Mormeau's comical blunder went past Christian without so much as raising a curl to his lips. So tormented was he by the blatant yet wonderful temptation put before him that he stood for some minutes in silence.  He did not like being tempted, nor did he like the fact that he was so enticed by the Baron's "kind" proposal.  He very nearly consented to his host's wishes, forsaking his soul and loving God, when his eyes, roving in desperation, came to settle upon the spine of a small, insignificant-looking book.

Slipping his finger between the two larger books that obscured the slim work which had so transfixed his already netted attention, he slid the booklet out from its place of anonymity and into his hands.

Once he had dusted it off with some air from his lungs, he allowed his fingers to massage the fine leather binding while his eyes discerned its most glorious title: *De Imitatio Christi!  The Imitation Of Christ*, Thomas A Kempis' brilliant touchstone of Christianity.  Only the Bible itself had a greater impact on those who would accept Christ as their Lord.  And here it was!  In the very pit of Hell, from the turmoil of his despair, here was a message that would give him renewed spiritual strength!

"'Tis times such as these," he said while looking at the small book that weighed so heavy in his palms, "that I see man's frailty in mine own weakness."

"Eh?" Mormeau blurted uneasily from the entrance.

"Even here," Christian continued, now addressing his tempter, "even in this dung hole, this monument to evil, lies evidence of God's good glory!" Raising the religious work to the Baron's face, as if by the reading of its title he should fall back and cower in fear, Christian proudly declared, "Anything you could offer me – be it all the riches, all the women, and all the knowledge: anything that I might ever desire – all of it is futile without God's love."

Vexed, Mormeau flung out his hand and tore the little book from Christian's fingers.  Pausing only long enough to perceive his guest's reaction, he ripped the work to shreds.

"It matters not that you rend the book unreadable," an unruffled Christian informed his host, "as the words therein are already known to me, and in so being are not lost by your action."

"That assortment of lies should have been burned a long time ago," Mormeau spoke in reference to the scraps of paper and bits of leather at his feet.  Of his guest, he asked, "Do you not find similar pleasure in any other book here?"

"I do not."

"As you like it not," returned the Baron as he moved aside in the entranceway and made room for Christian to pass, "then we shall take our leave of this place."

Christian brushed past him, emerging once more into the dining room. Although he professed otherwise, leaving the library was extremely difficult for him. With a rueful glance, he silently bid the hidden room farewell as Baron Mormeau restored its concealment by sliding the wall panel back into place.

Facing Christian, Mormeau pulled at his cuffs before announcing, "While we do not share the same taste in literature, I am certain we do so in festivity. It is said everyone loves a party. Do you exclude yourself from this truth?"

"It depends on the function, and the cause for its celebration."

"Good," the Frenchman responded warmly as he took Christian's hand and led him from the room in the direction of the antechamber. "I shall take you to such a gathering as I am sure you have never seen, nor ever will see."

As he allowed his enemy to conduct him to the strangely alluded party, Christian could not help but feel the weighty dread hanging in the air even as his hand felt lost in the icy fingers of Death.

# Chapter Nine

As Mormeau led Christian up the castle's staircase, the young man was seized by his repressed curiosity. "Why," he asked the Baron, "does Horst hold such aversion for rats as to relegate them to hideous confinement rather than commit them to death?"

Mormeau halted his climb and turned slowly on his heels. "Why is it you ask so often of so little that concerns you?"

"For as long as I am in this world everything concerns me."

"Then," the Baron smiled grimly, "you shall be relieved of your troubles shortly ..."

Ignoring the poorly veiled threat, Christian sought to sate his inquisitiveness. "Why does he hate rats?"

"When I found Horst," Mormeau began as he recommenced his ascension up the staircase, "he was dying at the side of the road. Already the Plague had ravaged his body, and the insects and rats especially had taken advantage of his weak state. That is why he is so grotesque, and that is why you shall take his position."

"If he so disgusts you, then why did you make him undead?"

Although he did not stop his stride, the Baron slowed as if he had been caught in a lie. "Why ... I do not know. Perhaps I was mad, or a bit merciful, or simply thirsty. I cannot recall." Picking up his pace, he then consigned the entire subject to sheer folly on his part. "Anyhow, it was one of my greater blunders. Imagine having as your manservant one who totally and completely repulses you at the merest sight of him. And he cannot engage me in conversation! His voice was chewed away, muted by the conquering rodents. I cannot appear publicly with such a monster."

"So you wish to enter into society once more."

"I wish more than to enter into society," his dull eyes sparkled. "I wish society to enter into me ..."

The chill that rippled down Christian's spine was long and painful.

Reaching the top of the stairs, they turned right rather than left, which would have taken them to Christian's quarters, and proceeded on into the ever winding corridor.

Coming upon a door not unlike any of the others in the castle, the Baron handed Christian his candelabrum and fished around in his robe's pockets for a key. On finding it, he inserted it into its keyhole and slowly turned. "I am afraid you are a little late for the party, my dear boy," he apologized through his sharp smile as he pulled down on the handle and pushed open the door. "About twenty years late …"

The flat air that welcomed Christian's nostrils reeked of molded perfume and deteriorating velvet. Before his eyes had even adjusted to the surprisingly well-lit feast hall, where centuries earlier knights must have banqueted and reveled to excess, he could smell that stench to which he had almost become accustomed – the subtle, musty scent of decay which so permeated not just the air of the Castel de Mormeau, but its very atmosphere as well.

While Mormeau moved on into the room, Christian stood transfixed in the doorway. He was indeed late for the party, as those gathered within were late of the party. His eyes were yet again submitted to a shocking exhibition of unholy proportions. Seated on either side of a large rectangular banquet table, far superior to that which took a position of prominence in the Baron's dining room, were the revelers who had come to party and had instead parted. Still bedecked in their finest threads – which now seemed a gross parody for age had laid bare, coatings of dust faded, and disuse stiffened the once valued raiment – the seasoned dead formed two rows of ten. By apparel only was it possible to ascertain that the women had been seated on one side of the table while the men held dominance over the opposite.

How many years had these deceased husbands looked on their deteriorating wives? Christian thought as he increased the impact of the tragedy for himself. How long had lovers gazed across at each other through vacuous eyes and with empty hearts, hearts filled only with dust?

Cosmetics, such as powder and rouge, did nothing to lessen the ravages of deterioration. In some instances it even proved worse, fostering the growth of mildew stalactites from the cheeks and chins of several of the ladies. In life, vanity promoted their appearance, in death it made it all the more horrid. Mildewed or not, all of the female corpses seemed ridiculous, nearly comical, in their wrinkled dresses and spoiled talcum.

Few of the men were spared any less a posthumous indignity. One in particular had the extreme misfortune of being placed under a crack in the ceiling. Whenever it had rained water had dripped down onto his neck. The moistness of his damp decay gave rise to a fungus which hung from his throat like some entwined beard. The flesh-colored fungi spread from just beneath his ever-yawning chin to his indented belly, clinging to everything in between, whether it be cloth or desiccated skin.

Surveying the feast that had never ended, Christian found with growing distress that the horror of it all was not in the time-caked bodies seemingly maintaining an air of joviality, but rather in his own unstirred emotions. Before when the Baron had exhibited such sights of morbidity he had felt anger, revulsion, and even pity for the victim. Now, however, he stood strong, appearing absent of a heart. My God, he thought angrily, his fury coming from what he saw inside himself and not around the dinner table, Mormeau has done what life and the Great Plague could not! He has effectuated in me an insensitivity I have for so long tried to avoid. The beast has forced me to relinquish that which I esteemed above all else about my person. He has relieved me of my sympathy.

"Do not stand there in the doorway like some whelp begging for table scraps," Mormeau admonished him from inside the room. "Come and join us! Here one is always late for supper."

Without budging, Christian demanded of his host, "And what atrocity did you commit here?"

Moving next to the table, Mormeau took what looked like a shriveled apple from its surface and held it admiringly in his hands. "I poisoned them all!" he crowed, his dark eyes fastened firmly on the spoiled fruit. "Is not it fantastic in its simplicity?" he spoke to the fruit instead of Christian. "I poisoned their food, their drink, I even laced their napkins with the vile stuff."

Christian stepped away from the doorway and drew closer to the table, his curiosity getting the better of him.

"They preserved rather well due to Horst's control of the rat population," added Mormeau as he placed the rotted apple in the open mouth of some poor woman.

"Just as your Avignon Popes corrupted and raped the Papacy as did Sextus do to Lucretia, you uphold your Gallic race's profanity and penchant for the abominable," the Englishman critiqued.

"Talk not of the cadaver of France," Mormeau warned, the intensity of his patriotism unmistakably etched onto his fearsome face.

Paying little heed to the Baron's threat, Christian sought to appeal to whatever humanity the Baron maintained, if he had ever had any at all. "How can you live like this?" he asked. "How can you live with yourself another day, let alone all eternity? Do you not feel anything for those you injure? Does nothing living spark your fancy? Renounce your wicked ways and black lifestyle! Take Christ back into your heart and ask God for His forgiveness!"

Mormeau's face soured. "You would preach to me?" he questioned his guest's reasoning, apparently outraged, seeing it as some form of insult. "You would sermonize one who was in life above you? One who held a station you could never even dream of attaining?"

Christian countered calmly. "Often 'tis the lowly soldier who bears the truth of history, not the corpulent general who lies safe in camp."

"How like the preacher," Mormeau shot back, "to congest his speeches with riddles and two-fold meanings. Forget not that you are speaking to a former Cardinal, transcended into an atheistic corpse. I know more than your puny brain could ever hope to comprehend. You refer to history; I am history. You strive for a paradise that is nonexistent; I dwell in a tangible Eden."

"You have the gall to berate me and the beliefs I hold dear?" shouted Christian. "You? You who mimics the appearance of an old tart and the posturing of womanhood rather than of manly strength. You scoff at me? Apparently the forfeiture of your life long ago also presaged the demise of your manhood. Your distaste in the abidance of all God's laws has led you to mock him even in your preference for wanton carnality of the most despicable kind!"

"Really now," the Baron disagreed, "I must protest. I only exercise that which you yourself declare: that of a competent man's assertion of his rights to choose. I do not discriminate against the pleasures one particular sex has over the other, but rather enjoy both, to the fullest extent my raw and beaten cock can allot me."

"Your hedonistic and Epicurean ways serve only to pave the very road you shall traverse to Hell, where all shall know of your name!" In a rage, Christian pointed his finger at Mormeau. "You seek only to defile, your existence is a direct affront to God, and you smell. I have not the stomach for you or your lies!"

"You have not the stomach for the truth! Say what you will about my good name, say what you will about me, only do not accuse me of not practicing what I preach! Can you be so bold as to make that same statement? I think not ... I know not."

Christian fumed at Mormeau's exemplary debating skills, honed in some French pulpit. He felt frustrated that he could not reach the Baron. Surely, he reasoned, though he had undertaken religious office for political motives there had to have been some part of Mormeau, however small, that had believed in the Almighty. Disturbed, he began to stroll about the table. Examining each eternal guest from their footwear to their wigs, which looked humorously oversized on such shrunken heads, he could not refrain from inquiring as to their identities. "Who are they?" he asked. "In whose corpses' presence am I?"

"My neighbors," Mormeau replied impassively. "Rich, aristocratic, and spoiled rotten." He allowed the blatant pun to sink in before finishing. "No one missed them."

"But why? Why did you murder them?"

"I am losing faith in your intellect, Chris. Do not disappoint me. Think!"

Slowly, eyeing Mormeau, Christian breathed, "You wanted their wealth."

"Precisely," the Frenchman clapped joyfully, "and lands." Moving across from Christian, the expanse of the table between them, Mormeau further elaborated. "You see, I invited them to my castle for some fine French cuisine. Evidently, it was too much for them!" Finding his witticism to have little affect on his company, he continued. "Anyhow, when each couple arrived I had them sign a parchment which I claimed was merely for my own personal amusement. Actually, what they signed was their properties – over to me. I rewrote the parchment heading later, making it into a deed."

"Did not the authorities get suspicious?"

"It was during your civil wars. As I said, they were not missed."

"Then why go through the trouble of creating a deed?"

"For future generations who desire proof of my holdings." Mormeau placed his hand on the delicate shoulder of a withered woman. "The last recorded owners shall have put their names, fully verifiable by those who study signature, upon a deed addressed to me."

Christian could not help himself. "Diabolical, if not genius."

A smile returned to the Baron's face. "So you see, there is more to me than meets the eye."

"Hardly," Christian shook his head. "All I see are two vacant chairs." He gestured to the ends of the table, where the seats were void of any neighborly remains. "You, obviously, sat at the head. Who sat at the end, partook not of supper, and in silence acted as co-conspirator in the achievement of your vile aims?"

Turning to the doorway, Mormeau responded apathetically, "Ask her yourself ..."

Whirling his head around to face what he already feared to be true, Christian saw the Lady Cassandra, dressed as she was when first they had met, poised at the room's entrance.

"You?" he gasped as if in want of oxygen. "Of course."

Though he had prepared himself for such a revelation upon realizing fully that Cassandra was in fact his dark lady, she that had plagued his dreams to nightmare and made sleep something to be dreaded, he still felt hurt in the face of her seeming complicity. How many have gazed as he, he grieved, how many eyes have lingered too long on the glory of the sun only to be swallowed up by the night?

As he approached her, leaving Mormeau with his congregation of the dead, the candlelight of the room began to flicker and slowly die. By the time he reached her, the doorway in which she stood had become the room's only source of light.

The Baron covered himself in the darkness. Quietly taking his seat amongst his coterie of corpses, he watched with amusement the commencing confrontation between his guest and his mistress.

"He made me," Cassandra pled in the face of her seething lover, "I ... I had no choice."

"We all have choices," urged Christian viciously as he pressed past her into the hallway, "save for you, who apparently never has and never will!"

As he hurried by her, she peered back into the darkened banquet hall and there found the Baron's two glowing red eyes staring back at her. Like twin stars they floated in the buoyancy of the dark: sinister points of light that bore through to the very soul. Creasing her smooth brow and biting her lower lip, she clenched her hand into a fist, held it up near her face, and shook it at the passionless crimson orbs. She then pivoted and chased after her wounded devotee.

"Chris, stop!" she called after him, "Chris?"

He feigned deafness and continued to walk away from her.

"Please, Christian!" she cried desperately, her voice choked by tears, "Please do not leave me!"

Her weeping having an effect on him, he halted his departure and, with his back to her, asked quizzically, "Why do you torment me?"

"'Tis not I," she sobbed, "but your own desires."

Wheeling to face her, he found that they were roughly ten feet apart, and was taken aback by her evident grief, which seized her so that she trembled and quaked as if suffering from a palsy. All he could utter, an utterance which was more an open query to God than a denunciation of Cassandra, was that which had concerned him from the beginning. "Why can you not be one of the living?"

"Let not such a whim of nature be a divider to our love," she implored.

"You speak of love? Your mouth hardly forms the word."

"Hardly, but enough so to your satisfaction."

He glared at her and she cast her eyes away in shame, flinging her shaking hands to her mouth.

"How could you allow yourself to become cold?" he demanded.

"Enough!" she shrieked as she threw her hands from her face. "I shan't go over that again! If I could go back and change anything, I would not!"

Christian was shocked. "How can you say that and profess innocence to the deed?"

Composing herself, she gulped down her sorrow and justified her response. "Had I not become what I am, what I have always freely professed to being, I would have died of age many, many years ago. Never to have seen your face, to have heard your laughter, to have made love ..."

Touched by her explanation, Christian's fury evaporated. "But ... but your eternal soul?"

Lifting her head high, and with a great deal of pride, she declared, "Had I had it to spare, for your eternal love I gladly would."

How cruel was fate that he should fall in love, and in return be loved, by a woman who was dead. Looking at her sadly, and battling valiantly the urge to take her into his arms and hold her for all time, he beseeched her for his freedom and his life. "If you love me," he said quietly, "then you will help me escape. Please, Cassandra, help the one to whom you have conveyed your love. If you'll not spare your soul, then spare mine."

"You are repulsed by me!" she wailed, cringing and hiding her face from him as she slowly stepped away. "You hate me! I shall destroy myself!"

"Cassandra, no," he weakly disagreed, "I didn't mean—"

"For you, Christian," she wept into her hands, "for your love, I shall cease to be a living torment! I shall become as I should be, food for the earth!"

He looked on her now with a new angle. No longer was she the perfect woman, the Heaven-blest beauty with skin of ivory and eyes of dark onyx, but a miserable, little wretch. She was not pleased with many of the aspects of her dark life, and the one person from whom she did derive a vast amount of pleasure was asking her to help him leave. Because his angel had fallen from the lofty height he had placed her and appeared less godly and more human, a companion in misery, he loved her even more so than before. He loved her more than he thought possible.

"I have waited many lifetimes for one such as you," the broken Cassandra spoke low and unevenly through her hands. "I've had a dream that when the darkness is over you and I will be lying in the rings of Heaven. Lifetimes of waiting, and I shan't wait for another." She tore her right hand from her face only long enough to point down the hallway at the banquet room. "I can't stand being alone with him always! Without you, I shan't go on."

"Nay, speak not of such things," Christian found his voice. "I'll not allow it!"

Gazing at him wide-eyed through her tears, Cassandra's face cracked into a smile that was careful not to display too much teeth. "You do love me!" she insisted joyously. "You do!" Rushing into his open arms, she buried her streaked face deep into his chest and threw her arms tightly about him.

Petting her head, he whispered into her hair, "Yes, I love you, by God I swear it!" Looking from the woman he held to the doorway of the banquet hall, he muttered, "Just as the Divine One was known as Christ Jesus while He walked this earth, so is the Prince of the Air thus named Mormeau." Taking her head into his hands, he gently lifted her from his chest and stared into her midnight eyes. "God damn the Baron for what he has done to you, for what he has done to the both of us! The darkness of night is as the lightness of day when compared with the black heart that beats within that beast's chest. As every fiber of my being commits to his dissolution, I shall see him truly dead!"

Pulling away from her angry lover, Cassandra excitedly encouraged his violence. "Yes!" she cried jubilantly, "Yes!" Grasping him firmly by the lapels of his jacket she gave him a slight shaking. "Slay the Baron, Chris!" she pressed him, "Slay the Baron and we can be together forever!"

Her sudden talk of murder with such relish and distinct joy pushed Christian back into his initial stance of appalled anguish. Releasing his hands from her head, he stood silently by and watched as she continued in his alienation.

"We can travel to many lands, Chris," she went on, oblivious to his change of heart, "and learn their ways and customs and histories, indulging in their societies. Once more I can entertain a ball! I haven't been in so long a time I've almost forgotten. Oh, Chris!" she cooed, "Say you love me! Say you … Chris?" She saw the change her words had wrought in him and realized she had gone too far. "Chris?" she asked rather confusedly as he backed away from her, plucking her hands from his jacket, "Whatever is the matter?"

His response was to simply stare at her with his watery brown eyes.

"Talk to me, Chris," she begged him as her voice began to waver once again. "Chris, what is wrong?"

"'Tis times such as these when I see man's frailty in mine own weakness."

"What?" she pled for clarity, "What say you?"

Without removing his aggrieved eyes from hers, he forcefully whispered, "Get thee away from me, woman. I know thee not."

"Chris?"

"Away I said!" he ordered, "Away from me, harlot! Nay, you are worse than a whore, far worse. Rather than your body, you have sold your soul!"

"No!" she cried hysterically as her face wrinkled in agony and her eyes flooded with tears. "No! No! No! No!"

"Leave," he coldly yelled above her denials. "Leave or I shall entreat you to what I have in store for your Baron!"

Cassandra cried uncontrollably as she stepped meekly away from him.

Unable to contain his pained rage, Christian ran to a nearby window and flung it open. Over the screeching wind he disdainfully asked her, "Wouldn't you prefer to exit this way?"

Arresting her tears long enough to speak, she sadly offered as her only excuse, "I love you."

"And I hate you!" he lied. "I hate you for what you've done to me. I hate you for what you've made me become! I have lost my heart to you; shall I now lose my mind? You are forcing my soul to mutiny! 'Tis said the eyes are a window to the soul, and yours are black, black, black! Leave, damn you to bloody hell, leave! I'll not let my eyes grow any darker than they already are!"

She began to withdraw from his presence, but before fully departing turned and faced him once more. "You shall always be mine, Christian," she said in a tone reminiscent of the haughty Cassandra he had originally come to admire, fondling Rebecca's locket hanging about her neck, "for you have tasted of me ..."

With that, she left him.

Watching her go was one of the hardest things he had ever had to endure. With her every step he wanted to cry out, to order her back into his arms. But he did not. He watched and waited until she had exited completely from his sight before buckling under the intense emotional strain and swooning to the floor. Propping himself up on his knees in the position of a penitent man, he clasped his hands tightly together and raised his head to the water-stained ceiling. He would never have what he wanted, his thoughts taunted him, never. There was no cure in Manasseh, only an evil far worse than any disease. And Cassandra would never be his. The woman who had inspired him from the time he was not much more than a child would go back to her realm of dreams. Justice would be if he did die tonight, for living out the rest of his days with only one night's remembrance of his love would drive him mad.

"Why, God?" he prayed aloud in a weepy voice, "Why must I be tempted on every level of my existence? Am I predestined for Hell?" He stopped only to stave off a rush of tears with his fingers before beginning again. "My God! Must I suffer scorching flames before I can reach cool waters? Must I trample barefoot over sharp shards of glass before my feet are rested on soft pillows? Must I be buffeted and beaten by temptations no man can endure?

I did not ask to be born, nor did I ask to be placed here, but here I am! Am I to fill some purpose, my Lord, before I reach my grave?" He paused to catch his breath and clear his eyes. "I love You, my God, I love You!" he nearly whispered, "And just as You beseeched Your Father to spare You, so do I You! Remember well those tears You wept in that somber garden, and take this cup from my hands!" Fearing nothing but the night storm, he carefully and painfully stood. "Alas," he sighed to himself, "I am as the lamb being led to the slaughter." Smoothing out his lapels and dusting off his trousers, he proclaimed tragically, "All that I have left is my soul, and I shan't lose it but hold on to it for dear, dear life. With both hands and every ounce of strength remaining, I shan't give it up!"

He then marched down the hallway as thunder began to knell from the ajar window he left behind. Coming to the entrance of the banquet hall, he slowed and peered in. Seeing nothing but pitch darkness, he resumed his brisk walk to the staircase.

In the darkened room where night so benignly hid its macabre occupants, Mormeau opened his eyes. He had listened to the lovers' argument by sitting quietly near the open door, eavesdropping in the shadows. Now he rose, his gleaming red eyes dancing in the air as he traversed through the dark and broke into the light of the doorway. Watching Christian as he strode away, he muttered to himself in amusement, "Perhaps I am Roman ..."

# Chapter Ten

Christian walked down the staircase a determined man. With every step that brought him nearer the first floor landing, his resolve grew. He must do as he had told Cassandra. He must slay the Baron Mormeau.

Although a noble notion, he was rational enough to realize that it would take a certified miracle for him to overpower Mormeau. Aside from the Baron's great physical strength and the seeming complexities involved in dispatching one who was already one with death, Christian was in no shape to do anything, let alone a violent murder. There was not a part of his body that did not ache or throb with pain. From his pulsing head to his blistered feet he was a shambles. The worst wound, however, was not outwardly apparent, nor would it be easily mended. It was no torn finger or bruised shin, but a broken heart. To say it was broken would even be misleading, for that suggested the possibility of repair. His heart had been shattered, splintered beyond fixing, by his believed betrayal at the hands of the Lady Cassandra. He would never be quite the same man again, and he knew it. A coldness had been nourished within him by the night's events. An emptiness which had always been filled, always replenished by Christian's personal love – even in the midst of London's carnival of horrors – was now prevalent in his bosom. When Cassandra had gone away she took with her all of his love. But she was no thief, for the love she took was hers to take. It was a love that he had saved and held locked away in his breast only for her. It was always only for her.

Stepping off the stairs, he took a long, hard look at the door which served as entryway into the castle. It was there, he thought, looking into this very room that I first laid eyes on the tangible Cassandra. This antechamber bore the distinction of being the place where I came face to face with a fantasy. Were it not for my cramped shoes, I would have pinched myself to see if I were dreaming. Pressing the vision of the near-naked Cassandra from his mind, he bolstered his fortitude with a gruff but hushed proclamation, "More a phantom than a fantasy." Diverting his gaze from the broad, wooden door and shifting his back to it, he began to seek out the Baron by starting with the first room presented to his wandering eyes – it was where the red beast would most likely be, where he had allowed his existence to be symbolically simplified in a color scheme. It was where he seemed human enough to hang a damaged likeness of his former self – it was his study.

Entering the red room, Christian once again failed to notice Mormeau, who having emerged from a secret passageway blended with the plush scarlet of the drapes.

"Come here, Christian," the Baron made himself known. "I should very much like to have a word with you."

Acknowledging his host's presence and power, Christian obediently approached him.

Gesturing to a chair just in front of him, Mormeau bade his guest be seated.

As Christian eased into the comfortable chair, he saw out of the corner of his eye that Horst had resumed a position in the room's doorway. Staring unemotionally through eyes tainted an off-yellow, the German monstrosity played the part of door effectively enough to force any notions Christian had about escape into the far reaches of his mind.

"Good," Mormeau commended his amenable Englishman. "Now, all I ask of you is your attention. Can you give me that?"

Christian nodded his acquiescence.

"Very well," Mormeau sighed, noticeably pleased that he did not have to compel Christian to agree with him. "Here is where we stand at this very moment. I offer you everything you desire, and more. I can give you the paradise you seek, here on earth." He moved from his drapery to directly behind Christian. Placing his hands on the chair's backrest, he stroked Christian's shoulders with his long nails. "All the pleasures of life are yours for the taking, forever," he whispered into the ear of his captive audience. "Yes, you must first die, but you will not notice death. How can one truly enjoy life when it is so fleeting? Nay, life begins after death! It is then when one has no worries and can take as much time as he wishes."

"You are presumptuous, sir," Christian chastened the merchant of death as he leaned forward in his seat and away from the Baron's sickening touch. "Judge not the living by the dead."

"It is you who is judgmental!" Mormeau spoke with a sense of exasperation. "I have experienced life as well as death, and cannot be judgmental, only honest, when I emphatically state to die is to live."

Shaking his head in disagreement and disgust, Christian concealed his face in his hands.

"Yes," the Baron granted as he transferred himself from behind Christian to a kneeling posture at the young man's feet, "yes, you must forfeit your life, but think of it as a burden being relieved, and of you, a prisoner being released.

Are not Sleep and Death brothers, being children born of Night? Do not fear death, embrace it!" Pulling Christian's hands away from his face, he delved deep into his brown eyes. "All I ask in return for my services is for you to simply be my friend, my companion."

"You ask far more than that, Baron. What you ask of me is something that no friend ever would."

Ignoring Christian's remark as if he had never heard it at all, Mormeau progressed in his appeals. "You shall act as my apprentice, a servant in my employ."

"You speak as if I have no choice in the matter."

"But you do not."

"But I do! You may make me like you, Baron, but nothing you could ever do will coerce me into aiding you in the taking of lives and the stealing of souls."

"You will have no choice there as well," Mormeau spoke ominously. "Publicly you will be my servant, but privately I shall treat you as an equal. What say you to that?"

Facial features contorting as he barely restrained the mounting anger within him, Christian replied, "You ask me what I say to your proposal? I shall tell you. I think that you are a scoundrel and rapscallion, and that your only concern for me is that through your machinations I lose my eternal soul."

"It is a pity you think that, my friend," a regrettable sounding Mormeau answered. "Truly, you spear me with your words."

"Then have some more. Your disgusting lifestyle leaves me cold. Reducing the human form to that of a parasite: feeding off the lifeforce of mankind, preying upon the sick, the old, the weary, the demented, and the dying. And upon the innocent children of the world, unto which no one since Herod has ever inflicted such wounds or acts of inhumanity."

Mormeau's matte eyes burned as he stood, looking down on his denouncer.

"Countless lives destroyed," an emotional Christian went further in his condemnation, "innumerable souls tainted, contaminated by your perverse blood lust. God be not a merciful Lord if He allows one such as you to thrive under His sun."

"But I do not thrive under any sun," Mormeau countered. "Be it the sun that warms the blood, or the Son whose blood was warm."

"Blasphemous pig! I find it difficult to believe the excesses of your villainy."

"What is to be believed and what is true are two different things, Christian. One is chosen, the other is not. You believe in God because you choose to do so, with me there is no choice. I am truth. I, not Christ, stand before you risen from the grave. I offer you what He cannot." Mormeau softly nodded his head in the manner of a wise man. "It would be prudent for you to take to heart the old maxim 'the truth shall set you free'."

Eyes downcast, away from the scrutiny of the Baron, Christian steadily muttered, "The only thing I shall take to heart is to put you back in the ground proper."

"Eh?" Mormeau tilted his head like some bewildered dog.

"I came to this town under good intentions, seeking a cure." The lowly apprentice glanced up at the Baron with a face full of spite. "I have come to realize the only cure here is me, that I am the town's cure, and cure it I shall."

"By annihilating me?" scoffed Mormeau. "Come now, surely you cannot think that possible. Even one such as you must realize the dire predicament you are in, the utter hopelessness of your position. Besides," he appended in a most sinister fashion, "you would not leave the town for the better, for it is a patient already lost ..."

Alarmed, Christian sat back in his chair. "Whatever do you imply?"

Obviously taking relish in his guest's dread, Mormeau paced softly over to his drapes and peeked through at the scourged town below. "I have taken precautions of a dubious nature," he spoke to Christian, but maintained his contemplation of Manasseh.

"Everything you do is of a dubious nature."

Mormeau turned and bared his pointy teeth at his sarcastic companion. "Early in the evening I realized you might not consent to join me fully and of your own accord. You are in need of some prodding." He let the drape fall and returned to Christian's side. "Because of your trepidation, I was forced to humble myself and enlist the aid of my townspeople, those pallid fools below whom up until now I merely weakened through my feedings, making the sunlight enemy to their frail eyes and malnourished physiques."

"You've made the entire town undead!" Christian blurted as he felt his stomach sink.

"Exactly," the Baron nodded. "I never intended them to be as me, those paltry peasants! Imagine me," he spoke with the outraged gall of a nobleman, "giving life eternal to a bunch of illiterates. It absolutely irks me to no end. But," he raised his eyebrows in hope, "there is still time for you to change your mind ... to have me reverse this travesty ..."

Christian knew what the Baron demanded of him, he knew that the innocent townsfolk were being employed as hostages against his soul. But he also recognized that now was not the time to engage Mormeau in argument.

He had to find out all he could about the red devil's actions in the event, however slim the possibility, that he might seize a chance to set them right. Controlling his indignation, he whispered through clenched teeth, "Go on."

With the deliberate slowness of a teacher, Mormeau expounded on how the science of the dead provided Christian an opportunity at rectification. "In the transition between the living and the dead, one must actually be dead to become undead. It usually takes between three to five hours after one's death for this to happen. In that time, the body is held in the clutches of rigor. When it is released, so is it that the dead may rise. Now listen carefully, Christian," he instructed solemnly, "for the townspeople of Manasseh have only been dead for, at most, two hours. Their bodies litter their houses and their places begin to stink. At your command, I will have Horst burn the town. Trapped slumbering in their lodgings, they will all be torched, their bodies serving as kindling for the fire."

"And this command you mention," Christian gravely observed, "is my consent. All this horror for my consent."

"Precisely," Mormeau grinned his beastly grin. "How did you say? The single most contemptible deed."

As his brow furrowed and his jaw locked, Christian tossed his glare into the fire. Watching the capering flame, he became aware of his own intense body heat, fueled not by what he eyed, but by the burning ire within him. His nostrils flared and his chest heaved to accommodate long and difficult breaths. His pores spewed forth droplets of sweat that beaded and rolled across his shiny face as his palms accrued a clamminess that could not be wiped dry. What would he do? he painfully deliberated. What could he do? Nothing. He could do nothing but comply with Mormeau's wishes; bartering his soul for the souls of the townsfolk, sacrificing himself for the good of all England, for God only knew what evils an entire town of Mormeaus would spawn.

The Baron had him, his mind sat aghast. The bloody French monster had him!

"Look at him, Horst," confided Mormeau to his manservant with evident awe. "See how pensive he is! How wonderfully intelligent he is! He is weighing the prospects at his disposal. If he consents, we shall torch the town; thus saving many souls, and many future lives and souls. If he dissents, he dies a needless death, knowing as he gasps his last breaths that his adamant refusals have unleashed upon his beloved country a blight that will erase even the memory of the Plague. Indeed, people will look to the years of pestilence as the good old days, when in death one stayed." He watched Christian stare blankly into the fire with an amazed joy that seemingly could not be contained. "He is defeated by his own goodness!" he happily proclaimed aloud. "Never have I seen love, compassion, and concern cause a greater agony! Never is there a better weapon than the internal goodness found in most men!"

The Baron's words scattered Christian's already disarrayed thoughts beyond all reasonable recollection. In desperation Christian reverted to his religion. "My God," he cried in torment, "what will You have me do?"

The holy appeal that escaped Christian's lips did not escape Mormeau's ears. It had the effect of souring the Frenchman's victory, of filching his moment of triumph.

"God will not help you!" he screamed at his seated company. "He cannot for He is dead! God is dead! He died centuries ago like some common thief, crucified upon a cross!"

"Through the power of God He was resurrected!" Christian vehemently disagreed. At this point he held to the only thing he perceived himself of having left, the only thing Mormeau could never take from him – his belief.

"If your God is so powerful, so almighty, how is it He can allow one such as I, a pariah even amongst demons, to grow fat off His children? His mass of flesh and blood upon which I feed, upon which I gorge myself, slaking my thirst to no end!" Wiping some spittle from his chin, he paused long enough to soften his frenzied verbal assault. "It will do you well, my son," he offered as he attempted to compose himself, breathing hard, "to learn as I have, and to renounce the Father, Son, and Holy Spirit ..."

Christian responded with distinct disgust. "Your vulgarities and obscenities are only surpassed by your blasphemies."

"And who are you?" Mormeau retorted, "Another Savonarola? Another reformer destined to fail? Or a lousy deceiver using the Church as nothing more than a ladder to advance his empty aspirations? You, sir!" he pointed an accusatory finger at Christian, "You have killed the townspeople! You have doomed them to live in death eternal! It was your obstinacy that forced my hand in the murder of the people of Manasseh! You dare berate me when you yourself do not come close to living up to your given name?"

"The lowliest whore could berate you, filth."

"Mock me, Christian, mock me," the Baron simmered, "for you have had your merriment, you have satisfied me of your flatulent piety. Now it is my turn to laugh! Now it is my turn to laugh long and hard when I see the expression on your bland face! For you are already dead, Christian! You are already a dying man!"

Christian maintained his poise, not wishing to give in to the Baron's pleasure. "If you refer to the fact that you are going to murder me, it comes as no surprise."

"Not going to, but have."

Despite his efforts, concern did register on his face. "What now, Mormeau?" he demanded.

"Let us say," the Baron began to dance a jig, "that perhaps, for instance, I placed a contagion of the Plague in your wine or in your stew?"

Christian's jaw fell open.

"Did you not wonder where it was that I got the tender meat for the stew?" Mormeau pranced melodramatically over to Horst. Sidestepping, he slapped the inner thigh of his manservant. "Perchance you partook of a section of Horst's diseased thigh? Or maybe a slice of his rump?"

"Monster!" Christian exhaled, "Vicious, deceitful beast! Do you think for one moment that I would believe you?"

"You yourself claimed earlier to be a believer in anything," Mormeau insisted. "Now you deny this? It is as I said: your belief is your choice, and you choose to refuse the truth! How quick you are to accept my evil and refute my good."

"That is because there is nothing good about you! And as for my beliefs, I never believe in anything without basis. Your allegation that you have done me a similar fate as you did those infinite guests above is without such basis. You would not risk damaging me in such a way when you freely confess that your diseased manservant, the position you intend me to fill, causes you such aversion. You would replace one loathsome servant with another? You expect me to believe that? If you do then you cast aspersions not on my intellect, but on your own."

"Believe, or rather choose, what you will, Christian," Mormeau talked in quiet, restrained syllables, "for I would not ask you to do any different than you have done all your piteous life." He moved forward and away from Horst. "You say that you believe only in matters which have a basis or foundation, presumably in fact. Then where is your basis in the belief in God? How can you justify such destitute superstition? By your own words you cannot!"

"By mine own words, nay! But by the words of the Holy Scripture, of the four Gospels attesting to the truth, love, and miracles of our Lord Jesus Christ! Of His humble life, impassioned death, and glorious resurrection! There, your foulness, is where I find my basis and justification!"

"Christ is dead!" the Baron screamed furiously at the top of his lungs. "He is dead, dead, dead! And may God strike me down if it be not so!"

Through a flash of lightning, Christian thought he briefly glanced fear on Mormeau's face. With the succeeding thunderclap such a notion was made obsolete.

"If you believe in the risen Christ," Mormeau jeered, "then why are you not on your knees before me? Am I not resurrected? Am I not worthy of your worship?"

"You are not worthy of anyone's condemnation, let alone their praise! God rose through the power of good, while you emanated from evil. To give you worship would be to bow before Satan, with whom I put you as equal in my mind." Christian slid back in his seat, comfortable with his reasoning and content in his convictions. "While I will not give you my adoration, Baron, I will give you my thanks."

"Eh?" a seemingly perplexed Mormeau mumbled, "What is this?"

"My gratitude to you, Baron," the calm Englishman clarified, "I thank you immensely. Whatever doubts or misgivings I have possessed as to the existence of God, you have solved. Where once my tongue was firm but my mind wavered, I now have unity. All the religious instruction in all the world is nothing compared to you, Baron. Should all be made clear as to what you are, the churches would not be able to accommodate the throngs. Your presence, if revealed, would convert more people than any epistle or gifted missionary ever could. You are indisputable evil, a living blasphemy. In the face of such conversant wickedness one can no longer dispute the existence of God. For an evil so complete as your own must derive from a greater source, a source that the Bible attributes to being in direct conflict with God. This is the bright star, whose fall from Heaven reflects your own fall from grace and whose tempting of Christ in the wilderness you continue in your torment of me." He wiped the sweat from his cheeks and dried his forehead on the sleeve of his jacket. "In your ceaseless attempts at seducing me, of trying to weaken the supports of my faith, you have only strengthened it. Your mockeries served only to reinforce my Heaven and your profanities only venerated my Lord. So 'tis in all truth when I say to you thank you, for you have made me a firm believer. Never have I been a better Christian."

Mormeau took in a deep breath. "Cassandra did mention that you were quite good."

Giving little thought to the Baron's lewd comment, Christian placed his arms on the chair's rests and braced himself for his host's reaction to what he was about to say. "If you want me, Baron," he spoke earnestly, craftily unveiling his speech, "then take me. Take me now."

Mormeau looked as if all reason had failed him. He stared stupidly at Christian, unable to even offer one of his snide remarks.

"Are you now deaf as well as dead?" Christian prodded him, "I said you could have me."

Treading lightly and never taking his suspicious black eyes from his guest's unrevealing brown, he strode to Christian's chair.

As he leaned over, as if to whisper in his prey's ear, Christian said complacently, "You may have me, but my eternal soul shall be His ... forever and ever!"

"Ahhhhhhh!" Mormeau exhaled his furor as he recoiled from the English neck, his eyes wild and lips curled. "Fool! As ignorant now as when you arrived!" He then bolted from Christian and rushed to his red drapes. Stumbling to a stop before a section of the drapery, he dug his hands deep into the luxuriant red, clutching two fistfuls of fabric. Maniacally looking over his shoulder at Christian, he shouted, "Do you not understand? Anyone can be a god! Anyone can be crucified like a pig!"

Like some insane artist exhibiting a new work, Mormeau flung the drape aside to reveal a sight that would offend Christian on all levels; spiritual, mental, and emotional. For there, resting against a sturdy window frame, was the crucified and excessively mutilated body of Cotton Smith-Patton, pierced through the wrists and feet upon an inverted cross.

On seeing his friend's form so abused and sacrilegiously situated upside down on two beams of wood, Christian rose from his seat in shock. He gazed at the man who he had only talked to hours earlier, who he had considered a friend, and who now was nothing more than several pounds of tenderized flesh fashioned into a grotesque mockery of the death of Saint Peter. Cotton's corpse was certainly more damaged than it had been when in the downstairs hallway. Mormeau had removed the Scot's nose and ears, and the pink thing projecting out of his mouth was not his tongue, but his penis. Cotton's tattered breeches were all that clothed his battered remains. Of the skin that was visible, not an inch went unmarked. His corpse was covered with scratches, bites, gouges, cuts, and bruises. The only part of him untouched was his left eye. How it stared at Christian in sorrow, as if scolding him for leaving his body to the Baron's devices! The general appearance of his dead friend, multiplied by the guilt Christian felt for allowing such a desecration of body to occur, forced him to flee.

Horst, evidently so taken by the Baron's handiwork that he actually cracked his partial veneer into a smile, did not halt Christian's flight from the room. Instead he stood grinning at Cotton's transposed crucifixion as Christian ran by.

"Horst!" Mormeau shrieked, pointing at his deficient subject, "Idiot! After him! Bring him back to me alive!"

Acting on his master's orders, the manservant zealously threw himself through the doorway and entered into pursuit.

Christian rushed to the nearest means of exit from the antechamber. The stairs would provide him with no direct cover and offer him only the weak sanctuary of the second floor rooms, and the entrance to the castle was too far away to be reached and unbolted before he would be apprehended. Therefore, in possession of a mind dizzy with emotion, he sought refuge in the dungeon.

Throwing open the dungeon door, he paused only to reflect that should he continue in the furtherance of his actions he would in essence be boxing himself in, the only exit from the place being from whence he came. His priorities were put in order, however, when he glanced back and saw the teetering monstrosity named Horst coming towards him. Deciding, ironically, that his best prospects lay in the torture chamber below, he tossed himself dangerously down the obscured staircase.

The little light that did enter the black of the dungeon illumined only up to about the third step; after that, Christian moved in complete darkness. As he faltered down the invisible stairs, he could hear Baron Mormeau's enraged cries issue from the study. "I shall split flesh and break bone!" the ignoble nobleman screamed. "I shall tear you apart, Christian! I shall torture you for hours and then make you as I am, so I can delight in torturing you for eons!" As Mormeau's words echoed off in the cavernous castle, Christian felt his blood run cold.

The speed which Horst initially conveyed in his chase was severely cut back when he began to descend the dungeon steps. The hindrance being his game leg, Christian was awarded additional time upon reaching the chamber floor. Recalling much of the room's articles, as they had been ingrained in his mind following the Baron's tour, he fumbled his way blindly to the Iron Maiden and there crouched behind her brutal beauty.

His vision becoming accustomed to the dark environment, he strained his eyes in the direction of the stairs. He did not have to wait long before seeing the radiating red gaze of the searching Horst.

Following the shifting of the glowing eyes, which unsettled him so that he pressed close against the Maiden, Christian ascertained that Horst had come to the bottom of the stairs and now moved freely about the torture chamber. A dawning fear flushed anew through the frightened young man as his mind dreadfully entertained the notion that the manner of beast in whose presence he was might be capable of perceiving in the dark, much like a bat. His worries were partially put to rest when the German apparently walked into one of the torture machines, causing a loud crash. Good, he thought hopefully, perhaps I may be able to slip past him in the darkness and find my way to freedom. This temporary rise in spirit lasted only as long as it took Horst to light one of the wall torches. Looking at the manservant as he held the flame high, Christian could only muse that even the dark did little to alleviate his gross disfigurement.

As Horst edged closer and closer to Christian, his penetrating eyes aided by torchlight, the living man began to scan wildly about for something to employ as a weapon, something to use for protection. His mad eyes sought a piece of wood or a link of chain, but nothing was within reach. Nothing, that is, but something which up until now he had loathed and reviled. Something which he had detested to the point of likening it to a physical embodiment of evil, he now praised as a gift from God. His unlikely salvation lay in a similarity he and Horst shared, a similarity of dislike. For there, at his feet, illuminated by Horst's own light, sniffed the curious nose of a rat.

The torch in Horst's hands projected chaotic shadows which, like the outside night, alternated between moments of placidity and instances of fierce turbulence. As he moved his towering, wasted form amongst the torture devices, looking for Christian, he highlighted the few twisted and contorted corpses still ensconced in their shackled agony and manacled death. The shade that was cast upon the walls from these tormented dead only magnified their never fading grief. Like wraiths, they stirred through Horst's movements, gaining rebirth through the power of his torch. Their silhouetted shapes shifted agitatedly across the masonry of the dungeon, conjoining with the silent screams of the impaled and a child's terrible wail in Christian's racing mind. These influences intermingled with the other actions of Baron Mormeau to attest and affirm the totality of his evil: the poisoned guests, the town depleted as if by a cancer, and the brutal murder of Cotton Smith-Patton. All these images tangled inside his head to form the likeness of the one tragedy Christian deemed above all others, the tearful face of the doomed Lady Cassandra.

Gingerly reaching at his shoes, Christian tried to catch the rat without making much noise. Dividing his sight between Horst and the rodent, he carefully flexed his fingers to within inches of the vermin. Closing the space between his hands and the little beast, he nearly captured it, but at the last possible instant it shied away. Damnable creature! he cursed it. Be you like the Jew, disavowing of your savior? The crackling cackle of flame told him the manservant was near now, and the smell of fire only hastened his panic. Holding open his palm as if offering something, the rat was drawn to him through its curiosity and hunger. It seemed forever that the thing crawled towards him, but once he felt the repellant tickle of its whiskers on his palm, he closed his hand firmly on its head and brought it quickly to his chest. There he cupped the rat securely in both hands and prayed the thing did not attract attention to him by screeching out loud. The price of the creature's silence was painful, for he allowed the frightened animal to bite his palms and fingers incessantly. 'Tis far better he draw blood, he thought in reference to the rat, than to have it drawn by Horst.

He waited patiently with the rodent until Horst was close enough to him and in such a position as to notice, should the rat be cast to the ground, the sacrificial rat and not Christian. As the big man swung the torch around, Christian let the rat fly through the tension-laden air. Landing at the rotted feet of the manservant, the rat tried to scurry to safety but was easily apprehended by Horst, who immediately scooped it up in his large hand. Holding his catch up to the light of his torch, Horst gave the tiny creature, which shrieked mindlessly as if in full realization of its plight, a thorough inspection. Satisfied that what he held was in fact a rat, he forgot all about Christian and began to lumber towards what Mormeau had called 'Horst's prison' near the stairs.

Peeking from around the iron dress of the Maiden, Christian perceived Horst as he set the torch down upon the dungeon floor and bent to unlatch the grating of his rodent keep. Removing the large carpenter's nail that served as a makeshift bolt, Horst lifted the grating upwards and let it fall back on its rusted hinges against the wall. The creaking of the grate was drowned out by the frenzied squeals of the rats contained therein.

They call to me, Christian irrationally contended within himself. They, like the spirits of the dead who still dance before me on these walls, cry out for my participation. He would never have a better opportunity to act — Horst was preoccupied with his perversion. Whether Christian would fight or flee was now inconsequential. What mattered was that he do either while he could. He looked to the stairs and knew that he could scale them before Horst became wise to his actions. But was that what he wanted? Was cowardly flight that which now tempted him? No, he thought. But what did fill him with extraordinary exhilaration was the prospect of slaying the mute beast before him. Do I commit that which I detest? Do I resign myself to murder for little more than self-gratification, the vengeance of those long past, and the salvation of things I loathe? Do I surrender unto violence and make false all that I have preached? While his conscience weighed the heavy moral and religious implications his passions proposed, his mind found solace in the words of an unlikely source.

*How can one kill that which is already dead?*

Taken from the very mouth of Baron Mormeau, this single expression helped resolve his conflict. For how could he perpetrate the high sin of murder when what he murdered had ceased living long ago?

Rising in the dark, Christian knew what he must do. Abandoning his hiding place, he began to slowly approach Horst, his eyes never faltering from the back of the giant's head. His pace quickened as he drew closer to the ogre, he no longer bothered to tread silently. The hectic lighting offered by the discarded torch, the chatter of the petrified rats, and the rhythmic clicking of his shoes intensified his already psychotic state. Hounded by fear, tormented by temptation, and rife with pain, Christian was about to fight back.

When Horst dropped the rat from his hand into his pit Christian was within feet of the mute monster. Perhaps it was the din of the ravenned rodents that covered Christian's advance, or the possibility that the manservant was as deficient in hearing as he was in speaking. Whatever the reason, Horst did not notice the Englishman until he was already upon him. Looking up with a sharp smile, he saw Christian, but had only time enough to react by forfeiting his crazed glee. With all his might, which was not necessary seeing how the German teetered on the edge of a hole, Christian pushed Horst forward, toppling the giant into the cavity of his own making. Wasting no time, Christian then slammed the grate back into place and stood upon it, effectively sealing off the ghoul's only means of escape.

Leaning his head heavily against the wall and breathing hard, Christian looked to the ceiling and cried woefully above the noisy rats, who seemed elated at having their tormentor in their midst. "Oh, Holy Father," he prayed, "forgive ... forgive me for what I have done ... forgive me for how I feel ..."

He felt good, too good for his own conscience. Casting Horst into the rat prison was in itself an unchristian act, but the pure euphoria he felt at having done so disturbed him all the more. Slowing his heaving chest, he calmed his flitting heart and attempted to shut the joyous rodent shrieks out of his mind. "Jesus, make them stop!" he pled. "Silence the recitals of my sin!"

It was then that he felt something cold brush up against his ankles. Fearing to do so, but forcing himself nonetheless, he glanced down at his feet upon the grating. What appeared to be long, white worms squirmed frantically about his shoes. It was only by gazing past this illusion and through the grate that he spied Horst's blazing red eyes glaring at him from the darkness. What he had originally perceived to be worms were not worms but the bony fingers of the fiend. He was trying to get out! his mind panicked. Hanging from the grate, he was still trying to get at me!

"No ..." Christian mumbled, peering down with increasing alarm. "No ..." All he could see were several desperately wiggling fingers and two flaming circles of eye, the rest of the manservant's ghastly appearance being thankfully lost to him in the dark of the pit. On feeling the grate abruptly rise a bit, despite his full body weight, he was once again pressured into fighting for his life. "Be gone, freak!" he shouted madly as he stomped viciously upon the loathed fingers. "Be as swallowed by your rats as you are by your darkness!"

His frantic footwork yielded satisfactory results. The aged and worn digits of the German monstrosity soon succumbed to Christian's hard heels and splintered, plunging Horst deep into his own horror. Christian watched until he could no longer see the behemoth's eyes glowering at him. The sudden hush of the rat's commotion told him they were presently at work on Horst. A few short struggling sounds echoed from out of the dark below, then nothing.

"The father devoured by his sons," Christian remarked. If ever there was a greater instance of God's own justice, he mused to the developing sound of hundreds of ingesting rodents, I know not of it.

Confident of Horst's gruesome demise, he stepped off the grate and walked to the stairs. Suffering from exhaustion, especially after so fervent an act, he slumped onto a step and buried his face in his hands.

The crackle of the torch mingled with the gnawing of the rats to soothe his quaking heart. Once the cloud of naivete, which obscured his mental processes, had been dispersed by regained sanity, the fires of resolve were again rekindled in the young man's bosom. He was of no consequence in this matter. What happened to him was insignificant. What was meaningful was the fate of those in the town. They, too, must be destroyed, he reasoned. And what of Mormeau, the cause of all this grief and misery, the villain who played with life and death as if engaging in a game of dice? He, also, must be stopped from further transgressions against the living. He must pay the price for turning from God, defiling the guiltless, and purloining the soul. *It is a price most dear, my bloody Baron, for the charge is eternal damnation. I shall be true to my words and see you mortalized, or by God I will die trying!*

Sliding his hands from his face, the blood of his rat bites smearing across his sweaty cheeks as though some form of ritualistic war paint, Christian leapt to his feet and dashed up the stairs with as much vigor as one would expect of an enamored suitor overdue for a rendezvous with his beloved.

# Chapter Eleven

Crouched before the flames of his fireplace, his narrow back tempting in its incognizance of a posed threat, Baron Mormeau appeared to Christian to be momentarily in Hell. From his vantage point in the study's doorway, the Englishman fancied that the blaze, which so captivated Mormeau's attention as to make him oblivious to Christian's scrutiny, would soon be licking the tender flesh of his soul for all eternity. Perhaps all that is needed here, he mused wickedly, is another push.

Revealing himself to be not as ignorant of his guest's presence as Christian hoped, the Baron spoke without veering his cold, emotionless orbs from the brilliance in front of him. "I knew you would dispatch Horst." Rotating his neck about like an owl, he motioned with a brief nod and offered, "Come, warm yourself. Join me by the fire."

Christian strode from the doorway to the fireplace. With some degree of concern he noted that Cotton's desecrated body had been removed from the room. Sitting on the floor next to the Baron, he saw that Mormeau held in his hand a poker with which he prodded the firewood into a continual burn.

"You cruel boy!" Mormeau playfully chided. "You have left me a vacancy. You must fill it," his white face reflected the orange firelight. "You must take Horst's place."

Unmoved, Christian stared into the flames. He recognized the fire's radiance, but felt none of its warmth.

The late storm outside was once again beginning to accrue its fury. Faint rumblings of thunder were raised to earthshaking crashes and occasional flashes of lightning became more frequent, often turning the dark night into day. The escalating wind presaged the complete dominance of the storm for the remainder of the night's reign.

"You must join me now," Mormeau's silky voice whispered under the strains of whipping wind and popping fire. "You have committed murder, one of the arch tenets of the Ten Commandments. Surely," he purred, "if there is a Heaven, your entry is most certainly barred now."

Christian's only reaction was to hold out his hand for the poker. Mormeau, smiling at his guest's apparent submission, obliged the quiet request and placed the handle of the poker gently in Christian's right palm. The mute youth then assumed the role of stoking the fire while the Baron was free to lecture.

"Christian," he began, touching the blue sleeve of his companion, "I wish to explain myself now, to rationalize some of my actions." He looked hard at the young man who did nothing but concern himself with the maintenance of the flames, letting out a pleased sigh when his hand was not removed. "That incident with the child," he spoke with the falter of regret, "was merely to show you the most horrendous of all evils. It was my hope that on viewing such a spectacle you might become numb to the lesser of my actions, that you would see the worst and grow the wiser because of it. I never intended your friend's death. I never wished him any harm, for he was nothing to me. You are all that has concerned me. I would venture to say that you and I are more alike than you would dare realize." Excessive thunder forced Mormeau to pause in his speaking. After a taut moment of rest, he recommenced his oration. "I know you will be one with me, Chris," he moved his face closer to Christian's expressionless features, "for I can sense which mortal shall be immortal. I have known for some time now that you would join me. It was inevitable ... never have I been wrong."

Christian pulled the poker from its place in the flames and held up its end for inspection. The blackened point was beginning to glow a faint red. Unsatisfied, he shoved it back into the fire.

Ignoring the actions of his young acquaintance, Mormeau went further in his barrage of words. "We will not be alone in our appreciation of the night," he revealed sinisterly, "for there are others ... others who call the dark their own." Sliding his free hand onto Christian's back, he softly began to rub. "Many friends have I, many friends have I made. In France, Spain, Gratz, and the Carpathians am I known. To some I am worshipped as a god, to others I am feared as a devil. You are quite fortunate, Christian, for I hold a title. To be with me would mean to avoid the haunting of old houses and the prowling of cemeteries, occupations which many of the undead sadly fill. To be with me would mean experiencing the very best the nobility has to offer. To attend their masked balls and mingle with their beautiful selves, to drink of the inbred purity of their blood!" Bolstered by Christian's unaffected attitude, the Baron was inspired to divulge the source of his funds. "We shall enter into society as befitting baronial men, for while the grounds below show no outward signs of harvest, the gold buried beneath renders them richer than the most fertile of tillage. How do you think I was able to maintain my anonymity? It was I who paid the people's taxes, of revenues which I myself doctored. We can relocate and do the same! There are many small hamlets and burghs in your country, many cut off and isolated from the concern of the larger populace ..."

The increasing patter of rain was heard against the study's windows as a torrential downpour broke over the castle.

"You were drawn here to Manasseh, to me, through latent desires as yet unrealized," Mormeau alleged in whisper. Smiling, he bared his sharp teeth as he looked at Christian with what resembled affection. Lifting his hand from his confidant's back, he softly began to stroke the living man's hair. "Your stubbornness was extremely annoying at first," he sighed pleasantly, "but I fathomed that it was only because you were denying the truth, that you were using religion as a shield against your true desires." He inched closer, his face so close to Christian's that should he pucker his lips a kiss would be delivered. "Cast down your shield," he exhorted passionately, his rank breath chilling the Englishman's cheek. "God can never do for you what I can." His hand dropped down and flipped Christian's watch from its waistcoat pocket. With a slight tug he emancipated the timepiece from its fob and as if it were trash tossed it carelessly into the very fire its owner had been stoking. "Consent to me and time means nothing to you. Nevermore will you have need of such depressing devices. What say you to that, eh?"

The pounding of rainwater against the windowpane filled the silence preceding Christian's response. Mormeau stared patiently, awaiting an answer as the young man sacredly withdrew the poker from the fire.

Gazing at its red-hot tip, which glowed as bright an orange as the flame from which it was removed, Christian finally replied to the Baron's query. Speaking with a zealousness not often heard, he uttered defiantly, "I would be assured of a place next to the right hand of God had I done nothing good my entire life but send your sorry soul to the very depths of Hell!"

Then, giving Mormeau no time to react, he plunged the heated poker into the Baron's chest.

Mormeau's scream was either one of agony or astonishment, but it was not shrill enough to drown out the nauseating sizzle of the poker as it scorched through his aged flesh.

Under the force of Christian's thrust, which utilized much of the youth's body weight, both men fell back onto the floor. Christian, maintaining a superior position atop the Baron, continued to push down upon the poker. Mormeau squirmed wildly in an effort to escape, but his aggressor held his place, driving the makeshift lance further into the undead bosom.

As lightning and thunder abounded, Mormeau thrashed and kicked at his assailant. Clawing Christian with his sharp nails about the face and neck and battering him with his pointed shoes, the Baron fought like a wounded animal. He grunted in exasperation as smoke began to erupt from his injury.

Coated with the intermingling of French blood and his own, Christian maniacally took the vociferous storm to be all of Heaven applauding his pious work. Screaming above even the clamorous thunder, he taunted the prone Mormeau, "Feel it burn?! Do you feel your foul heart burning?! 'Tis nothing compared to the everlasting fires of Hell, where you shall roast forevermore!"

Mormeau finally fended off Christian's onslaught, flinging his attacker over his head and into a small wooden table. A shattering proclaimed Coleswitten's collision as several pieces of glassware, including the wine decanter from which Christian had recently been served, toppled to the stone floor.

The Baron gathered himself to his feet, stumbling against the brick of the fireplace in a blundering attempt at keeping his balance. The heated poker, still protruding from his chest, had smoldered the breast of his jacket aflame. Patting at the fire spreading over his person, Mormeau frantically sought a more successful means of extinguishing the blaze. Hearing the tapping of the rain over the crackle of his burning, he rushed for the windows. As he raced to the saving rainwater, his haste caused the fire to propagate, swelling from his upper torso to his neck, and catching on to his auburn wig, thereby setting his head afire.

Christian watched the desperate Mormeau from his place on the floor, surrounded by broken glass and spilled wine. The ferocity he had only recently demonstrated had now left him. In its place was horror, a state of being which had become quite familiar to him. Looking at the burning Baron stumbling wildly for the rain, he felt not an ounce of pity, nor did he feel exultant, but rather sat aghast.

Nearing the windows as a human torch, Mormeau tripped over his own frenetic feet and pitched headlong into the scarlet red of his drapes. Plunging into the thick fabric, his wild strivings serving only to make the drapery his tethers, he pulled the material from its hooks and caused its full weight to come down upon him. Struggling against the heavy drape in which he was entangled, he finally buckled under its bulk and collapsed to the floor. His left hand, singed black, managed to rise from amongst the folds to quiver against the window before its nails screeched off the smooth glass surface and dropped out of sight, rejoining the rest of the Baron's concealed corpse.

After staring at the unmoving bundle of red for a time, Christian's eyes were drawn to a bright flickering stemming from the edge of a wall tapestry that hung near where the Baron lay. Apparently, in his exertions Mormeau had set a portion of the tapestry's canvas on fire. Burning quickly through the ancient artwork and corrupting the ornate design of its woven threads, the fire grew in prominence. Christian conjectured that it would not take long for the tapestry to fall from the wall and spread its flame to the carpet upon which he rested.

Slowly and painfully he stood erect. Brushing pieces of glass from his outfit and inspecting his wounds carefully with his fingertips, he looked with dread at the faintly smoking clump of dyed fabric that lay just before the window.

How funny, he thought with some frivolity, that despite all of Mormeau's ravings about the power of his immortal self, 'twas quite easy to do him in. Indeed, in the end, 'twas not I who was the prevailing factor in his demise, but rather a bit of drapery and a firmly fastened window!

Gingerly he proceeded towards the Baron's corpse. With every step that brought him nearer the body, his breath drew shorter. What if he was not dead? he nervously wondered. What if he still lived? Nay, he reasoned, attempting to put down such unsettling thoughts, an iron rod through the heart and a fire put to his flesh. There was no possible way, not even for one such as Mormeau, to withstand succumbing at long last to the Reaper.

Halting within two feet of the still cloth, he stooped and gazed down. The drape totally concealed Mormeau's upper body. His listless legs, being all that were left exposed, jutted out from underneath the red fabric and served to assure Christian that the Baron remained blanketed on the floor at his feet.

Reaching out, Christian intended to pull back the drape, but having second thoughts and second fears about seeing Mormeau again, instead withdrew his arm and straightened to a full standing posture. Cocking his right leg, he delivered to the corpse a well-placed kick. Pausing only to see the blow's reaction, he followed through with a salvo of exceedingly vicious strikes against the unmoving body, ceasing only because of the pain his right foot felt at having been used in such manner.

Mormeau's legs quivered, but not of their own volition. The aftershock of Christian's brutal verification of the Baron's death sent the nobleman's body into a fleeting palsy, which desisted as soon as Christian finished the venting of his anger.

Christian breathed a sigh of relief, "It is done."

How unencumbered he felt, how joyously tranquil was his spirit! Mormeau was no more; he had rid the world of a great evil and stood strong against the excruciating pangs of temptation. He turned from the covered carcass of a man he had come to despise above all others and shuffled his drained frame in the direction of the exit. He would leave this place, this place of untold horror, and never return.

Approaching the study's doorway, lightning helped him find his way and thunder bade him farewell. As the storm's adieu softened to a mild rumble, he halted his exodus for one final look at what remained of the arrogant Baron Philippus Mormeau. Glancing over his shoulder, he felt a tingling on the back of his neck as he eyed the prostrated figure.

Flickers of lightning flashed down upon the Baron's body through the exposed window. The pulsating bursts of brilliant luminosity created an odd effect whereby the prone Mormeau appeared to move. The animated stirring induced in Christian a brief shivering spell. Repeating over and over in his mind that the motion he observed was no more than a trick of light and shadow helped still his shudder. But as he turned from the drapery-enshrouded corpse, his eyes fell on the dead man's shoes, which appeared to be twitching. A prolonged explosion of lightning dashed any and all thoughts, however hopeful, to the contrary.

'Twas no deception of light! his mind cried out over his silent invocations. The Baron Mormeau yet lives!

He watched in benumbed awe and mute terror as the charred left hand of his inhuman host raised itself from the folds of the scarlet drape. In a slow, august style the blackened fist uncurled its ever-so-skeletal fingers, which due to the resculpting of fire now tapered to the points of his nails like the claws on the paw of some wild beast. Falling onto the red fabric, it slowly clutched a handful of drape and then quickly, as if mimicking the lightning, flew back, taking with it the entire section of cloth and exposing the horrid corruption of human form once again to Christian's unwilling eyes.

Rising in the midst of his guest's shock as if he had done nothing more than taken a short nap, the Baron gained his footing, stretched, and stood before Christian with a smile. The poker still protruded from his singed chest.

Even after all Christian had seen during his stay at the castle, after all he had seen while living amongst the disease-ridden streets of London, he still cringed at the sight of Mormeau. The entire upper left side of Mormeau's body was burned to a crisp. From his left hand on up to the top of his head, which, absent of wig revealed itself to be bald, was a nightmare of seared flesh and blistered tissue. Grayish-green pus erupted from his open sores only to simmer with a nauseating hiss upon his still smoking skin. Blood dripped like sweat from his cracked cheek and forehead, rolling to droplets under his split chin. The uniqueness of his damage was that it was reserved only for the left side of his body, his right remained perfectly untouched and intact. This disparity was no more evident than in the Baron's face. Almost with an exacting precision, the fire had destroyed the left of Mormeau's visage while sparing the right. A dark line of fissured flesh ran from his brow, down the ridge of his nose, to the cleft in his chin. To the left of this demarcation was devastation: scathed skin, rent nostril, shriveled ear, and an eye which was sealed closed. In its wake, the fire had left Mormeau a physical representation of his inner self. No longer did his outward appearance belie his internal evil, but mirror it instead.

"Christian," he crowed, "you are thoroughly disappointing, and yet ..." he grabbed the annoying poker in both hands and with an abrupt pull yanked it from his chest, "you always seem to strike a place close to my heart ..." With a sudden viciousness that betrayed the ire hidden under his composure, Mormeau flung the poker across the room at Christian, who did not flinch as the hurtling rod of iron missed him and clattered noisily to the floor.

The Englishman breathed with some difficulty, as if a fish drowning in air.

The Baron, perhaps inspired by his impaired vision, began to examine himself. Looking down at his hand, he could not bridle a slight gasp. His wounded limb prompted him to carefully feel his face with his pristine right hand, resulting in hushed cries of denial. The disfigurement being too much for the vain Mormeau to take, he shook with rage as he appallingly asked of Christian, "What have you done?!"

Swallowing nervously, Christian gulped down nothing but dry breath.

"What have you done to me?" Mormeau demanded from him. "Look at what you have done to me!"

Christian began to cautiously back his way out of the room, never taking his intent eyes off his enemy.

"You have ruined me!" Mormeau cried out in a voice choked with emotion. "Ruined!" Dragging his feet, he shuffled towards his attacker with open arms and a look of betrayed trust. "Christian," his voice quavered, "you have razed me! I, who only wished to give, who in return only asked for companionship ... friendship!" Milky-white drippings surged from his closed left eye, the liquid residue of an eyeball that had burst under intense heat, trickling down in pearly contrast to the sooty black of his cooked flesh. It appeared as if he were weeping.

Increasing the haste of his departure as the Baron moved closer, Christian stumbled against a chair. Initially leaning on it in order to maintain his balance, he took it into his hands and held it out in front of himself as an expedient defense.

Mormeau quickened his step and lengthened his stride, cutting the short distance between him and his quarry in half. "Look at me!" he screamed his insistence. "How could you do this to me?!" His black hand darted to the side of his face with which it was of equal hue. Shaking wildly, it began to tear into his scored cheek, removing a large chunk of steaming flesh. Holding the handful of pus-saturated and blood-simmered skin out to Christian, he bemoaned, "You have made me akin to Horst! You have reduced me to that which I have loathed!"

"I have made you as you are!" Christian yelled as he threw the chair at him.

Mormeau batted the chair out of the air and into a thousand pieces of splintered wood with one sweep of his powerful arm. "You shall curse your mother for your birth and your God for your life," he hissed. "You shall wish, nay, pray for the forfeiture of this world, for the blissful sanctity of crawling back into the womb. For what you have cost me I shall exact from your flesh, pound by bloody pound!"

"But you shall never have me! Never! Never! Never! That is the hell of your own making! That has you running for the womb of your mother, a jackal at best!"

"Speak not of my mother!" cried the Baron as he lunged for his fearful guest.

Before he could be taken into the burned man's grasp, Christian jumped back and out of the room, slamming the door closed as a paltry barrier between him and the demon within.

He knew he could not hold the door shut against the incredible strength Mormeau seemed to possess, so he frantically began to scan the immediate area for something with which he could defend himself. For a moment his eyes dwelt on the antechamber door, the entrance, or in this case exit, to the castle. He could probably make it, he thought with a glimmer of optimism, but what then? There was no escape from Mormeau, he himself had said it best in the study. No, the only way one could free himself from such an enemy was to rid that enemy of his life. He had to murder Mormeau and finish his reign of horror, put an end to his plans of future mayhem.

Returning his concerns to the study door, its handle held tightly in his grasp, he spied the thin but sturdy planks of timber that made up the door's frame. Set against the masonry in order to provide support for a wooden door within a brick wall, they were probably strong enough to make an effective pike-like weapon, yet easy enough to pull from their fixed stations. With one hand maintaining a steady hold on the door handle, he began to dig his fingers into the space between the wood and stone. The rushed pace at which he plied his fingers against the rough wood and unyielding stone chafed his flesh red. Content that he had wiggled his fingers to their extent, he initiated a desperate tugging on the age-old wood. From the start the length of board showed signs of weakness, of giving in to his demands. After a particularly intense expenditure of effort, he was rewarded as the timber divorced itself from its stones and leapt into his possession. He glanced at the hefty plank, eyeing the line of masonry nails that remained embedded deep within the grain, rust making them appear as if they were mere extensions of the carpentry. This would do, he thought, or rather hoped, as he examined its end; pointed to accommodate the frame's upper cross beam in a rudely fashioned corner, it would now serve as a form of stake to drive straight through Mormeau's breast. This would do.

Unclasping his grip on the door's iron handle, he distanced himself a few paces from the door, raised his homemade spear chest high, and waited nervously for the Baron to make his appearance.

What is taking him so long? he feverishly pondered. Why has he not shown himself? Moments before he had fled from Mormeau's presence. Now, standing alone before a closed door, he felt with identical eagerness the desire to see the Baron, to have him throw open his study's door and emerge only to be impaled once more. "Where are you?" Christian whispered thirstily. "I shan't miss your shrunken heart this time!"

His sweaty hands fixed as if by glue to the piece of framework held tucked under his right armpit, he developed a queasy, almost sickening feeling in the pit of his stomach. He had felt it before, at times during his life when the overbearing presence of evil came crashing down upon him. To some it was a form of the willies, a primordial sixth-sense warning system built into the body long before man had even instituted a spoken language. To him it was the very presence of his guardian angel: his whispering alert sending shivers throughout Christian, raising the hackles of his neck, and turning his belly to jelly. It was an intuition he had experienced more than usual upon arriving in this town, and nearly became commonplace on entering this castle. Quite simply, it was the foreknowledge of eminent danger. And at this moment he felt so encompassed by it, so girdled in its asphyxiating fear, that he nearly emptied his bladder into his pants.

Mormeau was near, it occurred to him. Very near.

His eyes darted from the door to the shadowed areas just to the left and right of it. Where was he? he worried. Where in Lucifer's low Hell was he?

Then it hit him, striking him dumb with horror. He was not in front of him, Christian's mind raced to catch up with his advanced senses, for he was ...

Behind him!

Spinning around, his wooden weapon pressed tight against his side, he came face to face with sheer terror.

Mormeau floated about a foot off the floor, and was close enough to him that he could feel, as well as smell, his rancid breath. No longer was it solely the burning eye that enticed Christian to falter, but the exhalation exuding from the Baron's cracked and blistered lips. On that breath one could catch a whiff of death, of the repugnant aftertaste of digested blood compounded by the unmistakable odor of rot. And just as the eyes of the Baron riveted one much like the serpent does its prey, so too did his breath, however repulsive, place one into a state of lethargy.

Christian gazed fully into the monster's ruined face. What was it about this man that so repelled and yet attracted him at the same time? he wondered in dangerous idleness. Was he so loathsome as to be fascinating? Or was this apparent contradiction the result of Mormeau's enchantment, much like his ability to drift upon the air or make appearances out of nowhere?

Shaking himself from his stupor and tearing his face from the Baron's leering homeliness he let out a desperate cry and swung at the levitating man with his timber shaft.

Raising his left arm, Mormeau protected himself quite easily from the blow and in the process snapped Christian's weapon in half across his forearm.

Christian looked in shock at the remaining piece of frame wood in his hands. Reduced to no more than two feet in length the petty portion of plank, little more than a stick, was his only means of defense.

"Know you by now that I cannot casually be slain?" Mormeau's voice, so close to Christian that he felt as well as heard each syllable, boomed like thunder. "'Til now I have been playing with you, as the cat paws the mouse before swallowing her entertainment. The mouse's fate is sealed with the feline's weariness, as is yours. I grow weary of your nonsense, boy."

The hole in Mormeau's charred cheek, the wound of his own making, suppurated every time he dropped his jaw to speak. Discharge dribbled down his chin and onto Christian's shoes. The hollow itself, formed out of his rage over being roasted, expanded and contracted with the Frenchman's every pronunciation.

"Why prolong the inevitable, Christian?" the Baron hissed at the subject of his anger, who stared not into Mormeau's eye but rather the talking wound in his cheek. "Give yourself to me now! Give yourself unto death!"

"Never!" Christian screamed as he stepped away from the Baron while smashing the wood still in his possession against Mormeau's injured face.

The blow landed well, striking the Baron across his crisp countenance and resounding with a loud whack. An added bonus was that the large nails that protruded from the piece of timber embedded themselves well into Mormeau's already tenderized flesh. One nail dug deep into the foul fiend's cheek, just below the spewing wound, while another sliced open his chin with a jagged cleft. The greater damage, however, was by a third nail, which pierced Mormeau's seared eyelid and revealed the emptiness it concealed.

Rather than struggle to pry it from Mormeau's sickly skin, Christian released the wood from his hands and backed away.

"Bitch!" the floating man spat as he tore the board from his face, releasing a spate of ichor from his fresh wounds that dripped like cold molasses. "Still you continue in the furtherance of my hideousness!" he shouted as he fractured the injurious wood with a single squeeze of his hand.

Before the first wooden splinters touched the stone of the floor, Christian was fleeing up the castle staircase.

"Run, Christian, run," Mormeau chided him, still suspended in the air. "Run your puny self ragged. You shall not escape from me, I shall have you."

Christian reached the top of the stairs and, glancing back at the serene Mormeau, stumbled to the right. He hurried down the dark hallway with reckless abandon, tripping into furniture and knocking things to the ground. All that concerned him was distancing himself from the Baron.

Nearing the end of the hallway he saw, with the aid of some well-placed lightning, the alcove of a doorway set inside the left wall. Heading directly to the door he found it unlocked, but stuck. Rust and disuse having sealed it shut he began to pound on it with his fists.

A sudden and unmistakable fear gripped him and he ceased his efforts at entry in order to peer down the blackened hallway. There he saw that single, glowing marble that was the Baron Mormeau's right eye. Although quite distant and small it was growing in size as it grew closer in proximity.

To further enhance the frantic man's fear Mormeau recited some obscure French rhyme. The lilt of the song's refrain, as well as its tedious iambic foot, was only heightened in its maddening monotony by the erratic eruptions of thunder, which jarred Christian to his very soul. "*A genoux, et dis Amen!*" the former Parisian gently sang. "*Assez mange d'herbe et de foin! Laisse les vieilles choses, et va! Le neuf emporte le vieux! La verite fait fuir l'ombre! La lumiere chasse la nuit!*"

Lightning occasionally bathed the area behind the Baron in light, thereby rendering him in silhouette and giving form and substance to that ever-approaching red eye. A discharge of the storm's white light showed the Baron still floating, gliding effortlessly in a vertical stance and at a leisurely pace.

"Mother of God!" Christian gasped in mindless invocation. He then threw himself savagely against the resistant door, thrashing upon its exterior with the entirety of his person.

"Christian!" Mormeau called out to him from the dark. "What is it that ails you, my cowering little Judas? How you have betrayed your savior?

How you nervously await my kiss of death? Or do you, even now, think of the virtuous Cassandra?"

On mention of her name Christian ceased his noisy attempts at gaining entrance into the room.

"Ah!" Mormeau resumed with a marked pleasure coating his words, "I see I have found your sore spot! You wish to know whether the good Lady is my daughter ... or my mother!"

He had hit upon the hidden conflict that had been raging inside Christian's conscience all night long. Who had created who? And was Christian to become another Mormeau, or another Cassandra?

"You seek to know all," the Baron continued in his taunting, "but desire this above conventional knowledge. For this is not a matter of the mind, eh? This involves that far superior organ, the heart. You seek to know who bore who into this world of everlasting night? Your heart cries out for either your Lady's exoneration or her culpability, but it cries out the same! Well, my conniving friend," he paused in order to heighten the suspense, "I shall never tell!"

"Bastard! Cruel, unremitting, bastard!" Christian shouted wildly with passion. "Be you a baron of blood who aspires to assume the throne of King of the Dead?! For all your titles I shall never bow before you except when 'tis before your legitimately lifeless corpse! I shall rid you of your illicit life as the laundry woman rids clothing of their wrinkles! I swear it be so, that before the dawn tames this storm the world will be rid of the Baron Philippus Mormeau!"

"Swear it with your life?"

"Aye, that I do!"

"Then I shall collect on your pledge and let you finally be with your mother ... in death."

In desperation Christian flung himself against the door. He pitched his shoulder into its stone-like wood again and again, his pace growing more rabid with the advent of Mormeau. He was almost upon him now, he fearfully surmised as the door's noncompliance nearly brought him to tears of frustration. I must not perish here! his mind gibbered. I must not die in this place, at his hands!

The stench of deterioration that preceded Mormeau's presence, that unforgettable odor that presaged the imminence of his lips' kiss, gagged Christian to the point of swooning. He closed his eyes tightly, hunched his shoulders in fearsome expectation of the attack, and gave the door one last attempt at allowing him ingress into the room. "Please, dear God," he mumbled as he cast his bruised shoulder once more against the door's oaken slats.

The door opened with a wide yawn, sending Christian spilling into the room and delivering him, however momentary, from the clutches of his foe. Quickly he rose and slammed the door shut, propping his own wearied self up to act as a brace against Mormeau's entrance.

A legion of bats, flapping wildly above Christian's head, screeched their disapproval at the invasion of their privacy. Like a churning black cloud they fluttered about the dank air of the room, swooping into his face for a closer look at their human intruder. He did his best to swat them away, noticing as his nervous eyes surveyed the little room that many more of the flying rodents hung suspended by the rafters.

He was taken aback by the appearance of the room, so much so that for the moment his thoughts neglected Mormeau and the pestering bats. The quarters, a duplicate in size and furnishings to Cotton's, the notable exception being its possession of a window, looked as if it had not been in use since the last stone was put in place within the castle's parapet. Dust carpeted the stone floor in so thick and profuse a nature that footprints were not easily left. The single object of note within the tiny room, a quaint canopy bed, lay in ruin. Its worm-eaten frame supported a mattress replete with tears and loose stuffing and its four posts stood crookedly. The canopy spread rested in tatters upon the mattress, having long ago capitulated to the pressing weight of dust and bat droppings. The only window lay open, and the sound of the pouring rain penetrated the room on a cold breeze.

Once again Christian was confronted with the horrid idea that just as in the town, so here were his hosts expecting only two visitors. The unkempt condition of this room, as with other areas of the castle he was not meant to see, compared to his and Cotton's rooms only reinforced this theory. 'Tis just as in the village below, he thought aghast. They knew in number how many to anticipate, how many rooms to prepare. But how? How did they gain such intuition?

His vain querying ended with a knocking at the door.

Silence ensued. What did Mormeau expect him to do? Ask who it was? The usually tranquilizing noise of the rain did little to soothe him as he heard only the beating of his aching heart and the coursing of his terrified blood.

A second round of knocking, this time the rapping more forced, more urgent.

"What?!" Christian was obliged to respond out of intense fear, perhaps also catering to his perverse curiosity.

"Might I come in?" The Baron's voice sounded weak, frail, almost defeatable behind the dampening of the door. "Christian, let me in," he appealed in an astonishingly pleasant tone. "Would you be so unkind as to bar your host entry into one of his own chambers?"

Christian again sought a weapon, something with which he could protect himself. The pointed posts of the bed were patently out of the question. Rot had effected them useless for even the buttressing of a sleeping body, let alone the piercing of elastic flesh and fibrous muscle. There was nothing else evident within the room, he realized with dread, that could be employed as a means of defense.

Just as his heart was about to take leave of him he noticed, through a glint of lightning, something situated on the wall above the bed's headboard. He strained his eyes in the dark to better make out what he had seen, but it was to no advantage. He shut his eyes and prayed for more lightning, but on opening them found only greater darkness. Then, as if in answer to his heavenly appeals, the wondrous moon peeled back her cover of cloud and shone forth her glorious beam into the small window and directly onto the spot where he stared. Perceiving it at first to be a shield of some sort, he gradually found it to be a decorative coat-of-arms. Perchance a remnant belonging of the previous owners, it displayed on its face an arrogant cock embossed with a raised sword.

A raised sword!

He instantly was reminded of Cotton's mean dirk, tucked safely away amongst his baggage. At once he reclaimed his spirit, finding new recourse in the caution of a dead friend. He had to get to his baggage, had to get to his room. And the only way, with the exception of walking past the Baron, was out the small window. He had seen before a narrow ledge that ran the length of the castle under its windows' sills. One could walk, quite carefully, from this room's window to his own.

Any hesitations he had pertaining to the possibility of falling to his death were quashed by another of Mormeau's interruptions. "Open up, Chris," he requested nicely. "I only wish to devour you. To rip the flesh from your bones and eat your innards. Oh, but I, the gracious host, will be gentle! You shall live long enough to see me pick your flesh from my teeth!"

Quietly falling back, Christian tip-toed tenderly from the closed door to the open window. His eyes never faltering from the room's entrance, he carefully hoisted himself up onto the wet ledge of the windowsill. Throwing one leg over, then the other, his body soon faced out into the storm while his head remained inside the room contemplating the doorway. Feeling the cold rain pelt his body refreshed him somewhat, it clarified his thinking. Eventually deciding it to be in his best interests to act, he turned his face from the room and dropped his gaze to the little ledge just below his dangling feet. As the wind threw him its fury and the rain began to welt his skin he let his hands ease him off the slick sill and gradually onto the slippery ledge. With little else but his balance and the fortuity of a few jutting bricks to keep him from being dashed below, he meticulously began to work his way towards his window.

The ledge was extremely hazardous, missing in some places and crumbling in others. The savage downpour had washed away much of the masonry's grainy adhesion, making every footfall a brush with disaster. The unworn bottoms of Christian's shoes only multiplied his chances of slipping, as did his shivering.

The rain so completely drenched him that his clothing seemed to weigh more than he did. The cold gusts that blew right through him were chilled all the more by the sopping of his attire. He felt that even if he did survive this night he would surely die later of the fever.

Cheek pressed close to the wall and fingers gripping wet stone, he made his way precariously around the corner of the castle. The blast that hit him upon turning the corner nearly sent him into the ground. Lifting his face against the agitated wind he was confronted with a fright that almost achieved what the turbulent air could not. For there, lined up in an even row before him, were the eternally disgraced remains of the impaled.

Twisting pathetically in the wind, like helpless paper kites, these vestiges of human life moved once more. Soused in rainwater that only rolled off what lingered of their tanned hides and exposed bone, their weather-beaten appearance glistened a ghastly white in the unkind rays of the setting moon. The rags that adorned their cadaverous forms flapped madly in the breeze like flags of surrender over lands left desolate by the wars of nature and the elements. Their rusted iron rods held them mercilessly steadfast in the relentless basting of the storm. This storm, as with the many others before it, would not free the desecrated from their ignominious perch, only profane them further.

Looking past the line of dead Christian could make out the windows of his turret room. To him, high on a ledge in the midst of a tempestuous storm and pursued by a monster in the guise of a man, the windows appeared as the very gates of Heaven, the keys to his salvation this night.

It sickened him to do so, but he had to take hold of the impaling shafts and brush past the suspended bodies in order to bridge the gap between his present position and that part of the ledge just beneath his room's window sill. There was simply no way to avoid contact with the corpses or their means of execution. After slipping his hand off the first cadaver's rod he glanced at the brownish red stain left across his palm. Was it simply rust, the oxidization of the iron through prolonged exposure to the elements? Or was it dried blood, the desiccated leavings of a fluid once pumped by the man's heart? He uttered a silent prayer for the poor soul, whose remains he turned from in revulsion, and for the souls of his associates in ignominious death.

And so it was that he continued on in this way: carefully planting his feet on the wet ledge, squeezing past the oblivious deceased, and always on the lookout for Mormeau. He had passed seven shells of men, an odious task he would not soon forget, before arriving at the rounding face of the turret.

His long hair, dyed a rainwater black and clumped and plastered to his head by a bonding of wetness, whipped his face a bright pink and impaired his vision.

The bitter storm, now turning aspects of his own body against him, forced him to fight harder to attain a place at his cherished windows. Inching his way around the hazardous curve of the turret he came upon the first of three impaled skeletons. He was familiar with these three, having seen them before from his bedroom.

His left foot slipped off the slick ledge and he frantically struggled to regain his balance in the midst of a driving gust. Grabbing the first corpse's impaling rod, he steadied himself and recovered his unstable footing.

Maneuvering around the first corpse he came within inches of the thing's face. Peering into the void of the dead man's sockets he saw, if but for a moment, all that Mormeau claimed actual death offered – nothing. Lowering his gaze he found to his dismay an abandoned bird's nest, probably of a species of swallow, lodged in the skull's mouth. How strange 'tis, he mused, that there are things which find life even in death.

Successfully navigating around the nest man he slid his way prudently to the next corpse, which lay directly below one of his windows. Taking this corpse's iron rod into his hands just as he had done with the others, he began to swing himself around the body when the ledge beneath gave way in a sudden crumbling of masonry and mortar. Frantically digging his feet into the side of the turret wall to keep from putting his full weight on the metal shaft, he fruitlessly fought against the rain-glossed brick with his smooth soled shoes. Failing in his valiant attempt he hung from the shaft as impotent as those he imitated.

Taunted by thunder and mocked by lightning he began to painstakingly pull himself up. He dared not look down at the broken ground that lay far beneath him, dared not contemplate how it would break him should he let go of the rod his hands fastened to. Here I dangle from an upraised pole of iron, he thought miserably. Shall I fall, or be struck by lightning?

As he exerted pressure on the rod while lifting himself it buckled under his demands and twisted downward, compelling him to hold on for dear life as his hands, now clasped to a shaft slanting towards the ground, started to slide off.

With rainwater acting as lubricant, the corpse whose impaling rod Christian clung to began to slip down the pole and onto the terrified Englishman. While its weight was of little consequence, for most of its mass was gone, the psychological burden of being harassed by a corpse nearly drove Christian to the insanity of letting go. In desperation amidst the chaotic storm he risked his life by removing a hand from the rod and pushing at the imposing cadaver. During a fit of deranged panic he forced his hand through the mouth of the corpse, his lunacy ripping the head from its brittle neck. The viciousness of this act succeeded in freeing the corpse from its captivity upon the rod. The body, or what remained of a body, spiraled on the wind down to the cracked terrain below. The head of the dead man remained with Christian, his hand lodged firmly in its mouth.

"God, why have You not helped me?!" he demanded of the turbid night sky as he hung precariously with one hand, a bellowing thunder chastening him for his audacity in questioning the motives of the Almighty.

Shaking the seemingly biting skull from his hand and sending the bothersome corpse's head to rejoin its body broken below, Christian initiated a renewed effort to right himself. Digging the points of his shoes into the wall and simultaneously hauling his soaked self up, he managed to reach out and latch on to his windows' sill. Once he had ensured himself of his grip, both on the sill and the rod, he brought his feet up one at a time and secured his footing on a portion of ledge which remained firm and unyielding. Content in his balance, he released the detestable iron rod, adding to his hold on the windowsill. When the soundness of his grasp was doubled upon the little ledge, he raised himself to a full standing posture and looked in on his shadowed room through rain-streaked glass.

Although his quarters were quite dim, and the reflecting light of the moon off the glass decreased his visibility further, when he squinted he could make out his baggage: undisturbed and strewn about his bed as he had left it.

God be praised! he rejoiced as he pulled on one of his window's frames, only to find it resistant to his touch. Peering in he saw all his windows to be latched closed, effectively locking him out. "Damn it!" he cursed under his breath as he rattled the window to no profit. His safeguard, not only in the weapon concealed within his room, but the shelter of the room itself, was denied him by a few panes of glass. He did not chance breaking the glass with his own fist for fear of slicing his wrist, so he hurriedly sought other means of obtaining entry.

He did not have to look far. The last of the three corpses which lined his windows was situated just to his right. It was the first of the corpses he had seen when gazing out only hours earlier. It was the first corpse to get his sympathy and now, as the wind whistled through its hollow head as if granting Christian free license to do with it as he wished, it would be the first of its kind to actually assist in carrying out their revenge. "Better sympathetic than empathetic," he nervously quipped as he plucked the cadaver's head from its body in an impromptu decapitation. "God forgive me." Employing the skull as a makeshift hammer, he shattered the glass of the pane nearest the latch, pounding away sharp shards that remained in the frame's casing. Placing his hand through the opening he undid the latch. Pushing with what strength remained within him, he forced open the window. Dragging himself inside, he rested amidst the broken glass with his skull hammer clutched firmly in his right hand. "Thank you, my friend," he whispered in all sincerity to the disembodied head held as though it were Yorick. "While no one saved you, you may yet have delivered me." With that, he tossed the helpful cranium out and to the wind. "Farewell, whoever you were!" he yelled after it. "May you finally find the peace for so long you were denied!"

Moving from the windows, he strode with increasing speed to the baggage surrounding his bed. Snatching up the first leather satchel he tore it open, only to find clothes. Discarding it, he opted for the next two articles of luggage, which contained his necessities: a shaving kit, writing utensils, his mother's pots and pans, and his father's woodcarvings. As he excitedly reached for the last valise, recognizing it now as the bag he sought, a queer feeling made him look to the windows.

Gliding through the broken window on a crest of wind was the burned, bloody, torn, and wet Baron Philippus Mormeau. His single eye radiating a piercing red that all but mesmerized Christian.

Outside, the lightning and thunder died down. Only faint rumblings and short flickers of light remained of the pompous majesty that was once the night storm. It was the natural prelude to an act of violence, the epilogue to a book written in blood. It was the calm before the true fury of the night.

They faced each other silently, roughly twelve feet apart, before Mormeau pointed to the bag in Christian's hands and promised, "That will not save you from what I am going to do to you."

The Baron was grotesque to the fullest extent and beyond. Hovering slightly above the floor, his royal raiment ragged and blackened even to a beggar's eye, he was the epitome of all that was odious. Even at such a distance his stench was strong. Brought to Christian's nostrils by the wind that blew into his room from behind Mormeau, the smell was a mingling of decay, burned clothing, flesh, and blood. It caused the bile to rise in Christian's throat almost as much as Mormeau's appearance.

His eyes lingering on the loathsome baron, despite an intense desire to shield them from such wretchedness, he opened the valise.

"And where is your God now?" Mormeau scoffed as he began to float towards Christian. "Does the war in Heaven have Him so preoccupied that He cannot spare His wayward lamb from sacrifice?"

Slipping his right hand into the valise, Christian felt for the dirk.

"You are speechless in the face of Death? You?" the Baron remarked as he drew nearer, his stink preceding him, growing to an unbearable odor. "Have you no proverb or biblical quotation to mark the occasion of your murder?"

His fingers finding no dagger within the jumble of undergarments, Christian grew nervous. For the first time since Mormeau entered the room, he took his eyes off the Baron. Where was it? his mind screamed so loudly it echoed about his brain. Where was Cotton's dirk?

"What is it you seek?" Mormeau built upon the man's evident fear. "Some religious fetish to protect you, some holy charm to ward me off? Nothing can protect you, for you are a lost cause. The god you worship is called Self."

Groping wildly through the bag, Christian's index finger brushed upon something sharp. Wincing happily at the bite of the blade he followed the thin metal up to its abbreviated tang and from there clasped his fingers tightly around the leather-wrapped handle of the Scottish weapon.

"I trust you have made your peace?" the Baron mocked.

"That I have," Christian answered evenly. He thanked Heaven above for Mormeau's reek, for it diminished much of the hypnotic power of the fiend's ruby eye. "I hold no malice toward thee, Baron," he continued rather favorably, "for you are merely existing as best you can." Recalling how Mormeau soaked up flattery like a serpent basking in the sun, he decided to feed the thing some lines, no matter how ridiculous they sounded. "I am honored that you considered me suitable for your companion. I apologize for the trouble I have caused, and for my mistreatment of you and of the kindness and genuine hospitality you have shown me unselfishly." He held out his left hand while his right maintained its grip on the dirk, which remained concealed in the valise. "Please," he implored almost laughably, "accept my hand in friendship and in death …"

Mormeau seemed confused as to his prey's behavior. Perhaps passing Christian's conduct off as nothing more than the disturbed rambling of an unsettled mind, his perplexity melted into amusement. "It is a shame one such as you, one filled of promise, should throw it all away," he spoke rather regrettably. "Like a raindrop into the sea, none will remember you but I. I shall never forget you."

Take my hand, Christian mentally commanded him, and I shall render you as Samuel did Agog – all hacked to pieces. From your murder I shall arise anew, released from the flames like the phoenix I shall rise above all temptation. Your blood, foul as it is, shall serve as my baptism: a rebirth borne of violence. In destroying the last vestiges of my morality, I shall destroy you. Now, take my hand. Take it and I shall take yours!

Again they stared at one another. Christian, his left hand upheld to the earth-defying Mormeau; and Mormeau, gazing down at Christian through that one, unreadable, scarlet eye, let the stillness rule and the tension torture.

Finally, as usual, Baron Mormeau ruptured the quiet. "I shall take your hand, Monsieur Coleswitten, and with honor at having engaged such a worthy adversary." He floated forward and took his guest's hand into his own charred palm.

"Charming to the last," Christian remarked as he clasped his tormentor's hand, steadying Mormeau for the kill. He allowed the Baron to come in close and low, fangs bared and eye blazing with an intense blood craze.

Just as Mormeau was within inches of his precious carotid artery, Christian wrestled the dirk from the confines of its bag and wielded it expertly, its swath cutting deep into the Baron's neck. Blood gushed from the severed jugular and a gasping Mormeau retaliated by tightening his squeeze on Christian's hand, popping a few of his assassin's bones.

"Die! Die! Wretched beast!" Christian cried out in pain and madness. "Perversion of the supernatural! I shall put an end to your abominations!" He tore the short sword from the Baron's percolating neck and was instantly covered by a misting of blood. Angling his face down and away from the brackish spray, he pulled down on Mormeau's crushing hand, uttering prophetically, "If the hand offends thee, cut it off!" And in so saying so did, bringing the dirk's blade to bear upon the Baron's left wrist, severing the black appendage as if cleaving butter.

"Villain!" Mormeau shrieked like a woman as he cupped his amputated wrist, black blood rushing from his cleft veins onto the floor. "Deceitful little monster! Judas!" With his right hand he whacked Christian across the face with so much force as to send the sturdy man flying through the air.

Crashing to the ground, a dazed Christian allowed the dirk to slip from his hand and slide out of reach. He felt as if he had been struck by the moon itself, a thunderous blow that left him nearly senseless. The pain in his neck told him he had come close to having his vertebra snapped and the salty taste in his mouth betrayed more damage than his jaw's present feeling of numbness suggested. He lifted his throbbing head and saw Mormeau descending upon him like the bats he had so recently left. Glancing deliriously about in the dark for Cotton's dirk, he found he still clutched the Baron's cindery extremity.

"Rob me of my hand, and I shall rob you of your heart!" Mormeau screamed as he angled through the air towards Christian.

"Take what is yours!" Christian shouted back at him, throwing the severed hand into the Baron's face.

Rolling to his knees, he began feeling in the dark for the dirk. On impulse he thrust his hand under the bed. Just as Mormeau was upon him, his fingers retrieved the weapon from its unwanted concealment and he whirled in aggression, slicing the Baron's midsection open.

The smell that escaped the wound in Mormeau's gut forced Christian to cover his nose and mouth. The scent of moist decay, the spoilage of body organs long in disuse, induced the air to a rankness found only in morgues. Bursting forth from the gaping cut were the fetid intestines, curled and black like a nest of asps.

Clutching the profusely leaking stump of his left forearm and trying vainly to push his absconding intestine back into his abdomen, Mormeau drifted back and away from his quarry, his thirst for blood giving way to his injuries.

His attention centered on his wrecked physique, he failed to see the table behind him and subsequently toppled over it, falling on his backside. His blood loss, an extreme desertion of the vital fluid, weakened him doubly; for it not only deprived his body of its proper functioning, but caused him to languish in a hunger he could not abate. The dark blood flowed from his throat, wrist, and stomach as if he were an infernal spring, giving forth freely a substance sustaining to life from a creature committed to death. Clamping his right hand down upon his left wrist to contain the bleeding, and cocking his head to close the tear in his throat, he spoke with defiance. "It is not the pain," his voice gurgled through the blood draining in his neck, "for I feel little. It is the dishonor you inflict upon my person. Look at me! I shall not be able to go anywhere!"

"When I am finished," Christian uttered boldly as he got to his feet, "the only suitable place for you to go shall be Hell!" Making that his rallying cry, he rushed at the weakened Mormeau, assailing him with a plenitude of blows from the dripping dirk. Chopping and hacking away in a blind fury, venting his anger at the world and God with every stroke, he decimated the Baron's appearance past the point of recognition. Outside, thunder and lightning gathered for a clash befitting such butchery. Pieces of Mormeau flew about the room and Christian was drenched in the fiend's blood, yet still the wicked man lived on. "Die! Damn you!" an exhausted Christian commanded, or rather pled, as excited spittle shot from his mouth. "Die already!" His blade heavy in his hands and awash with blood, he brought it to his side and took a weary step back to survey his work. He must have struck Mormeau a hundred times.

The Baron sat propped against the overturned table, his legs reduced to splintered pieces of bone and muscle and his arms mere stumps. His clothes were cut to shreds and blended indiscriminately with his oozing body, sopped in blood as Christian was in rainwater. Bulbous gobs of fat bulged from puckered wounds and stringy sinews and bands of muscle slung from rent armpits. His burned face, once only partially ruined, was now a crossroads of slice marks, his nose being sheared off in their making. He sat in his own blood, an outpouring of which it seemed ten men had been slain instead of one. Despite it all, he still managed to keep a strange composure about himself. With a half smile and a roll of his slightly closed eye, he whispered, "Your Christ would have died by now."

"Still you insult God?" Christian asked in amazement at the man's continued profanation. "I have the right mind to leave you this bloody mess. For you to spend your centuries a detestable, helpless little leech."

"Your compassion would not allow it ..."

"My compassion, sir, is dead. You have seen to its murder."

"Then be done with it!" the jumbled remains of a man directed as if he still possessed any power at all. "You are foolish if you seek to use my death as a means to your redemption, for you cannot be redeemed when there is no Redeemer!"

"Perhaps the reason you lash out against God, given the opportunity," Christian thought aloud, looking directly into the mutilated man's eye, "is because you are not sure there is no God, just as I was not sure there was a God."

"You seek to torment me."

"As you have done me."

"Always the good Christian," Mormeau spat, his bloody spittle clinging to his sneering split lip.

"Change not the subject," Christian directed him with the point of the dirk.

"God is dead!"

"Say it enough times," the soft-spoken executioner responded as he stepped closer and raised his long knife above his head, "and perhaps you will believe it, Cardinal."

"You shall not leave me be?" The once-haughty Baron asked, fear painting what remained of his features.

"Nay, I shall send your soul to Hell."

"Then to Hell with you, sir," an indignant Mormeau shot back, his voice breaking and hissing through the hole in his throat, "and may you always be damned!"

"Nay," whispered Christian as if in church, his blood-sprayed face serene, "'tis you, sir, who is to be damned."

He brought the dirk down one final time, shepherding it through Mormeau's neck and decapitating what was left of the Baron. As Philippus Mormeau's head rolled into a corner and his lifeless body slid from the supportive tabletop to the floor, thunder and lightning joined in a concluding signal of departure.

The vicious Baron Mormeau was no more.

Now that the job was finished, the dirk weighed a thousand-stone in Christian's hand. Not out of lassitude, although he was in a state of extreme weariness, but rather disdain, he let the elongated dagger drop from his hand and splatter into the immense puddle of deep maroon in which he could not help but stand.

The blood continued to seep from Mormeau's slaughtered carcass as Christian waded through it to his bedside. So dense was the filthy liquid that it rippled over the tops of his shoes as he walked. And its stench was that of the river Styx.

Relaxing his unwinding form onto the mattress of the bed, he pulled his feet out of the growing lake of dark red and reclined his bruised head against a bedpost. In his arm he cradled his left hand. Perhaps broken, but certainly fractured, pain would not allow the hand to be flexed in any way.

Through eyes half shut he surveyed the residue of his rage. The goddess moon permitted enough light to enter for him to see that Mormeau was parted out across the room. Near the bed lay a hand, by the door a foot and partial calf, and loose portions of flesh and bone were in abundance. The syrupy blood covered much of the carnage with its own horror, swallowing up divorced fingers and partitioned limbs under a murky blanket of congealing stagnation.

One element of the Baron's body that escaped this blood bath was his detached head. Set in a corner behind and to the left of the overturned table, which acted like a dam by offering the discharging blood no recourse but to meander towards Christian's bed, the head lay on the side damaged by the fire. Still fearful of the bodiless Mormeau, Christian gazed into his eye and rejoiced when he saw not a glimmer of red. Despite missing much of what one would construe as being human, Christian's dirk having thus robbed him, Mormeau seemed, at least through the untouched eye, to be at a strange peace.

Closing himself to the massacre he had made Christian felt the shadow of his fear, of his concerns, and of his doubts leave him. He felt as if the weight of the world, a weight self-imposed, had fallen from his shoulders. The old Christian lay a scattered mess before him, dead in Mormeau. In murdering the Baron, he had committed a fractional suicide, killing off that part of him he detested. He could now leave this place a free man, a truly free man. Confronted by darkest temptation he had emerged with his faith not only intact, but strengthened. Tonight he had not only fought with Mormeau, but against himself. And he had been victorious on both counts.

He was in the process of falling into sleep, a sleep he anticipated to be lacking of nightmare, when he believed he heard in a vague, dying rumble of thunder the laughter, or weeping, of a child.

Sitting erect in an instant he was forced yet again to confront the evil of Mormeau and to put his life once more on the line. As the wind outside began to swell and gather itself for yet another onslaught of storm, Christian whispered frighteningly aloud, "The town!"

# Chapter Twelve

Christian fled his room of bloody disarray. In the space of a few minutes it had come to exemplify the entire course of events that had taken place during the unquiet night. And as the blood of the Baron Mormeau slipped into the cracks and crevices of his guest's floor, so did the creature of eternal darkness become one with his very abode.

Rushing down the perilous staircase, Christian nearly slipped to his death because of the lubricating film of blood left on the soles of his shoes. Even still, he thought madly, the treacherous Baron tries to take my life!

Leaping to the ground floor before even completing the stairs, he bounded over to the front door of the castle. Please, he prayed, let it be open! To stay trapped in this place for one second longer than necessary is to flirt with the blade of the Reaper!

For a second he halted his actions. The antechamber felt noticeably warmer than before. In the dim light the crack under the door to the Baron's study glowed in brilliant waves and a stifled popping was heard.

A fire! he correctly inferred. Please, God, Your hand has been on my shoulder this night! Do not let me perish now by a fire of my creation! Let this door be unlocked! Let me emerge from this hell with my much-awakened life intact!

He threw back the bolt, turned the door handle and, much to his relief, was released from his prison and allowed out into the demonic night. However fierce, the outdoors were a comfort to him, for it in no way compared to the ferocity he had just weathered.

Dashing from the doorway he raced through the resisting walls of wind that assailed him as he crossed the courtyard. Finding the coach and horses left exposed on the side of the castle, he quickly set about freeing the steeds. Shivering from the cold, the horses welcomed him with grateful neighs.

Undoing the wet leather straps that hitched the animals to the transport was no easily accomplished chore. After a moment's struggle, the carriage rolled back against the wall and the horses were liberated. Christian had to hold on to one of the frightened beasts as it shied from his grasp.

Grabbing a thick clump of the mare's soused mane, he pulled himself up onto its slick, black back and steered the horse in the direction of the courtyard entrance, the second horse following.

As the horse under Christian saw the way out of the confining walls of the castle grounds, it broke into an excited gallop, spurring the trailing horse into a competition for departure. Both creatures raced Christian through the wide entranceway and down the winding road to the town.

Looking behind him as his mount bucked and his matted hair trembled in the wind, he saw the lodgings of his nightmares beginning to burn. The fire set in the Baron's study had spread quickly, emerging through heat-fractured windows to tender the leaving guest a farewell. He wondered as he glanced back to the deserted road how an edifice so constructed of stone and mortar could catch and keep a fire. Perhaps the rotted woodwork, he hypothesized, the weathered kindling of furniture and fabric, all colluded to bring about the erasure of a monument to the evils of age and the ravages of time – a cleansing fire to gut the memory of atrocities committed and to revert to ashes bodies long abused.

A fire, he reflected, that must also be set to the town.

Easing the jittery mare to a brisk trot, Christian entered the town of Manasseh with caution as his guiding principle. He knew what must be done and done quickly.

The riderless horse racing alongside never slowed in its pace, leaving him with its companion in the midst of a town as dark as its midnight hide. He watched the solitary horse as it bolted through the bantam town and out onto the open road, fancying upon its back the ghost of Cotton Smith-Patton before its blackness was absorbed by the dense night.

Looking up, he saw with some comfort that the moon, although partially covered in cloud, was still with him. Dropping his eyes he surveyed the town and found the only window illuminated by candlelight to be set in the inn. Navigating his dissenting horse to the lighted building, he dismounted. Before approaching the inn on foot, he turned to the quivering horse and gave it a calming stroke along its neck, whispering in its ear, "Don't be afraid, for we'll leave this place shortly." He then turned and stepped up to the shut door.

A thousand thoughts rippled through his mind as he stood before the door. He had his life, his freedom – why jeopardize that? Why not flee this area and consign those ignorant enough to have allowed Mormeau to become their neighbor to the Hell they deserve? Because, he reasoned, he did this not for those within, nor for himself, as he had done with the Baron. He did this for those whose innocence would make them prey, whose only crime would be to leave a window unlatched, tarry too long after dark, or trust a pallid stranger with a peculiar grin. What he was about to do was for people who would never know the extent of his heroism, people who would never even recognize their savior in the street.

As his hand touched the cold metal of the inn door, he was struck by the image of the little afflicted child he had allowed to sleep in his bed. He would return with no cure for her, he thought sadly; she would die like the rest. But while he could no longer prevent the death of a life so precious, he could forestall numerous deaths of a far more sinister nature. A permanent quarantine, irreversible, was needed in order to stave off a disease that continued to kill long after its host had expired. The cure that was worse than the disease was in fact the greatest affliction of all, unadulterated evil.

Perhaps coming to this town had been by an act of God. While he had found nothing to release the death grip of the Plague, he had been enlightened as to the existence of a very real threat and was presented with the opportunity to combat it. Actually, what he now waged against was of far greater significance than the Plague, for it not only robbed those of their lives, but of their souls as well.

"The Lord works in mysterious ways," he muttered under his breath as he pulled the handle down and opened the door.

He was confronted with a ghastly sight, the lifeless bodies of the townspeople strewn here and there across the inn floorboards. Some lay in piles like dirty laundry while others stretched out in solitary repose. Outwardly, their corpses gave the appearance of a peaceful and deep sleep, although when they awoke they would be anything but peaceful. Christian was thankful that none rose to greet him.

It seemed to him that Mormeau, perhaps to save time or because he was lazy, had collected all of the Manassehans in one place. The inn was so packed with pasty, white bodies that even though many were stacked upon one another there was still no way one could enter the inn without traversing upon human remains. That was the true horror, he reflected, that they looked to be asleep, but the very setting prevented this from being so and only added to the weight of the atrocity.

He could see well because someone, probably Horst, had lit the candles on each dirty tabletop. It seemed shockingly fitting to him that the residents of such an unkempt town should now lie collecting dust themselves.

His eyes locking onto the figure of a little boy, dead in his mother's arms, propelled him to finally enter the inn of the damned. Stepping lightly on the bodies, for he could not step over them, he tried his best to respect the forms of those passed on. In this manner he bridged the expanse between the doorway and the bar.

On reaching the bar, he swung himself over the counter, picked up a candle, and crouched down behind the bar itself. He had some idea as to what he wanted to do and knew he had to find something flammable. He had to destroy these remains as quickly and as assuredly as possible, and nothing fit the bill better than a mass cremation. Ah, he breathed easier, here was what he sought. He reached under the counter and proceeded to remove several medium-sized kegs.

The small barrels contained ale and lager that had gone bad long ago. What Christian had learned from having a father who drank was that after time the ingredients in an alcoholic beverage separated. The barley, whey, water, and hops gathered at the bottom while the alcohol, in its pure form, settled on top. He hoped this was the case with the contents of these long-fermenting kegs.

Cracking one keg marked as beer open with his fist, he was greeted by a pungent and thoroughly disgusting odor not unlike the kind he had become used to. Taking this keg, he began to pour out the liquid inside over the unflinching dead. Christian blanched as he spilled some of the spoiled beer into the face of a deceased old woman. When that keg was emptied, he opened another and went through the same ritual. He continued this practice until all kegs save for two were discharged of their rancid contents over the corpses on the floor.

From his place in the center of the room, he realized that the people had actually fallen where they had stood, that they had probably formed in a line to be drained by Mormeau. He shuddered at standing most likely where the Baron had, where only hours earlier these people had taken part in a procession that led to their demise and the devastation of their souls.

Placing the two sealed kegs on a table near the inn's entrance, he searched for a lantern or something with which he could keep and protect a flame from the bullying gusts that still prevailed outside. Finding such a lantern in a corner surprisingly not cluttered with the dead, he raised it up and dusted it off. Carefully placing a single candle in it, he closed its window and set it upon one of the unopened kegs.

Looking over the morbid scene one last time, adding little details to a memory already cluttered with images of the freakish and grotesque, he reached for one of the candles that, through their dripping wax, stuck to the tops of the tables. As he attempted to unfasten it from the smooth wooden surface without burning his fingers, he tried also to block the sight of the townsfolk, some still in the frozen frolic of rigor mortis, from his thoughts. He succeeded only in detaching the lighted stick of wax from its wood grain.

These were once people who learned, loved, and laughed — who gathered round the fire at night to tell of stories fantastic and deeds impossible. Who bore children and reaped fields, who lived honestly and worshipped humbly. Who were set upon by an unspeakable thing from Hell, an evil beyond their simple comprehension or defenses. They did not deserve to die, just as their corpses did not deserve the indignity of a mass burning. Defiling the dead through defiling the living, he whispered in his mind. Those of Mormeau's ilk suck the dignity out of death as they do the bloody marrow from their victims' bones. They dishonor their prey in life by seducing them unto death, and in death continue in their disgrace by making the dead their kin. In this state of existing in quietus, the newly dead add further to their disrepute by preserving the outward appearance of life, thereby destroying even their memory in the minds of family and friends.

Such thinking reinvigorated the seething hatred and disgust he held for Mormeau. Squatting on the backs of the dead, he placed the flame of the candle near the alcohol-doused shirttails of a late farmer. Gazing into the man's peaceful old face, he felt almost powerless to touch the candle to the cloth. What had this night done to him that he presently found it so easy to set fire to an entire town? He had preserved his life, but had he lost his humanity? He fought against these inexplicable thoughts that invaded his mind by setting his free hand on the old farmer's mouth. With his fingers he peeled back the colorless lips and regained control of his senses — for there, inside the man's mouth, sat two pronounced canine teeth.

Christian's firmness in his conviction would no longer falter. He was only righting a horrible, horrible wrong — a wrong that would grow even more horrific if he did not take steps to terminate it here and now. It did not matter what he was reduced to doing in order stop the vicious cycle started in France. Regardless of his own barbarism, his was a means of bringing about a better end, of ceasing evil's influence and fathering a greater good.

With this urgency of duty ruling his thoughts just as Mars reigned his passions, he removed his fingers from the dead thing's lips and tilted the candle to the shirt's hem.

It was then that he saw it.

Roughly five paces in front of him a man stiff with rigor began to move. At first it was so slight as to be imperceptible, a mere spasmodic quivering of the fingers. This gave way to a general shaking of the hands and upper arms, a seizure of epileptic proportions in a prone figure empty of life. Within seconds the trembling had spread throughout the whole of the corpse and the dead man wriggled on his back like a tortoise overturned.

My God! he thought as fear raced from his heart to his head. They are waking! Their true sleep is over and now they begin their rise into a darkness forevermore! They shall do to me as I have done to their father!

Controlling himself, he remembered the candle in his hand. Just as he was about to touch it to the body of the farmer, those corpses upon whose backs he squatted began to stir, setting him off balance and making him fall on his backside. Everywhere he heard the waking of the dead; floorboards creaked, tables overturned, dust was thrown into the air. All around him bodies writhed and contorted, stretching out of their hellish slumber and shaking off the sleepy shackles of death. He was surrounded by an entire town of burgeoning Mormeaus, by children born not of sex but of death.

Thrusting himself forward, he reached to have the flame of the candle light the farmer afire. Amid all the noise and quaking, reining in his terror and deaf to the gasping of the undead, he outstretched his arm and neared the saturated shirt with the flame. He was within an inch, the heat of the candle fire beginning to smolder the fabric itself, when the farmer's cold, dead hand shot up and grabbed his wrist, forcefully placing a stay on his efforts to burn the man's body. Christian tried to scream as the farmer dazedly lifted his head from the floor and opened his white eyes, irises hidden, into Christian's, but the sound got caught in his throat. As the dry orbs rolled in the thing's skull and the familiar pitch black irises appeared as two swirling Stygian pools, Christian's shriek was released.

The demon that now resided in the shell of a former man focused its eyes on Christian and the entire countenance of the farmer changed. No longer did it seem pacific and smooth in its composure, but wrinkled and spiteful. It looked on the man whose wrist it held with utter and unexplainable contempt, possessing a hatred that knew no bounds save for the furnaces of the Devil's dark domain. It showed its fanged teeth in anger and let out a hiss that sounded like blood turning to steam upon the hinges of Hell.

As the monster started to pull him closer, Christian took his unrestrained hand, the one Mormeau had wounded, and used it to topple a nearby table onto his enemy's chest, giving him time to wrench his wrist free. Driving the burning end of the candle forcibly into the farmer's shirt, he set the vigorous corpse alight as quickly as if it were a bale of cotton. Turning from the flaming farmer, he rushed away on the churning multitude at his feet.

Stopping before the open door, he rolled the kegs he had set aside out into the night. Taking up the lantern in his good hand, he was tempted to look back before leaving, to see the farmer flailing about and spreading the fire to all the dead, but chose not to. Perhaps fearful of turning into a pillar of salt, or of seeing in those last moments people ablaze and not the monsters held within, he walked out and closed the door behind him. Retrieving a plank of wood, he thrust it so between the door handle and the door frame that none could open it from within, effectively sealing all of those trapped inside to their true fates.

The fire unfolded fast, the wind blowing from behind the inn already bearing its heat. The flickering golden light coming from the two front windows grew in radiance, as did the sickening sound of burning grow in loudness.

From within Christian could hear above the flames the cries of the doomed, newly born and returning unto death. Their screams were hideous and evoked no pity from him, sounding as if they emanated from the farthest bowels of Hades. He stood there in the wind, silently observing his work.

He had begun to feel a bit righteous, slightly heroic, when from the flames came bursting forth vestiges of humanity. Some wailed for their loved ones, while others to a god that had allowed this to happen. Their weeping was moving as they vocally searched amongst the fire for their beloved.

Outside Christian turned from the inn. Despite all his efforts to the contrary, tears chilled his cheeks. In time the voices crying from the fire would fall silent, being overcome by the crackling of flame and the exploding of heated glass. But in his mind they would echo forever – forever calling into the night.

His horse had not deserted him, and on it he rode throughout the town, using the flammable alcohol residue contained within the kegs and the candle protected in his lantern to set fire to every standing structure remaining in the cursed town of Manasseh. He did not feel it was necessary, for he believed all of the town to be burning in the inn, but rather safe.

And so it was that the man who had come to save all of England razed a little country town. In effect, he had done what he was sent to do.

After the last of the houses were ignited, Christian steered his nervous steed towards the road that led out of town. Looking back at Manasseh, he saw that the darkness was overcome by the appetite of the fires. The smoke that blended high into the black sky carried on it the souls of the townspeople; released from the stigma of damnation they wafted into Heaven.

Gazing past the exaggerated bonfires of Manasseh to the structure that sat upon the hill like a giant tombstone, he eyed the Castel de Mormeau. Built of mortar, stone, blood, and misery, the fortress that entertained Death as a guest appeared to be a mammoth candle. Light all the night, he thought. Be a beacon to those who have lost their souls.

The feeling he had simmering under his breast – that of goodness, of rightness – made him complete. All his life he had searched for something, anything, to give him a sense of purpose, of worth in the world. It was ironic that he should find his destiny here, in an obscure town that excelled only at death. He had been foolish to think that he could achieve personal satisfaction through the Church, or that an accumulation of wealth would really leave him better off. What a person of his conviction needed was a quest, a lifelong journey to wage a war against an evil as yet unrevealed to many. As he led his mount onto the rough road he felt a surge of exhilaration burst within him. He had found his life's calling. It would offer him adventure and knowledge, and he would be doing the Lord's work. He would seek out and destroy those relatives of Mormeau, those bound through blood by a thirst for blood. In old cemeteries and ancient crypts, deserted castles and run down towns, he would find them. In their places of rest – their graves, coffins, and dark abodes – would they quake in fear of their discovery. How he would go forth and destroy them all! None shall be spared, not even the ageless beauty of Cassandra. But to kill her, he realized, would be next to impossible.

Oddly, he thought of his possessions left to the fire of the castle. All his belongings, all he owned in the world save for the soggy clothing on his back, had been eaten by the flames. Good, he decided, for just as the prophets of old forsook many things in their worship of God, so shall I follow their example. I reject all things material and embrace all immaterial!

True, he would miss the mementos of his mother and father, and the little trinkets and books he had come to love, but they would be kept alive in his memory, just as Cotton would be – forever ingesting his ale and spouting his worldly philosophies.

He rode on into the dark of early morning, long and hard on muddied trails. He had to reach Bantingham before sunrise, to lie next to Rebecca and tell her of this night and the impact it had in the shaping of his life from this time forward. He loved her, he finally conceded, and she could join him if she so wished.

Oh, what a glorious night! he concluded joyfully. For in the space of an evening he had resolved all of his inner conflicts. He now firmly believed in God and His Heaven with an unwavering zeal. He had conquered his own personal demons and for the first time in his life actually liked himself. And greatest of all, he had realized his love for Rebecca. No longer was she an ignorant girl good only for a roll in the hay, but the very heart that pumped his essence. He loved her, yes, he loved her completely.

As the hours of darkness began to wane, he pushed his black mare harder, galloping dangerously fast on the sodden roadway. He had to reach Bantingham by morning light, his mind repeated over and over, he must be with Rebecca while the moon still governed.

What had taken virtually half a day's travel with Cotton he covered in little more than a few hours. His mount flew from Manasseh and into the bounds of Bantingham, slipping through the early dark like a ghostly arrow. All the while Christian clung to its back as the abdicating moon reflected off the beast's shiny hide. He felt as though he were astride the wind, covering miles in a single gallop.

A light rain sprinkled his dampened self as the lady above wept tears of adieu. The rushing of the wind as he sliced through only multiplied the shivering of his rocking bones as he sped onward to his destination.

To Hell with Stemmons, he thought arrogantly, let the Devil have his lot! The gout-infested sow had endangered his life for nothing more than the scant chance of monetary gain and the possibility of saintly notoriety. Cotton was right when he had condemned Stemmons, claiming that he and Christian were merely pawns in the fallen priest's game of holy deception. No longer would he be a party to Stemmons' outrageous conduct; no longer would he overlook the man's obvious failings. The first thing I shall do upon returning to London, he mused wickedly, is to blind myself to the oaf's collar and beat the vile shit out of him!

Overhead the candescent globe that had presided over an evening of indefinable fear passed slowly from her nightly dominion, slipping behind a dark veil of rapidly flowing cloud. Its brilliance being dimmed to a hue, the land was plunged into darkness.

The shrouding of the moon made Bantingham more difficult to see, for at such an early hour no windows shone forth with candlelight, and Christian was upon the town before even realizing it. Jockeying his steed to the village tavern, he dismounted and left the horse that had carried him so ably through the forest to its own will.

Walking up to the door of the tavern, he did not bother to knock, for by the darkness within he could see that none were awake to let him in. Trying the door handle, he was surprised to find it unlocked. Burglary in such a small village probably being nonexistent, the owner bothered not with barring his door.

Entering the quiet of the tavern, a quiet surpassing even that of the sleeping village, he stepped lightly and closed the door gingerly behind him so as to not roust anyone from their slumber.

Rebecca lies above me, he thought happily as he removed his drenched jacket and flung it casually to the floor. I must wake her and tell her of my ordeal. He ascended the stairs rather sprightly, with a minimum of creaks, and soon found himself in a contained state of excitement just outside her closed door. He thought of knocking, but wishing to rouse his lover with his lips rather than his knuckles, gently opened her door and slipped inside.

The small room nearly blinded him with a beam of dying moonlight that cut through the dark, angling along the near wall and filling a corner with illumination. As his eyes adjusted to the contrasting white light, the shadows of the room became darker to him and he had to find Rebecca's bed through memory.

He was beginning to grow warmer now, not simply through being out of the chilly morn but by being situated so near the object of his affections. He called to her softly, "Rebecca! Rebecca! 'Tis Christian ... I have returned! I have returned as promised!"

From out of the pitch-dark came the ecstatic and startlingly sudden response, "Christian!" She spoke his name as if he were what she desired most, as a child might cry out for sweets and a dying man for absolution. "Christian," she said again, this time in a satisfied whisper. "Oh, my dear, dear, Christian!"

He could hear, but not see, her rise from her bed and approach him. To facilitate her entry into his arms, he stepped against the wall and into the moonbeam.

She came into the light abruptly, her nude body enhanced by the magical glow of the moon. They hugged and he could not repress putting his feelings into words. "Oh, 'Becca!" he sighed joyously into her ear, "I do so love thee!"

"And I thee, Chris," she reciprocated his sentiment. "Ours is an eternal love, a love that shall last forever!"

He could feel the smile on his lips increase to the point of threatening to break his face in half. He was so utterly happy, so content to be safe in the arms of love, that he failed to notice deriving no heat from her body. He held her face in his hands and looked into her shaded eyes, planting a kiss upon her welcoming lips. On impulse he began to lavish her with kisses, weeping tears of joy as he whispered, "Yes! Yes! We shall never part! Never divorce our hearts!" His intense kisses led him from her face to her neck and from there dropped to her chest, when his lips touched upon a cold band of metal. Ceasing his amorous advances, he examined the chain of gold and found not his cross to be dangling from her neck, but her locket. Recoiling in alarm, he asked fearfully, "Where did you get this?"

Glancing down, Rebecca responded absently, "Why, silly, you gave it to me, remember?"

Suddenly feeling the coldness in his arms, the bottom dropped out of his stomach. Scrutinizing everything about her in the unflinching light of the moon, he raced to prove his intuition wrong. Staring deep into her eyes, he saw those eyes! Bereft of life or compassion. Confronting his inner denial, he roughly forced an inspection of her neck. The right side, the side exposed to the moonlight, revealed nothing.

"Christian!" she giggled. "Whatever are you doing?"

His turned her about so that her back faced him and her left side was awash in light. Pulling back her hair from her shoulder and pushing her head to the right, he saw what he feared.

Two perfect puncture wounds lining the carotid.

"No," he breathed helplessly. "No!" And while his remonstrations were barely above a whisper, his soul's scream could be heard in high Heaven.

Rebecca pointed to her bed, which lay hidden in shadow, and lovingly asserted, "She did that to me."

Following her finger, he affirmed what he already suspected. For emerging from the obscurity was Cassandra, naked in all her perfection.

Christian stared blankly at the guileful Lady as she cracked her lips into a seductive smile. It was a smile he had seen a thousand times, a smile he could never escape.

"She loves you too, Chris," Rebecca continued, never taking her eyes from Cassandra. "We can all be together, the three of us ... forever and ever."

With those words, Christian felt his knees buckle and his support leave him. After all he had been through, this final offense was too much for him to bear. He fell against the wall and slumped to the floor, a fit of hysterical sobbing overtaking him.

Rebecca knelt in front of him, placing her hand tenderly upon his knee. "Don't weep, Chris," she implored him. "Be happy. We shall be together now forever. That is what you wanted, isn't it?"

Between his profound crying, Christian broke into sporadic bouts of crazed laughter. Raising his tear-swollen eyes to Rebecca, he reached out and stroked her impenetrable face, lamenting, "What have I done? What have I done to you?"

Kneeling beside Rebecca, Cassandra placed one hand on her fellow female's back and her other on Christian's head. In response to her touch, Rebecca turned and greeted her Lady with an amorous kiss.

Parting from Rebecca's lips, Cassandra moved close to Christian's face. Playing with his tangled hair, she peered into his saddened eyes. With an unmistakable fondness, she pressed her lips against his puffy cheek and murmured, "I told you you were mine ..."

As tears shook his body like torrents released from a floodgate, his breakdown was complete. As the final traces of reason abandoned him, he was left with one disturbing thought. All night he had stood firm against the lure of evil, battling against such inducement on all levels of his existence. And yet it was not the darkest villainy that defeated him, but the desire to be with a lover. It was not evil itself that overpowered him, but what he had taken to his heart. In the end, he was defeated not through the force of evil, but by the power of love.

As everything he had raised within himself came crashing down, all he could do was babble about his betrayal from above. "Why, God?" he demanded impotently. "Why have You allowed this to happen? Why? Why?"

All he received in answer to his emotional query was the soft tickle of Cassandra's lips as they slipped from his cheek to the tender flesh of his neck.

In the dark sky spread out above the quiet village of Bantingham, the moon once again drowned in a sea of cloud.

# Chapter Thirteen

Father Samuel Stemmons rolled his great girth off his flattened mattress and sat for a while at the side of his bed. He wiped the sleep from his eyes and the sweat from his forehead before rising to urinate. As he emptied his bladder into a bucket near his bed, he cursed having to rise so early. He had to get up before sunrise in order to bless those Catholic dead before the dead carts spirited their stinking corpses away. It also had to be done at so inopportune a time to avoid Protestant jeering, and, as was the case with many he visited, to keep concealed the religious leanings of many of London's wealthier inhabitants.

Shaking his diseased penis, he spat a wad of phlegm into his shoddy toilet before turning away. The open sores on the shaft of his phallus oozed a green pus that looked very similar to the gob of phlegm left floating in a virtual ocean of urine. The piss bucket had been in need of a dumping for days now, but Stemmons was too lazy to carry it to the door. He did not mind the smell anyway, for the stench of his own body overpowered much of the waste's odor.

Slithering into his frock, which used to be an off-white but through staining and sweat approached a medium gray, he began to ready himself for his daily chores. Lifting his sole crucifix from its place of sacrilege above the headboard of his bed, he flung it into his prayer bag on the table.

I hope that fool returns soon, he thought angrily in reference to Christian, for when he does I'll never have to administer Last Rites to pathetic dolts or fumble with ornate benedictions to an unfathomable sky.

He was just about to reach for his sandals when a knocking at the door caused him to freeze.

He analyzed the knocks. They were not rushed or seemingly urgent, but rather even in number and in tone. He called out to his unwanted visitor in a guarded voice, "Who's there?"

From behind the oak of his door came a calm reply that lent a face to the priest's unknown caller. "'Tis I, Father Stemmons – Christian."

Momentarily stunned, for he had not expected the youth's reappearance for some time, he shook himself free of his befuddlement and rushed to respond.

Throwing open his door, his eyes were welcomed by a wet, bedraggled, and thoroughly awful-looking Christian Coleswitten. "My boy!" he exclaimed upon taking in his damp and ashen acquaintance. "Heavens above! What has happened to you? You look a mess!"

"Might I come in?"

"Why yes … yes, of course!" Stemmons stood aside and his guest entered. As he bolted the door behind them, he caught sight of some of the bloodstains that still remained on Christian's clothing. The rain had not washed away all of the blood that had spotted him and some faint discolorations, particularly upon the collar of his shirt, maintained a vibrancy of freshness. On seeing the blood, Stemmons instantly feared the worst. The weakling never made it to Manasseh, he erroneously presumed, a failure just like his father before him. "I had not counted on your return for several days," he attempted to get to the bottom of things. "What has happened?"

Christian stood with his back to the profane priest. "Everything."

The utter finality with which the young man spoke his words chilled Stemmons. "You did arrive in Manasseh?"

"Yes."

"But you have been gone for little longer than a day! Where is Smith-Patton?"

"In a place far better than here."

"Do not confound me with riddles, boy," Stemmons scolded, plainly irritated by Christian's weird attitude. "How could you travel from here to there and back again in a day's time?"

"How can you allow the evil of rust to stain the Christ of your crucifix?"

Well, now, the overweight clergyman thought with much disdain, how his retorts have soured with his looks. Don't take that high-and-mighty tone with me, wastrel! And don't you dare continue in your lack of respect for me by talking with your back turned! You had better have brought me good tidings, Christian, or I may not be liable for what I might have done to you.

As if reading his degenerate mind, the subject of his mental threats spoke in a low, barely audible, but thoroughly snide voice. "I have what you seek …"

"What was that?" a suddenly inspired Stemmons asked, his wide, glazed eyes indicating that he had heard his visitor's utterance but only wished to hear it again. "What say you?"

"I have what you seek."

"The cure!" Stemmons cried happily. "You have the cure!"

"'Tis worse than the disease …"

Jolted from his euphoria by Christian's peculiar reply, Stemmons angrily approached his rude guest. "What mean you by that, Christian?" he said as he put his fleshy hand on the cold man's shoulder. "Where is it?"

"I have it."

The vein just above Stemmons' right temple began to show. Aside from being upset with Coleswitten's baiting, his gout had started acting up, probably due to the excited rushing of his blood. Biting his lower lip to keep from giving Christian a tongue-lashing he breathed deeply. Minding his temper, he asked his guest to clarify the ambiguity of his speech. "Christian," he muttered, "what is it you possess? The cure for the Plague?"

"What 'tis you seek ..."

Such a response failed to elucidate the nervous Stemmons, causing him to explode. Yelling at the back of Christian's head, into the tangled mess of moist hair, he shouted arrogantly, "Enough of your trifling! If you have what 'tis I request, then give it to me, foolish boy! Give it to me now!"

"Yes, Father," Christian said with an obedience tinged by malice, "as you wish." Pulling Stemmons' flabby hand from his shoulder with an icy grip he spun about quickly and glared into the portly man's surprised face.

"My God!" Stemmons sputtered as his astonishment rapidly dissolved into fear. The face he stared into belonged to no one nor no thing he knew on earth. He could not take his beady eyes from the blazing coals that burned for his attention. His jowls quivered at the hint of pointed fangs and his terror led to the discovery that he had not discharged all his bladder held. The thing that stood before him, that held his hand in so puissant a grasp, was not Christian but the Devil incarnate. "God!" he cried once again to a now urgently fathomable Heaven. "God have mercy!"

"No!" the entity that was once Christian Coleswitten screamed. Dropping the deviate cleric's sweaty hand and fastening his fingers onto the frightened man's broad shoulders, he drew his obese prey to his mouth. "No!" he repeated insanely before latching his sharp teeth onto Stemmons' thick neck.

At the moment of feeling the pricking of his throat flesh and tapping of his artery, Stemmons collapsed into an unconsciousness from which he would never recover.

Holding the dying priest's body up, Christian continued in the quenching of his unholy thirst. As he sucked and lapped at Stemmons' generously spurting carotid, the frothy red matching the hot ruby of his irises, a teardrop rolled down his cheek and into the smear of gore that coated his chin.

Was his tear just the watering of an eye splashed with salty blood, or the agony of a soul lost?

"I will call the grave my father,
and the worms that eat me I will
call my mother and my sisters.
Where is there any hope for me?
Who sees any?
Hope will not go with me when I
go down to the world of the dead."

JOB 17:14

# Author's Notes

It should be quite apparent by now to the reader that this story dealt with vampirism, however the word "vampire" was never used. There is a twofold explanation for this: one historical, the other by choice. Upon doing research for this novel I was surprised to discover that "vampire" entered the English language only as recently as the eighteenth century. The time setting for my tale being the late seventeenth century disallowed for the English characters to refer to Mormeau and his kindred as vampires. And while I could have had the French Baron or his learned Lady reveal their true titles, I chose not to. To have the protagonists of this story deal with an evil that is virtually unknown to them (although the well-traveled Cotton does claim some acquaintance with their lore) I find to be among the greatest horrors of all. How much more terrifying it is when one does not know his enemy. This is one reason why I purposely omitted any "Van Helsing" type characters. It seems that in all horror tales, there is one character who is knowledgeable in the area or aspects of the occult in which the heroes find themselves. I thought it would be thoroughly haunting to write a book that lacked this particular personage. In the course of the novel, it is Christian who must overcome the vampires armed with nothing more than his intellect and wits. This is why it takes him so long to dispose of Mormeau, a virtual trial-by-fire execution which was crafted to encompass the three main ways to dispense with a vampire: impalement through the chest, burning, and dismemberment or decapitation.

One may notice an ambiguity concerning some of the characters, most notably being the vampires. It was my intent to create a work in which the reader could become actively engaged, where upon the finishing of the novel certain details would still hound one's conscious thoughts. This is why I steeped the book in symbolism, which is probably literature's greatest device. I have always favored works of a symbolic nature, for it is usually up to the intelligence of the reader to locate and then translate the symbolism in relation to the entirety of the tale. Again, I have tailored much of my symbolism to the wants of the reader. If one chooses to investigate this book further, to analyze place and character names, the words they speak, or the actions they undertake, they may do so and gain additional insight. If one wishes to simply take the novel at face value, as nothing more than a good – if chilling – read, then one may do so as well. I have written this book to be read, and therefore written it for the reader. It is ultimately you who must conclude the cycle I have begun, and it is you who has final judgment on all facets of the book.

When I set about writing my first novel I was posed with several decisions. In what genre would my story be classified? With what would it be concerned? And in what style would I write it? It was instantly obvious to me that I had very little choice in the area of genre. Horror has always come naturally to me, probably due to my growing up with Hammer films, and it provided me with a perfect venue to showcase my imaginative side. Once this was decided, I then had to pick what kind of horror: psychological or physical? I found both in the vampire. The allure of vampirism lies not in its bloody appetite, but in the masking of its evil. The vampire, usually, looks not unlike us. We find ourselves attracted to them, an attraction which often turns to repulsion when their true selves are disclosed. I chose to accentuate this disparity by mildly transforming my vampires when they were ready to attack. It should be noted at this point that although I have not made my vampires slaves to their legend (i.e. fearful of garlic, crucifix cringing, casting no reflection in mirrors), that is not to say that this is not so. Rather than do what many authors have done and change vampire lore to their specifications, I chose instead to not deal with it at all. There are no mirrors in Manasseh with which to prove or disprove a vampire, garlic is never mentioned, and crucifixes are misplaced for no reason other than poor judgment. In the area of the killing beams of day, Cassandra states she no longer enjoys daylight simply because it reminds her of her life. But once again, is she being truthful? That is up to you to decide. In legend, the vampire can change into animals and mist. I did not approach this directly, but there are parts in the book (most notably the number of wolves and the mysterious appearances the vampires make seemingly out of nowhere) where the reader is led to make their own assumptions. I did allow my vampires to have glowing red eyes, levitating capabilities, and, of course, lengthy fangs for the express purpose of depicting their evil as forcefully as possible. That is where I found my supreme pleasure in the telling of this tale, in the depiction of the duality of evil, how one moment these demonic creatures can seem every bit as human as you or I and in the next be at home with the lion, tiger and other wild beasts. Vampires do not always look evil, but when they do, they must epitomize the very furnaces of Hell.

In most vampire myths, the authors choose to concern themselves with only one facet of the legends. They often play up the sensuality and eroticism of the vampire while diminishing the religious implications. Temptation for many victims of the vampire lies in sexual innuendo. I did not want my character to forsake the equally enticing prospect of abandoning the yoke of religion, and in turn of decency, for mere sexual gratification. Christian Coleswitten had to be tormented by more than just a desire to copulate, but to renege on his convictions as well. I have often pondered, who is happier: the simpleton, or the genius? Easily it would have to be the simpleton, for his mind is less cluttered with annoying details and the constant pressuring of society's expectations. For Christian, giving up the demands put upon him by people, government, Church, and self far outweigh the pleasures of the flesh. To be free of all cares and worries, to be free from death itself, now that's tempting! To increase Christian's burden, as well as to not neglect the eroticism of vampire stories, I included the temptation of the seemingly perfect Lady Cassandra. Christian is a character who is tormented, as he himself states, on every level of his existence. To me, he is one of the most pathetic characters – a man destined, despite all his aspirations and goodness, to do nothing but fail.

In researching the vampire mythos I read many scholarly books about vampirism, as well as many interpretations by other authors. The majority of stories I found repetitious, if not amusing. It seemed to me that the qualifications for a vampire had to be a Slavic birth, a noble ancestry, and a cape: in other words, a poor facsimile of Count Dracula. Let me now state that I hold Bram Stoker's Dracula in the highest regard. I consider it not just the greatest horror novel ever completed (mine included), but one of the greatest novels ever written. Dracula became the foundation for my own tale. I took those aspects of it I loved, primarily the castle and its character interaction, and integrated it with my own concept. My only other source of inspiration, aside from a few great quotes from Shakespeare and Montague Summers, was J. Sheridan LeFanu's Carmilla. Here, LeFanu presented me with the vampire as told from the female perspective. Rather than choose between a male vampire and a female vampire, I was compelled to employ them both in my story. Readers of Dracula and Carmilla – and those who haven't read these works are truly missing out on some great literature – will recognize some flourishes in the characters, settings, and depictions in my novel. I did not copy, but only sought to embellish my tale with those peculiarities of both books that I took to heart. If horror writers had a Bible of their own, then Carmilla would be the Old Testament and Dracula the New.

In the writing of my novel, while I chose to leave much discretion to the reader, I did not wish to forsake the expected norms of the horror genre. The old castle is there, as is the deformed manservant and cursed town. Most of the principle action takes place at night, and the hero is somewhat naive as to the ways of the supernatural. Within this framework I worked; yet I peppered this quilt I was making with some common sense. Legend demands that vampires rest in coffins. This seemed trivial to me, so once again I found a way of not

319

addressing it; the majority of the tale takes place at night, when they wouldn't be sleeping anyway. Mormeau would have to be an aristocrat in order to maintain his privacy. It was either that, or he'd be prowling the graveyards, as surely he couldn't live in as urban a center as London. A vampire without a title would have it exceedingly rough. Also, both Mormeau and Cassandra are my own odes to the characters of Dracula and Carmilla, both of whom were of noble birth. It was here that I played off the vagueness of the vampires. I ask the reader, are both Cassandra and Mormeau equally evil? If not, who is worse? Which of the two is truthful? Is Cassandra the wronged beauty she so vigorously protests to being, and is Mormeau really the one pulling the strings? Once again, I defer to the choices of the reader.

It is ironic that I was in fact coerced into setting my own conceptions of a vampire tale to paper through the viewing of a bad vampire movie. I chose to set my tale in a gothic setting within an historical context. Whenever possible, I maintained the tone of the novel by employing only appropriate wording. In this I am indebted to Samuel Pepys, whose diaries were not only a source of proper linguistics, but of day-to-day activities and historical occurrences which took place during the Great Plague. The Plague I found to be excellent for atmosphere: how much more tempting for Christian is vampirism when he is confronted daily with death and despair? England was chosen as a location for no more than its long association with gothic horror and the fact that the Plague reigned there during the particular timeframe in which I wanted my story to occur. The Baron was made French in order to play on the age-old hatred between the British and the French, and thus add a further conflict to the storyline.

I wrote this novel while attending college. In between classes and studying, work and rest, I would type bits and pieces into my word processor, rejoicing at the completion of a chapter or the surpassing of a hundred pages. It has taken me well over two years to complete this wretched labor of love, and I am beholden to those who have supported me in my undertaking. I now give thanks to God for allowing me such family and friends, and I hereby thank those people close to me for their attention, interest, and continued support (in particular Kyle Russell, who assisted me in "trimming the fat" and in procuring a polish edit). I have strained to make this book as perfect and faultless as possible, but do acknowledge that it isn't flawless. It was my main intent that the story stand on its own, that it thrill, chill, and perhaps sadden those who read it. All I have written of is a clash between good and evil, and ask that any incendiary remarks contained herein be taken in the context that this is a work of fiction and nothing more. Once again I give thanks and praise to my family and friends, and to you, who have honored me with the reading of my novel.

Kenneth Miller